SILHOUETTE

RYAN ALCOCK

SILHOUETTE

A catalogue record for this book is available from the National Library of Australia

Under the moonlight

My view, and those around me,

Is death's silhouette

Anonymous

FRENCH GUIANA

FIRST REPORT: SNACKS AVAILABLE

There was definitely a storm coming in. The clouds were like dark grey marshmallows that had been hurled by the hand of God against the midnight blue sky, coming in over the Pacific Ocean with an anger that suggested they had been wronged and were determined to get their revenge. The midnight was appropriate, if not exact, but it was still warm and muggy. Melissa Andersson, having just left her home in Stockholm where the temperature was a far more bitter two degrees below zero, wondered if she was going to get sick by changing climates so quickly.

She was glad that she had decided to wear just the denim shorts and loose white t-shirt she had opted for, but she clung a little closer to *Phare de l'Enfant Perdu* just in case the militant clouds decided to unleash on her.

Her meeting on the little rocky outcrop that contained the Lighthouse of the Lost Child was a last-minute decision. Her instructions were relatively simple. Travel to Cayenne, meet with a contact from the DGSE and investigate.

Investigate what? That, it turned out, was the question.

She had arrived in Cayenne, having flown there directly from Paris, and booked into the Lodges Balourou. There she spent the day by the pool, dressed in a red bikini which highlighted her tan. With her long legs and blonde hair, and wonderful Swedish accent, she looked like a typical backpacker. She received a number of appreciative glances from fellow residents, and when she had sauntered out through reception at around two in the afternoon, the desk clerk gave her a big grin and informed her she had a message.

Phare de l'Enfant Perdu – 11.30 pm

Mission goal one, achieved.

Getting to the Lighthouse of the Lost Child was surprisingly simple, and she was able to catch a lift to Tonate (or more accurately Macouria, the commune a few kilometers north-west of Cayenne). There she was able to find out where the lighthouse was, and set off on her walk. In truth, she was lucky to get to the outcrop when she did, as the tide was starting to rise and she realized that she would soon be cut off from the mainland. There was a rundown little cabin, but she had no real desire to spend the night there, and so she hoped that her contact would arrive very soon.

Now, as 11.30 came around, Melissa took a deep breath and checked her phone for the millionth time in the hopes that it might bring some miracle. The waters were getting more and more choppy, and she understood clearly why the lighthouse was needed.

"*Je n'arrive pas à croire que l'on puisse avoir du réseau cellulaire ici,*" came a voice, and Melissa turned to see a tall, handsome man dressed in a navy polo shirt and dark trousers coming across the rocks towards her. "*Parles-tu français?*"

"I prefer English," she replied.

"That works for me as well," he grinned. "Maximilien Travere. Max to my friends." He held out his hand amiably, and Melissa took it.

"I feel underdressed," she admitted, suddenly a little self-conscious of her appearance.

"I think you're dressed perfectly," Max said, and Melissa raised a perfect eyebrow. "For what you're about to do," he added.

"You are dressed for our excursion better than this guy," came another voice, whose accent was thicker, the more curious French Guinian accent, as opposed to Max's more vanilla French accent.

"This is Gendarme Benoît Royer, of the Maritime Gendarmerie. He has been my contact here," Max grinned.

"Contact for what?" Melissa asked, her voice calm. "Honestly, I have little idea of what is going on. I was told you would be able to provide me with some background."

"Do you see that?" Max asked, pointing out to the black ocean beyond the lighthouse and into the darkness. Melissa followed his finger and squinted slightly, but could only vaguely make out a light. "That is the light of a, uh, how do you say?" Max turned to Royer.

"Rig," the gendarme supplied. "There is a rig there."

"I didn't know there was oil in French Guiana," Melissa said, surprised.

"There was," Royer said. "But it dried up. It wasn't the success everyone hoped for. Most of the companies are pulling out to see if they can go somewhere…anywhere else. This area is pretty much dried up."

"That rig, however, is not an oil rig," Max clarified.

"What is it?"

"That is the million-euro question."

"I have a boat," Royer said. "Over by the deeper waters.

We can get on board and go for a little trip."

"Could you not have left from Cayenne?" Melissa complained.

"We could, but we're aiming for this operation to be low key," Max said.

"As a result, I'm piloting a motorboat myself," Royer grumbled.

"You know this place used to be a prison site, yes?"

"The country?"

"The entire country, yes. But this lighthouse was punishment," Max held out his hand as they walked across the rocks. Melissa had to admit that some of the path was a little treacherous, and she slid her hand into his gratefully as he helped her towards the edge. "They would send three prisoners here and the prisoners had to keep the lighthouse going. Once, the prison administration forgot about the lighthouse and the prisoners there. One of them died from starvation. Of course, the light extinguished as well. So, the other two built a raft and decided to escape. They made it to Cayenne, but were found and arrested for escaping." He grinned again at this, and Melissa couldn't help but grin back.

"This country is brutal," she reflected.

"Brutal, yes," Royer called out, "but beautiful, I think. It's savage and rough. You don't get anything like it."

"That's true," Melissa had to admit. In Cayenne she felt a lot of French vibes, as though she were in a smaller part of Paris, watching diners eat on the sidewalks of cafes. In Tonate, however, it was a very different world. The poverty was far more obvious.

They had made it to the edge of the outcrop, and sure

enough, there was a dull grey motorboat, about 20 meters long. A small gangway allowed access, and Royer quickly walked up and onto the boat, heading for the pilot's cabin. Melissa followed, with Max behind her, pulling up the gangplank. The sound of the crashing waves was so loud, Melissa couldn't hear the boat start up, but she felt it shudder and once inside the cabin, the noise was muted. Royer gave her a small smile, and held out his hand. On it were two pieces of chewing gum.

"Trying to give up smoking. Thought I'd try gum."

"Uh, no," Melissa wrinkled her nose.

"Not nicotine gum. I can't afford that. Just the standard." She smiled and accepted the offer.

"Have you got files on a man named Heroux?" Max asked as he came into the cabin.

"Possibly," Melissa said. "We usually get them sent to us," she added.

"Of course," Max smiled. "Interpol is just a distributor of files. I think, though, you have a few of your own." Melissa shrugged, and Max's smile widened. He looked around the cabin, and then went over to a locker which he opened and removed a laptop. Then he brought it to the small table in the center of the room and activated it. A few taps brought up a man in his late forties, possibly early fifties. He looked weather beaten and had a scar on the side of his face, while is black slick backed hair was grey at the temples. There was a lack of warmth in his eyes, but Melissa supposed she might be judging harshly based on a single picture. "Heroux. Known mononymously. He's French, and worked as a mercenary for a while in Afghanistan. Possibly gun running. We suspected he might have ties to Librada Cisneros, but we could never quite prove that. Of late he has been more legitimate, apparently. That rig out there is, allegedly, for archeological exploration."

"Allegedly?"

"We don't entirely believe that," Max affirmed.

"We did a pass by of the rig when it was set up, and there were a few things that surprised us about it. Firstly, it doesn't look much like any rig we've ever seen before," Royer added, looking back to them as he steered the ship. "It's pretty much one big white cylinder. There are windows, but you can't really see anything through them, and we did send a drone over the top, but all we saw was a helipad, and a farm of solar panels. It's self-sufficient, but there must be a fair bit of power being pumped through it."

"Now, perhaps you might think we are being judgey on a man because of his past," Max said affably, "but we can't work out how this operation was funded. And that raised some flags."

"What's he looking for?" Melissa wondered.

"He claims that pirate ships sunk here. And he may be right," admitted Max. "But it seems odd to build a semi-permanent complex to look for something that would be fairly limited, with an unlikely return."

"And you want Interpol to gather information?"

"We would very much like that," Max said. "But we thought you might like to look into the actual issue itself."

"Look into?"

"If it's OK with you, we will take a little underwater dive to take a look at the rig from below water level," Royer said.

And this time it was both Royer and Max who grinned at

her.

Melissa looked at herself in the mirror that was on the cabin wall, and was fairly confident she had got the diving suit on correctly. It had been a while since she'd had to go deep sea diving and it wasn't her favorite thing in the world; honestly, if she needed to be on water, she preferred to be quite literally on it, rather than in it.

Nonetheless there were no reservations as she walked up the steps of the boat from the cabin to the deck; rather a resolve that she was prepared for whatever was going to come her way. She was a trained Special Response Operative for Interpol. She wasn't going to waste time fretting over getting her hair wet.

On deck, Max had finished putting various bits of diving gear onto Royer, and he turned satisfied, lifting up the tanks to sling over Melissa's shoulders.

"You've done this before?" he asked cheerfully.

"Sure," she nodded, turning her back to him to receive the tanks.

"We go down and straight forward," Royer said, and he was chewing on something, which he promptly spat out over the rail. Melissa wrinkled her nose at the action unable to hide her distaste, but said nothing. Royer was very uncouth, she decided. "When we get there, I think there should be an intake pipe that we can get into. We stick together and try to get in, then we see what is there, and then we get out."

"That sounds good, given the fact we'll be trespassing," Melissa said sourly.

"The Maritime Gendarmerie sent a formal request to Mr

Heroux, but he has chosen to refuse our politeness," Royer scowled. "Personally, I think we should just board him in force, but Mr Travere doesn't think it's a good idea."

"I don't think it is either," Melissa agreed, but Royer simply snorted, and headed to the back of the boat, where he sat on the edge. Melissa turned to look at their target, and realized they were a lot closer than where they had been, though now the boat had stopped, and they were simply bobbing, possibly even moving away from their destination. She came over and sat beside Royer, turning to look into the dark waters below. As a child she had read a scary story that included the phrase "inky black depths". Seeing them now triggered an association to that horror and sent a shiver went up her spine.

"Should we be looking out for, I don't know...caiman?" Melissa asked, a little nervously, trying to recall what was in the waters.

"No, you're pretty safe out here," Royer said, surprisingly sounding concerned. "The Black Camin are mostly inland. There's a lot of interesting sea life out here, but not much of it is dangerous. If you're lucky you might see a Giant Oceanic Manta Ray, but these days, the microplastics in the sea are more dangerous to them than we are."

"You ready?" Max said, handing her a mask, and she nodded. With a reciprocal nod, Royer held up three fingers and counted down, falling back when the last finger went down. Breathing calmly, Melissa fell back as well.

The pair plunged into the ocean, the weight of the tank helping her to dive lower. Royer hadn't been wrong; as soon as they broke the surface, schools of colorful fish scattered, moving away from the disturbance, afraid at what might have joined them in the depths. For a moment she was distracted by the sea life that she could see, but when Royer turned on a torch, she quickly refocused and followed her new partner.

Royer wasn't wasting any time, and headed directly towards their destination. Melissa followed beside him, making sure to remain calm in her breathing, and glad she had tied her hair back, so it wouldn't float around her head. She was grateful for the light as the ocean was quite dark, and in his dark suit, Royer looked like just another shadow around her. At one point she thought she might have seen a Green Turtle, but Royer didn't slow, and Melissa felt a stab of disappointment that she wasn't able to go and check for sure.

Royer's smooth underwater swimming was stronger than Melissa had expected, and she found herself working harder to keep up with him. She felt it had taken little more than ten minutes to finally get to the rig, and there she was surprised to find that it was almost exactly what Royer had described. A great white cylinder that seemed to have been dropped into the ocean. She placed her hands on the cylinder and though she couldn't quite tell what material it was, she was surprised that it felt less like metal and more like some sort of lite plastic.

In fact, it almost seemed like it had been placed around the rig to prevent people from seeing in. She realized she had lost sight of Royer, but caught a dim light, and started to make her way towards it. As she moved, out of the darkness, a massive mouth opened in front of her, and she squealed, kicking back in fright. A hand on her shoulder caused her to squeal again, and she turned to see Royer's face in front of her, his hand moving up and down in the water.

She turned back to see that the giant mouth belonged to an enormous brown fish, a permanently downturned expression on its giant freckled face. It seemed to realise it was quite close to the plastic barrier, and turned to swim away, passing close by her. Melissa watched as the fish made its journey, seeming to take forever before the final fin flicked past her, and she shook her head, disappointed in herself.

Royer gave her a thumbs up, and she wearily returned it, before he pointed down. She nodded, and the pair swam lower. They stooped when he pointed to a large, circular ingress in the plastic wall, and then pointed to it, motioning to go in. She gave another thumbs up, and he dived forward into the tunnel, the light guiding their way.

They entered the tunnel, and Melissa ran her hands along it, noting that this time it was definitely metal. Not far into the tunnel, they came across a metal grill, and Royer handed the torch to Melissa. She held it up while he first tested to see if the grill would easily come loose, and then ran his hands around the edges, before finding a catch which he released, and the grill opened. Together the pair then entered, with Royer taking the torch back.

By now they were both far more careful than they had been before, and the pair continually looked around as they made their way, checking to see where they were and what options were around them. Not usually the type to feel claustrophobic, Melissa had to admit that the chill she had on entry wasn't going away, and she shivered again, worried that she might have unwittingly entered her own coffin.

Melissa Andersson decided she had lost track of time, so she wasn't entirely sure whether it had been a short trip, or forever when Benoît Royer held up his hand and pointed up. She looked up and realized that there was a tunnel extending upwards, complete with rungs, and guessed that they had found their entry point. Royer was already removing his oxygen tanks, taking a few breaths before he sealed the breathing apparatus and grabbed the ladder. It was all very ad hoc, and Melissa was nervous about it. She didn't like operations that weren't well planned; she wasn't used to them. This was far too casual.

Despite this, she followed Royer's example, removing her own tank and depositing at the bottom of the tunnel, before reaching up and grabbing the rungs. She quickly followed Royer, climbing higher until suddenly she was above water level and no longer needed to hold her breath. Royer climbed down a little to talk to her, and she recoiled at the smell of the nicotine on his breath – someone wasn't trying hard enough on the plan to give up.

"We go up," he said. "We take a look around, we see if we can find out what is going on here. Then we are out, yes?"

"This is your operation," Melissa said, irritably.

"Then we separate, it will be quicker. Let's get in and out and we don't have to waste time." She nodded, wondering what on Earth they would discover. Royer climbed up the rungs again, quickly getting to the top where there was a wheel which he spun before pushing open the hatch it unlocked. Turning back to Melissa, he gave her a nod, and then pushed the hatch open and climbed out of the pipe. Melissa followed, but was astonished to find that Royer had already disappeared. She replaced the hatch and sealed it, before scanning the room she was in. There were two doors, opposite each other, and one was slowly closing, so she guessed that was where Royer had gone.

She crossed to the other and tried the handle, easing it open gently, so she could get a glimpse of what was beyond. It seemed to be a control room, and there were a few people walking around, though it seemed that at this time of night, it was just the skeleton crew. She paused and wondered if it was a good idea to wear her wetsuit, but as the other option was her red bikini, she decided there was no real choice.

Melissa pushed the door open cautiously, and stepped through, but as she turned to survey the area, she looked straight into the eyes of a security guard. They eyed each other up for a moment, and she could see his brain working overtime, trying to decide if what he was looking at was acceptable.

"Just checking the valves," she said, indicating the suit.

"Sorry," he said. "I don't think we've met."

"All good," she replied, a lot more confidently than she felt. "It's a big rig. Dr Klara Friberg." She held out her hand, and he shook it with a smile. Her cover name slipped off her tongue without even trying, having used it fairly regularly over the past few years.

"Gabriel Neri," he said. "You're a lot more personable than a lot of the scientists here," he added.

"Well, take me out for a drink sometime and you'll see I'm very different to these guys," Melissa laughed, and Neri followed suit.

"I may have to take you up on that, Doc," he grinned. "I gotta get back to work, though."

"See you around then," Melissa smiled easily, and he waved, before turning back to continue his walk. Melissa set off in the opposite direction, hoping that it wouldn't seem unusual. Fooling a security guard was one thing, but she was unlikely to be just accepted as a scientist by the actual team itself.

As she passed by the various computers that were on display, she looked around to try to get some idea of what they were actually doing on the rig. She couldn't see any sign of pressure readings, so they weren't searching for oil. She also couldn't see any tracking equipment, so they weren't following vehicles. The computers did seem to be measuring things. When the text caught her eye, she paused to look at one of the displays. It seemed to be measuring temperature of some sort, but the measurement was 9000. Regardless of whether that was Celsius or Fahrenheit that was ridiculously hot.

What on Earth could they be doing that required heat to that extreme?

And yet, everything seemed so legitimate. But if that were so, why not just declare it to the authorities? Why build an offshore rig that no one could see to hide legitimate research and investigation? Royer and Travere were right; there was something not quite right about the rig.

"*Puis-je vous aider?*" a voice came, and she turned to see a balding middle-aged man in a cardigan approaching her.

"*Pardon,*" she replied. "*J'étais juste curieux.*"

"*Qui êtes-vous?*" the man demanded, though he was still more puzzled than alarmed. Melissa opened her mouth to say something, when suddenly an alarm rang out.

"*Intrus!*" a voice rang out over the intercom, and

Cardigan-man looked at Melissa in shock. Without a second thought, she stepped forward and punched him hard in the gut, winding him and forcing him to the floor. She ran to what appeared to be the main entrance for the computer room, looking around to see that the scientists inside were baffled and looking at each other for clarity.

Presumably, someone had stumbled on Royer, Melissa reflected, as she pushed the door open to see people running back and forth along the corridor outside. It couldn't have been her, because Cardigan-man hadn't time to raise an alarm. She pondered on her options, which really amounted to abandon Royer, or try to get him out. She could try to use her authority to get out of their dilemma, but perhaps Royer had already claimed his identity as a Gendarme, and that obviously had little effect.

Perhaps it would be better to get back to Max and hope they could negotiate something. She turned, only to find herself looking down the barrel of Gabriel Neri's gun.

"What's going on?" he asked, and she realized with relief that he was raising it to go outside.

"I don't think the intruder's immediately out there, Gabe," she said, gently putting her hand on his gun and lowering it.

"Right, right," he nodded, and it suddenly hit Melissa that he was probably in his early twenties; inexperienced and naïve.

"You stay here and look after these guys," she said. "I'll go and see if the rest of security have the intruder under control." He nodded, relieved that someone was going to think for him, and she pushed the door open, and stepped out.

Once in the corridor, she wondered if she had possibly made an error. People who she assumed were security guards were running down the corridor, all dressed in black, with bulky vests and handguns clearly on their belts. The corridor itself didn't particularly lend to hiding, as the wall she was on was featureless, blank and beige, interrupted only by the occasional door. The wall opposite, however, had a number of pipes running along it, as though someone had forgotten to actually the build the wall that should have covered up the workings behind it.

One of guards that ran past her, briefly looked at her and then shouted "*Retourne dans cette pièce!*" But he didn't stop to make sure that she had obeyed him, so rather than going back inside, as the last guard passed her, Melissa crossed quickly and tried to see if there was a way to get into the pipes and stay slightly better hidden. She was quite slim, and so she dropped to the ground and discovered she was able to slide underneath the bottom pipe, which was particularly large, and then, with a great deal of effort and agility, she maneuvered herself around and was able to stand on the other side of the pipes. It wasn't ideal, and there was not a lot of room at all there. Equally, if someone noticed her, there was no chance she was going to get away from them.

Crossing her fingers that her new hiding place would keep her safe, she made her way down along the pipes as quickly as she could. Luck, it turned out, was in her favour, as she was not noticed by any of the (admittedly very few people) walking along the corridor, and the corridor took her to where she wanted to go – not that she had known where that was initially.

The corridor opened into a large room, and she was able to slide along the pipes, which still ran along the walls, though she noticed that at the midpoint of the wall, a number of them all took a sharp right turn and moved away to the center of the room. She was also aware that the pipes themselves were heating up, and wondered how much hotter they would get.

9000 degrees?

Near the entrance way, security had formed a circle, and Melissa wondered if she could perhaps use the pipes to climb a little higher. Deciding to risk it, she reached up and grabbed a pipe to pull herself up the wall, her feet sliding between pipes as she went up to create footholds. She was not remotely surprised to see that the circle had formed around Benoît Royer.

He was on the floor, spitting out blood, and clearly having been on the receiving end of a particularly brutal beating from a big bald man with a gold earring, grinning every time he delivered a blow. Melissa's heart caught in her throat, her pulse increasing as she tried to contain the panic that was building inside. She had backed herself into a corner in a situation that was clearly both unfriendly and unpleasant. Logic dictated that she escape and get away as quickly as possible, and yet logic was fighting guilt at the thought of abandoning Royer.

But then, what was the worst they would do? Beat the living shit out of him and then send him on his way? It wasn't great, but it might even allow for the Gendarmerie to actually move in and do something.

Her thoughts were interrupted by the arrival of a new man, wearing a white shirt and a beige suit. He was white, unlike most of the rest of the people in the room, and his black hair was transitioning to grey, particularly at the temples, but it was his face that caught the attention. He was clean shaven, with intense grey eyes and a craggy face. But the face was deeply scarred, as though he had been attacked by a pack of vicious animals.

"I know who you are," Melissa heard Royer say, and she realized that there was a deep hum in the room that had perhaps masked her colleagues voice up until that point.

"I don't know who you are, friend," came the response from the scarred man. "Perhaps you might enlighten me?"

"I'm a gendarme," Royer said, and there was a flurry of movement from the security guards, though the scarred man just seemed amused.

"Do you not bother to follow the rules, Mr Gendarme?" the scarred man said.

"I don't know what you mean?"

"The gendarmerie aren't famous for breaking into perfectly legal operations," the scarred man replied. "Or perhaps you think we aren't perfectly legal?"

"You're supposed to be archaeologists," Royer spat. "But you're no archeologist, Heroux!" Melissa's eyes widened at the name, suddenly understanding who she was looking at. This was the mercenary, then. Heroux was still looking amused, however.

"You want to know what we are doing? That seems like a fair call, Mr Gendarme." Heroux turned and looked up, waving to someone. Melissa craned her neck to see what he was looking at, and realized that the room had a second level, which was being surveyed by a number of people behind large windows. There was a whine, and on the floor at the center of the room, a large circular door irised open.

Melissa could feel the heat in the pipes start to build up and she realized that something was about to happen. She couldn't stay where she was, though, and fighting against her natural instincts, she began to quickly move back the way she came. When she got a certain distance, she risked dropping and pulling herself back out from the pipes. As she came out, she heard a scream from coming from the room she just left.

She didn't need to ask who.

Melissa pelted back down the corridor, ignoring the looks from the one or two people who she passed. She paused for a moment, suddenly not quite sure which door she had come in from, but then thought she recognized the pipes she had slid under and raced over to the nearest door, pulling it open.

Gabriel Neri was standing at the door, and she felt relief flood through her, realizing she had made the right choice. Neri was, however, pointing a gun at her. Her brain automatically noted it as a Colt M1911. Not surprising. Lightweight grip, minimal recoil, accurate and much used by security firms.

"Gabe?" she said softly, and was delighted to see a small flicker of doubt in his eyes. It was enough, and she quickly brought her hand up, knocking the gun aside, and allowing her to use her other hand to punch Neri hard in the throat. Neri dropped to his knees, and Melissa turned to retrieve his Colt.

There was, however, a foot on it. A foot in a well-polished, and quite expensive shoe. She looked up the beige trousers to see the damaged face of Heroux looking down at her.

"Another gendarme?" he said, the amusement from earlier still in his voice. "So nice to meet you. You should have stayed with your friend. You would have got to see our operation first hand. Before becoming part of it."

Security guards moved into the room, with one – the big

24

man who had given Royer his beating – grabbing her arms and hoisting her up.

"I'm not with the Gendarmerie. I'm with Interpol," Melissa said, hoping that it might be some deterrent against what Heroux intended to do.

"Oh, that's a pain," Heroux sighed. His voice was nowhere near as deep as it should have been, Melissa thought, somewhat absurdly. "I suppose I shall have to call two different numbers to register my complaint." He turned to the two security guards holding her. "My friends would you please show Ms Interpol where Mr Gendarme is. And then, would you ask Mr Wilcox if he would be so kind as to give her the same demonstration?"

"Yes sir," came the quick response. Now Melissa was unable to quell the panic, and she struggled, hoping to find some way of escaping the grip of the security guards, but it was clearly not to be.

"My people will come looking for me!" she said, hoping against hope that something might change Heroux's intentions.

"I shall make sure to have snacks available for them when they do," Heroux said with a smile. "Goodnight, Ms Interpol."

CANADA

FIRST REPORT: BLACK HOODIE

Not for the first time, Dana Spectra stood in front of a mirror regarding her appearance and nervously finding herself coming up short. She was dressed in a black bikini, which had a neon yellow "S" on it, that seemed duplicated, with the second one spinning out from the original, but somehow linked in, like an Escher painting. Over it all was a large black, zip up hoodie, with the same double "S" on it over her left breast. The theory was that it would look amazing as the basic hoodie was dramatically removed to reveal the string bikini beneath.

However, her leg would be exposed for the entire event, and that was always the bit that made her nervous. She twisted slightly to see if Jeremey's concealer was doing its job and keeping the scar on her thigh hidden. It seemed obvious to her (or obvious that something was being covered up), but Jeremy had given her his usual reassurance that she was being silly and that it couldn't be seen. He had also pointed out that surely she shouldn't be bothered about a scar, given all the drama she had been through the previous year.

"You almost fell from the tallest building in Seoul," he had said as she judged his work critically. "I can't believe this is the thing that still bothers you."

"I know," she replied witheringly, but she couldn't help

her idiosyncrasies. Besides, that had been ages ago.

"Ready for action?" came a voice beside her, and Dana turned to see Asha at her side. The pair had begun following each other on Insta some months earlier after Dana had been fascinated with one of her videos that seemed to be set in the middle of a jungle, and had amazing wildlife. Coincidentally, the influencer had also been invited to be one of the faces of Shadow, a new drink that was being launched by entrepreneur Silhouette Moreau. In some ways the pair were quite different, Dana's impressive 5'11" height contrasting with Asha's 5'5" in the same way that Dana's long strawberry hair was the opposite of Asha's dark bob. The strawberry colour was a new thing, a test of the waters as the stronger red began to fade. She didn't hate it, but she had to admit that her fans weren't overly keen. Bella, staying on top of her social media as she was now demanding payment for (surely sisters were obligated to help out for free?) had informed her that there was a swell of passion for the blonde to return, and Dana supposed she would go back to it at some point.

Certainly, the photoshoot she had recently done had been met by a degree of disappointment from the artistic director, who archly asked, "I thought you were a blonde?" However, given his artistic vision required artistic implied nudity with another model, there was a limit to how much he could complain about.

And, having said all that, she'd recently met singer Luna Rochique, and was quite impressed with the woman's blue hair. Maybe she should try that to really stir up the fan base.

"Are you?" Dana asked, her trademark smirk playing on her lips. For Asha, modelling was going to be a totally new experience, having never done it on a professional level before.

Her outfit seemed to be what Dana was missing, dressed in a similar black bikini, but with baggy, black cargo pants hanging off her hips.

"I think so," the smaller girl replied. "In some ways it's nice to know that people will see me without instantly replying their feelings."

"Wait for a few hours," Dana sighed. "As soon as pictures from this event leak, you can guarantee that the paparazzi will be making an assessment of your appearance. And on social media, they're not being mean, right? Just honest."

"Just calling it like they see it," Asha laughed, playing into Dana's sarcasm.

"We chose to be in the public eye, we shouldn't be surprised when people make comments about how we look," Dana continued, her laughter now escaping.

"Ladies, whenever you're ready, we are," came a voice with a Canadian accent. A tanned woman with short, dark hair had entered the dressing room, a clipboard in hand and pods in ear. Along with the other celebrities who were representing Shadow, Dana and Asha followed the woman out of the room.

Dana had never been to Montreal before, and as such, when her manager, the sardonic Christa Adams, had contacted her to let her know that a brand opportunity had come up, the fact that the promotions were kicking off in Canada had been a big selling point. Since her stock in the industry had increased over the past few months, the offers had been coming in. Nothing on the level of *Digné* just yet, but still, she was enjoying the chance to actually select her next ventures, rather than needing to say yes to everything in order to establish herself.

"This won't last forever," Adams had warned, her right eyebrow arching. "You have to play it carefully if you want to survive. It's all very well to explode overnight, but it's not much stick if it fades within a year."

"Stick?" Adams looked at Dana witheringly, and Dana repressed a smile.

"You're saying I should keep agreeing to every offer?"

"We'll be selective, but not too picky. Everything's just picking up again, post COVID. We need to be ready for anything," Adams replied, though Dana wasn't sure she could see the difference. "Are you still in therapy?"

"What?"

"Don't make me repeat myself."

"I still go, yeah. If that's OK." Dana felt vulnerable at the comment, unable to remember when she had told Christa she was seeing a counsellor. Had she even?

"It's just not a great look if lots of people know about it," Christa replied.

"Well, that's on society," Dana said defensively. "Maybe I should be the face of mental health awareness!"

"Maybe you should. I'll look into it, if you like. But it would be as a spokesperson." Adams suddenly paused. "Actually, that's not such a bad idea." Dana fought to stop rolling her eyes, regretting opening her mouth. She definitely wasn't prepared to open up about her experiences to the world, and she was fairly certain that there would be certain people who would have something to say if she were to suddenly start talking about it.

"Today, though," Dana said, hoping to get Adams off this

particular track.

"Ah, yes, there's a new energy drink coming out. Shadow. Every heard of a man called Silhouette Moreau?" Dana frowned a little at the name. It did seem familiar but she couldn't remember exactly where she had heard it before. "Billionaire who is very keen on recycling. Owns a lot of recycling plants around the world, but donates millions to cleaning up some of the bigger problem beaches."

"Oh!" Dana exclaimed. That was where she had heard the name before. "He was on a documentary, wasn't he? About pollution on beaches on South Pacific islands, or something?"

"Yes, I think he has dedicated himself to destroying the, uhm…what's it called?" Adams clicked her tongue, trying to drag back the memory. "Trash Island?" she guessed.

"Great Pacific Garbage Patch," Dana said, looking up from her phone, where she had already started googling it. "There's a bit of a fight, isn't there. Some scientists think that there's a whole ecosystem developing there that could be destroyed if they get rid of the garbage."

"Probably," Adams shrugged, clearly showing her disinterest in the planet's pollution. "Anyway, he's invited you to be one of the faces of Shadow. The whole Miss Green Earth thing last year made you pop up on his list. That and that ridiculous cat," Adams scowled at the last thought, though Dana couldn't help but grin.

"Dine is the reason I'm here," Dana said proudly, the little cat's black face leaping straight to mind.

"No, a lucky photograph of your bracelet is why you're here," Adams responded, taking the wind out of Dana's sails.

"Anyway, it's moot. I'm giving you the option. If you want it, I'll let them know. There're photoshoots, advertisements, the lot. And a series of launches, of course. You probably won't have to do them all, as I think there's a couple of other ambassadors. But the ones you are needed for, you wear the merchandise and talk about how important saving the planet is. First stop is Canada, I believe."

"Well, it does sound like my thing," Dana admitted. "Sure, sign me up."

From the outside, standing on Pl Jean-Paul-Riopelle, the Palais des cogrès de Montréal looks like someone zoomed in on a stained-glass window. Five rows of multicoloured glass sit above the entrance foyer, with its much simpler doors and plain glass windows, ensuring that if one were on the inside when the sun was in the right position, one would be bathed in different colours. The top left-hand corner of the building façade, however, is different – a pixelated image of a hand reaching across, in different shades of blue. Located in Ville-Marie, precisely 1001 Pl Jean-Paul-Riopelle, the building is an impressive 184,000 square metres.

The foyer entrance, though, is a slightly more depressing set of eighties glass doors, framed by aluminium. Once through those doors, the foyer itself is impressive if for nothing more than the sheer size of it. Cafes are scattered throughout it, along with an actual art gallery. The building contains a number of what are described as thematic zones, including The Cottage, and The Station; the former looking like a wooden children's play area, while the latter is seating designed to mimic an alpine ski lift.

The actual convention rooms start on level 4, but Silhouette Moreau had rented out The Marquee on Level 7 for the launch of Shadow. This was on the roof of the building; a giant white marquee situated on the Terrace, nestled in between the greenery and stone paths that wormed around giving entrance to the different rooftop options.

Dana Spectra, on arrival, had been quite overwhelmed by the Palais, and as she, her good friend and make-up artist Jeremy Gordon, and her little sister, Bella, made their way inside, flashing lanyards with the Shadow logo on them to staff who helpfully guided them to their destination, Dana decided she had definitely made the right decision.

The Marquee had been set up for a small fashion show, with a catwalk running down the centre, surrounded by chairs, with enough space between for waiters to bring drinks to the various guests that were present. Bella North-Spectra had been to enough of these events now to confidently leave her sister and make her way to the seating area, where she found a spare seat and sat down to watch the show. Another man came to sit beside her, and Bella gave a passing glance to see who he was – he was bald, with a greying goatee and a round, happy face, though in truth there was no smile. In fact, he seemed slightly tense, and Bella wondered what might be his issue. She caught a glimpse of his lanyard and saw that it had the letters VIP on it – her own had "Special Guest", but there were others with simply "guest".

Bella played on her phone for a while, waiting for the moment the show would start, and sipping on a lemonade. She had asked if she could get a milkshake, keen to pursue her search for the best vanilla milkshake in the world, but had been politely refused.

"I wanted one as well," the bald man beside her said, with a cheerful grin. "Tom," he said, sticking out his hand. "I mean, just saying hello. Nothing, nothing…" he paused, clearly realizing he had dug a hole and was unlikely to get out of it. "Sorry," he finished, withdrawing his hand.

"I wasn't scared," Bella said, and held out her hand. He gave a small smile and shook it. "Bella. I'm one of the model's sister."

"I'm just a," he paused, as though uncertain about what he was. "I worked on Shadow."

"You worked on the drink?" Bella asked, surprised.

"Uh, no, I'm a chemist. Engineer. Uhm, well…" Again, it seemed like he wasn't sure what he was supposed to say, and he nervously played with the card on his lanyard. "I'm on the board. A specialist. On the board."

"You must be excited for the launch," Bella said, hoping that she could go back to her phone.

"Yes, absolutely." He grinned in a way that made him look like he was a long-suffering husband on an old British sitcom. In fact, Bella mused, he spoke like one as well. The awkward conversation was blessedly cut short by the arrival of a staff member distributing what looked like an order of events. Bella took one, though Tom declined.

The lights dimmed, and a lectern set to one side of the catwalk lit up, bathing the man standing there in a spotlight that he seemed entirely comfortable in. He was tall, but not just in height, where he comfortably conquered six foot. His demeanor and attitude gave him an additional height that had him dominate those around him. His suit was a black that was so perfect, light seemed to glide off it. It was expensive, and Bella wished Dana were sitting beside her to inform her what it was, but more importantly how much it cost. The shirt underneath was a pristine white, but the man's own skin colour was also black, and not a light shade. His head was bald, his teeth as bright as his shirt, and both ensured that the man's age was hard to determine. He was also, Bella decided, very good looking.

"Good evening," he announced, and his voice was warm, like honey. "*Bonne soirée.*" His French was faultless – not that Bella knew any better – but his voice lacked a specific accent. When he spoke French, he sounded French, but his English was not strong enough to be English, American or Australian. It was a more neutral accent, and Bella guessed that most people in the room would imagine the man came from their own country. "My name is Silhouette Moreau, and this is my party." There was a round of applause, and Moreau raised his hand, graciously. "Please, don't applaud. I haven't asked for your money, yet" There was laughter at this.

"Ladies, gentleman and those that don't identify as either, we are at an important crossroads in the life of our world," he continued. "Many of you sitting her have heard me say this before. Probably many times. But I won't stop, and while there are those in governments who aren't interested in what I have to say, or label me a millionaire with a mission, or even put me beside a teenage activist saying that I lack a proper understanding of what we speak, I will continue to use what power and influence I have to make people listen to what is going on.

"We have problems with our wildlife. Problems that we

have caused, thanks to the plastics that we have used and the reluctance to spend money to try to fix that problem. I know some of those who have as much, if not more money than me, will talk of trying to save this planet, but are more interested in trying to increase the human population, than finding a way to repair the damage that we have already created. Some may see me as the kind of person who is disinterested in humanity, more interested in the flora and fauna around us, but those people are wrong. This race, this wonderfully inventive and astonishing race that has risen above everything around it, should continue. But it can't if it doesn't respect that the world we stand on is as important to us as the cars we drive and the phones we are addicted to.

"Silhouette Inc has been developing plasma pyrolysis processes in the hopes of destroying plastic right down to the microplastics that are getting into the wildlife both on the land, in the sea and in the air. Already we are about to launch a ship that has a plasma arc generator, sending it on its way to the South Pacific to clean up one beach at a time. It is not a process sponsored by any government, nor is it funded by any United Nations efforts. It is one man who has been lucky enough to have a lot of money, who can then put that money into assembling a team with some of the most intelligent people on the planet. A team that will help save the world.

"But you can't live in a capitalist world without giving some leeway, am I right?" Moreau grinned a huge grin, and the audience gave an appreciative chuckle. "Shadow is our energy drink. Not made from plasma, obviously, but with enough ingredients to ensure that you can get that energy boost you need to keep working into the night. And as for the bottle, well, this is the good part. It's made from a plastic that has been designed to degrade into a small lump which can be either be destroyed by the plasma arcs, or reused for other plastic products.

"We're gonna show you some of our other merchandise, some great clothing and some amazing swimsuits modelled by some very familiar faces. Well, familiar to anyone who isn't as old as I am." Another round of laughter. "Guys, sit back, enjoy the night, eat, drink and definitely be merry, and come talk to me. Donate, if you want. I definitely won't say no. Thank you so much, and now let's take a look at that merch!"

The lights dimmed, putting Moreau into blackout, before around the stage a number of different coloured illuminations began to bring the stage to life. Bella found herself excited by the sudden change in music, and she sat up to pay more attention. Annoyingly someone popped a champagne cork somewhere, and she looked across the room, catching sight of a woman who probably was responsible.

She also frowned at the weird burning smell that suddenly pervaded her nose. What with strange noises and strange smells, she wondered if the whole fashion show was going to be ruined, and when the man beside her suddenly rested his head on her shoulder, she realized it definitely was.

Angrily, Bella turned to the man, and then paused, seeing the hole in the man's head, and the blood seeping out of it.

To her shame, she screamed.

Dana was the first to go out on stage, and she placed her left foot against the step, ready to move up and onto the catwalk. There had been a brief run through earlier in the afternoon, but Silhouette Moreau had said he wanted a somewhat relaxed attitude to the whole thing.

"You're the experts, right? You know how to make things look good. I just want you guys to go up there, show off the clothes, encourage a bit of a buy, but *have fun*! That's the most important thing of all. Have fun."

"I'm not an expert," Asha had muttered to Dana, and the taller girl laughed in response.

"You'll be fine. You look sick in that. Just get up, show off the boobage, and people will want to buy."

"What boobage? My followers are always disappointed by my bikini pics, I tell you," Asha giggled.

But as the lights dimmed, and Dana adjusted her weight to make sure she was ready for the first step, she heard her sister scream. A song by Luna Rochique started to play, but Dana was already through the entrance portal and onto the stage, quickly scanning for her Bella. She saw her sister, saw the man slumped beside her, saw the bullet in his head and quickly swung around to the other side of the room.

Someone in a black hoodie was clearly running.

Caught at a crossroads, Dana's mind worked overtime. Whilst the fall in Korea seemed like ages ago, being the target of an assassin seemed much closer, and her blood chilled as she wondered if someone was still out there to get her. Or worse, were they trying for her family? Her brain cycled through her options, but her emotions were running wild, trying to override her logic. Logic clearly highlighted the best option to take: report to the police what she had seen. But Emotion pointed out that by the time she had done that, the culprit would be well and truly in the wind. On top of that, everyone's attention was on the dead man, and no one was looking as the person ran.

Dana leapt off the catwalk and quickly ran through the pathway to the doorway, pulling it open and racing after the escapee.

She was grateful for the decision to wear sneakers, having guessed that it would go with the bikini, but as she hit the open air, her legs were bit by the cold, and she wished she had been given something warmer to wear.

Pelting for all she was worth, Dana followed the person she believed to be the shooter, and tried her best to follow the stone paths that were on top of the Palais, but Black Hoodie was easily making her own way around, heading directly for the doors that led to floor seven of the Palais.

Dana was catching up, and by the time she got through the doors, she saw the shooter pushing their way through the crowds that were milling about in the foyer, trying to get to the escalator that would take them out of the building. Dana noticed for the first time that Black Hoodie wasn't particularly tall, which made it difficult as they merged with the crowds.

The model continued her pursuit, pushing her way through the throng of people to get to the escalator, feeling like she was stuck in honey, and noticed that the shooter was running down the escalator in an attempt to get ahead. Dana shoved past the people standing still, eliciting a number of rude retorts, but Dana simply bellowed, "Get out of my way!"

This was enough to make the shooter increase their own pace, and soon Black Hoodie was on the fifth floor. Dana cursed as she lost sight of Black Hoodie, and tried to get down quicker. As she hit the grey carpeted foyer on the lower floor, she caught a glimpse of the clothing she was looking for, and realised that they had already begun their descent to the fourth floor on the escalators. As Dana approached, she noticed that there were a set of stairs beside the escalator, and she ran down them, immediately regretting her choice. The escalators and stairwell went down to the second floor, rather than the third, which meant Black Hoodie had an advantage on the escalator, no matter how small.

Biting her lip, Dana decided to do something silly and launched her bum onto the silver rail running down the centre of the staircase, and the soft fabric of her own hoodie allowed her to slide with surprising speed down the rail. As soon as she hit the horizontal path, she leapt off and ran to the next diagonal rail, jumping on and sliding down again. To her delight, she began to shorten the gap between her and Black Hoodie, and at one point, she saw Black Hoodie risk a glimpse back over their shoulder.

By the time Black Hoodie made it to the second floor, Dana wasn't that far behind and she ran, ignoring the pain in her legs as she did more aerobic exercise than she had done in a while. When Black Hoodie reached the escalators to take them to the first floor, and the Viger entrance, Dana was just seconds behind.

"*Arrêt!* Stop!" someone shouted from behind, but Dana continued to run down the escalator, close enough to Black Hoodie that she was almost able to grab the hood. Before they had reached the bottom, Black Hoodie surprised everyone and leapt over the side of the escalator. Dana tried to get to the edge, but two or three men were suddenly in her way, and cursing she pelted down the escalator, looking around at the bottom for where her target had got to.

The Hall was full of people and there were black hoodies everywhere. Dana paused, her breath ragged, but she couldn't see any sign of her assumed shooter. As she realised Black Hoodie had gotten away, she was suddenly shoved roughly to the ground, a knee in her back and her arms pulled awkwardly behind her.

"You're under arrest," a man said, his Canadian accent obvious. Pushed against the cold concrete of the floor, Dana let out a word that she would definitely not be comfortable using in front of her mother.

SECOND REPORT: SUPER MODEL

It was a surprisingly comfortable interview room, Dana reflected, as she sat back in the chair and enjoyed the fact it wasn't a cold, hard metal one, but rather one that was nicely cushioned. She hadn't been handcuffed, and though the table in front of her was metal, the room wasn't a boring pale blue or green, but rather a friendlier off-white. The traditional mirror ran along one wall, but all in all, it was rather pleasant.

And someone had provided her with some Montreal Police tracksuit pants, so she didn't have to spend all her time in her bikini. Thank you, Montreal, you are a wonder.

The door opened, and a man and a woman walked in, both wearing suits, though the man was the only one with a tie. He looked to be the senior, slightly older than his partner, and bearded. There was quite the intensity to him. The woman was more relaxed, but definitely not less on the ball. She was the one with the folder that she tossed onto the table as they walked in.

"We wanted to talk to you about what happened at the Palais," the man said, genially. "But before anything happened, we got a call and told we weren't allowed to talk to you." Dana was a bit disappointed he didn't end the sentence with "eh?"

"Well, the obvious question is, why are you then?" Dana said, raising an eyebrow.

"Everything that happened was a bit weird, and someone was murdered," the female detective said. "So, you can probably understand why this is an issue for us."

"I didn't murder...whoever it was," Dana said. "I was literally behind the stage waiting to go out onto the catwalk. Asha will vouch for me."

"She did," the female detective affirmed.

"But why did you run?" the male detective asked. Dana noticed that the female detective had sat down, but the male remained standing, holding his own manila folder. So, tell the truth? Admit the assassin might have been trying to kill her or Bella or..

"I saw the killer. I thought I'd try to stop them," Dana opted for.

"That's very civic minded of you," the male detective said, though he was clearly suspicious. Dana fought to keep the smile off her face, deciding it was unwise to look smug.

"Look," she said, shrugging, "I don't know anything about the call that said you can't talk to me, and I'm more than happy to help, but I didn't murder anyone and I didn't want to and...well, that's it, really. I just saw the shooter run off and I went after them."

"You're Australian, right?" the female detective said.

"Yes," Dana nodded.

"You were arrested for creating a public disturbance in Australia as well, weren't you?"

"I rescued a cat," Dana sighed, putting her head on the table. "I didn't want this cat to get hit by a car, so I...held up some traffic. It wasn't the end of the world." The two detectives regarded her carefully.

"Weren't you also involved in Librada Cisneros' death?" the male detective asked, and Dana fought from rolling her eyes.

God, would people let it go?

"No," Dana said. "I was in his beauty pageant, I was on his yacht once as a guest, and had nothing to do with when it sunk, or when he died." That was Interpol's lie, but she was happy to propagate it.

"Then there was the death of that model a few months later, right? You were there for that as well?" The male detective looked at her, and Dana felt a stab of a billion emotions. Suddenly she wished she was with her therapist.

"I was. Are you writing my biography?" she said, her tone becoming far more acidic. "Can I ask who was murdered?"

The detectives exchanged a look, and Dana was sure there was surprise in their reactions.

"You don't know?" the female detective asked.

"No, that's why I asked."

"He was on the board for Silhouette's company, apparently." This time it was Dana who was slightly surprised.

"Did you get a look at the shooter?" the male detective asked.

"He was wearing a black hoodie, and I didn't really see him from the front. He was short though."

"Short?"

"Shorter than me, anyway," Dana said.

"You're quite tall," the female detective pointed out.

"Well, yeah, but this guy was at least a head shorter than me. Actually," Dana suddenly realized, "you said that Asha vouched for me?"

"Yes, she did."

"Well, I think the shooter was probably about her height." Dana sat back, happy with her timely nugget of information.

"But you didn't see anything more than a short guy," the male detective said, and Dana was disappointed he wasn't more impressed. "Sure it was a guy? It couldn't have been a woman?"

"I don't know," Dana admitted, and now she was a bit disappointed with her performance. Could it have been a woman? The clothes were baggy so it wasn't clear to her really. She sat back in her chair and sighed, but then the door to the interrogation room opened, and a man walked in. He was short, with curly black hair and very white teeth, but was definitely dressed off the shelf. Dana smiled, recognizing Karam Narogin immediately. Narogin was an ASIO analyst, and had inadvertently become her contact with the Australian intelligence community, who had agreed to let Narogin be her handler, for want of a better word; though Narogin would have been quick to point out that he didn't handle anyone.

"Karam, what a surprise," grinned Dana.

"Interview's over folks," Narogin said, the weariness in his voice immediately obvious. "I mean, you were told not to talk to her at all, but that's fine. Just ignore Australian governmental requests. You do you."

"I did say they could talk to me," Dana said. "I have nothing to hide, and they were just doing their jobs."

"Out, detectives," Narogin said, and jerked his thumb to the door. Both detectives were clearly disgruntled, and the female was about to say something, but clearly thought better of it, and they left the room.

"Wow, look at you being all forceful and assertive," Dana said, her grin never fading.

"Why do you have to be such a pain in my ass?" Narogin complained, sitting down at the table. "I was really having a nice day, Dana, until you came up on the system as having been arrested for disturbing the peace. And, oh, what a surprise, was also being held for questioning in regards to a murder."

"You keep track of Canadian police?" Dana asked surprised.

"Interpol keep track of Canadian police," Narogin sighed. "They caught your arrest and informed us. I had to then immediately get on a plane and come here."

"I have been here for a considerable time. Locked up in a prison cell."

"A holding cell. And Canada is pretty good, all things told."

"It was one of the nicer holding cells I've been in. How come you didn't bail me out when I was arrested for rescuing Dine?"

"Disturbing the peace in Brisbane with regards to a cat doesn't really concern us. Disturbing the peace in Montreal with regards to a murder is slightly different," he drawled sarcastically.

"Well, thanks. Am I free to go?"

"You are. But," and he paused for a moment, glancing at the mirror. As he continued, he held up his hand to cover his mouth, and dropped the volume of his voice. "Do you know anything about the murder? Honestly?"

"No," Dana replied, doing nothing to conceal her words.

"I didn't lie to the police. I didn't even know who the victim was."

"So why chase after the killer?" Narogin said, no longer hiding his words or his frustration.

"I don't know," Dana sighed. "I just thought someone should do something to stop the killer getting away. And I could. I mean, it could have been Bella, right?"

"Your sister? Why would anyone want to kill her?" Narogin said, clearly puzzled.

"What?" Dana snapped.

"She hasn't done anything to warrant an execution, has she?" Narogin replied.

"And the other guy did?"

"And I did?" Narogin sighed, realizing the point Dana was making.

"It's more likely that someone was targeting the actual victim than a random coming along and shooting a guy in the crowd, don't you think?" He paused looking at her, and Dana opened her mouth, before shutting it and nodding.

"Good point," she admitted.

"Come on, let's go," Narogin sighed, getting up. As Dana stood up, she had to admit she felt more than a little stupid. It certainly made more sense that the poor guy had been targeted, rather than she or Bella had been. But the question then arose, what had he done to get murdered?

Coincidentally, or perhaps not really, right beside the Palais des cogrès de Montréal on Rue Saint-Antoine is a much taller, and much less interesting grey brick building, which looks fairly dull on the outside, but on the inside is far lusher. The guests for the launch of Shadow were being accommodated in Le Westin hotel, high price accommodation for what were considered to be high price guests. Entering the long, rectangular, brown and beige lobby dressed in a hoodie, track pants and barefoot, Dana felt decidedly under dressed. She was not surprised to see that more than a few people glanced her way, and she cringed a little as a few phones were brought out and photographs snapped.

Typical, she mused. Karam Narogin came in behind her, and she was annoyed that despite the fact he looked as though he had slept in his clothes (which, to be fair, was probably true), no one paid him the slightest bit of attention.

On the left of the entrance, past the ceiling-less room with the escalator to the upper floors, there was a waiting room. With a number of dark grey, leather arm chairs, and lighter grey couches, the room was occupied by several people Dana immediately recognized. Both Bella and Jeremy were sitting, waiting somewhat nervously, but to her surprise, the dark figure of Silhouette Moreau was also there, along with what Dana presumed was his personal security, looming in the background and virtually advertising their jobs. Surprisingly, one of the security guards was a woman with long dark hair, dressed in a suit and tie that was immaculately tailored. Dana could see tattoos poking out from her sleeves, and it looked like her picture might be under "resting bitch face" in the dictionary.
Even more surprisingly, in the chair that had its back to her, was her manager, Christa Adams. Adams leaned around the chair to see what everyone was looking at, and raised her eyebrows when she saw Dana.

Dana affected a meek smile in the hope it might make

some of them happy, but the look of worry wasn't easily removed from most of their faces. Adams, however, simply looked slightly annoyed.

No change there then.

As Dana walked over to the group, Moreau was already getting up, and walking towards her.

"Dana, I am *so* sorry," he said, and he embraced her, much to her surprise. She hadn't been aware that they were on hugging terms. "I can't believe that this would happen. And in my own launch. It's horrible, absolutely horrible."

"I'm sorry for your friend," Dana said, and Silhouette released her. For a moment he looked genuinely puzzled, but then he nodded.

"Thank you. Thank you, Dana. He will be greatly missed. We weren't enormously close, but the death of a colleague is not something to brush off." He looked concerned for a moment, before seeming to brush it off. "I'm just horrified your sister was in danger." Bella gave the same meek smile that Dana had given earlier. "You must stay as long as you need to in order to get over what has happened," Moreau continued. "Food, drink, accommodation, your flights back. Everything is on me. Absolutely everything. Do not hesitate for a moment to do something that will relax you. All of you." He graciously extended his arms, clearly indicating Bella and Jeremy, though he did also look at Karam and Adams and nodded slightly. "Dana, I have to go. I have to attend other matters in regards to my dear, departed friend. But I hope that we will see each other again soon, and I hope that you can stay with the Shadow product. I know it might not be easy, but I am happy to talk to you about anything that can help make it better." He leaned forward and kissed her on each cheek, before embracing her again.

"Thank you," Dana whispered, and Silhouette Moreau smiled genially.

"Chillo," he called, and Dana saw the tattooed woman look up, but Silhouette was already walking away without looking back. His security detail followed, ironically Moreau's other, other Shadow.

"Absolutely fucking incredible," Christa Adams said, and Dana wasn't sure whether she was impressed or annoyed. "You have a bizarre knack for creating publicity in a way that I wouldn't have thought possible." She held up her phone, and Dana caught a brief glimpse of the words *Hero Model Tries to Catch Killer!* "Honestly," Adams continued, "you can't buy this sort of publicity. It's incredible." She shook her head.

"Real-Life *Super* Model," Bella said, grinning as she held up her phone to display another headline. "Get it? Supermodel. Like Superwoman. But a model."

"I get it," Dana muttered to her little sister.

"Right, well, I'm getting back on a plane to make sure we can ride this momentum. There'll be interviews, I'm thinking. Lots. Phone's already ringing off the hook. You'll start as soon as you've got changed, fair?"

"Oh, well, uh, of course," Dana shrugged. "I mean, definitely fair."

"Don't waste time with this. The news cycle might pass by soon, and everyone will forget. Let's get your face out there." She turned and headed for the entrance. "I'll get them to do the interview here so it looks good," she called back over her shoulder.

"Police interrogation to public interrogation," Narogin chuckled. "Nice way to live, Spectra. You OK?" He directed the last question to Bella, and she looked a little surprised to be remembered.

"Yeah," she said.

"Good," Narogin said. "I'm going too, Dana. Please try not to get arrested again in Canada. I don't wanna come here again." He shook his head and headed after Adams.

"Who is he?" Bella asked, and Dana opened her mouth to reply, before pausing.

"He's with the Australian consulate," Dana said, deciding that was an easier answer than "He's with ASIO, but he's my handler, so he sometimes acts for ASIS as well. Do you know what those are?"

"Right," Bella shrugged.

"I'm glad you guys are both OK," Jeremy said. "Because, obviously, I'm mad keen to dine out on expensive food, and get drunk on rich people's booze. We should eat, right?"

"We should before Christa has me on *News of the World*," Dana sighed. "I need to get changed though. I'm tired of looking like a hobo. Let's just get room service." She headed for the escalator, but was held up by a voice calling her name. Turning, she saw the figure of Asha running up to her.

"Dana, what the fuck, babe?" Asha gushed. "I mean, honestly!"

"I know," Dana grinned, and the two women hugged.

"You are a fucking legend. My socials are exploding. They want more pics of me and you. Honestly, it's crazy."

"It's been weird, right?" Dana said.

"Can we go?" Bella asked, and Dana shot her a look.

"I can't believe you just ran. Like, you just kicked those heels off and you're pelting after that guy. What are you, Dana?" Asha gushed.

"No heels, Ash," Dana chuckled.

"Don't ruin a good story!"

"Dana," Bella repeated, grabbing her sister's arm.

"What?" Dana snapped, unable to contain her irritation.

"Can we go to the room?" Dana glared at her for a moment.

"Oh man, you were almost shot, right?" Asha said, moving forward to take Bella's hand. "Honestly, kid, are you OK? That was mental, right? You're incredible."

"Thanks," Bella muttered. Dana frowned, puzzled by her sister's behaviour. It wasn't like Bella to be so introverted, but now she wouldn't look Asha in the eye, and almost seemed to recoil at her touch. "Please?" Bella asked again, and Dana nodded. She felt a stab of guilt and wondered if she wasn't taking her sister's emotional state seriously enough. A woman she barely knew was being more sympathetic than her own sister.

"It's cool, babe, honestly. Take her to the room, give her a break. You both need it." She leaned forward and kissed Dana on the cheek. "DM me before you leave, right?" Dana nodded, and took her sister's hand, heading for the escalator. She waited until they she felt they were out of earshot, before turning to her sister.

"Are you OK?"

"She's probably just stressed," Jeremy said, bringing up the rear of the two girls.

"I'm fine?" Bella said.

"What about that…thing with Asha. You couldn't even look at her. What was with that?"

"Dana," Bella started, and then paused. They had reached the top of the escalator and all three stepped off. "Dana, who is that girl?"

"That's Asha. She's an influencer. You know that," Dana said. "Why?"

"Dana, she's the assassin."

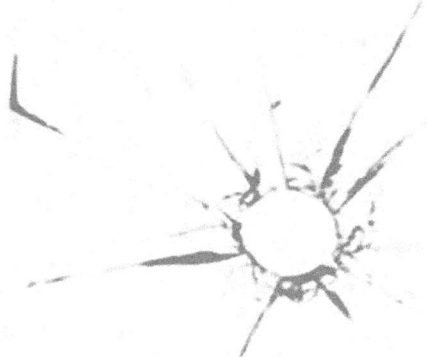

AUSTRALIA

FIRST REPORT: AMPED UP

"I'm beginning to think I'm cursed," Dana said, somewhat dramatically even to her own ears. She looked out of the window of Dr Prass' office, onto Queen St Mall in Brisbane, and wished that she could just go and do some retail therapy to solve all her problems.

"Who have you cursed?" Dr Prass asked levelly, though Dana didn't believe she was buying into it.

"Well, Guin would still be alive if I hadn't got involved in the whole Green Earth thing," Dana said.

"You didn't kill Guin," Dr Prass pointed out. "You were asked to take part, so you didn't actively seek out the problem. Arguably it would have occurred whether you were there or not."

"Gary," Dana replied.

"But again, you didn't kill Gary," Prass argued. "He was killed by someone else in a hospital. Had you not been there, the person who was shot in Japan would have died, so death was almost inevitable, whether you were there or not."

"And then Boom, and I know, I didn't kill him. I know that, I do. But you know, you can't walk through life with people dying around you and not think, I'm the common denominator here. I'm the connection." Dana left the window and flopped down in a chair opposite her therapist and let out a sigh. There were others, but Dana didn't give Dr Prass all the information for fear that she might be labelled insane and locked away. The dark-haired face of Illya Tymoshchuk briefly appeared in her head, and she cringed slightly. She'd not ever brought Illya up with Dr Prass, and she really wasn't sure why.

"I think," Dr Prass said, annoyingly reasonably, "that you're taking on a lot of responsibility for things in your life that you don't have much control over. I thought that you had decided you were happy with being a part of this world of espionage?"

"I did," Dana admitted. "I am happy. I mean, it's exciting, and I've always felt that I never quite understood Dad's job, but now I feel I do a little better. I understand why he does it, and why he thinks it's important, and I like that feeling. I like…" Dana paused. "I'm making it sound like it's a cheap thrill. And that's not right."

"No, I'm not getting that," Dr Prass replied.

"It's important. I like the feeling of making a serious difference and helping people. Not that I think modelling is pointless and worthless, but it's a different thing."

"You don't have to justify yourself to me, Dana. Are you trying to justify things to yourself?" Dana buried her head in her hands.

"Maybe?"

"If I were to guess, and I may be completely wrong, and if I am, then correct me," Dr Prass smiled, "but are you worried about Bella?"

"She was so close to being murdered. That guy was probably assassinated by an expert and that saved her life, but what if it wasn't an expert? What if it was some idiot thug that pulled a gun and shot in that direction but missed and killed her?

And if I had my gun, I'd have been able to stop that assassin. He could be in custody right now. Like, I'm not trying to brag, but my aim is amazing. Genuinely. No crumbs left." Prass frowned, but let the comment slide. "And it's not even like this is the first time Bella's almost been..." This time she stopped because she physically couldn't bring herself to say what almost happened on Cisneros' yacht. It was the whole point of seeking therapy and her inability to say it aloud told Dana that she still needed it. "And then I *was* actively targeted by an assassin, and what if that's still going on? What if Bella is a target to get to me?"

"It feels to me like this whole lifestyle change, this whole," Dr Prass paused, searching for the right words, "this whole refocus is moving in stages. You've confronted this world, been dragged into it and forced to kill to save your life and to save Bella's. Then you had to confront yourself, and how your lifestyle works in relationship with this new path. Can you have both? Should you have both? Now you're seemingly approaching a third stage. Confronting the safety of those around you. You've entered this world in an unorthodox way. Most people consider this and make decisions and give it a lot of thought. You dived into the deep end and now you're trying to work out just how far you can swim."

"So, what do I do?" Dana asked.

"Well, you know I can't answer that question for you," and Prass gave a sympathetic smile. "You have to decide what you want to do. The feelings of satisfaction and of completeness... do they balance the feelings of fear and concern for those around and those that you love? And if you feel that they do, will you be able to live with that choice?"

"Urgh," Dana groaned out loud, eliciting a laugh from her doctor.

"We're at the end of our time, Dana. But I'm glad you came back. It worried me when I hadn't seen you for a while." Dana pulled a face.

"I'd thought I was coping," she admitted. "But then the Shadow thing happened, and there was something in Russia," Dana shrugged, not willing to get into that particular issue. "I just needed help," she admitted.

"I'm always here," Prass smiled.

"Did you unfollow Asha on my account?" Dana asked, unable to keep the outrage from her voice. Bella looked up, with a gaze that only a teenager can muster at the height of their hormonal anger.

In truth, Dana had decided she was probably about ready to move out of her parent's home and into her own. She had sized up a couple of apartments that interested her, both in Brisbane and other places, but she hadn't quite decided where she wanted to go, and in truth, she was a bit scared about moving away from her family. Christa Adams had told her repeatedly that she needed to consider moving countries, as it would be easier to grow her brand in Paris, LA or London, but Dana liked the idea of being an Australian model. Others had done it, and though she wouldn't put herself in the same league as Elle or Miranda, she certainly aspired to be like them.

But while she was still living under her parents' roof, bursting into her sister's room was a perfectly reasonable option, especially as the two had rooms pretty much opposite each other in the corridor that led to the bathroom at one end of the house.

Dana was holding up her phone as though it were the proof of her assertions, but Bella, relaxing on her pale purple bedding, barely turned her head at the interruption.

"Well, sorry to be the voice of reason, but I don't think the optics look good if you're friends with an assassin." Bella stopped, before restarting with perfect timing. "Another assassin." Dana let out a gasp of exasperation.

"She's not an assassin, for god's sake!"

"I know what I saw, Dana," Bella insisted, and Dana could feel the teen sass coming off her sister.

"Seriously, how is that even possible? She was literally standing behind me when that guy was shot," Dana said, and noted that her voice was higher and louder, and she felt a little like she was losing the argument.

"Was she? Was she really? In the dark you're certain of that?" Bella's look was nothing short of a throwdown, her eyes more challenging than anything Dana had come up against in the past. But Dana was absolutely certain. She remembered standing on that step ready to go up, and she had just spoken to Asha, and then the lights went down, Silhouette did his bit, the music amped up, and the shot rang out.

But Silhouette's bit wasn't exactly short, was it?

"If you can't do what I want you to do, then maybe I should do my own socials," Dana snarled, and her heart immediately regretted it as she saw the hurt in Bella's eyes.

"Then have your stupid fucking phone and do your own stupid fucking job and get out of my *fucking room*!" Bella screamed. The phone was thrown, and when Dana turned to collect it, the door slammed shut with enough force to know at least one picture had fallen off the wall.

Dana felt sick to the very pit of her stomach. She and Bella had never fallen out like this before. In fact, after Kimba, Dana had been determined to make sure that she would not fail Bella, but now she definitely had. And yet she couldn't understand why Bella was so insistent that Asha was a killer.

Though, Silhouette's bit was quite long...

Asha had been there when Dana stepped up to go, right?

Right?

The phone hadn't shattered, which was nice. She wandered into her room, and did a search on how to contact ASIO. Hesitant, she made a decision and dialled 13 ASIO.

"Welcome to ASIO Brisbane, how can I help you?"

"Uhm, I'm trying to get in touch with Karam Narogin," Dana said, feeling a little silly.

"I'm afraid it's against policy to connect you to anyone directly, and we cannot confirm or deny if anyone by that name is working for us," came the response, which was surprisingly sympathetic.

"Oh right. I'm just...I'm Dana Spectra and I'm...I'm sorry," Dana said.

"The model?" came the response.

"Yes, I mean...yeah, I guess."

"Wow, a huge fan," gushed the response on the other end. "So impressed with you saving the cat. Amazing."

"Thanks," Dana said. "I'm sorry to bother you."

"I'm sorry I couldn't help," came the reply, and Dana hung up. She needed to fix things, she decided, and she wouldn't be able to do that unless she knew exactly who it was that had done the assassination. And for that she needed help. She supposed she could always contact Interpol, but she wasn't particularly keen on that option.

To her surprise a little green dot started to blink in the corner of her phone display, and she paused for a moment before pressing it. The display melted away, replaced by a new one and now it was clear she was receiving a call from Karam Narogin.

"Hello?"

"What do you want?"

"Sorry?" Dana couldn't quite believe her ears.

"What. Do. You. Want? You called me. Why?" Narogin sounded annoyed, as always. "Also, why not just call me directly? Why did you try to go through the ASIO switchboard?"

"I didn't know I had your number," Dana replied, defensively.

"I made me a contact when I set up the alternative OS," Narogin said, and Dana could hear him shaking his head at her ineptitude.

"I'd forgotten about that," Dana admitted, and she wondered if he banged his head in frustration. "I need to meet with you," she continued.

"Now?" Narogin asked, and Dana suddenly realized she wasn't sure where in Australia Narogin actually was.

"Well, as soon as I can," Dana said.

"OK, well, how long will it take you to get to the Mall?"

"Queen St Mall?" Dana asked, and it was her turn to sound surprised.

"Yeah, I can be there in about fifteen," Narogin said.

"OK," Dana said hesitantly. "It might take me thirty, but I'll go now."

"OK, thirty. Jimmy's." With that he hung up, and Dana looked at her phone curiously. She would definitely have to explore the under-OS more, she decided.

SECOND REPORT: INFORMATION BROKER

Jimmy's-On-The-Mall is a nice restaurant that, location wise, lives up to its name, situated just off the side of the direct center or Brisbane's Queen Street Mall. Two stories, open air, with some rather nice greenery scattered around to suck up the ultra-urban vibe, the restaurant's food is perfect, particularly for those catching up on a weekend before they set out to other events. Dana liked the place, though she was often nervous about going in light of the fact that on one particularly drunk night, she had gone there late, with friends, and it wasn't until the next day she realized they had all got up and walked out without paying. Ever since that day, she was worried that someone was going to tap her on the shoulder if she ever dined there and remind her she still owed money.

As Dana strolled up, she saw Narogin on the bottom floor, sitting at a table looking lonely. She preferred the upper level, but guessed that definitely wasn't Narogin's scene.

"Hey," she said, sitting down opposite him.

"Hi," he replied, and sounded weary. She wondered if it was to do with work or her. Or both. Hopefully not both.

"I need your help," she said, and leaned forward across the table.

"What are you doing?"

"I figured this might be top secret," she said with a

frown.

"Oh right," Narogin rolled his eyes. "Go on."

"You seem particularly annoyed to see me," Dana said petulantly.

"I do have a job, Spectra," he said. "You aren't my sole portfolio, you know." He raised an eyebrow and she felt suitably chastened.

"Sorry. I need to know who killed that guy in Canada," Dana said.

"We're looking into it. And by we, I mean the Canadians. They have their own thing, it's their jurisdiction, etc etc." Karam Narogin shrugged.

"Don't you care?"

"When you do what I do, you come to terms with the fact that not all your problems are wrapped up in a nice little bow," Narogin said.

"Oh yeah, I understand," Dana nodded, and she wasn't being glib. Her trip to Korea had taught her that rather brutally. Ironically, having reached that conclusion, she found herself in a situation where she could have the answers. Nonetheless, she was happy now, controlling the things she could control, and letting go of all that she couldn't. "But this is different. For me," she added, hoping not to offend.

"I don't know what you want me to say exactly," Narogin said, though he wasn't exactly unsympathetic.

"Do you know where I might find the assassin who did it? Or how I would go around finding out? Like, is there an assassin's website or something?" Even as she spoke, she decided what she was saying sounded stupid, and was therefore somewhat surprised when Narogin didn't laugh her out of the restaurant.

"Sort of is, sort of isn't," Narogin said.

A waiter interrupted them to ask if they would like anything to eat or drink, and while Dana just opted for some water, Narogin was clearly keen for lunch, and opted for a premium beef burger. When the waiter left, Dana opened her mouth to say something, but Narogin shook his head.

"There are actually some websites that do advertise assassination requests," Narogin explained. "However, most of them are done through intermediaries to avoid anyone's identity coming out, and giving everyone plausible deniability. We keep an eye on the websites where we can, but they often get shut down and started up again somewhere else, so it can be tricky. That said, the death of Tom McAteer was not advertised on anything we picked up."

"That was his name?"

"Yeah. He worked for Moreau."

"I remember," Dana nodded. "So there's no way of finding the assassin?"

"Assassins don't just gather together and chat about jobs," Narogin said, and this time he absolutely was condescending.

"Alright," Dana said snarkily.

"But," Narogin started, and he looked conflicted. They were interrupted by the waiter bringing drinks, and when the waiter had gone, Narogin had seemingly resolved his inner conflict. "There's this woman. In France. She's," he paused, searching for the right words. "I suppose she's a socialite.

69

DeeDee, they call her. She holds these big parties, big names attend, very fancy, invite only. You know the drill." He sipped at his drink before continuing. "There have been rumours for a while that she's connected to some of the shadier underworld figures. We suspect she might be an information broker, and she uses the party to disseminate information. I say *we*, I mean ASIS. And even then it's a big guess on their parts. Nothing has been proven one way or the other and Salomé Hélène Delacroix-Dennel doesn't give anything away at any point."

"I think I've heard that name before," Dana admitted.

"Oh, didn't she collaborate with some designer on a DD collection?" Narogin asked.

"That sounds right," Dana agreed. "But you think she knows?"

"No idea," Narogin said. "It's a long shot. A very long shot. But," he shrugged. "Maybe. If anyone does, she's not a bad place to start."

"OK," Dana said. "I guess I'm going to France. Can you give me the address?" Karam Narogin looked at her wearily, then pulled out his phone and started writing a text message.

"Be careful, Spectra," Narogin suddenly looked up. "Look, we've always assumed that DD is a hangover from the old days of espionage. Cold War sort of thing. Polite but dangerous. We could be very wrong. If you're going after her, be very careful. *Very* careful." Dana nodded at Narogin, and stood up. She appreciated the advice, but her mind was made up.

Dana stood at the door to Bella's room, and raised her finger to knock on it. There was a whiteboard on it with the word "No!" written in big letters. She could smell the scent of rosewater coming from the room, and suspected that her sister had lit a candle. Part of her had been tempted to just leave, but she couldn't do that. She wasn't going to leave her sister having fought with her, and there was too much to do to hope that might just go away rather than fester.

But it had been a rather painful fight. Balking slightly at having to behave like an adult, Dana knocked at the door carefully.

"Who is it?" came the response and Dana cringed slightly, wishing it had simply been "Come in."

"It's me," Dana replied, and there was a pause – a long pause – before Bella replied.

"Go away."

"Bella, I need to talk to you," Dana said, wondering if she should just push the door open and risk further upset. The pause this time was longer, and Dana could feel her stomach lurch slightly with nerves. Suddenly the door opened and her sister was looking up at her. Dana suddenly realized that she seemed to be a little taller, a little thinner in the face. Not quite as waifish as she had once been. Had she not noticed her sister growing up?

"What?"

"I'm sorry," Dana said, softly. She had gone through what she wanted to say a lot on the drive home, with a billion different variations presenting themselves, but it wasn't until she was standing in front of her sister that she decided there was only really one option. "I'm really sorry. I have to go. To France. But I don't want to go having fought with you. And I should take you seriously. And, I don't appreciate you as much as I should, and I know that." Tears had begun to sting her eyes, and Dana suddenly realized how much she meant what she was saying. Bella held her sister's gaze, but her eyes were also glistening.

"I'm sorry too," her sister said. "I should have asked your permission before unfollowing your friend." Dana grabbed the smaller girl and hugged her hard, and felt the hug in return. "Why are you going to France?"

"The only way to prove you wrong is to find out who actually did it," Dana said. "So, I'm going to do that."

"I'm not lying, Dana," Bella said, and this time it wasn't petulance but pleading.

"I know," Dana acknowledged. "I know. And," she swallowed as she accepted the truth of what she was going to say, "maybe you're right. Maybe I'm wrong and she wasn't there. Maybe I made a mistake. But the only way I'll know that is if I find out the truth."

"Please be careful," Bella replied.

"I will," Dana assured her sister. "But I do have to go shopping and buy something before I go. And maybe, given that I don't appreciate or even pay my social media manager enough, maybe I should buy her something as well." Dana paused and then kissed her sister on the forehead. "Wanna go shopping?"

Later that evening, with a bag packed full of things that Dana thought she might potentially need on her journey, and a bank account lighter, thanks to Dana's desire to buy her way back into her sister's good graces, the model lay back on her bed and contemplated her trip to France.

Go to the party, find out who was hired to kill Thomas McAteer. Easy enough.

On a whim, she typed McAteer's name into Google, and

was curious when a number of different people were brought up. She scrolled through them, looking for any possible mention of Silhouette Moreau as well, and clicked on the first link that had potential.

Dr Thomas McAteer B.App.Sci, MA, MS, PhD – Head of Research, Silhouette Systems

Dana scrolled down a bit to read more about the man and was intrigued to see that he was on the board for Silhouette. She wondered what that entailed, and decided it was probably just money, and lots of it.

So someone had gone out of their way to murder a board member, and the head of research. Who would want a research scientist dead?

Experimentally, she typed Dr Thomas McAteer controversy and pressed search. To her surprise there were a few articles that came up but not to do with his assassination. Most centered around a comment that had been made regarding a fellow academic.

"Dr Growlin's accusations are ridiculous and probably slanderous. To suggest that I have had any inappropriate financial dealings is an affront to me and an insult to all the hard work that I've put into every business I've ever worked with. My professionalism has never been questioned before now, and to have this sort of accusation made is deeply offensive."

Dana flicked down a little further.

"I'm hope Growlin is satisfied with their outcome, but it doesn't resolve the problem and pretending it's just going to go away doesn't help anyone. And I said their, so it should make them happy."

So, potentially an embezzler or someone who liked a side hustle, Dana mused, but at the same time he wasn't alone in his sentiments, so it was unlikely any hitman aiming to balance the scales would start with a fairly obscure…Dana looked at the article again…nanotech researcher. There were certainly more notable targets than Dr McAteer. No, Dr McAteer's past convictions were unlikely to be the cause of an assassination attempt.

As she laid her head back on her pillow, her eyes began to close and she had one last thought as morphea overcame her: If Bella was right, why would Asha want to kill anyone?

FRANCE

FIRST REPORT: RAISE FLAGS

The address that Karam Narogin had written down was an obscure one, and after some research, Dana had finally worked out where exactly she needed to go, and more importantly, when. Narogin's information also told her that Salomé Hélène Delacroix-Dennel's soirees were held on the first Saturday of every month. That gave Dana two weeks to prepare herself, and so she took the opportunity to get herself ready for the trip, and to inform Christa that she needed a week of freedom, which Christa wasn't tremendously impressed by.

True to her word, Christa had Dana on a number of television talk shows, where she awkwardly talked about why she had decided to pursue an assassin in Canada. A few live linkups to other countries were scattered between appearances on television shows in Australia, culminating in a seat on *The Project*, where she was quizzed about what had happened, and then posed important questions like what level of crime would prompt her to actually jump off the catwalk. Dana had tried to contain her irritation with the presenter when that question was asked, but when she pointed out that someone had actually died, the discussion seemed to be cut short and that was the end of it.

Christa Adams was dismissive about the performance.

"The news cycle is almost over anywhere," she said.

"But you just came across as someone who gives a shit about the person who died, which is more than those morons did. You're the one who looks good, so it's a win." Dana had felt somewhat relieved about that, though she did reflect that Adams herself had shown surprisingly little care for the deceased.

Though, in fairness, that was Christa Adams. There was nothing particularly new about that. She was right, as well – a number of posts on social media led with a *Someone Died – The Model Who Cared.*

And so, on a certain Saturday morning, Dana watched the countryside rush past her as she sat on the train that would take her from Paris to Vernon. She had briefly contemplated the idea of flying her new Maclaren 720S Spider to France to drive, but on discovering just how much it would cost for that to happen (even with the idea of shipping it back), and all the paperwork required to drive it in France, she gave up on the idea very quickly. Buying the car had definitely not impressed Colonel Indigo Spectra; flying it to France to drive around in would have given him a conniption.

As they left Greater Paris, Dana watched the countryside turn green as fewer and fewer houses appeared on the land around them. It was a glorious morning, really, with the sky absolutely clear – a nice change for France – and the ground a rich, verdant green. The odd little farm house dotted the land, and then every so often they would pass by a small village, which was invariably not a stop that was planned.

Vernon itself was a small town, that reminded Dana a little of Via Cantonale, the small village she had visited when she was in Switzerland while on the run with a woman who would later turn out to be an international thief. As she arrived in the train station, however, she revised that opinion. Vernon was more modern, though not particularly up-to-date, and lacked a lot of the charm that Via Cantonale had. There was a little bit of local colour, and the village wasn't unpleasant by any stretch of the imagination. It just wasn't particularly exciting. As she exited the train station and surveyed the quiet little village around her, she decided her opinion was pretty much on the money.

She had booked a room at the Hôtel le Normandy, and after catching a taxi there, she checked in. It was *fine*. In fact, from the exterior the building looked quite cute, with its pale salmon walls and dark roof. She was even slightly impressed that some gold rails had been set up at the entrance, trying to give it a more exclusive feel. What was more scenic, though, was the fact that opposite the hotel was an old fountain, complete with very dark, almost sacramento green water. Inside the hotel was slightly more typical, though she quite liked the look of the old-fashioned wooden bar with its deep red carpet and stained-glass partitions. Her room was also *fine*. A large double bed sat between the brown walls, though she did have a window that allowed her to look out over Vernon, but in truth that was pretty much all there was in the room. She put her suitcase on the collapsable rack that was provided for that purpose and then sat on the end of the bed, looking directly at herself in the mirror opposite.

Recently she had dyed her hair red, but she noticed that her natural blonde was starting to grow through, and she decided she would dye her hair again before she went to the soiree later. With a little help from her phone, she went out and was able to track down a pharmacy where she bought herself the dye she needed, and then returned to the hotel.

As Dana pushed the door to her room open, she paused and looked around the room. There was something out of place, she mused. She closed the door and looked around, her mind trying to figure out what her eye was seeing. Everything seemed the way it had been when she left. There was even the slight crumple on the bed where she had sat earlier, looking at the mirror.

Slowly she made her way around the room, stopping when she got to her mahogany travel trunk. Suddenly her brain caught up and she realized that when she had left, the trunk was facing the bed, and yet now it was facing the mirror. It had been turned, 90 degrees. The bed still had the crumple in it...

Someone had been in her room. Flicking the dials, Dana unlocked her suitcase and opened it, and immediately realized someone had been through her things. They were all packed neatly away, but she could see a black G-string on the top to the left of the trunk. That was something she would never do – she always put her G-strings between her other knickers so they didn't disappear in amongst all her other clothes.

Quickly she went through the suitcase, searching for the case that had been given to her by Narogin to hide her gun when she was going through security. The box was there, and Dana suspected that someone had tried to open it, but when she put her thumbs on either side and the box flipped open to reveal the golden Glock inside, she knew that whoever had been in her room had been unsuccessful.

It did raise some interesting questions, however. Why was someone going through her stuff? Presumably it was known that she was in Vernon, but why did that raise flags? For the first time in a while, Dana suddenly felt exposed, and she wasn't quite sure why.

Regardless, it appeared that she was to be expected at the party. With a sigh, Dana headed to the bathroom.

SECOND REPORT: SERIOUS CONVERSATIONS

Having been told that Salomé Hélène Delacroix-Dennel's were the sort of thing people were desperate to get into, regardless of which side of the law they sat on, Dana realized if she was going to get through the door, she would have to make an impression, and as such, her shopping trip with her sister resulted in the purchase of a teal J Angelique Disa dress. It was an odd design that seemed to be a midriff top that only went over one shoulder, but also tied into the skirt; which itself seemed like a piece of fabric that wrapped around and came together at the same point, leaving quite a leg slit. The dress was also, to a degree, sheer, and as such Dana's teal underwear was visible at a certain angle. It was definitely the right outfit to make an impression, and with her hair once again a fiery red, the dress' colour complemented her perfectly.

Makeup was not an issue. Over the years, though she would always make sure that Jeremy was on hand to do her make up for any professional event (because he was genuinely just that good), Dana had picked up a certain number of pointers on what to do with her makeup. On a long excursion, Dana would bring her Victoria Secrets' 4-in-1 Train Case to ensure she was ready for any situation that she could handle, but of late she realized it was safer to have a backup. Never leaving her travel trunk was her Bescher Puffer Beauty bag. In it was everything she needed to enhance her features; It Cosmetics' Bye Bye Undereye, Giorgio Armani Luminous Silk Foundation and Glow blush, Urban Decay Inks Easy Ergonomic Liquid Eye Liner Pen, Lancôme Hypnôse Doll Eye Mascara and the Urban Decay All Nighter Vitamin C Setting Spray. It wasn't exactly her best arsenal, and it certainly wasn't anything close to what Jeremy would have, but under these circumstances it was perfect.

Hiring a car in Vernon hadn't been particularly difficult, but getting one that suited the vibe of what she was trying to achieve was a completely different story, and ultimately, she was lucky enough to get hold of a BMW M5. The car boasted the first all-wheel drive system for the BMW M series, and as Dana drove through the streets of Vernon, heading out of the little city, she felt the car purr beneath her. Jeremy had laughed at her when she had bought her Maclaren, but she decided she was beginning to appreciate sports cars a little more, and there was definitely something fun about handling a car that was designed for speed rather than day-to-day fuel efficiency.

She drove along the Avenue De L'île De France, heading towards the large roundabout that would indicate she was leaving Vernon. The avenue was a simple two-lane street, houses on either side cementing the rural feel of the place, though by the time she came to the roundabout, these too disappeared. The roundabout itself was a cute little thing, with six flags flying in front of a what looked like a curious wooden wall. Dana didn't recognize any flag outside the French one, and briefly wondered what the others were for.

As she continued on the Avenue, the greenery on both sides ensured she couldn't see the Seine, even though she was aware that it wasn't too far from her on the left.

The Rue du Val d'Aconville was helpfully well signed, and Dana eased the car right, heading down the narrower road, looked over by thoughtful trees on either side. Green fields stretched out, their lushness wasted at the time of evening that Dana was now driving through, with even the horses ready to put up for the night.

Dana's destination, however, was not too far from where she was, and so when the stately house appeared through the trees, she slowed down a little more to make sure she didn't miss her turn.

The house was hidden behind white walls, but there was an open gate which led to what was effectively a parking lot. As Dana pulled her car in, she saw that the party was definitely in full swing. By the exit from the lot, two men stood wearing black suits, both looking uncomfortable, and Dana thought she saw the shape of guns underneath the men's left arms. She wasn't surprised that Salomé Delacroix-Dennel had security, but she did wonder what the extent of that security was. For the first time she wondered if she should have thought her expedition through a little more, but it was now far too late.

She walked up to the guards, neither of whom seemed to be interested in stopping her going through, and as she passed them, they did nothing more than check her out. That was fine; it was all the attention she needed.

She entered a large courtyard, a road circling around it, and Dana realized that there were another two entries into the house, though these were hidden, designed to be part of the wall that set up the barrier. Directly opposite her was a two-story house, orange with a darker roof, walled off from the courtyard and having its own little courtyard. The party, however, was in the building to her left, a four-story manor house, in the same pale orange as the smaller house opposite, with an entrance that was accessible via a set of stairs that flowed out under the canopy. There were other entrances on either side of the building, but these weren't where Dana was going. She strolled across the courtyard, heading for the grand entrance, cutting a striking figure as she did. More security stood by the steps, and again they did nothing more than cast a glance over Dana. She wondered if any of them had been the one who had gone through her room.

She approached the staircase to the entrance and began to walk up, a little cautiously, wondering what the security guards would do. In her bag, was her little case with the golden Glock, though if they decided to grab her, she would have very little time to actually do anything. Her heart in her mouth she continued up the stairs.

At the top, two burly gentlemen in tight suits and tighter features, peered at her. One opened his mouth, but to her surprise, the other simply shook his head.

"*C'est bon, tu peux entrer,*" the one who shook his head said, and they both stepped back. Dana smiled slightly at them and continued through, her heart beating uncontrollably. It had been easier than she had anticipated, but without doubt, way too easy.

She stepped through the large wooden double doors into a massive entrance hall that looked like something out of a dream. The hall was marbled, a beautiful white with black veins, pillars of the same reaching up to the high vaulted ceiling. A giant staircase started at the center of the room and flowed towards the upper level, where people were milling around, engaged in idle conversation and happy chatter.

For the first time in a very long time, Dana felt completely out of place. She was used to opulence and soirees, but there was something about this one that made her feel as though she was very unprepared.

As she looked around at the multitude of people, she began to take in some details that explained her feelings. A man in the corner, tall, dark and scarred, had a suit on with something clearly jutting into the coat at the back. A woman, middle aged, dark-haired and harried had her phone out, as she wondered around, looking for people and having serious conversations. On the upper level she saw a mountain of a man with a bald head and an expensive, handmade suit. She couldn't make out his face, but for all his size, he looked like a shark, with the people around him zipping back and forth, trying to avoid getting eaten.

They may have looked like they were enjoying the party, but they were very dangerous people. *Very* dangerous.

A man walked past her carrying a tray of flute glasses, and he paused as he reached Dana, cocking his head as he put the tray forward. She smiled a little and took a glass, knowing full well it was champagne, a drink she didn't particularly care for.

She noticed there were egresses on either side of the room, and decided that she wasn't going to go to the upper floor. Instead, she headed to her right, walking out of the room and into another, more stately room.

This one was wood paneled, full of cushioned chairs that looked terribly expensive. She saw a chair her brain wanted to call a Louis XIV, but she wasn't entirely sure. It certainly looked as though it were something from the 18th century. Elegant and old-fashioned chaise lounges were also scattered liberally around, and most chairs were occupied by people who were both rich and on a mission.

How would she find anything here? Where would she even start? Feeling overwhelmed, Dana started to realise that she had made a mistake in coming to France. Maybe a mistake in trying to track down the assassin in the first place.

Maybe she would have been better off contacting Broadsword and Interpol, she mused. Her mind virtually made up to leave, she was suddenly interrupted by a very elegant, French voice.

"Dana Spectra, what an *absolut* delight."

THIRD REPORT: SALOMÉ'S WORLD

The woman standing before her was dressed in something she didn't remotely recognize (though it was gold and violet, was a perfect fit and looked divine), had a glass of something fascinating in her hand (it wasn't champagne, but bizarrely it was also gold and violet). Deciding it could only be one person, Dana bowed her head slightly.

"*Madame Salomé Hélène Delacroix-Dennel*, it's a pleasure," Dana said, taking the gamble.

"*Non non*, just Salomé to my friends, and I am sure that we will become such," the woman said, beaming at Dana.

"Not DeeDee?" Dana asked, and Salomé pulled a face.

"If people address me as such, I know they are either law enforcement who seized upon a very boring nick name, or my mother," and Salomé burst out laughing, a rich peal that filled the room.

Dana had to admit she found the woman fascinating. She had no idea what age she was – definitely over thirty, but unlikely to be over seventy, which left for a pretty wide age bracket – and this wasn't helped by the steel grey hair bundled in a braided bun. Her face clearly had lines, but when she smiled the lines deepened, and Dana wondered if laughter lines were all they were. "You have no idea what an honour it is for you to attend my soiree," Salomé continued, and Dana found herself liking the woman despite herself. "So many people come through my door, but so few have such a fascinating story to tell. Please tell me," and Dana braced herself for the inevitable question about Librada Cisneros, "how is that *exquise* pussy of yours?"

"I'm sorry?" Dana asked in shock.

"Err, did you call him Dine?" Salomé queried, apparently not noticing Dana's reaction.

"Oh," Dana said, and suddenly wondered if the question had been deliberately designed to be off-putting. "He's fine, thank you. He's getting quite large."

"Ah, I follow you on social media and see that beautiful pussy all the time," Salomé said, and she linked her arm into Dana's. "But now, you must tell me what has brought you here. We are friends, yes, definitely, and so we are not here to deceive one another. How can I help someone who is so gorgeous and so popular?"

"You're way too kind," Dana said, and she was surprised that she was blushing. "I uh, well…" All of a sudden, she didn't want to say why she had come. In that moment she felt childish and immature, like a five-year-old who declares their intention to run away from home, but makes it to just outside the fence and then sits down to wait. As it turned out, however, the surprises were not going to stop.

"Oh, my dear, but of course, you are still shaken by the shooting in Canada? How thoughtless of me not to ask if you are alright, after that horrible incident." Dana looked at Salomé and gave a wry smile. She may have looked full of concern, but Dana was now fairly certain that she was being cleverly played.

"I am fine, really," Dana said, "but I am worried about the shooting. I was a target a few years back." Salomé said nothing, waiting for Dana to speak, but she did guide the younger woman out of the lounge and back into the hall. "So I've found it difficult to let go of what happened."

"Understandably," Salomé said neutrally.

"Someone suggested to me that I might find some," Dana paused, trying to find the right word that wouldn't offend. "Help, here."

"My dear, you don't have to be so coy," Salomé said, her voice a veritable ooze of suppressed delight. "We are not here to deceive one another. You want to know if someone has been hired to kill you? I have friends in low places, it is true. There is someone who might be able to give you what you need. Hopefully he is not the man who has been given the contract," she laughed and it was delicate in a way that reminded Dana of a small waterfall in a rainforest. Sort of…sprinkly… "Come, come."

To Dana's surprise, Salomé continued her walk from the main hall into the room that was to the right. This room had a very different feel despite the fact that to all intents and purposes it seemed to be precisely the same room, just in reverse.

Salomé, however, had it filled with tables where a number of people were playing a variety of games, all of which it was clear there were bets on, and none of which were probably legal. But it was clear that Salomé lived by her own rules and no one was going to question her. Dana wasn't sure exactly who was at the soiree, but she wouldn't have been surprised if it turned out that law enforcement officials were present. Sometimes it seemed the worlds of enforcement and destruction were just two sides of the same coin.

It had been some time since Dana had set foot inside a casino, and vaguely thought the last time was in Monaco. Well, legally anyway. She supposed that technically she had also been to an underground casino on Korea, but the less said about that the better. Not that Salomé's version was not exactly any more moral.

She was guided across the room, through a variety of tables populated by rich people getting rid of money at a high rate. Somehow, Dana suspected that the house won a lot more in Salomé's world than it did in the big cities.

"They play for secrets, you know," Salomé said pleasantly. "Each and every one of them gives up something to play and it is a secret. I have no need for the money but I do like to know what is going on. Everywhere." Her voice never seemed nasty, never contained a single trace of menace, and yet Dana suddenly realized she was being told an underlying message.

"I'm not sure what I could offer you, if I'm honest," Dana said, guessing correctly. Salomé smiled broadly at her.

"I have, for you, just one simple question I would like answered. It's not even particularly important. But it is a curious oddity that bothers me. So it has *become* important because I don't have enough information to..." Salomé paused in her walk and seemed to search for words. "*C'est un problème simple, mais ça m'énerve de ne pas connaître la réponse.*" Dana frowned, but Salomé laughed. It was a light sound, again without danger, but at the same time soulless.

"If I can answer I will," Dana said carefully.

"Do you know very much about Dr Thomas McAteer, the

man who was killed in Canada?" Dana raised her eyebrows slightly, wondering why Salomé was so interested in a research scientist. Presumably she already knew as much as Dana did, and yet there was something more she wanted to know.

"I didn't really get to know him, if I'm honest. My sister was the one sitting next to him. He just told her his name, but didn't say anymore. I assume he wasn't lying." Salomé looked at her, no emotion on her face, but Dana sensed she was keen for the information. "I think he was on the board or something," Dana said. Salomé's face was neutral, and leaving Dana uncertain as to whether the older woman was satisfied with the answer or annoyed. Or simply bored with the conversation.

"The board? Of Silhouette Moreau's company?"

"I think so," Dana said, wondering why that was significant. "I'm not sure why you would even bother to assassinate him."

"Indeed," Salomé agreed, and Dana realized she simply wanted a piece of the puzzle that she didn't have filled in. "If you find out why, please, do tell me. I would be fascinated to learn. And you are always welcome at my house, at any time," she said. Salomé was once again in full flight, and it seemed as though she had always intended to go the way she was going. Her destination was a card table, where a beautiful young woman dressed in a black silky swimsuit with white cuffs, was dealing cards to the very large man she had seen earlier.

Up close he was just a little more terrifying that he had been from a distance. He was very big, very bald and his eyebrows were dark and furrowed, hovering above two cold blue eyes. When Salomé arrived, he raised one eyebrow, allowing him to briefly take in his host, before he tapped the table in front of him.

"*Dix*," the croupier called as she dealt a queen face down in front of the big man. "*Six*," her own card followed. "*As*," and an ace was placed down in front of the Big Man. She dealt herself a card, but didn't bother to call it, instead, she pulled the cards in and pushed a pile of chips towards the Big Man.

"*Monsieur*," Salomé said, "would you be interested in being joined by another player? She's quite keen to meet you." The big man looked over at Dana and then regarded his chips thoughtfully.

"Sure," he said, his voice as low as Dana expected it to be, though she was a little surprised to discover he was American. For some reason she had thought he might be English or European. "I'm assuming you're not playing for cash," he said, and Dana felt a little awkward as she realized she had nothing in front of her on the table.

"*Mademoiselle Dana* will be covered by the house," Salomé smiled. "Your information will be of equal value. Just bet as normal." Salomé gave a smile to the croupier, who nodded her understanding and was discretely no longer at the table. Carefully, Salomé dealt out a card to each player.

"*Dix*," she said as she laid out the Jack of spades in front of the big man. "*Six*," as the matching six came out. Dana sighed a little, suspecting she had made a very big error.

"*Deux*." Two of hearts – this time it was the big man who looked irked. "*Neuf*." Nine of clubs. Dana bit her lip deciding she definitely hadn't thought this through. When he tapped the table, Salomé dealt a card.

"*Trois*," she intoned, and the annoyance remained on the big man's face. Dana paused, and hesitantly tapped her nails on the green table surface.

"*Dix*," Salomé said neutrally, and put the King of diamonds on the table. She placed a number of chips on the table, equal to what the big man had initially put down, and pushed them all towards him. Dana glanced at the tall woman, who simply raised an eyebrow. Two more cards were tossed onto the table.

"*Sept*." Seven of diamonds to the big man. "*Cinq*." Five of diamonds to Dana. Two more cards followed. "*Neuf*." Nine of clubs to the big man, and Dana watched him wince slightly. "*Deux*." Two of hearts. Dana closed her eyes and rolled them to herself. 16 plays 7. What a disaster. At best she could get 18. The big man tapped the table without hesitation, and Dana wondered if he had a rule he stuck to, given that the 16 had unimpressed him. "*Deux*." The two of clubs. Dana tapped the table. The ace of diamonds hit the table. "*As*," Salomé said, and looked at them. The big man regarded Dana thoughtfully, aware that he was the one in the awkward position. He waved his hand slightly, content to sit on 18. Dana bit her lip slightly, and then tapped the table.

"*Trois*," Salomé said, as she dealt down the three of diamonds. Dana's eyes widened in surprise.

"Well risked," the big man said, and though he wasn't smiling, there was no anger in his eyes. "How can I help you?"

"I understand you know a lot about what goes on in the, uhm," Dana struggled to find a phrase that didn't make her sound green. "World of murder." This time the big man did smile.

"A little, I suppose," he acknowledged.

"Do you know anything about the assassination at the

Shadow launch last week?" The big man looked across the table to Salomé and gave a laugh that was a short bark. "Oh subtle, Salomé." Salomé raised her hands innocently, but Dana got the feeling she had definitely been played.

"He was a scientist that worked for Silhouette Moreau. There was a hit put out on him earlier in the week. I was contacted but," the big man paused for a moment, a smile creeping across his face, "they couldn't afford me."

"But they contacted you? He was the target?" Dana asked, curiously.

"Oh yes," the big man said. "They wanted the job done by the best. So, they contacted me first."

"Then who?" The big man shrugged.

"I don't care about my leftovers."

"Are you sure you were first?" Salomé asked gently. "I'm surprised they didn't approach Man Garam." The barking laugh came again.

"Alright," he admitted. "The client contacted them after me. I did check."

"Or the client contacted you after Man," Salomé said, and the big man narrowed his eyes.

"I was first on the list, I assure you."

"So, who," Dana started, but the big man put up his hand.

"No more questions. Unless you want to play for them," he added. Dana took a deep breath, and Salomé shrugged at her. The big man slid all his chips into the center of the table, and Salomé widened her eyes slightly.

"Ooo," she said. "Unfortunately, I do not think the house

could cover your bet *Mademoiselle*. I do not think you have any information that could be worth that much."

Not for the first time in her life, Dana's exterior became fixed – cool and composed, an act she had developed when she learned that hiding your true feelings was essential in the modelling industry. Do you like this outfit that is made of left-over bicycle parts? It's a work of art (*Who the fuck would wear that???*). Did your tit just fall out when you were on the catwalk? Possibly, but the outfit was totally worth it (*God, please don't let that get on the internet!*)

Her brain kicked into overdrive, as she scoured through everything she had learned since her meeting with Justice, and a number of things came up that she suspected would interest Salomé Hélène Delacroix-Dennel. What was she prepared to sacrifice? Or perhaps, who?

"It's been a pleasure," Salomé said to the pair, and she turned to walk away.

"Chalice," Dana said quietly, and Salomé stopped where she was. She turned back to Dana and looked at her.

"What," she started to say, but Dana cut her off.

"Only if I lose," she said, and the big man barked his laugh. Salomé narrowed her eyes, and then a broad grin crossed her face.

"You are fascinating," Salomé whispered. She reached for the shoe, and Dana noticed that the croupier from before had been resetting the table while they waited. Salomé slid out two cards.

"*Dix*," she said as the king of spades was tossed before the big man. "*Neuf*," she said, and the nine of diamonds landed in front of Dana. "*Dix*." The ten of diamonds landed in front of the big man, who smiled broadly. "*As*," Salomé said, and the Ace of clubs landed in front of Dana. The big man was already waving his hand, and yet there was a shadow on his face that made it clear he wasn't entirely satisfied with his own actions. It would be madness to call again on 20, thought Dana.

But if she didn't it would be a draw, and they would play again. Maybe. Unless the big man didn't think it was worth his time. Closing her eyes, Dana tapped the table, her French manicure standing out against the green.

"I hope your information is worth 50,000 euros," Salomé said, and there seemed to be an edge to her voice. "I should very much not enjoy being made a fool of." Dana turned to look at her, and tapped her fingers again, meeting the older woman's gaze.

Without even looking, Salomé slid a card out of the shoe and tossed it over to Dana, casually, but with enough flip it landed face up. Dana glanced down at the card.

The Ace of Hearts.

"You are both extremely lucky, and extremely ballsy," the big man said, and there was an admiration on his face. "Unfortunately, it's all been for nought. The truth is I genuinely don't know who was after me, if that's the question you were going to ask. I am sorry."

"Ah, such is the nature of the game," Salomé sighed. "And now, *mademoiselle*, what do you know about Chalice?"

"Oh, no," the big man interceded. "She won. You got your money, Salomé. The girl gets and gives nothing." For the first time since meeting her, Dana saw Salomé was genuinely angry. And yet the big man remained stoic, and for whatever reason,

Salomé slowly nodded.

"Very well," she muttered. And then, like a sudden shower, the anger was gone. "You are probably my two favourite people," she said, gushing. "Dana, you must stay and enjoy yourself. See me before you go, because I must have you come back in the future." She turned to the big man. "You, you delightful man, I hope will enjoy yourself as well." He bowed his head to her and she returned the gesture gracefully, before turning and walking away.

"Thanks for the game," Dana sighed, standing up.

"Ms Spectra," the big man said. "That's who you are, correct?"

"Yeah," she nodded.

"I can't tell you who was third on the list. But I can tell you who the victim was exactly." Dana raised her eyebrows.

"He was a scientist, right?"

"Oh yes. But he was working on something very specific. If he had been successful, it would have revolutionized Silhouette Moreau's business. Plasma pyrolysis."

"Wait, so you're saying…"

"Killing McAteer wasn't really anything personal. It was to cause problems with Moreau's business."

"Someone has a vendetta against a billionaire philanthropist?" Dana asked, incredulously.

"I know," the big man chuckled. "It certainly doesn't narrow the list down, at all." He got up from the table, casting an imposing shadow over Dana as he blocked out the light. "Though," he added thoughtfully, and for the first time, Dana saw a glint in the big man's eyes, "it's curious that Silhouette Moreau's old partner is now his rival in the recycling business. You may have heard of him; Andre Hémery." Dana narrowed her eyes.

"Why would I have heard of him?" she asked, genuinely puzzled.

"Oh, I thought his company was one of the sponsors for the Miss Green Earth pageant that you entered. TWT, I believe it's called." Dana realised in truth she hadn't paid much attention at all to the sponsors of the Green Earth pageant, though was sure they would have been told at some point.

"Tomorrow's World Today. Curious that, don't you think?" the big man twitched a muscle near his lip, hinting at a smile, and then turned and walked away. Dana too got up, but her mind was racing. Andre Hémery rang a bell for some reason. As she headed to the door, she got her phone out and randomly flicked to H in her contacts list. When she saw it, she stopped.

Hémery, Ophélie.

The gorgeous model representing France at Miss Green Earth, and whom Dana had become firm friends with. It could be just a coincidence, she thought.

A coincidence that one of the models in the Miss Green Earth pageant has the same name as the owner of one of the companies sponsoring it?

She didn't need to be a spy to know that a connection like that was a coincidence too far. It was time to go back to Paris.

FOURTH REPORT: FAVOURITE NEICE

"*La vache!*" Ophélie Hémery stood in the doorway to her apartment, her mouth open in shock. "Dana! *Mon œil!*" The *younger girl threw her arms around Dana, wrapping her in a bear hug, and exposing the fact that beneath the satin dressing gown, she was wearing nothing but a small, black G-string. Dana hugged the girl back, a grin across her face, before* Ophélie kissed her on both cheeks, and then firmly on her mouth. They had a complex relationship, Dana decided, recognising that the French girl had a crush on her and Dana had to admit she didn't find the idea unappealing, but at the same time, she was trying hard to not be quite as easy to jump into bed as she used to. Poor Ophélie. If they'd met two years earlier, the pair would have definitely slept together by now.

"I am so excited to see you," Ophélie gushed dragging Dana into the apartment. "I'm surprised you even kept my address."

"I said I wanted to see it," Dana protested, which was absolutely true. She had been sent a few pictures of Ophélie's apartment when the French model had bought it six months earlier, and was waiting for an excuse to go to Paris to see it. Now she had the chance, she was quite excited.

The apartment was on Quai Charles Pasqua, the top

floor of a rather boring beige looking building that was high enough such that Ophélie's apartment looked across the trees that lined the street and the median strip, and delivered a beautiful view of the Seine. There was something quite peaceful about the river, though Dana was under no illusions about the state of it, regardless of the potential future development that might be put into it.

"What do you think? *C'est craignos*?" Dana looked at her blankly and then laughed.

"I don't speak French. Is that good?"

"Is the apartment good?" The girl looked at her, and Dana suddenly wanted to hold her, because with her round face and messy blonde hair, she was ridiculously cute. Dana looked around and had to admit the interior of the apartment was infinitely nicer than the exterior, and much more moder. In many ways it served a minimalistic vibe, with tall white walls, and rooms separated, curiously, by opaque dark glass that gave the hint of what was behind it, without giving anything away. The main lounge into which she had entered was sunken slightly, a step away from the dining space and the entrance. The furniture looked white and luxurious, and the black television attached to the wall seemed slightly out of place in amongst the heavenly décor of the rest of the lounge that she was in.

Scattered around the room, ensuring the television didn't look too awkward, were a number of pieces of art, and Dana was curious to see that there was a selection of five paintings on one of the walls that saw each of them in a dominant colour, but were nude paintings of different figures. One was definitely Ophélie, while the other...

"Is that me?" Dana asked in astonishment, as she pointed to a reclining figure, her legs splayed, in a world of sea green.

"Do you like it? A friend painted them for me. I thought they were curious and mysterious." Ophélie grinned, standing next to her own painting, and pulled her gown apart to expose her breasts and give a better comparison. Dana simply laughed out loud.

"I mean, it's incredible," she admitted.

"Dana, I am glad you like it. You are staying here, yes? We are going out tonight. Oh, it's going to be so much fun. I will see if there is anyone who will join us. There will be. Everyone is desperate to meet you."

"We can do all those things, but I have an important question to ask you first," Dana said, and took her friend's hands. Ophélie frowned, a little surprised at this, but didn't flinch. "Do you know someone named André Hémery?"

"Uncle André?" Ophélie asked, a little surprised.

"That's your uncle?"

"My uncle's name is André," Ophélie said, nodding.

"Does he own, uh," Dana paused, but Ophélie continued.

"MDA," and Dana frowned. "*Le Monde de Demain Anjourd'hui,*" Ophélie continued. "Oh, I think it is TWT, no? Tomorrow's World Today."

"That's the one," Dana said. "Yes, him."

"Well, of course I do," Ophélie smiled.

"Is there any chance," Dana started, and felt immediately guilty, "that you could find a way for me to meet him?"

"Dana, what is this about?" Ophélie asked, curiously.

"It's," Dana started and then stopped. She felt awkward, remembering how she had bustled Ophélie off in Japan after they had been hunted by Snake Eyes.

"You are involved in something again," Ophélie said, and Dana thought there was a little bit of judgement in her voice.

"Maybe," Dana admitted.

"*C'est nul*," Ophélie said, and Dana didn't need a translator to know that it wasn't good. "Of course I will help you," Ophélie continued. "But I worry for you. I don't want anything to happen to you. Not like…" She stopped speaking, unable to say the name that was on her lips, and Dana knew exactly why.

Ophélie had a breakfast appointment, but invited Dana along, and Dana relaxed on the sidewalk of the Dandy Kitchen while her friend met with someone who looked very professional, but at the same time the epitome of ennui. Dana sipped on a cup of tea and watched Ophélie get particularly animated while her colleague seemed remarkably disinterested in everything she was saying, and bored by most everything else. She had no idea who they were, but they were fascinating.

About forty-five minutes later, Ophélie got up and came over to Dana's table and sat down, raising a perfectly manicured eyebrow.

"Fun meeting?" Dana asked, smirking.

"*Oui*," Ophélie said, smiling a little. "What is your manager like, Dana?"

"Oh," Dana mused. "She's very efficient. Very business. No sense of humour."

"This must be something that all managers require," Ophélie sighed. "Shall I take you to Uncle Andre? I have to go to another meeting apparently. It is a late decision, but I have time to keep my promise to you."

"Sure," Dana agreed.

"And then tonight we go out and enjoy ourselves, *non*?"

"Definitely," Dana agreed. She actually was quite keen on the idea of chilling with her friend, and Dana was glad that her excursion had driven her to Paris. If she could find out a little more about what had happened with the assassination, then she could return to Australia, satisfied. Ophélie's meeting with her manager did remind Dana that she had a job as well, and she feared looking at her phone messages in case she had missed something important.

Ophélie summoned a taxi and they left the Rue St Denis, which Dana was quite frankly happy to do. The Dandy Kitchen and its nearby hotel were of a high quality, and she very much enjoyed them, but the Rue St Denis area itself was somewhat seedy, and on arrival Dana had been tempted to ask what on Earth would possess Ophélie's manager to want to meet there. The Dandy Kitchen explained that, but still, Dana reflected, the Dandy was doing a lot of heavy lifting to give the area any respect.

The headquarters of Tomorrow's World Today, was on the Rue de Rivoli, one of the main streets of Paris that stretched roughly north-west to south-east, though it wasn't so much a forty-five degree angle as a thirty degree slope. None of the buildings on the Rivoli were particularly tall, but there were a lot that were clearly several hundred years old, though advertising and some of the more modern street signs did try and destroy the façade that Napoleon had fought so hard to create.

One such sandstone building had a bottom floor with a grey, concrete front that was only interrupted by the windows and an extremely incongruous yellow sign with a very bright flower sitting on top of it. The concrete was interrupted, however, by two pillars on either side of an impressive Mahogony double door with large brass handles, and equally impressive brass doorknocks, though both rings were locked into place and could no longer perform their original functions. The pillars stretched up to two cherubs, wrapped in loose togas, holding aloft the balcony above.

Approaching the building, Dana noticed that above the ground floor were a series of balconies, making her wonder if they weren't approaching a hotel, but when the taxi edged to the sidewalk (somewhat illegally), she recognised that they had approached the offices they needed to be at. Rather surprisingly, Dana saw that there was nothing more than a small black plaque on the door indicating that they were at Tomorrow's World Today.

Ophélie breezed towards the front door. Dressed in a Burberry short sleeve black dress, she looked as though she could have been a business woman on her way to work (a very well-dressed business woman, admittedly). Dana had eschewed her signature white-collared black A-line dress, and was wearing what some might view as a school uniform – a collared white shirt, with deep red neck tie, a Revolve woollen beige vest, and a Halara high waisted check, red, pleated mini skirt. This was complemented with somewhat thicker than usual stockings, and a pair of black Tony Bianco Danni slingbacks; not particularly high heeled, as she was already a few inches taller than Ophélie and had no desire to highlight their height difference any more than necessary. Indeed, with Ophélie's Jimmy Choo pointed pumps, the pair were almost on the same height.

Once through the main door, Dana was surprised to see the interior reflected the exterior. For some reason she imagined that the old-style front was nothing more than a façade for a much more modern interior, but inside there was the same sort of architecture; luxurious, sumptuous and grandiose. Tomorrow's World Today seemed to look a lot like Yesterday's World, if their headquarters were anything to go by.

"*Bonjour. En quoi puis-je vous être utile?*" smiled the lady behind the reception desk. And it was a desk. Rather randomly the room had a single desk at which a young lady sat. Her hair was pulled back into an efficient bun, and she had a single tablet on her desk, which seemed oversized for what it was being used for.

"*J'aimerais voir mon oncle,*" Ophélie said, and as the receptionist looked back at her blankly, Ophélie added: "André Hémery." The receptionist's eyes widened.

"*Un instant s'il vous plaît.*" The receptionist tapped on the tablet for a few moments, and then looked up, but before she could say anything, Ophélie said one word.

"Ophélie." The receptionist nodded, and Dana couldn't help but smirk at her friend's arrogance. Ophélie turned back to grin at Dana and the pair giggled slightly. To Dana's surprise, a door at the end of the corridor burst open and a man stepped out. He was comfortably in his fifties, thin, wiry, with dark hair that was flecked with grey, and a matching beard, both of which seemed slightly out of control.

"Ophélie! *Ma nièce préférée!*" He came up to Ophélie and embraced her warmly, and the hug was returned.

"I am your only niece, Uncle André," Ophélie said without a smile. "This is my friend Dana. She doesn't speak French, but she wanted to meet you."

"Oh, Dana, I have heard so much about you. And I think you are now the face of Shadow, yes? I would have loved you, but of course, I have my own amazing model," he grinned, keeping his arm around Ophélie's shoulders. "Come, come. Let's go to my office. Michelle, please organise hot drinks, nibbles, whatever we must have."

There was an effusiveness and energy about André Hémery that was not easy to dislike, but Dana couldn't help notice that his comments to Michelle – presumably the receptionist – were made without even looking back at her. He had Ophélie's arrogance but without the grace that came with it. With all that, however, there was something slightly odd about his relationship with his niece. She didn't' seem quite as comfortable with him as one might expect, and though she didn't flinch at his touch, there was a tolerance rather than warmth between them. Ophélie might be André's favourite niece, but Dana suspected that he was not Ophélie's favourite uncle.

André led them to the end of the corridor where they found the elevator doors, and Dana noticed the clash between the metal of the doors and the wooden walls around it. By the time they got to André's office, the modern world had begun to overtake the building, and while the walls and their trappings still remained on the top floor, a number of glass fronts, metal tables and computers crept like a mould throughout.

One set of glass walls clearly housed André's office, and it was undeniably huge. As they walked inside, the walls suddenly went opaque, turning the office from a large open space to greet all into a much smaller room ruled over by one man.

"Well, this is an unexpected pleasure, and I can't help but wonder what has brought it about," André said, the smile on his face not quite reaching his eyes. Dana looked at him thoughtfully, wondering what he might be getting at, and Ophélie also noticed the slight difference in him.

"Oh, I," Dana started, but André held up his hand.

"Can I guess?" he asked. "Is it something to do with a certain event in Canada?" Dana frowned a little at the comment.

"You know?"

"It is in my world, Dana," André said. "Of course I know. Silhouette Moreau's top scientist is murdered at the launch of his Shadow. You were there, of course. But I can't understand why you are here. Do you suddenly work for the *gendarmerie*?" He was still smiling, but there was definitely an edge to his voice, and on making his comment Ophélie's eyes turned away, and doubt clouded André's face.

"I don't work for...the police," Dana said and hoped that her hesitation could be put down to her translating *gendarmerie*, "But my sister was almost murdered. She was sitting right beside the guy that was killed. And I want to know why, and I was hoping you might know something." She paused and then added "Because it *is* your world."

André Hémery sat down on one of the couches that were near the entrance to his office and indicated that the women should sit down on the couch opposite.

108

"I don't know much about it," he started. "I know that Thomas McAteer was a pioneer in his field, and I would have loved to get him on board. I wish that I could give you further information, but I honestly have no idea." He paused, as if deliberating over something, before finally coming to a decision. "I might possibly have some information for you. But I won't be giving this information out to anyone other than you, you understand. I know that you want to find out why your sister was in danger, and that is why I will say this, but outside of that." He waved his hand, throwing the idea away. "You should talk to one of my staff. His name is Ian Bryce. He's in my financial division. He might be able to help."

There was a knock at the door, and André called out for the person to come in. Dana briefly glanced up to see a figure walk in, though she was wearing a hoodie, and Dana couldn't clearly see her face. It made her realise that everyone had been dressed pretty casually when they had entered, meaning that André was rather the odd one out in his organisation, looking far more well-dressed than any of his employees. She guessed that it was probably a deliberate thing, not least as he was, she suspected the, the face of the company.

That said, it also made her realise that she and Ophélie were ridiculously overdressed.

"It's not that I know anything, but there was something that puzzled me. I couldn't quite put my finger on it – I have been quite busy – but I did get Mr Bryce to have a look into it," André continued.

At which point the hooded figure who had entered pulled out a handgun and shot him in the head.

Unsurprisingly, Ophélie screamed as bits of her uncle were splattered around the room. Dana, who had her handbag with her, immediately reached in and pulled out her golden Glock, targeting the hooded figure, and cursing herself for not being more alert. The figure was already running away, though this time Dana had the upper hand. She was at the door, stopping it from closing as Hoodie ran through the office, but there were a number of obstacles in Hoodie's way, preventing him from getting anywhere quickly.

In addition, it turned out there was a security guard on the floor as well, and Dana saw him make his way across the room, heading towards the exit in an attempt to cut Hoodie off. Rather unfortunately, Michelle from reception entered the room (perhaps wondering what was going on with the food and drink she had sent up), and Hoodie kicked out a roller chair, knocking the person on it to the floor, but sending the chair into Michelle, who rather savagely fell.

Hoodie grabbed Michelle and swung around, putting a gun to the poor girl's head, who promptly gasped in fear. Dana didn't lower her gun, and once again felt the confidence she had in the past as she aimed at Hoodie's exposed shoulder, confident she would be able to wound Hoodie before Hoodie could do any damage.

At that point, however, the hood came off and Dana's draw dropped.

Bella had been right. Standing before her was Asha, her auburn hair swept back, her eyes dark and stormy. She looked at Dana, but rather curiously there didn't seem to be a hint of recognition. Instead, she snarled, shoved Michelle to the ground and fired wildly at the security guard, though there was no chance she was going to hit as she didn't take her eyes off Dana.

But it was enough. Enough for the security guard, and everyone else in the room to drop in fear, and enough for Asha to make her escape.

But the simple revelation of her face had been enough to prevent Dana from pulling the trigger. In the background she registered Ophélie's sobs and the cries of the people around her. Michelle was hugging her knees crying, and the security guard was picking himself up, already on the phone.

But it was far too late. Asha had escaped.

FIFTH REPORT: WHISPERED CONVERSATION

"You're aware that you have bookings and work to do?" Christa Adams said down the phone, coldly and without any sympathy.

"Yes," Dana said patiently, sighing a little as she sat in yet another police interrogation room. Fortunately, this time she wasn't under arrest, but she was beginning to be far too well acquainted with what was going on.

"In two days' time, Dana," Adams spat, and Dana slumped back in her chair.

"I know. Where, again?"

"For fu… Melbourne. There's a fashion launch on for Egyptian Tomb, and you're fronting it."

"I'll be there, I promise," Dana said. "I'll book my flight as soon as I can, and head straight to Melbourne. You can assure them I'll be there."

"And what do I say about the preparations?"

"You've already said something," Dana replied, feeling a little smug as she knew her manager would have. At the same time, she knew it was unwise to be quite so smug, so she shut her mouth quickly.

"Yes, but that's not the point. Get your act together, Dana. You're not quite up there enough to be able to pull shit like this, do you understand?" Dana was about to reply, but Adams cut the connection and Dana winced slightly.

"*Bon jour*," said a warm voice, and a gendarme entered. He was average height, with dark hair and oddly blue eyes that contrasted with his olive skin. "Dana Spectra? I am a big fan. Not that I have much to do with modelling or anything, but you are quite," he smiled without finishing the sentence, and Dana wondered if he was trying to hit on her. "What can you tell me about the incident?"

"I was catching up with a friend, we went to see her uncle and then...someone walked in and shot him." Dana tried to look more disturbed than she felt, but the gendarme didn't seem particularly interested one way or the other.

"You don't know why?"

"No idea," she said truthfully.

"He is not connected to the murder you witnessed in Canada?" the gendarme asked, and Dana paused before answering, her mind already putting two and two together.

"I don't think so. I don't really know." She said nothing more, and the gendarme looked at her thoughtfully. Why would the French police service be curious about a connection to a murder in Canada? Interpol must be involved, Dana mused. She wondered who might be watching the interview.

"Did you see who it was? I understand that the killer's face was exposed." Dana's brain once again kicked into overdrive as she wondered exactly how to approach this.

"Not really. I think it was a woman, but I'm not entirely sure."

"Ah, you do not assume gender?"

"Oh, no, I just...don't know." Dana shrugged, and the

gendarme smiled, but Dana got the impression that he didn't entirely believe her.

"Well, I don't think I have any more questions, but I can always contact you if I do, *non?*"

"Of course, I'll be happy to help."

"You are going back to Australia soon?"

"Tomorrow, at the latest," Dana said.

"Perhaps that is for the best," the gendarme said, and Dana didn't have any doubt this time that she was being subtly redressed for what had happened. "You may go whenever you like." Dana stood up and straightened her vest, before walking out with as much dignity as she could muster.

"Dana!" Ophélie called to her as she entered the foyer of the police station they had been brought to, and Dana was relieved to see her friend, enjoying Ophélie's hug that seemed to exude relief, concern and the need for attention. "I was so worried about you."

"I didn't do anything," Dana smiled, holding her friend. "It's fine."

"But you had a gun," Ophélie said, and Dana put her finger to her friend's mouth. No one had mentioned the gun, and Dana had stressed to Ophélie not to do so. She was hoping that she could leave without anybody bringing it up, and if she was lucky, it would be a quick escape. She had no desire to call on Karam again if she could help it.

The two walked out of the station hand-in-hand.

"What now?" Ophélie asked.

"I understand that you probably aren't up to partying anymore," Dana said with a sad smile. "I'm so sorry about your uncle."

"Oh, it's fine," Ophélie said, a little to Dana's surprise. "Honestly, we didn't get along particularly well, and I hardly ever saw him outside of Christmas. That's why he was so surprised to see us when we turned up. I'm just in shock. I didn't particularly like him, but I certainly didn't want him to get murdered. Especially not in front of me."

"I feel it's my fault."

"*Vas-y mollo*," Ophélie tutted. "How can that be? No, tonight we will go out and party."

"Before we do, though," Dana said. "Is there any chance of meeting with that Ian Bryce guy?"

"Who works at the company? We can go back and try," Ophélie shrugged. "But please, then we go out."

"To eat?"

"*Se bourrer la gueule!*"

Michelle was no longer working on the reception desk when the two models returned to Tomorrow's World Today, but there was a young man who seemed to be practicing boredom as a new sport. When they walked in, he was barely able to look over his phone at the pair.

"*Oui?*" he managed to drawl.

"Can we talk to Ian Bryce, please?" The young man looked up at them under hooded eyelids, and then sighed a very long sigh.

"There is no Ian Bryce working here," he finally said.

"There is," Ophélie snapped. "My uncle told me he works here and we should meet him." The young man signed again, and put his phone down with significantly more effort than was needed. He tapped the tablet in front of him and flicked down some pages, before finding something.

"He is not here," he finally said.

"Address," snapped Ophélie.

"I cannot give you that," the young man started, but before he could do anything, Dana leaned forward and grabbed the tablet from him, and started scrolling through it. "Hey!" The receptionist shouted, but Ophélie simply leaned forward and pushed him back into his chair.

"*Laisse tomber,*" she said with a grin. He seemed about to get up again, but Ophélie turned and glared hard at him.

"*Pas de souci,*" he shrugged, and pulled his phone out. Dana didn't catch the rest of his statements as he started mumbling to himself. Dana, meanwhile, was going through the files on the tablet and finally found what she was looking for – the personnel file for Ian Bryce. She showed it to Ophélie who nodded.

"I know it," she said. "Merriwether?" she said.

"What?" Dana asked.

"Ian Merriwether Bryce," Ophélie pointed out. Dana grinned at her friend, and tossed the tablet onto the table.

"Have a nice day, *monsieur,*" Dana smiled.

"*Casse toi!*" came the response, and Ophélie widened her eyes.

"Do not even ask," she said, grabbing Dana and heading for the door.

As they left the building, Dana was sending a text message to Ian

Bryce, having realised that he may not have actually gone home already. She had memorised his number from the same file, and quickly fired off a message:

My name is Dana Spectra. B4 he died, Andre said I should talk to you about an assassination in Canada.

As soon as she sent the text, she felt stupid and bitterly regretted it. There was no way anyone was going to take that sort of text seriously. Rather than get any help, she'd probably immediately targeted herself as insane and someone to avoid at all costs.

Curiously, though, the three little dots started pulsing. Meet me at the Dirty Dick now.

"Do you know the Dirty Dick?" Dana asked her friend. When Ophélie opened her mouth, there was a twinkle in her eyes, and Dana put a finger to Ophélie's lips. "Do not even, girl." Ophélie pouted at her, then grinned.

"It's a bar, not far from here. I'll try to get us a cab." She stepped forward to the edge of the street and scanned back and forth before waving. A black car with a "Taxi Parisien" sign above it moved through the traffic with the reckless abandon of someone who is convinced that everyone else will get out of their way, to the symphony of a number of angry horns. This didn't stop the driver, who pulled to the edge of the pavement and gestured for the women to get in the car.

"You've been before?" Dana wondered, as they climbed in and Ophélie spoke to the driver.

"Dana, I've been to *every* bar in Paris," grinned Ophélie, sitting back as the car launched into motion. "Well, all the important ones. If I haven't been there, it's probably rubbish."

Dana couldn't help but laugh at her friend, but then caught herself.

"Are you sure you're OK about your uncle, Ophélie?" she asked quietly. Ophélie stopped and turned to her friend.

"You care so much," Ophélie said. "Thank you." She squeezed Dana's hands before continuing. "Honestly, I am OK. I am dealing. I think after Gary I am able to cope with this sort of thing better. And I wasn't lying before. Uncle André and I didn't have the closest relationship. Stop worrying." She leant forward and kissed Dana surprisingly tenderly on the lips, before turning and pointing. "Look!"

They were approaching a wooden building front with the words "Dirty Dick" in big red letters above the door. Dana had to admit that what she was seeing was not what she had expected. The wooden frames looked scuffed and battered, and the panelling below the large window front seemed to be designed to look like bamboo.

"Wait," Dana said cautiously. "Is this a tiki bar?"

"Of course," Ophélie grinned, as she leaned forward to hand over a card to the driver for payment. "Didn't you know?"

"I haven't been to every bar in Paris, have I?" Dana said pointedly, though Ophélie just laughed. The pair got out of the car and headed up to the door, pushing on it to go in.

"Should we get Flamingos on Acid?" Ophélie enthused. "Between us. Or a Scorpion bowl. Wait, do you like cognac? There was something, right?"

"Rum," Dana muttered absently, looking around the room they had walked into. It was a cozy room, wall papered in green palm tree print, with one corner dominated by a strange wooden inset, guarded on either side by totem poles. Somewhat at odds with this were the couches scattered around, all furnished by small little tables that had red candles on them, burning away. The bar was also wooden, with the same (presumably deliberate) scuffing, and odd lightshades that seemed to mimic something seen in an old movie set in an unknown jungle. Its base was sculpted to look like bamboo, and it was directly to their right when they walked in. Ophélie headed towards it, while Dana looked around to see if she could see Ian Bryce.

It wasn't particularly busy, though Dana suspected that may not have been the norm. A few couples were engaged in a sweet evening, while three business man sat on stools at the bar being a little louder than they probably thought they were. Needless to say, that suggested that the man sitting by himself in the corner of the room was probably Ian Bryce.

He was not what Dana had expected. In some ways she thought he might have been bookish, thin and nerdy, but Ian Merriwether Bryce was probably in his mid-thirties, dressed in a suit, but without a tie, and was surprisingly good looking, in a classical sort of way. He had well styled dark hair, and a solidly square jaw. Dana strolled across the room, aware that she had caught the attention of most people as she did, and sat down in front of Bryce, who looked at her in surprise.

"Hi," she said, offering her hand. "I'm Dana."

"Right," he replied, and his voice was very definitely English; that sort of English that you associate with old time movies or the villains in American science fiction – very polite, very correct. "Ian Bryce." He took her hand and Dana couldn't resist it.

"Ian Merriwether Bryce," she said, and Bryce flushed red, which was impressive given that the light above them had essentially cast the entire room in that colour.

"How do you know that?" he asked in astonishment.

"We had to get your number and someone at Tomorrow's World Today helpfully gave it to us." Whatever reaction Dana thought she would get from that information, Bryce's response was definitely not that. He immediately looked as though he were a deer caught in headlights, suddenly fearful. Then he stood, looking around, taking in the surroundings perhaps much better than he had before.

"You don't have to panic," Dana said, leaning forward to pull him back into his seat. "I'm not here to cause you any problems."

"Then why are you here?" he demanded.

"Someone assassinated a scientist, and almost killed my sister in the process. I've been to a very strange party in the countryside and that pointed me to André Hémery, who pointed me towards you. I don't know what you can tell me, but at this point I'll take anything." Bryce regarded her carefully, seemingly weighing up whether it was worth his time to invest in her or not.

"Your sister?" he finally said.

"She was sitting right next to the guy who was killed," Dana said.

"And then Uncle André was next," came Ophélie's voice as she sat down beside Dana, placing a drink in front of her. Dana's was in a glass that was thick and patterned with a disturbing tiki face, leering out at her. The drink itself looked pink-ish and Dana took a small sip, enjoying the flavour more than she expected.

"I'm sorry for your uncle," Bryce said. "I liked him. A

great deal. He trusted me."

"To do what," Dana asked. "What were you looking into, exactly?"

"You are right," Bryce said, his tone measured. "The payment to kill Thomas McAteer came from Tomorrow's World Today. But it wasn't with André's knowledge. He didn't approve the payment."

"Who did?"

"That's the thing," Bryce shrugged. "I've looked into this. Been looking into this as soon as André asked me too." Dana frowned, and Bryce realised he needed to elaborate. "When the murder occurred, at the launch, André was worried we might get the blame. He didn't want the police or Interpol knocking at our door and asking awkward questions. So, I was told to get our finances in order. That's when I discovered the payment, and that's when I realised it had come from us."

"But you don't know who made it?"

"I have no idea who approved it. I didn't think it was possible, but it looks as though someone got in and deleted the data."

"Who could have done that?" Dana persisted.

"Well, honestly, any of the executives, and fifty percent of either the finance or IT people."

"That doesn't seem very secure," Ophélie pointed out.

"It's not a huge list of people," Bryce protested. "And they are all supposed to be trustworthy. But I suppose…" He let the sentence hang in the air, and the Dana and Ophélie unconsciously mimicked each other as they sat back in their couch and crossed their arms.

"Look, I know it seems pointless, but I do have information that can help. I couldn't work out who authorised the payment, but I know who the payment went to." Bryce looked at the women, who both sat eagerly forward. "And I know this is going to sound crazy." Dana fell back into her seat, already sensing that she was going to be incredibly disappointed. "The money was paid into the account of something called the Four-Fold Crown." Ophélie looked back to her friend, who shrugged in return.

Dana glanced around the room, suddenly realising that there was music playing, not fighting with any of the conversations, but filling the gaps where silence was starting to build. The businessmen were in it for the long haul; god only knew what drink they were onto, but their ties were no longer on, and they were discussing things *very* passionately.

One of the couples had left, while the other one was having a whispered conversation. Dana smiled slightly to see how happy they were, and when he frowned, his partner shook his head and whispered again, and he nodded in understanding, the smile returning to his face. Suddenly he gripped her thigh and started talking excitedly too her, and she laughed, unable to stop herself.

Dana found herself envious of the pair and for a moment wished that she could have something like that. A freckled redhead popped up in her mind, the lilt of an Irish accent, but Dana buried it.

"Do you know what the Four-Fold Crown is?" Dana asked, leaning forward again.

"No idea. Just that it is based in the Congo."

"The Congo?" Ophélie said, sounding as surprised as Dana felt.

"Yup."

"Which one?" Ophélie continued.

"Sorry?"

"Which Congo?"

"There is more than one Congo?" Bryce said in surprise.

"Republic and Democratic Republic," Dana said.

"Oh, ah," Bryce hesitated. "The one that speaks French?"

"They both speak French," Dana scowled.

"How do you know that?" Bryce said curiously.

"We were in the Miss Green Earth pageant," Ophélie said witheringly. "We learnt a lot about the world for that."

"Oh."

"So, somebody paid the Four-Fold Crown – an organisation in a Congo – to assassinate Thomas McAteer using Tomorrow World's Today money," Dana said, and looked at Ophélie, who looked back expectantly. "I guess I'm going to a Congo," Dana mused.

"Can I come?" Bryce asked, and Dana looked at him in surprise.

"I feel I need to know more. To find out more about what happened. For the sake of André."

"I will come as well," Ophélie announced grandly, as she sipped her drink. Dana narrowed her eyes at her, suspecting that she was tipsy.

"You're not going anywhere," Dana said to the younger girl. "We're going out tonight, then you have work you don't have time to give up." Ophélie pulled a face, but knew that Dana was right.

"And me?" Bryce asked.

"Sure, you can come. But I don't know when I'll be going exactly. I have some work to do, or my manager will kill me. Give me your number, and I'll let you know what's going on." Dana paused, and shook her head. "We don't even know where we are going yet," she sighed.

"We know where we are going now," Ophélie said cheekily. "Moulin Rouge is very close." Dana giggled, and the two girls got up, Bryce standing up as well, though both turned to him and their looks immediately had him back in his chair. Dana held her phone out to him, ready for his number to be placed in.

"Not you, obviously," she said unnecessarily. He handed the phone back, and Dana took it with a smile. "Be ready for my message," she warned.

"Let's go!" Ophélie almost shouted, and the two walked out, arm in arm.

SIXTH REPORT: OVER DRAMATIC

It was, Maximilien Travere decided, all a little over dramatic, really. No one in the Intelligence community really believed that anyone operated like they did in the movies, and yet every so often you came across a situation where reality was actually slightly stranger than fiction. Max felt he was in that situation now, as he sat in a room that definitely could have been a bit lighter had someone bothered to open the blinds, in front of his boss who looked harassed and concerned, with two men and a woman in the background shrouded in darkness and looking mysterious. Max half expected the older of the two men to light up a cigarette and start smoking eerily.

"Essentially, the point is that Benoît Royer is dead," Eugène Sauvageau said, and Max looked at him accusingly. Sauvageau had the decency not to look him in the eyes. They had already had this conversation, and Sauvageau knew the answer.

"Yes," Max replied. "I believe that to be the case."

"Based on?" The younger of the two men spoke up. His voice was higher than Max expected it to be, and he couldn't help but notice there was a sauce stain on the man's pale-yellow tie. Obviously he'd had a nice lunch before he came to this particular inquiry, which was embarrassing to the say the least.

"I waited the allotted amount of time, and followed the

plan we had in place. In fact, I waited a little longer than what we had laid out, because I don't like to leave anyone behind."

"But you didn't go looking for them?" the younger man said, taking a seat beside Sauvageau. Max wished they'd had name plaques to identify them, but annoyingly they were just mysterious.

"That's not the way we work," Max continued, and the younger man made a noise that clearly voiced his disgust.

"Benoît Royer was a good man," the younger man said, and there was a general sense of exasperation around the room.

"No one is disputing that," Sauvageau said, looking across the table.

"He was exceptional," Max replied, reading the Deputy Director's look accurately. "His knowledge of the area, his commitment, all were amazing. That's why I think he was murdered." The last sentence caused the younger man to sit back in his chair, but the Deputy Director didn't react. He'd heard it all before. Curiously, though the other two people in the room also didn't react.

"He was murdered by this," the younger man waved his arms.

"Heroux," Max supplied.

"I assume you think Melissa Andersson was murdered as well," the older man spoke for the first time. He turned to look at Max, and though he had a friendly face, there was an intensity to his grey eyes.

"I believe so, sir," Max said, not entirely certain why he felt more inclined to show respect to this mystery man than the more annoying representative of the *Gendarmerie*. Or perhaps he did, he thought to himself, repressing a smirk.

"Can I ask if you discovered anything?" the older man asked. Max was suddenly struck by how good his French was, considering he clearly wasn't.

"Nothing of any real value."

"So, what do you want to do, exactly?" Deputy Director Sauvageau asked, and all four behind the desk turned their attention directly to Max for the first time in the hearing.

"I think we still need to find out exactly what Heroux is doing on that rig, sir," Max said. "If for no other reason to find out what happened to Royer and Andersson. Neither of them deserves to just disappear, their fates unknown. They deserve better than that, and I want to give it to them. And I want to know what Heroux is doing and why it is such a mystery. The only thing I was able to discover is that rig is giving off a lot of heat, far more than it has any right to for someone doing an archeological dig. I think it's important to know why."

"I'm inclined to agree," the older man said.

"Are you going to send in any more help for us?" the Deputy Director asked without turning his head. To Max's surprise, the woman suddenly opened her mouth as though she had something to say, but the older man touched her arm and she fell silent. Max wondered who the woman was. Presumably she worked for the man from Interpol, was Interpol herself, but what was her interest in his investigation?

"Maybe," the older man said. "But all I'm saying is that I think we should give Mr Travere the opportunity to continue doing what he's doing. Perhaps we may even have an additional lead for him. In which case we would, of course, supply that information."

Max frowned at this unexpected news.

"We are not providing any more bodies to be disposed of," the younger man snapped, and the Deputy Director nodded, a degree of irritation passing across his bald head.

"Very well," the Deputy Director said. "I don't think there's anything more than can be gained from this meeting. Max, you and I will talk. Thank you, gentleman." He paused as he remembered the lady. "Thank you all," he corrected.

"I might sit in on your meeting, if you don't mind Deputy Director?" the older man said, though it was less a question and more a statement.

"Of course, Broadsword," Sauvageau replied.

Broadsword? Max Travere wondered exactly what was going to happen at this meeting.

"I just need to go back, sir," Max insisted, leaning forward to Sauvageau, and causing the Deputy Director to sit back as though he were worried Max was going to attack him. Savageau had decided to talk with Max immediately after the hearing, and now they were in his slightly more comfortable office at the Directorate-General for External Security: Action Division's headquarters in Noisy-le-Sec. From the outside 141 Boulevard Mortier, 20th Arrondissement, Paris looked rather boring – a two-story bland gray building with darker trim (so bland, it's colour was named gray. Not Pearl River or Pewter, just gray). The only reason it stood out was the fact that a long stone wall ran from other side of the building to the corner of the block it was on, and the fact that the middle of the building was fronted by a number of mirrored windows, the bottom floor of which could open to allow cars to pass in and out. If pressed, one might say it looked vaguely military, but in truth it just seemed like an overelaborate entrance.

Looks, of course, were deceiving, and inside the building was much more interesting, a more dynamic set of offices, some with quite lush furnishings. Some, of course, were *steel* and full of very clever people pouring over computers, tablets and papers. Computer screens displayed maps of the world, all of which had notes and tags indicating a variety of different things, from the location of agents and operations, to what the current stock market was in each country.

Deputy Director Eugène Sauvageau would check on all of these at certain points throughout the day to ensure that he was abreast of what was going on, so that (heaven forfend) should the director contact him to ask him anything, Sauvageau would know precisely what was taking place. When he had received the report that informed him a member of the gendarmerie and an Interpol agent had disappeared, he felt his stomach lurch, and he wondered if he had got sick. When Broadsword had contacted him, he knew the phone call wasn't going to last long.

Now, Maximilien Travere sat in the comfortable chair opposite Sauvageau's desk, while Broadsword himself sat at the back of the room on one of the two more comfortable armchairs that were positioned in case Sauvageau had to meet with someone of great import. The President himself had once sat in one of those chairs, though that was another conversation that had ended with Sauvageau sitting on the toilet until he was certain it was just nerves rather than diarrhea.

"Can I ask," Broadsword said, and the two DGSE officers turned to look at the man from Interpol, "what could possibly be producing the amount of heat you suspect is there?"

"I have," Max paused as he tried to think how to answer the question properly. "I'm not sure. There are a number of options, but I suppose what concerns me is that it might be nuclear."

"Could it be something more plasma orientated?" Broadsword said, and Max frowned before turning to his boss, his eyes questioning.

"You think you have a lead?" Sauvageau asked.

"Not me, as such," Broadsword grinned. "I know someone who is currently looking into the assassination of a plasma scientist. And I'm not a big believer in coincidences, as you yourself probably aren't."

"What has this person discovered?" Max asked.

"I'm not sure. Honestly, it's all a bit up in the air," Broadsword shrugged. "But I suspect that she might contact me any day now, and if she does, then I'll have more information."

"She's a bit of a wild card," the dark-haired woman that accompanied him said, speaking up for the first time. She was clearly American, and though her French wasn't as good as Broadsword's, it was still quite comprehensible. "She's not one of ours, but she is a…" The dark-haired woman looked to Broadsword, who smiled.

"A friend," he completed. "Someone I trust."

"So, what are you proposing?" Sauvageau asked.

"Obviously my priority is to discover who assassinated Melissa," Broadsword said. "Oh, and the gendarme, of course. But I'm happy to wait until my associate gets in touch and I'll find out how far she has got with her investigation. She's quite determined."

"And you'll send her to me?" Max asked.

"If her investigation is indeed tied into yours, then I'll definitely point her in your direction. I know that they might be two completely different situations, but I find that sometimes you have to follow your gut, don't you?" He smiled at this, and Max nodded.

"Well, you two organize contacts and all the rest of it," Sauvageau said, waving his hand at the trio, "and Max, you can keep me up to date with what is going on."

"Perfect," Broadsword said, standing up. Sauvageau stood up as well and crossed the room to shake Broadsword's hand and then the hand of the woman with him. The trio then left the Deputy Director's office.

"This," Broadsword said, "is Justice Kennedy. I'll leave her to liaise with you, shall I? She quite likes France." Broadsword smiled at a private joke, though Kennedy seemed to scowl slightly.

"Delighted," the American muttered. "And you?" she asked, more directly.

"Oh, I'll wait for my phone call," Broadsword said, his smile never leaving his face.

"You're so confident she's going to call," Kennedy said, raising an eyebrow.

"There's only so much ASIO or ASIS will do for her," Broadsword replied. "Me on the other hand. Well, I can do anything."

SINGAPORE

FIRST REPORT: RAISE FLAGS

Dana pursed her lips slightly as she looked around Changi airport, and took a deep breath, enjoying the aromas. Without doubt, it was her favourite airport in the world, and it held a lot of memories for her, particularly in recent years. She wouldn't be able to see the Butterfly Garden without thinking of Shira Langlois, or Tiffany Chandler or whatever her name actually was. And of course, it was the location of her first meal with the man that she knew as Alan, though that might also have been a pseudonym, despite his assurances to the contrary.

Terminal 4 of the Airport was the most recent addition and without doubt it was built with a specific eye to catering to the millions of people who used the airport every year, taking into account the ways to pass the stop over time for anyone making connecting flights. Given that the airport is the largest hub for Asia, that was perhaps a very wise decision.

Dana found the escalator she was looking for, and as she ascended, she took a look back down to see the check in desks that were organized, very neatly, into seven different rows. The blue and teal of the desks made it a little lake in the burnished tan of the floor in general. It was evening, and so the artificial lighting was necessary now that the giant window wall was no longer letting in any sunlight. Nonetheless, Dana found it quite beautiful.

At the top of the escalator, she turned right and headed along the purple-carpeted pathway, but was almost immediately at her destination – the Aji Ichi Sushi Bar. The entrance to the bar was on her left, but there was seating on her right, and sitting at a table right beside the glass railing was the person she was having dinner with.

He was in his early-forties, wearing a light suit that refused to be either white or beige, with a blue collared shirt and no tie. He was a few inches taller than her and was bulky, though he seemed to have lost a little weight since she had last seen him. His grey eyes were framed by spectacles, and his greying hair was thinning, but there was a handsomeness about him that appealed to Dana, and she knew that, despite herself, she very much enjoyed his company.

It was just a shame that he worked in an industry where you couldn't trust a word out of his mouth.

"Alan," she said with a small smile, as she sat down opposite him.

"Dana," he replied, and seemed genuinely delighted to see her. "I can't believe you called. I mean, I wish you would more often, but I understand you're very busy." That was exceptionally true. After her night of excitement with Ophélie where the two had ended up back in her room, barely dressed, but sadly too tired to do anything more than fall asleep, Dana had returned to Australia and got into a number of work projects. For a fortnight solid, she had travelled the country working, but in that time, she had made an important phone call, and requested some time off for travel. The phone call was to a man she had met on a plane, and who turned out to be an important figure in the Interpol hierarchy.

"I'm sure you're busy as well," Dana countered, to which he shrugged dismissively. Dana wasn't sure whether Alan's office was in Singapore or if he just liked the country, but she wasn't remotely surprised when he agreed to meet her, and less surprised when he suggested Changi Airport. It was possibly convenience, possibly nostalgia, but when he suggested the Aji Ichi Sushi Bar, Dana began to wonder if he simply liked the food.

"Drink? My shout, obviously. I'm having Hakushika Nadajikomi Dry, but you're welcome to whatever."

"Bundaberg Root Beer?" Dana asked incredulously as she looked through the menu.

"Your part of the world is very well represented," Alan smirked mischievously.

"I don't know much about sake," Dana admitted.

"Ah, well, Junmai is a rice only sake and tastes a little savoury. The Ginjyo is slightly more fragrant, and the Daiginjyo is quite fruity. Dassai 23 tastes sweet, almost like honey. You should try that one, actually," he grinned.

"You are being very grand," Dana said, a little pointedly.

"Well, it's so infrequent we see each other, I should definitely make the most of it," Alan replied. "Though I assume you have a specific reason for the visit, rather than just a catch up."

"I need help, and I don't know who to turn to," Dana confessed.

"Your father?"

"I don't think it's a good idea. I think," Dana paused. "I think I need to go to the Congo, and I don't think he would be happy about that."

137

"I don't think I'm happy about that," Alan said, and Dana noticed that his affable demeanour had frozen instantly. "What on Earth do you want to go there for? And when you say Congo, I assume you mean Congo-Brazzaville?"

"Do you know anything about an organisation called the Four-Fold Crown?" Alan sat back in his chair as a little robot glided up to them, a dish of food on the top of its three trays. Alan removed the dish and put it on the table, pressing a button on the "face" monitor of the short device, sending it on its way.

"It's a cult," Alan finally said. "At least that's what we think. We've not really got a lot of information about them, based on the fact that they are in the Congo." He paused, and then said, "and by Congo, I mean the Democratic Republic, Congo-Kinshara. We don't get a lot of cooperation from police in any of the Congo's, but when it comes to Congo-Kinshasa you can say that cooperation is virtually zero. So, whatever they know about the Four-Fold Crown remains something of a mystery. Why, Dana?" When they had met in the past, Dana had always felt their relationship was of equals, but for the first time, Alan was giving her "Dad" vibes.

"I think that they were responsible for the assassination of Thomas McAteer in Canada," Dana said.

"And of André Hémery?" Alan asked. Asha's face flashed before Dana's eyes as she remembered the lack of recognition when their eyes had met. Dana hadn't told Bella anything on their return, but the truth was she now had much more doubt about the events of that day in Canada. And maybe, just maybe, her sister had been correct. "Negitoro on Garlic Toast, by the way. Try some." Alan slid the plate he had just got forward, and

Dana took one, smelling the wasabi as she picked it up. She bit into it, the tastes of the avocado, tuna and wasabi creating a rather delicious mix.

"The money came from his company," Dana said, and Alan nodded.

"That makes sense," he murmured.

"You knew?"

"He was on our radar. It's not my case, but my understanding was we couldn't get a subpoena for his banking records. Most judges thought it was a fishing expedition. There was no evidence. But are you saying the money went to the Four-Fold Crown?" Dana nodded, and Alan sat back in his chair, his face unreadable. He frowned slightly, and then lent forward to the conversation again. "So, you want to go to the Congo to find them?"

"It's insane," Dana agreed. "But," she paused and wondered if she should just confess the truth about Asha. "But this has hit home twice," she lied.

"You'd need visas. And it might be best to fly into Congo-Brazzaville and then cross the river into Congo-Kinshasa. Though that might not be the greatest idea either. It's going to be ridiculously dangerous." Alan shook his head, and sat back again.

"I don't particularly want to do this, but," Dana stopped again, and Alan narrowed his eyes at her.

"I'm assuming you know something that we don't," he said casually, before picking up his chopsticks and taking a piece of sushi. There was an awkward pause as Dana fought with herself over whether to trust the man in front of her.

"Sorry," she finally said, but Alan's face betrayed no

emotion whatsoever.

"Look," he said, "I'll help you, but I really think this is a bad idea. A very bad idea. There are certain areas of the world which I would definitely advise against travelling, and truthfully the Congo is two of them." He took another piece of nigiri, clearly enjoying it. "But you're relatively resourceful and a big help. And we may need your help in the future, so I'll pull some strings, make some requests. I might even try to see if there's any chance, I can send someone along with you. But for the love of God, Dana, please be careful." Dana smiled, and reached forward to squeeze the man's hand.

"I promise I'll do my very best. Not least because my agent has more work lined up for me, and I'll get into big trouble if I'm not there to make her money."

The look on Alan's face made it clear that the joke was not appreciated in the way she hoped it would be.

CONGO

FIRST REPORT: LARA MULLER

Brazzaville was *poor*. Poor in a way that Dana had never really understood the word. She wasn't stupid, she wasn't even entitled, but Dana hadn't quite appreciated how good her life was compared to the way other people lived, and as she sat in the car that drove her to the French Embassy in Brazzaville, it hit home in a way that it never had before.

Thanks to Alan, it had taken mere hours to sort out her trip to Brazzaville – although perhaps it would be more accurate to say that it had taken mere hours to sort out Dr Lara Muller's travel to the Congo. When she had been presented with the documentation, Alan had informed her that it was all under the name of Lara Muller, a doctor with *Médicins Sans Frontières* that was now Dana's new alias. When Dana had pointed out that she probably wasn't old enough to be a doctor, Alan had dismissed this, pointing out that "Lara" was actually older than Dana, but was still young enough to be idealistic.

Dana had taken the opportunity to tell Alan about Ian Merrywether Bryce at that point, and Alan scowled a little but then seemed to come to a decision and nodded his consent. It was a curious look; the face of someone making a calculation, but Dana wasn't sure what the calculation was, and she wondered briefly if Alan had decided he could use another asset. Or worse, something more disposable. Either way, before she knew it, Dr Wyatt Fichera was joining Dr Muller on her journey. When Dana had asked how Alan had found out so much about Bryce to make the fake documents, he replied – somewhat drily – that Merrywether was a fairly uncommon name.

They had flown into Maya-Maya airport, the Republic of the Congo's international airport, and while it wasn't anything particularly special, it was certainly of a comfortable standard that when they disembarked, both strolled through without a second thought. They were comfortable, the airport was *familiar*. Even on the outside it looked quite swish; another monolith of concrete and glass with sweeping curves and air-conditioned comfort to protect those from the uncomfortable humidity outside.

There was a tall man in a suit waiting for them on their arrival, and he quickly took them to a black car. Alan had made it clear they would be taken straight to the French embassy where they were going to meet someone who would give them further help in getting to their destination. This was the trip that made Dana more aware of what the country was like. As they approached the Embassy, the roads were fine and the countryside was beautiful, but getting there required them to go through some of the less salubrious areas of the city, and it was here Dana saw the streets that were covered with dust, and the buildings that were held together with tarpaulins and rope. Markets lined the road with families haggling over fruit that they couldn't afford to buy in one of the shopping centers.

"It's not like where you from, huh?" the driver said with a big grin. "Don't worry. Most of the city is more comfortable for you. You like, yes?"

"J'habite à Paris," Bryce said, and the driver grinned again.

"Est-ce que c'est beau? J'aimerais visiter," the man replied, and Bryce nodded, before Dana looked at him.

"Oh, sorry. We should speak in English. My friend doesn't speak French," he added, and Dana rolled her eyes slightly. She had got to know Bryce a little better on their journey, but he had a habit of pointing out her flaws as often as he could, in a way that he thought was endearing, but which Dana felt was patronizing. She even began to wonder if he knew he was doing it.

"No problems, no problems," the driver said, the grin never leaving his face. "Look, we are back in the city. Good news for a big-time girl like you." Dana fought the urge to punch them both in the face.

He was right, though. The streets were once again well maintained, with green sidewalks, or rails allowing people to walk without getting too close to the traffic. Which, Dana reflected, wasn't particularly bad either. In a city of over 11 million people, she was surprised that it didn't seem crammed.

The driver pulled onto a road called Rue Alfassa before coming up to a building with a very large yard, and more noticeably, two men at the front in dark uniforms, carrying very obvious guns. As the car approached, the driver wound his window down, and one of the officers grabbed a two-way and spoke into it. Almost immediately, the gates in the fence around the building that they were waiting at, swung open and the officer waved them through.

The building itself was white, with stone columns at the corners, and giant square entrance ways potted around the outside. Dana looked out as the car drove along the driveway towards the entrance, and marvelled at how impressive it was. Sometimes Dana got the impression that many of the world's capitals had started to homogenize, gearing themselves up towards a global population that wanted to travel without feeling uncomfortable at any point. Brazzaville seemed to be caught at a midway point, with the some of the city moving in that direction, while the rest of it remained stuck the way it was. And almost not by choice.

The driver courteously opened her door, and Dana exited and glanced at the driver who helpfully pointed out the direction they needed to head in. She made her way to the small set of stairs, checking to see that Bryce was following, and headed up to the main entrance which again had two black-clad officers on either side, though this time one was cheerful enough to give her a smile as they went in.

Inside the large entrance hall, there was a desk where a young woman sat typing on a computer. Bryce moved up to the desk and leant forward, surprising the woman, who looked up at him. He started speaking in French, and she nodded before finally something clicked, and her nods became far more definite and assertive.

"I told her that we were here to see someone. She's on it," Bryce said.

"Oh thanks," Dana said snarkily.

"I didn't think you could speak French," Bryce protested.

"And presumably she couldn't speak English?" Dana asked, driving her point home.

"*Bon jour!* Hello," came a voice, and the pair looked up

to see a man walk towards them. Dana guessed he was in his thirties, with dark hair and dark eyes. He was wearing a maroon polo shirt and beige trousers, and there was something undeniably magnetic about the man. "Maximilien Travere," he said, a genuine smile on his face.

"D...Dr Lara Muller," she replied.

"Of course," he said. "I've heard a lot about you. And...?"

"Oh, I'm Dr Wyatt Fichera," Bryce said, sticking his hand out and seeming very uncomfortable with the resulting handshake. Dana was slightly more surprised at how comfortable he was with saying his pseudonym, but then, having travelled with him for this long, decided he was quite enjoying himself playing spies.

He was probably going to end up dead, Dana mused pessimistically. If anything, she'd learnt that this life wasn't a joke.

"So, I was asked to plan a trip for you, with some basic information," Travere said, and Dana smiled a little. Dana raised an eyebrow, but Travere beckoned them into a door that was behind the reception desk. When they entered, it turned out to be a small conference room, and Travere beckoned to the chairs, taking one himself.

"I am Max," he added, sitting down with a small smile, and Dana cringed a little. "I'm with the DGSE," he added, and Bryce's eyes widened. "Don't stress, Ian," Max laughed. "The Directorate-General for External Security has no interest in English accountants. No offence."

"Dana Spectra," she said. "And you obviously know Ian Bryce."

"Oh, I know all about you too, Ms Spectra," grinned Max.

"Our mutual friend gave me your file. In the strictest confidence," he added. "It's a fascinating read." Dana frowned, but Max continued on. "So, the trip, based on the aforementioned basic information."

"Sorry, it's a bit in the air," she admitted.

"Our mutual friend asked me because I have as much knowledge on the Four-Fold Crown as the best of us. Which is to say, not much, if I'm honest. Though if you're telling me they are running some sort of assassination-for-hire gig, I have to admit I wouldn't be totally surprised. They are very mysterious."

"Who are they?" Dana asked, intrigued.

"Well, hopefully you can tell us that," Travere said, and his face was serious. "Honestly, all we know is that they are some sort of cult in the middle of the Congo. I can't tell you who they are or why they are there. Well, I guess why they are there," he shrugged.

"But," Bryce said, "you must know the origins of an all-girl cult in Africa. Surely that would be unusual." Travere looked at him curiously, before continuing.

"Well," he said, "not if they just appear overnight." He reached for a nearby tablet and activated it, reaching forward and hitting a button on the table which brought a screen to life on the wall beside them. Dana turned to look at it, and saw that a map of the region had come up. There was something niggling at the back of her brain, but she couldn't quite put her finger on it, and as she started to examine the screen, she lost her train of thought.

The map showed both Congo-Brazzaville and Congo-Kinshasa. Dana studied it, not quite realizing how close to Kinshasa they actually were.

"The Congo river pretty much divides Congo-Brazzaville from Congo-Kinshasa," Max began, and then paused. "Apologies if you already know this. I'm not trying to patronize you." He gave an easy smile, and Dana found she was warming to the man immediately.

"No, this is all new to me," Dana said.

"There were difficulties when Belgium wanted to claim their part of the territory for themselves, so that's how the split occurred. It's a long story, not worth going into, but Congo-Kinshasa is bigger than Congo-Brazzaville. So, the information we have is that the Four-Fold Crown have their, uhm, retreat?" He paused and frowned. "I have no idea what to call it. But they live somewhere around the Kwa River, which comes off the Congo at a little place called Kwamouth. That probably makes a lot of sense really," Max grinned. "There's a little village called Ngabe on the Brazzaville side, because obviously Kwamouth is on the Kinshasa side. More obviously," and at this he flicked his tablet and the map changed from a standard blue and green map of the Earth to one that was red and orange. "You can see that everywhere around the Kwa River is regarded as a very bad place to go by most governments. It's deeply unpleasant."

"Is Kwamouth safe?" Dana asked, and Max shrugged.

"I think given the ongoing conflict, and the inability or lack of interest by the government in controlling the violence would suggest it is anything but." Dana swallowed slightly at this, and she glanced across at Bryce who had gone a little pale.

"The idea of you being with *Médicins Sans Frontières* was that they might be inclined to leave you alone, but if I'm honest, I don't think it will make much difference to them. The

149

violence is deep rooted, and they want something so badly they will kill for it."

"What...?" Bryce opened his mouth to say, but Max shook his head.

"Justice," he replied simply. "The upshot is, we would prefer not to go into Kwamouth. But we need to go somewhere between here." He got up and walked over to the screen pointing to a part of the map that had nothing on it. "Kwamouth is here, Libonge Djoko up here," and he moved his finger up, "while Puemba is down here," and his finger moved down. "There's a road that goes from Kwamouth to Puemba, but the government advises against using it."

"So, we go to Ngabe?"

"Ngabe has a little tourist hotel, would you believe? Just across the river from a town that its own government advises people not to go to. Strange world," Max mused. "So, we go down the Congo, and we stop at Ngabe. Restock, rest and relax. Then we have to take one of two risk options." Max turned away from the monitor and looked to his two guests. "We can either take the road to Puemba, stop before we get there, and head into the forest, or we can take the river Kwa to Libonge Djoko and stop before we get *there*, and then head into the forest."

"Our choices are to get shot by some militia, or play it safe on the river?" Bryce said, but Max gave him a look.

"The river isn't safe. Not from the militia, not from crocodiles." He went back to his tablet and sat down, leaning back in his chair with a small smile on his face. Dana wondered if he planned to make them uncomfortable, or was he just trying to emphasise how dangerous the situation was. Not for the first time she was beginning to wonder if this had been such a good idea.

"You can back out," Max said. "No one will think any worse of you for doing so. It's very dangerous, and that is not a joke. We're going to be taking a safe boat, and one that won't be overcrowded like so many we will see on the Congo, but that doesn't mean that journey will be a joyride. And no matter what, we then have to go through the jungle to get to this place. It's going to be a long road. I'm happy to take it with you, but…" The shrug again, and he reclined in his chair.

"If we go to Kwamouth, we won't be going into the town, right?" Dana asked.

"No, we'll pull up on the banks, and then head across the land to the road."

"Without a vehicle?" Bryce pointed out.

"We could acquire one if we ducked into Kwamouth," Max suggested. "Going into the center of the village might be risky, but on the outskirts, assuming we don't come across any gangs…"

"We can't do it without a land vehicle," Dana said, and Max nodded his agreement, but said nothing. "We have to get one from somewhere. The chances are better in Kwamouth than in Libonge Djoko, I'm guessing."

"If I'm honest with you," Max said, "we have no idea what Libonge Djoko is like. It's not been mapped or photographed by anyone recently. At the moment it's a district where some people live. But how many? Who knows. Do they have cars? No idea. But, if they did, it's unlikely they would be in a great condition."

"Kwamouth it is, then," Dana said.

"Are you sure you want to do this, Dana?" Bryce asked, and Dana looked at him with a smirk.

"Lara," she corrected. "Dr Lara Muller."

SECOND REPORT: RIDICULOUSLY OVERCROWDED

They had spent the night at the Radisson Blu M'Bamou Palace, which was a slice of proper luxury that Dana genuinely felt slightly guilty about having seen the drive into the city. It was easy to put poverty to the back of your mind if you didn't know how close it actually was, and now that she did, she felt a little bad for living it up (and realistically, for free, given that someone was paying her bills, though she wasn't sure exactly who). Bryce didn't seem to have the same sort of guilt and Max had smiled at her as though reading her mind when they approached the hotel.

"Make the most of it," he smiled, his accent adding to his cool, suave demeanour, "because as of tomorrow I guarantee that you will be worlds away from all of this." At which point, on cue, the multi-story building came into view.

"How many times have you been to the Congo?" Dana asked Max, suddenly curious about his familiarity with the area.

"Oh, a few times here, only once to DR Congo," he said. "The DGSE is the same as your ASIS, so I work outside of France most of the time. We still have a lot of interest in Africa, and it doesn't serve us to not know what is going on here most of the time. As it happens, I was doing some work at the Côte d'Ivoire so I was asked to pop over and do our mutual friend a favour."

"Is that where you plan on going back to?" Dana asked.

"Once I've made sure you're on your way and you know what you're doing," he grinned.

"Wait, you're not going with us to the Four-Fold Crown?" Bryce suddenly asked.

"I'm afraid not, my friend," Max said, his shrug becoming almost second nature. "But I have confidence that Dana will keep you safe. She is very resourceful and determined, and I promise that if anything happens, I will return to see what I can do. I did say this was risky," he added. "It's not going to get less risky, I promise you."

As the sun set, Dana decided to go for a swim, and Bryce came with her, to look around, though as Dana stepped onto the wooden deck, she noticed that the look around seemed to concentrate somewhat on her navy-blue Sommer Swim Harper Top bikini, or perhaps, just her ass. To be fair he wasn't the only one, as there were a few guests reclining in the deck chairs, and a number of the men were inclined to look. As usual, Dana was more concerned about the scar on her thigh and so she quickly made her way into the water to hide it. Once immersed, she told herself off for being so silly.

As the evening sun dropped, so did the temperature a little, but Dana could feel the humidity making no effort to go away, and so she laid back and enjoyed the coolness of the water. In truth, as the lights came on both in the pool itself and on the deck, it all looked rather beautiful. People could be forgiven for wondering why there should be any concerns about going to the Republic of the Congo.

Once out of the pool, Dana dried herself down and put on some activewear - a Lululemon set in the same navy blue as the bikini – and then went to the gym where she started to do a proper workout, which was something she felt she hadn't done in a few days. She guessed she would probably not have to stress too much about trying to keep fit over the next few days, but today she wanted to do it properly.

Bryce remained with her, an ever-present shadow and after half an hour walking, sweat dripping off her face thanks to an air conditioner that seemed to struggle with the atmosphere outside, Dana finally turned to Bryce and channeled her exhaustion to him.

"Ian, what are you doing?" she said, grabbing her towel and wiping her face.

"I'm just…" He couldn't finish the sentence, instead just indicating the gym as though it were a traditional hang out spot for people. Though maybe it was, for him, Dana supposed.

"I feel like you're a puppy waiting for me to feed him. Like, literally my kitten isn't this clingy," Dana said, and Bryce's face fell slightly.

"I'm sorry, I'm just…"

"Can you stop finishing sentences on *just*, please."

"Tomorrow, are you worried?" he finally asked, and Dana felt a pang of sympathy. She took a deep breath and toyed with how to answer, before finally settling on honesty.

"Yeah," she admitted. "Definitely. I think it's going to be scary. Like, really scary."

"And you're telling me that some model from Australia is prepared for that?"

"Well, you could explain why some accountant from Paris has a desperate urge to find out why his boss was shot,"

Dana said. "Seriously you could leave it up to the police, but instead you're here. I don't get it. And yes, I could leave the almost assassination of my sister to the same police, but in this case, I know they aren't going to look into it any further. But you," Dana said, and looked at him pointedly. "You don't know any of that."

"I have my reasons," Bryce said. "I don't want to go into it just now, but," he paused and then came to a decision, "I want you to know that I'm not going to let you down. I'm going into this for a good reason."

Dana looked at him for a moment and decided that she had probably judged him harshly on the flight to Brazzaville. And she shouldn't be judgey just because he was checking her out in her bikini; after all he certainly wasn't the only one, and it wasn't like she hadn't perved on hotties in the past.

"You know there's a nightclub here, right?" she asked, and Bryce looked at her in surprise. "It'll probably the last time we get to go partying for a bit. Maybe we should take the opportunity." She gave him a small smile, and his shocked look changed to a matching smile.

"That sounds cool. Dinner first, though? I'm hungry."

"Let's check out what the Radisson has to offer," Dana grinned.

As it transpired, they had to travel to *Port autonome de Brazzaville* in order to get on their boat, and it wasn't that far from where the Radisson was, which was another blessing as when they stepped out into the humid world outside the airconditioned comfort of the hotel, it was clear that the traffic was not going to let up. In actual fact, it had backed up considerably, and Dana reluctantly suggested that they walk to their destination, which didn't seem too far on Google maps. Bryce, however, was not quite as excited about the trip, not least because it turned out he was one of those people that sweated almost instantly. Barely five minutes into their journey and his shirt was sticking to him as he wiped the sweat from his forehead. Dana sympathized, but glad she wasn't suffering the same way.

The walk wasn't the easiest either, as it turned out, given that the road and the sidewalk seemed to blend almost into one, and despite crossing to the other side to get a wider sidewalk, it became clear that people were parking there as well. The whole city seemed to give off a vibe of salmon – the colour, not the fish. There was something orangey-pink about everything, be it the road, the sidewalk and even some of the building. Old fashioned wooden buildings with mismatched windows sat snugly between multistory buildings bearing the blue glass that those buildings always seemed to. And yet the 5G building made sure that there was an orange painted concrete path on the front of the building, almost as if the designers finished and suddenly realized they hadn't given the colour scheme the proper Brazzaville consideration.

The more they walked, the scrappier the city became, concrete walls now cracked and stained, wooden fences around buildings that were crooked and wonky, and again the buildings looking more and more in a state of disrepair. And yet, weirdly enough, it was in this part of the street they came across the Casino, which had Chinese writing on it, meaning Dana had no idea what the name of it was.

It was Bryce who first noted that they were getting looks,

and when he tapped Dana on the shoulder to point it out, she nodded. At the back of her mind, she had registered the looks, but Bryce was right in that they were attracting attention now, rather than just looks of appreciation or interest. When they came to a path between buildings that seemed to lead down to the port, Dana decided to take it, and hope they were doing the right thing. Anything to get them off the busy Amilcar Cabral Ave.

It turned out to be the right decision, and they came across the port relatively quickly. *Port autonome de Brazzaville* was sort of what Dana expected; not particularly modern, just concrete everywhere, with gangplanks leading to further concrete piers and jetties. All sorts of boats were docked, from three story steamers that were ridiculously overcrowded, to much smaller fishing boats. In front of the long just-yellow warehouses, big cranes sat waiting patiently out the front to stack their freight onto the long flat ships that would be moving them around.

Dana knew that somewhere along the Congo bank there was a ferry that could take them to Kinshasa, and consequently to the Democratic Republic of the Congo. She wasn't sure, however, if it departed from *Port autonome de Brazzaville* or from somewhere else.

"Do you know where we're supposed to go?" Bryce asked, and Dana looked around, feeling tense. Most of the time she didn't mind the situations she was in, but when things felt like they were getting out of control, and that she didn't immediately have a solution to the problem, she felt her stomach tense up. She took a few deep breaths, remembering what her therapist had advised and refocused on the situation. She had made the decision – and indeed advised Bryce to do the same thing – to pack all her things into a single, quite large, sports bag that she wouldn't feel bad about losing. She reached around it, grabbing and pushing, and sure enough she could feel the shape of her special gun case.

"Hey!" came a voice, and they turned to see a large policeman walking towards them. He was wearing dark blue shirt and pants, with a black vest packed to the hilt with a variety of tools, though his hand was resting on something slid into a holster, and Dana was under no illusion of what it was. He had a browny-green beret, and was wearing sunglasses, which made him look a little like he stepped out of a 1980s cop movie, but the look on his face indicated he wasn't playing games. "Who are you?" he asked, his accent thick.

"We're," Bryce started and Dana butted in, suddenly worried Bryce might have forgotten their cover.

"Dr Lara Muller," she said, sticking her hand out. "*Médicins Sans Frontières.*"

"Dr Wyatt Fichera," Bryce said, though he didn't bother sticking his hand out, as the *gendarme* clearly had little interest in shaking Dana's.

"Why are you here?" the cop said, his hand not straying from the holster. Dana wondered why he was so interested in them. How had he known they didn't speak French?

"Oh," Dana started, but then breathed a sigh of relief when she heard a familiar voice.

"*Hé boss!*" came the familiar voice of Max Travere, and Dana heard Bryce's exhalation of relief. "*Ça baigne?*" The *gendarme* immediately seemed to move his hand, but before he could say anything Max was speaking again. "*Vas-y mollo. Ces*

159

gars-là sont tous bons. Ils ont un bateau là-bas." To Dana's surprise he got closer and closer to the *gendarme* with every sentence, and then finally he held out his hand. The *gendarme* could see as clearly as Dana that there was something in Max's hand, and it obviously had meaning, as he shook Max's hand and then shook his head, before walking away. When he was far enough away, Max turned and gave them a smile. "So many countries where you can easily buy the police off. Not singling out the Congo, by the way. There are plenty in Europe."

"But not France," Dana said with a smirk.

"Oh of course not," Max looked wounded. "The French are the model of incorruptible." He gave her a grin, and clapped Bryce on the arm. "Come on. Let's go to the *Dame Rouge*."

Travere took them down a walkway to one of the concrete piers where three boats were anchored. One was a small thing with an elderly Congolese man sitting at the prow holding a fishing rod, though whether he was awake or asleep was a mystery, but he seemed to definitely be fishing. The second boat was bigger, but perhaps less impressive, less a boat and more a platform, a number of Congolese were moving an enormous amount of produce that was on the pier onto the boat. They chatted excitedly amongst each other, grinning and laughing and having fun, despite the manual labour in the increasing heat. But it was the third boat they went to – easily the largest of the three, but at the same time, nothing that suggested it was rich and impressive. The *Dame Rouge* was a fishing boat as well, but it was much bigger than the elderly man's. This one was larger and had a crane on the back with a net attached.

"It's bigger on the inside," Max grinned, possibly in a

way that he thought was reassuring. "You guys can get in, head down, get under cover if anyone asks too many questions." He stopped and looked around, before suddenly yelling out: "*Ntamba!*" Travere waited a moment and then bellowed the name out again. This time, from below decks, came a friendly face with a straw Panama hat ignominiously planet on the curly black hair.

"*Boss!*" he said delightedly, coming up to them. He was wearing a brightly coloured shirt and white shorts, though both had hand prints on them where he'd clearly been working and needed to wipe grease.

"This is Lara and Wyatt," Max said. "This is who you're taking down the river."

"Ah, the crazy people who want to go up the Kwa!" Ntamba said with a smile.

"Bernard Ntamba," Max said, and Ntamba shook hands with both of them. "I've told him about how important it is to get into Libonge Djoko."

"A lot of sick people there," Bryce said, and Dana looked at him, wondering if he realized there was a chance he would now have to elaborate on his point.

"Ntamba will tell you there are sick people everywhere," Max interrupted smoothly, ending the conversation. "But we gotta do the best we can."

"Let me help you get your bags on board," Ntamba said, but Dana shook her head.

"It's all good. I can carry mine." Ntamba turned to Bryce, but Dana sharply added, "So can he," and Bryce immediately looked chastened.

"Well, that means I get the last bit of work on the boat

done. As soon as it's finished, we can set off. Everything's in order." He smiled at them, and turned to Max, who clasped his arm and looked at him as though they were communicating through telepathy.

"OK, well I'll be on my way," Max said. "Good luck you guys." He paused and then said, "I mean that." A final nod, and Max turned to leave, without looking back.

"I'll just complete that work and we can go," Ntamba smiled at them. "Not long now and we'll be on our way."

Dana looked out to the Congo and took a deep breath.

No going back now.

THIRD REPORT: REAL CONCERN

Possibly due to the activity at *Port autonome de Brazzaville*, Dana was surprised at how quickly it petered out as they began their journey, and two hours into the travel, the river was surprisingly calm, with very few people on it. Occasionally Dana saw a small canoe with passengers and invariably a bag or container making its way along the river as well, though not at the speed the *Dame Rouge* was travelling. With that being said, Dana felt annoyed that they seemed to be travelling slowly, but with the banks of the river nothing more than vast tracts of deep, rich shades of green forest on either side, there was the notion that they weren't making any headway at all.

Ian Bryce, it had turned out, wasn't a great traveller and was sitting looking distinctly pale towards the back of the boat. Dana smiled sympathetically at him when she caught his eye, but wondered if he was unwell from the boat or from something he had eaten earlier. In truth she herself was feeling a little queasy, but she wasn't certain it was the boat.

She was also slightly regretting her choice of attire, as although the t-shirt and shorts kept her cool, she was being bitten by something. She was fairly certain it was a mosquito, but she couldn't slap it fast enough. She had lathered some insect repellent on her bare skin after the first thirty minutes of feasting, but was still itchy from the bites, and hoped it wasn't anything worse than simple irritation.

She made her way to the helm, having decided it was time for a proper chat with Ntamba. As she got to the front he smiled at her.

"Dr Muller, hello, hello," he said.

"Ntamba," she acknowledged.

"You can call me Bernard. That's my first name."

"Oh," Dana said, slightly surprised for some reason. "You should call me Lara." Her new name bounced off her tongue easily, and she decided she quite liked being Lara Muller. *Dr* Lara Muller, even.

"What makes you want to go up to Libonge Djoko?" he wondered. "You're with, uh, *Médicins Sans Frontières,* right?"

"Yeah," she said, remembering her briefing from Alan before she left Singapore. "There are issues there. We don't know much about the village there, but they need help."

"Everyone in DR Congo needs help," Ntamba said, a little gloomily. "It's not a nice place. You know when we get to Kwa, we're going to have to go past Kwamouth. It's not a nice town. Dangerous."

"We thought it might be easier to go through Kwamouth and then take the road to Puemba, rather than take the river to Libonge Djoko," Dana said, a little worried that the plan was going to change.

"Yeah, yeah," Ntamba nodded. "I don't know, though. I think I'd rather face the crocodiles than the Yaka."

"The Yaka?" Dana asked curiously.

"One of our native peoples. The Mobondo militia is

mostly Yaka."

"It's that bad?"

"The government have got so many problems with
Rwanda and the M23 rebels that they have forgotten about the
problems of the little people, especially at Kwamouth. The Yaka
just kill. Mostly Teke, but sometimes I wonder how they know the
difference." His smile had gone, and now Ntamba just kept his eye
on the river ahead.

"You're Teke?" Dana asked, and the smile suddenly
returned.

"No, *mademoiselle*," he grinned. "Definitely not. I'm
Sundi. I know what you're thinking," he continued. "Aren't the
Sundi and the Teke enemies? Not for years. And I don't think
murdering civilians is a proper way of fighting." Dana decided not
to point out she wasn't remotely thinking that, and instead decided
to approach her real concern head on.

"So do you really think the river is the best way to go?"
Ntamba shrugged, eerily like Max was prone to doing.

"Depends on what the crocodiles are up to," he said,
and pointed ahead. There was a canoe in front of them, and Dana
noticed that the people on board had pulled up their paddles and
were instead now just coasting.

"Look," Ntamba urged, and pointed again. Dana
followed his finger as best she could and as she narrowed her
eyes, she realized she could see something in the water near the
canoe. Once, as a child, she and her family had visited
Rockhampton in Queensland, and taken the opportunity to go to
the famous crocodile farm that was there. Her sister – her
biological sister – Kimba, had been fascinated by the crocodiles,

but Dana had been terrified. When she looked into their cold reptilian eyes, the lumpy skin and hideously toothed jaws made her think she was looking at a proper dinosaur. She had seen fear in the eyes of other animals in the past, but there was no fear in that crocodile's eye. Later, when it leapt out of the water to seize on the chicken that was suspended above in the crocodile show, Dana had shivered. Kimba had as well, but she gripped her sister's hand and Dana saw the awe in her eyes.

The Congolese on the canoe weren't stupid, and the crocodile lost interest in the canoe as the *Dame Rouge* approached, swimming away from both. It wasn't hungry and wasn't in the mood to fight for its food.

"I think I'd prefer to deal with the Yaka," Dana murmured.

Dana found the next few hours a strange affair. Neither of her fellow crewmates were particularly talkative, with Bryce definitely not coping with the boat trip, while Ntamba was constantly on the lookout as they sailed. Dana wasn't sure exactly why he was on edge all the time, but she was prepared to listen to what he said rather than assume he was over cautious. He definitely knew what he was doing better than either she or Bryce did, and she had instinctively come to trust Max Travere; given Max had recommended Ntamba be their guide, Dana transferred that trust to Ntamba.

They had a simple lunch of bread and fruit and Dana put some together on a plate and took it to Ntamba, who took it appreciatively.

"I might have forgotten to eat if you hadn't brought me

food," he grinned, and started to dive into the bread with enthusiasm. Dana suspected that was probably a bad idea given the man wasn't particularly carrying any extra kilos in the first place.

"You seem on edge a lot," Dana said. "Is there something we should be stressing about?"

"I might be paranoid," Ntamba said, "but I'm fairly certain we're being watched." He looked across to the DR Congo side of the river and Dana looked, but couldn't really see anything beyond the sea of green. "Every so often I think I see a car driving along." Ntamba elaborated, and Dana raised her eyebrows. "It's probably nothing," Ntamba said. "This place can get to you after a while. We only have a few more hours to go. Hopefully we'll be there before it gets too dark and you can relax at the tourist spot. Have some dinner and a swim. Then we go to Kwamouth."

"You really think we should go on the Kwa?" Dana asked.

"I'll do whatever you tell me to, Dr Lara," Ntamba grinned again. "But Kwamouth…*effrayant*." Dana looked at him, and then glanced across to Bryce, who was clearly desperately hanging out to get to dry land and have a rest. He'd probably prefer to make the trek along dry lands tomorrow, but at the same time, he's also probably prefer not to get a bullet in his brain. And what was it she had decided about Ntamba?

"OK," she said. "I'll take your advice. We'll go along the Kwa. How long will that take us?"

"Only about an hour, I reckon." Dana was slightly surprised by this. She had suspected that the journey along the road to Puemba was going to take longer than that, and from there they would have to trek into the jungle to find where the Four-Fold Crown might be. Ntamba's plan seemed much quicker.

"Are you OK with that, Wyatt?" Dana asked, managing to remember his fake name at the last minute.

"I honestly just want to get off this boat," Bryce moaned.

"You'll be fine, boss," grinned Ntamba back at him. "Once you get to shore, you should go shit, eat some fruit, go for a swim. In that order. Don't go shit in the pool." Ntamba laughed uproariously at that, but Bryce was clearly not that amused. "Hey," Ntamba suddenly said, and he grabbed Dana by the arm. "Look," he said, and nodded his head to the DR Congo bank. He passed Dana pair of binoculars, and Dana used them to look across the waters.

Through the branches and leaves, there was something moving. It was definitely not natural, sharp lines and green, but a manufactured green. When it pushed forward a tail light was visible. Dana dropped the binoculars and looked at Ntamba.

"Are they looking at us?" she wondered.

"Maybe not the same car as before," Ntamba said. "Maybe they are chasing something. I dunno. Do you believe it's coincidence Dr Lara?" Dana looked at Ntamba and grimaced. They chances were pretty unlikely all things told. She looked up through the binoculars and froze as she saw a face looking back at her with their own binoculars. He was big, bald, scarred and bearded.

And then the trees obscured the view.

The evening had definitely settled in by the time they had reached the *Site Touristique de Ngabé*, which was every bit the holiday destination Ntamba had suggested it might be. As Ntamba brought the boat up to the bank, women in bright yellow t-shirts and coloured skirts waved at him, with one launching her canoe from the shore to come the short distance to the boat.

"What have you brought us, Bernard?" the woman asked, and he grinned his by now familiar grin at her.

"Some guests from *Médicins Sans Frontières.* You have a booking for them, right?"

"Oh, of course, of course," the woman smiled. "Come, come, get on board, I'll take you ashore and away from this horrible fish smelling boat."

"And when you've settled them, you have a booking for me too, yeah, Jeanne?" Ntamba said, and there was a twinkle in his eye. Jeanne was clearly older than Ntamba by at least a decade, and she gave him a look that spoke volumes of the friendship they had and the disinterest she had in his flirting.

"You couldn't afford to have a booking with me Bernard Ntamba, and that's true," Jeanne said with fire, though it was quickly dissipated by Ntamba's raucous laughter. Dana and Bryce got gingerly onto her canoe, and she helped transfer their bags across. Soon they were on shore – much to Bryce's intense relief – and Jeanne took them to the main building.

They passed through rows of wooden huts which looked beautiful, and there were people wandering around, clearly enjoying themselves.

"I wonder what you do out here?" Bryce mused. Dana had noticed some jet skis on the shore when they arrived and suspected that there was quite a bit to do. Certainly, if all you wanted to do was relax in a beautiful environment that was not your own, then you could do worse than come to the Congo. She slapped at a mosquito and realized she needed to do her insect repellent again.

Well nowhere was perfect.

Forty minutes later, Dana stepped out of the shower in her cabin and hugged the fluffy white towel to her naked body, enjoying the feel of it as it absorbed the water from her body. She paused to look at her face and for a moment was appalled. Quickly she went to her bag and rummaged through it, finding her Bescher Puffer Beauty bag, and was glad to find that she had packed moisturizer and cleanser inside.

It would have to do.

Having donned another rather plain t-shirt and shorts that she had purchased in Singapore and lathered up in insect repellent, Dana left her cabin to head for the communal cabin where she would be able to get food. Her path there took her past the pools, both lit up rather beautifully for the evening, surrounded by a number of deck chairs in which a couple of the other guests were seated. Dana also noticed that there were a few other Congolese scattered around the place who didn't look like tourists, but she wasn't quite sure why they were there. Ntamba had made comment about the fact the place had a more cultural feel and that you could sit with elders during the day in a room that was, in his words, Coca-Cola red.

She decided to alter her path and walk around the pool – or more accurately pools, as there was a large rectangular one, with a smaller one beside it, closer to the shore. She skirted around both pools, enjoying the soft blue light emanating from them, and at one point knelt down to run her fingers through the water, enjoying the coolness of it.

As she stood up and continued on her journey, she saw an older man sitting a little way off, looking across the bank of the Congo. Dana paused to look at what he was saying, and thought she could see fire on the bank opposite, but it wasn't particularly easy to make out. She went over to get a closer look, and as she did, was more certain that something was burning on the bank opposite.

"More death," the older man said, and Dana wondered if he was speaking to her. There was clearly no one else around, but she wasn't sure that necessarily meant he was talking to her, or just making a general comment.

"In Kwamouth?" Dana asked, hoping she wasn't intruding.

"Death stalks that village," the old man nodded. He turned to her and patted the ground beside him, and Dana found herself doing as she was told, and sitting down. "Bernard says that you are going to Libonge Djoko." Dana looked at the man who gave her a very familiar grin at her surprise.

"You're Bernard's dad?" she asked, hoping she wasn't making a mistake.

"Of course," the man said. "Where do you think he gets those good looks from?"

"We're just providing help there," Dana lied, though feeling slightly bad about it. "But we're trying to go to somewhere sort of between it and Puemba."

"Ha," the old man barked. "You're looking for *La Couronne Quadritête*!"

"What?"

"The four headed crown. That's what you want, isn't it?" He looked at her triumphantly and Dana thought that her shock at his accuracy had confirmed it.

"Is that why they need help?" she replied cagily, and her approach was successful.

"Of course it is. There is something evil about that place," the old man said. "It's like a plague. It's not Congolese, you know. Not just not Sundi or Teke, but not Congolese. Not even African. It's just *wrong*." Dana frowned slightly, wondering if they were talking about the same thing.

"You've seen it?" she asked, hesitating before deciding on *it* to describe the unknown.

"Yes, it's a *pyramide* just sitting there, all black and *effrayant*. Only women there. You know that?"

"No, I didn't," Dana said, but then her brain corrected itself and she realized she did know that. How did she know that? "The pyramid is between Libonge Djoko and Puemba?"

"Yeah, if you start from one and walk to the other you will find it. You can hear it before you see it."

"Hear the women?" Dana asked, puzzled.

"Hear the *pyramide*," Daddy Ntamba relied. "The sound of the spirits trapped within it."

"Wait, are you saying it's haunted?"

"There is so much death in the Congo. They are all there, in the *mfinda*. You can hear the *bisimbi* when you are there. They still walk in the *mfinda*, but I think they know *La Couronne Quadritête* are evil and they don't like it. They try to warn people." Daddy Ntamba turned to Dana and gave her a deep look. "Maybe

172

you should listen, *mademoiselle*. I can see that you want to help. See it in your eyes. In your heart. But people like you often have a tragic story mapped out for them. I think it would be sad for that to be your story."

"I think so too," Dana said glibly, but she had to admit she was somewhat shaken by what Bernard's father had said. He had turned to look out to the river again, and Dana wondered if he had been praying before she had interrupted him. "I'm just going to…" she started, but the old man interrupted her.

"Have some food. Enjoy your night. Tomorrow will be a long day if you are going to find the *Couronne quadruple.*"

Dana nodded and got up, feeling a lot more shaken than she thought she would.

FOURTH REPORT: RIGHT, BITCH?

The following morning, Dana had breakfast at the communal hut with Bryce, who was looking much better than he had the previous day.

"Thank god for the shore, then?" Dana said with a grin.

"Very funny," Bryce replied. "Your problem is that you're so young. You think you're indestructible."

"Oh please," Dana groaned. "You can't be much more than ten years older than me. Don't tell me that when you hit thirty you suddenly have to stop taking risks."

"No, you don't, but you get some common sense."

"OK, Boomer," Dana chuckled. "You ready to go, or do you want to have a nana nap so you have enough energy to cope with the day."

"Ha ha," Bryce responded. "I suppose if all I had to do was look pretty and drink I'd probably throw common sense out the door as well."

Dana decided that it was time to make sure she had collected all her things, and left before she lost all her goodwill to her travelling companion. With that done, Dana headed to the main hut to discuss payment, but she was assured that Max had taken care of everything. Please come again, they insisted, and Dana decided that she quite wanted to. Even as she was leaving, she saw that *Site Touristique* was coming to life, with the guests starting to decide on their first activities for the day. There were tourists being taught how to get their fishing gear together, while a number of teenagers were running down to the shore, presumably with the intention of using the jet skis.

Dana was also able to check her phone, something which had become a luxury. On the Congo there was no reception at all. She had been shocked when her phone pinged at her as they entered the Wi-Fi of the hotel, and realised this would probably be her last chance for a while to connect to the outside world.

Jeanne, the woman who had taken them from the boat to shore the previous night, was already there, now dressed in a bright red t-shirt, chatting with some of the other staff who were preparing themselves for the teens with the look of anyone in the world who knew what excitable kids were like to confront.

"You want to go to that no-good Bernard?" Jeanne said with a smile.

"I didn't realise he was such a worry," Dana said good-naturedly.

"Oh, that man," Jeanne shook her head as she reached forward to take Dana's bag and balance it carefully in the canoe. "He thinks he is God's gift to women. The problem is, he is, if you know what I mean," Jeanne added conspiratorially. "There are too many women on the Congo who know Bernard's charms. He won't get around me though. I have sorted out his father, and I will sort him out too!" She laughed at this, and Dana couldn't help but laugh with her, infectious as the laughter was.

Bryce joined them quite soon after and the pair were

back on the *Dame Rouge* quite quickly.

"Well, well, well, if it isn't my favourite world savers, and my favourite boat woman."

"Boat woman indeed," huffed Jeanne. "You be careful out there today, Bernard. The world is ready to knock some sense into you."

"What are you talking about?" Ntamba said laconically. "Don't tell me this is some old superstition you have heard from my old man."

"Sometimes he knows more than he lets on," Jeanne replied, and Dana was surprised to see she was being quite serious.

"He just likes to be mysterious. Creates an atmosphere that women think is cool," Ntamba said, but Jeanne pouted at him.

"Be careful all the same," she warned, and even Ntamba seemed surprised now.

"Yeah, OK," he said, and she nodded, before using her paddle to push away from the *Dame Rouge* and head back to the *Site Touristique*. "She's in a strange mood this morning, don't you think?" Ntamba said to the others, though they both shrugged, neither having enough experience to say one way or the other. "Right," declared their guide. "We have a journey, probably no more than an hour. Maybe more. But not much more. We move on up, keep our heads low and then we get you two to Libonge Djoko. Or wherever it is from there, yeah?"

"Sure," Dana agreed, and Bryce nodded along with her. Ntamba gave them a wink, and started up the *Dame*'s motor. With a lurch, it moved forward, heading starboard to the Kwa River. They crossed over the Congo, Bryce staring intently into the river.

"Looking for something?" Dana asked.

"Hippos," came the reply and Dana stopped herself from speaking, suddenly wondering if there were actually hippopotamus around.

"Hey Bernard, are there hippos around here?" she asked, feeling slightly self-conscious about looking stupid.

"No Dr Lara," came the cheery response. "You all good here. They are up near Burundi, a way up there." He waved, but Dana thought it was far too general to be a specific direction, and didn't take it in. "No, all you got to worry about are the crocs. So don't stick your hand in the water Dr Wyatt, huh?" For the first time that morning they got a blast of Ntamba's joyous laughter, but he reigned it back very quickly. Dana looked around and noticed that they had started to enter the Kwa, and they could make out Kwamouth without any difficulty at all. Some small children stood on the banks and watched them. One waved cheerily at them, and Dana waved back, which prompted the others to wave as well. She felt a sense of sadness to see such innocence in a place where there was definitely none.

They travelled the next fifteen minutes in silence, and then for the fifteen minutes after that, whenever one of them spoke, another looked warily around and that forced them back into silence. After thirty minutes, they mutually decided it was time to converse, but as soon as Bryce opened his mouth and said "Well," Ntamba immediately put his hand up to Bryce's face, having come from his wheelhouse. Bryce looked annoyed, but Dana looked at their friend and frowned.

Ntamba held his hand to his hear, and the other two strained to hear what Ntamba had. Over the beating of her heart, which was the only thing Dana seemed able to take in, they heard an engine revving.

Ntamba went back to the wheelhouse, and when he returned, he was carrying a pump action shot gun. Dana's relationship with guns tended to center around handguns, but she recognized the Mossberg 500 pump action. Ntamba nodded reassuringly to his passengers, presumably worried that they thought he might shoot them, and then headed to the back of the boat and the crane. Dana looked past him and saw a motor boat making its way up the river. Much faster than they were, she grabbed the binoculars to see and saw that there were five men on the boat – all heavy, all thugs, and all carrying guns. But not handguns or shotguns; even though Dana wasn't an expert, she recognized the Sig Sauers they were carrying.

Dana hesitated for just a moment, and then opened her bag and grabbed out her gun case, unsealing it with her fingerprint, and pulling out the golden modified G48 Glock that she had been given as a gift.

"Get under," hissed Ntamba, and Dana nodded, opening the hatch that led below decks and clambered down the ladder, her gun now tucked into her shorts. Bryce appeared and Dana beckoned him to join her, but he shook his head and closed the hatch. For a moment Dana wondered what the hell her new friend was doing, but decided to make the most of her situation.

On the deck, Ian Bryce watched the new boat get closer and closer. There were five men on board, and he risked a glance at Ntamba, who seemed to know exactly what was going on.

"You should probably go down to, Dr Wyatt. Keep your

head low. This will get nasty." The boat continued to approach and Ntamba pumped the gun, firing it into the air, but above the heads of the boat approaching. To Bryce's astonishment, he saw the boat begin to slow.

"Where do you think you are, *mon ami*," came a guttural voice from the new arrivals. "You're on our land and you shoot guns at us?"

"You have big guns. I'm easily scared," Ntamba called back.

"How about you tell us what you are doing here and then we decide if you can stay, or if you should go back to your home, huh?" the voice returned.

"We're doctors," Bryce called out, and the men on the boat raised their guns.

Could they hit me from that distance? What's the range on machine guns?

"Doctors?" came Guttural. "What sort of doctors?" By now he had made himself clear – a big man with broad shoulders and a bald head, a single gold earring in his left ear, and a cigarette somehow staying on his lip as he spoke.

"Just the usual kind. We're here to help out with some sickness at Libonge Djoko."

"They don't need help," Guttural argued back.

"Are you a doctor?" Bryce retorted, and wondered where he got the inner strength to say that.

"Kwamouth needs doctors," Guttural said.

"Why?" Bryce asked.

"The other one died," Guttural said, and there was a ripple of laughter amongst the men on the boat.

"You need to go back to Kwamouth," Ntamba said.

"Or what *mon ami*?" asked Guttural.

Ian Bryce had to admit he wasn't sure exactly what happened next, but it was quick, fast and furious, and he wet himself as it went down. He had been watching the approaching boat, when a shot rang out, and temporarily deafened him, so he suspected it must have been from Ntamba's gun. Why the boatman had done it, he had no idea, but regardless, for one of the men on the boat, his chest erupted into a blossom of red, and he dropped his gun and fell to the ground. The other four reacted without thought and bought up their guns, and Bryce had no idea why, but he dropped to the ground.

Ntamba fired again, killing a second man, but this time the bullets ripped through him and he fell to the ground, blood frothing in his mouth as he tried to feel where his wounds were. Bryce crawled across the boat to him, and Ntamba looked at him with fear and tears in his eyes, and Bryce embraced the man who held on tight.

As the three remaining men came on board the *Dame Rouge* from their boat, Bryce could feel Ntamba's strength ebbing away, and sure enough when he released the man, the eyes looked back at him sightlessly.

Don't worry, boss.

"Stand up, doctor," Guttural said, but he dragged the last word out. *Doc-tahh.* "You know, I could have sworn that there was somebody else on this boat." Bryce was hauled up to a standing position as Guttural grabbed him by the shirt and lifted. He was surprisingly strong.

"Well, who are you with?"

"No one," Bryce said.

"Did you piss yourself, Doc-tahh?"

"Yes, I did. I'm terrified. You just shot my friend."

"You shot two of my friends. Do I look terrified?" Guttural leaned in, and Bryce could smell breath from a mouth that hadn't had the teeth cleaned in a week, at least. The man reeked of sweat and blood and smoke; a cigarette somehow balancing on his lip. "Anyone else, here Mr Murderer?" Guttural asked, with as much care in his voice for the fate of Bryce's friends as the mosquito that landed on his neck.

"There's no one else where," Bryce whispered. Guttural looked at him, and then without any warning smashed his hand into Bryce's face, knocking him to the ground. Bryce could feel the blood coming from his mouth and nose, and wondered if something had broken.

"Maybe pussy boy is telling the truth and he's alone, but I don' think so," Guttural announced. "You," and he pointed at one his men, who looked back with a face that didn't seem to be immediately obedient. "Go down, find out what's going on. If there's anyone down there, kill them." The thug looked back at him, and then nodded, heading towards the hatch and pulling it open. Slinging the machine gun over his shoulder he descended below deck. Above him, Guttural moved to look down and see what was going on.

The thug paused as he decided which way to go, and opted to head aft, where there was really nothing but storage space. It was a quick look, and he couldn't see anyone else. Then, he turned and headed towards the stern of the boat, down the little corridor, but there was a door on either side.

"Hurry up, I'm bored wasting my time," Guttural called down. He paused, but then was surprised that he didn't get an answer. After a minute passed, Guttural frowned. "What the fuck is he doing?" he muttered.

And then he paused and turned around moving over to Bryce. Grabbing the Englishman, he hauled him up and looked into his face, spitting. "Did you lie to me, Doc-tahh?" he snarled.

Suddenly a shot rang out, and Guttural's remaining thug dropped with a scream of pain, grabbing at his knee. Guttural swung around, bringing his gun to bear, but he was stopped.

"Don't do it," Dana Spectra's voice rang out clearly. "Drop the gun and turn around very slowly." Guttural paused, finding himself in the awkward position of holding Bryce with one hand and trying to get his gun with the other. He twisted his head and saw Dana halfway out of the hatch, her gun pointed at him.

"So, you are a murderer too, huh, bitch?" Guttural said, and Dana gave a small smile.

"Your friend down below is still alive, and he's going to live," she said indicating the other man. "But you are going to drop that gun and release my friend."

Guttural weighed up his options and dropped the gun, however, he didn't release Bryce. In fact, as he turned, he twisted to get Bryce in front of him. Dana climbed slowly out of the hatch, never lowering her gun.

"Guess we got an Afree-can stand off," Guttural said, mangling the pronunciation. "Cause you don't want to shoot your friend, and I don't think you're that good a shot that you would risk taking it, right? Right, bitch?" Guttural moved backwards slightly, but paused when he realized he was at the edge of the deck.

Bryce, meanwhile, pleaded with his eyes.

Please help me, but for the love of God, don't pull the trigger.

Dana, on the other hand, seemed slightly preoccupied with what was behind Bryce, which annoyed him, because he was unable to turn and see. And then, to both Bryce and Guttural's surprise, Dana raised her gun a little more.

"You wouldn't fucking dare," hissed Guttural.

Dana squeezed the trigger.

The bullet found its target with unerring accuracy, going over Bryce's shoulder but straight through Guttural's who squealed in a surprisingly high voice for someone who spoke so low generally, and he let go of Bryce to grab at his shoulder. Even as he did, Dana moved forward quickly and pushed at Guttural, who staggered back and fell into the water.

Guttural tried to shout something but his mouth was full of water, which he desperately tried to spit out.

Bryce, meanwhile, had seen the same thing Dana had earlier – the cold, yellow eyes of a crocodile regarding the boat with a degree of calculation. The eyes had moved closer, and the shadow beneath the water made it clear just how big this particular crocodile was. Bryce suspected it was bigger than most, possibly as long as 5 meters.

As Guttural splashed, the crocodile opened his jaws, and it was when Guttural's hand hit the creature on the side of the head as he struggled in the water, that he finally realized just how much danger he was in. Guttural screamed as the crocodile's jaws clamped around him, and then suddenly the creature twisted, and Guttural was dragged with it as it turned in the water.

Both Bryce and Dana looked away, unable to watch.

Dana turned and pointed her golden Glock at the thug on the deck, who had gone pale and silent as his boss had become crocodile fodder. When the other thug climbed out of the hatch, rubbing his head where Dana had clearly dealt him a blow earlier, Dana spoke.

"Get out of here. Get off this boat and go back to where you come from," Dana snarled.

"You aren't doctors," the able-bodied thug said, but Dana just looked at him.

"We're very well trained in *Médicins Sans Frontières*," Dana said coldly. "Tell people not to fuck with Dr Muller in future." The thug nodded and turned to his friend, who reached out for help to get back on the boat. Dana waited until they were well on board and heading away before she finally turned to Ntamba's body and knelt down to touch his face.

"He saved my life," Bryce said. "You both did."

Dana simply closed their guide's eyes.

FIFTH REPORT: AN ANGEL

Bryce had been able to pilot the boat a little further down the river, and admitted he was grateful the controls seemed to be relatively straightforward (and perhaps more importantly, he didn't have to do very much other than steer and accelerate. The other thing in their favour was that they weren't too far from Libonge Djoko.

Within half an hour they had discovered their destination – or more accurately they had discovered what they thought their destination was. The maps had indicated that there was nothing else in the area, so presumably the small little village they had stumbled upon was it.

And it was *very* small.

Bryce decided to steer the boat straight up to the shore, the only part of the bank where the trees weren't growing over it, making it impossible to get to shore. Dana scanned the area for crocodiles before she readied herself to jump off the boat and into the shallow water to get to the shore.

"What do we do about Bernard?" Bryce asked, and Dana paused. In truth the same thing had been playing on her mind and she had continually pushed the question away because there was no answer that made her happy. There was no realistic way they could take the body with them, and it would have been extremely dangerous for them to even consider it. But it seemed so disrespectful to leave the corpse on the boat and never speak of it again.

"We've got two options," Dana said to her friend. "Either we leave him here and let the authorities know as soon as we get into contact with them, or we set the boat on fire."

"What if we need it?" Bryce asked, panicked, and Dana nodded grimly.

"There was some ice down below," Dana reflected. "Maybe we could take him down there and the ice might help preserve him until we can get the authorities to retrieve him."

"Maybe," Bryce agreed. "Though remember we're in DR Congo now, Dana. We're not likely to get much help from them." Dana sighed and beckoned to Bryce to help her move Ntamba. With the awkward task completed, they jumped off the boat and made their way to shore, catching the attention of some of the locals who looked at them with a passing interest, though not enough to say anything or engage.

Dana took in the small village and counted seven huts. She wasn't sure if this was the sum total of Libonge Djoko or simply a smaller part, but either way it was clear the place was definitely not a thriving metropolis. The huts themselves were very basic, with no glass in the windows, and no doors, save for maybe a piece of cloth hanging down.

The strange thing was, that while she had felt Brazzaville was poor and uncared for, it was clear that Libonge Djoko was much poorer, but definitely didn't feel that way, and the village did not feel uncared for at all. This was home to a group of people who were content to live a simple life. She wondered if they avoided the militia groups that were in constant conflict around them, or if they had to sacrifice something in order to be ignored.

"Hello," Dana said, waving at them, and to her surprise, one of the men sitting on a stool out the front of a hut – an older man - waved back and gave a friendly smile. "Do you speak English? *Parlez-vous français*?" She was delighted when he perked up at her French, but he clearly didn't understand her, and turned to shout something into the hut behind him. The door-curtain was pulled aside and a younger man came out with a face of confusion, but then saw the newcomers and enthusiastically responded. Dana sighed as she realized she had no idea what he was saying.

Bryce, however, was clearly in his element and began to talk, indicating Dana at one point (indeed she heard "Lara Muller" and so recognized she was part of the conversation). The younger man nodded, and turned to the older man and some other villagers who had gathered around, clearly translating the conversation for them. Bryce continued and when he said three words Dana actually understood – Four-Fold Crown – there was a wave of panic over the group, some making gestures that seemed designed to ward off evil, while a few even walked away from the conversation.

The younger man responded to Bryce, and then Bryce turned back to Dana.

"They know of the Four-Fold Crown, but they essentially described them as demons," he said and Dana frowned.

"What, do they mean? The members of the Cult are demons?"

"No, the actual Four-Fold Crown. Apparently its four

187

women who run the cult, and they are the demons. This is Adoua. That's Ndongo, his father. They all know about the Crown. Apparently, there's a pyramid they operate out of." Dana shook her head in surprise, almost unable to believe she had heard currently.

"A pyramid? Like Bernard's father said?" Bryce frowned at Dana realized she hadn't told him the story.

"I guess so," Bryce said, shrugging. Dana sighed again as her conscience kicked in, anticipating what was to come. She had planned to do what Ntamba's father had suggested and make a line for Puemba, hoping that her phone would be able to guide her, but her phone had virtually no reception now, and that was seemingly going to be very unlikely. The possibility that Adoua might be able to, or at least know someone who could guide them to the Crown was their best option, but she already had a huge amount of guilt over Ntamba, and to add to that list was not going to sit well.

Suddenly she felt very drained. The heat around her, her clothes sticking to her awkwardly, the fact she felt very hungry all of a sudden, and the possibility that she had come all this way, gone through so much, simply to have to come to a dead end because she really had no right to put anyone in the position of death just seemed too much.

Her thoughts were interrupted by the old man – Ndongo – poking her on the arm, and holding a bowl out to her. She looked at the bowl which seemed to have water in it, and Ndongo grinned at her, miming drinking. She gave a smile to the little, old man and ignored her better judgement and drank from the water. Ndongo patted her on the arm, smiling, and Dana's smile grew as she handed the bowl back to the man.

"The water's OK, you'll be happy to know," Bryce said. "Adoua has assured me that it's all safe. They get it from the plants or something. He offered us some fruit and bread if we'd like it as well. Not quite what you're used to eating, I know, but still." Dana looked at him, cocking her head on the side.

"Not quite what I'm used to eating? What's that supposed to mean?"

"Well, big time model like you. You dine out at all the best places." Dana scowled.

"I ate with you last night, remember. It wasn't first class."

"It wasn't fruit and bread either," Bryce chuckled. Dana rolled her eyes.

"You shouldn't be so quick to judge people," Dana huffed.

"I must admit you were a dab hand with that golden gun. Where did you even get that?"

"It was a gift from a girlfriend," Dana said. Ndongo and Adoua had returned, bringing with them some bowls, and Dana noticed that a few kids had brought out some small stools, which they put down and indicated the travellers should sit. As she did, one of the children – probably no older than seven – reached out and touched Dana's hair, curiously. Adoua spoke to Bryce and Bryce laughed.

"They think you are an angel," Bryce said. "The kids, obviously. Not the adults. They aren't idiots."

"I am an angel," Dana pouted, and turned to touch the boy's black curls, which he giggled at, and ran away to a friend, suddenly embarrassed. As Dana ate the first bit of bread (which was *not* what she was expecting, but at the same time not terrible, so she wasn't devastated) she felt a little revived. The simple display of hospitality was helping a lot and she focused herself on deciding what the next course of action would be.

"Can you ask Adoua if they can tell us in which direction we need to go to get to this pyramid?" Dana asked, between mouthfuls of a banana which had been given to her. The banana had been green, but her surprise it was quite ripe and tasted amazing. She saw that there was a dish that seemed to have pineapple and decided that was definitely next on her list of things to gorge on.

Bryce relayed Dana's request, and Adoua nodded, but then spoke back to Bryce. Whatever he said was not well received by Ndongo, who grabbed at his son's arm and spoke to him in whatever language the pair usually used. Dana suddenly wondered what language they actually did speak here, and also how Adoua knew French. Adoua was probably in his thirties, and Dana wondered if he had left the village earlier, and on his return had become their spokesperson.

The family discussion was heated and Ndongo was not happy, glaring at Bryce when he had finished. Adoua continued his discussion with the Englishman, and eventually Bryce turned back to Dana.

"Adoua is going to take us there, though Ndongo isn't happy about it. As you could probably tell. But he is, and apparently, I'm to blame for it."

"Well, I didn't ask him," Dana pointed out, and Bryce looked at her from under a frown.

"Neither did I," he said pointedly. She shrugged and

smiled sweetly. Adoua had some more to say, and Bryce nodded. "Adoua says we can leave as soon as we've had our fill, so that's good, I suppose."

"I suppose so," Dana agreed, and quickly grabbed the bowl of pineapple before anyone else could.

Secretly Dana was enormously reassured that Adoua had agreed to take them on their journey, and was feeling a lot calmer as a result. Before setting off on the trip, she had gone back to the *Rouge Dame* to get some more bottles of water that were on the boat, and also to get the medical kid that was there. When she had returned, Adoua shook his head and said something to Bryce who turned to her with a grin.

"Adoua thinks you probably shouldn't go into the jungle like that," he said, trying to lose the grin. Dana looked at him puzzled.

"What do you mean?"

"Put your shirt on," Bryce said. Dana looked at them for a moment, and then realized what they were talking about. While she had been on the boat, she had taken the opportunity to change into the Muki activewear she had brought with her – a midnight blue seamless ribbed longline crop top and matching leggings, wrapping her shirt around her waist so it wouldn't continue to stick to her uncomfortably. However, she realized that having bare arms might not be ideal as they walked through a forest full of mosquitoes and leeches, and so obediently put her shirt back on, buttoning it up. Almost instantly it clung to her bare belly and arms, but she put the discomfort out of her mind.

Adoua had been wearing jeans before, but now was wearing a shirt, and Dana hadn't noticed Bryce take his shirt off at any point, so he was ready as well. Adoua went over and grabbed his father's hands, resting his forehead on the older man's, and then waved to the other villagers. Dana wondered if Adoua's mother was around, but decided she didn't want to pry, so she left it alone.

Adoua beckoned them to follow him, and he led them through the small village, before turning at the second last house and heading into the jungle beyond. There was a confidence about the man that suggested this wasn't the first trip he had made and the point at which they entered the jungle certainly seemed to be a well-worn path, rather than a completely new entrance.

Bryce looked uncertainly at Dana and she shrugged, before swallowing her resolve and moving into the jungle after their guide.

SIXTH REPORT: MILITIA GROUP

Perhaps the thing that Dana had least prepared herself for in the jungle was the darkness. The further they entered the jungle, the deeper they got into the foliage and forest, the darker it became, as the trees above wove their branches together to sew a ceiling of leaves that cut out the light as effectively as any concrete wall could. Half an hour into their trek, and the light desperately reached down to them through the tiniest gaps, creating little beams, like lasers.

Thanks to the insect repellent, she had been left relatively alone by the bugs, but every so often she chided herself as she walked through something just a little like a filament and jumped at the possibility something else had landed on her. She and Bryce had got extremely lucky, she realized, to not only find someone who knew what they were talking about, but who was actually game enough to take them into the forest. Adoua was a godsend, and Dana had no idea why he was so actually keen to help. Though he spent a lot of time talking to Bryce, the Englishman hadn't translated most of the conversation, and Dana wondered if he had told Bryce the reason he was keen on their mission.

Initially they had talked, making small jokes about the trek and being more serious about how often they should stop and how much water they should be drinking. Curious about the trees around them, Dana had even asked Adoua through Bryce what they were, though the communication gap between them caused confusion with the answers; Adoua didn't know what the trees were called in any language other than his native tongue, and so he couldn't give them the French for what they were after. Bryce, surprisingly, was able to point out mahogany and ebony trees, and even knew a cinchona tree. However, at the point where Dana lost track of time, the conversation had dried up, and they were simply hauling themselves through the jungle. Dana tried to remain vigilant, but again, the spiderwebs reminded her that she wasn't being remotely as conscious of her surroundings as she should have been. Bryce seemed to be holding up better than she was, though when he stumbled, she realized perhaps she was giving him more credit than she should.

At one-point Adoua suddenly stopped and raised his hand. He gestured to them to move back into the shadows, and Dana stepped back a little, trying not to get into the undergrowth, but at the same time clinging as close as she could.

She peered around, trying to see what it was Adoua had seen, and then to her shock she saw three men walking through the forests, machetes in hand, slashing at the growth in front of them. They were dressed casually, in boots and t-shirts, with dark pants, but over their shoulders were machine guns, with belts of ammunition around their necks like scarves. Two of them looked older, possibly in their forties or fifties, their hair peaked and grey, while the third was much younger, possibly not even in his twenties. He had a dark look across his face, a nervous energy about him as though he were keen to kill.

Then, to Dana's shock, three more figures came up behind them. They were children, barely older than ten, carrying guns that were almost as big as they were. They didn't have the darkness of the older boy, but at the same time there was still something haunted about their appearance. One of them pointed to something which Dana couldn't make out, but the three giggled all the same, which earned them a reproachful glare from the older boy. The two men turned and said something and they moved forward, slashing through the growth.

The trio waited, Dana not willing to make any movement until their guide had given them an all-clear, though as she sat patiently, she was sure she saw a snake glide down the tree in front of her, and she shut her mouth, willing the snake to either not exist or go in a different direction, away from here.

With time having lost all meaning, Dana wasn't sure how long it was before Adoua turned to Bryce and whispered something, making several hand gestures. Then he waited and Bryce turned to Dana, clearly the news needing to be relayed.

"I suppose you know that was a militia group," Bryce started and Dana looked at him causing him to nod apologetically. "Obviously they've gone on their way. Apparently, we're not too far from the Crown's pyramid, but we have to be careful not to draw attention to ourselves. Not that I'm saying you would, I'm just telling you what Adoua said," Bryce added trying to cover himself. Dana bit back a sarcastic response and the three stood up and continued on, all three of them looking back over their shoulders to see if the little group they had crossed was going to follow them.

Dana would never know quite what Adoua believed "too far" was;

by the time the guide put his hand up once again, Dana wasn't certain whether they had been walking for ten minutes or over an hour. The jungle had become one big repeating cycle of trees, bushes and shrubs. Dana was at a point where she desperately wished for it all to be over, tired of the walking, the heat and the humidity, and the constant weariness of never knowing what was near them. Off in the distance she could occasionally hear the trumpeting of an elephant, while at one point they neared two okapi, who regarded them with soft dark eyes. Dana had paused, marvelling at the animals, with their bizarre striped legs, brown bodies and white faces. A low growl, however, had caused Adoua to encourage them to move on, and Dana realized that there might be far more dangerous things nearby than the militia.

Finally, and to Dana's eternal relief, Adoua turned and put his hand on her arm, giving her a smile. He took her by the hand, and led her slowly forward, and Dana looked ahead to see that there was a clearing; a surprisingly big clearing. Even though she had been expecting it, she was still astonished to see the pyramid at the center.

It wasn't as big or as imposing as the pyramids at Giza, but this one was more bizarre as it was incongruous and out of place in the middle of the rainforest. Dark grey, perhaps almost a strange purple in colour, the pyramid lacked any distinct markings on the outside. Perhaps even more incongruously, there seemed to be a chimpanzee on the top of the pyramid. It was reclining, enjoying the sun that was coming through thanks to the lack of foliage above it.

"Did the Crown build it?" Dana wondered, not sure if she expected an answer.

"There are pyramids in the Sudan," Bryce muttered. "Like, up north. I don't really know anything about the whole Nubian culture, but I didn't think there were any below the Central African Republic." Adoua suddenly shushed them and pointed again. He had lost his humor, a great concern replacing it.

The chimpanzee had stirred itself, repositioning so that it could see what new disturbance had been created down below, but on seeing it was just more human beings it actually yawned, before scratching its grey-black fur and resettling, still keeping an eye on the new arrivals. Just in case.

The group that had walked into the clearing were immediately clear to Dana, who looked at the little militia group they had encountered earlier and found herself holding her breath, completely unconsciously. All six members had their weapons ready to go, including the two little kids, which Dana found just a little sickening. Adoua made a strange gesture with his hand and Dana wondered how superstitious he might be.

At the base of the pyramid, a door opened and someone walked out. A woman, based on her figure, wearing a black suit that was figure hugging and completely enveloping. Even her head was covered by a balaclava of sorts, with just a gap for the eyes. She looked like a ninja, if that ninja had only access to activewear.

"Go away!" the woman said, and Dana was surprised to find the voice annoyingly familiar. "*Va-t'en!*"

"*Non! Tu dois partir. Nous nous emparons de la pyramide!*" came the response, and there was a pause as silence settled over the area. Up above them, the chimpanzee watched with curiousity, wondering how it would play out.

"*Dernière chance*," the woman said. "*Partez maintenant, ou subissez les conséquences.*" Bryce turned to Dana, but she stopped him from speaking. She didn't know exactly what was said, but the message was clear enough. However, at that point, one of the older men and the younger man both fired their guns, hitting the woman in the chest. Dana forced herself to stay still, but to her surprise Bryce was leaping up. Both she and Adoua grabbed him and pulled him back down, though he still struggled.

Meanwhile, the door to the pyramid opened, and another figure stepped out, dressed the same as the first. Before anyone could do anything, however, she had was firing a gun, and Dana realized the figure had entered with the gun raised. The militia men dropped, all of them dead, including the two kids.

Dana felt sick at the sight.

To her shock, Bryce was once again up and this time was too quick for them to hold back. He was running into the clearing straight at the pyramid and screaming. Dana turned to look at Adoua, but their guide was panicked, and he backed away, his hands up, shaking his head and muttering. At one point Dana was sure she heard "*Je suis désolé. Je suis vraiment désolé,*" but wasn't sure what it meant, or even if she had heard it correctly.

She turned back to the clearing to see what was going on, and her mouth dropped in shock. The woman who had shot the militia dead had pulled off her hood, and standing before them, gun still in hand, her short dark hair framing a familiar pixie face was Asha.

There was no doubt it now, Dana reflected. There was no room for misunderstanding. Asha had killed Thomas McAteer and Bella was completely right all along. Bryce raced up to her and embraced her, but even as she did, more women dressed in the same black outfits were appearing, presumably coming from other entrances to the pyramid, and they were all armed with a variety of guns that Dana suspected probably came from militia groups they had captured. Already some of the women were going over to the dead militia men and looting their corpses.

The woman that the militia had shot was, it turned out, not dead. She was picking herself up and Asha turned to help her. Dana realized that the women's outfits must have been made from some sort of bullet proof material, as she could see where the bullets had embedded themselves into the woman's chest.

At that point Dana also realized that she was surrounded as well. Two of the black-clad women came forward and pointed their guns at her, and Dana reluctantly raised her arms in surrender. One of the women came forward and roughly grabbed Dana's backpack, pulling it from her. There was an odd smell coming from her, like the scent of a flower, but with the hint of burning, as though someone had perhaps burnt roses or some other flower to create the scent. It was a surprising relief from the smell of the jungle.

She was roughly shoved forward, and despite the warm embrace that Bryce had initially received, He too was now a prisoner of the women.

And they were women, all of them. It was like they'd stumbled on a cult of…

"Ohhh!" Dana said out loud, her brain suddenly kicking in. "Oh, I've been an idiot," she reflected, shaking her head.

Suddenly she realized what it was all those days ago that had bothered her. Bryce had said that the Four-Fold Crown was a cult of women, and yet no one had said that at any point, so how could he possibly have known that?

Only if he had already been in contact with them somehow. And Asha was a member of the Crown, and was clearly in some sort of relationship with Bryce.

Which was odd, because Asha had never mentioned a partner before ever.

The woman who had been shot finally stood up, and Asha turned to her and asked her if she was alright, to which the bullet-ridden woman nodded, clearly wearily. With some effort she reached up and pulled her hood off.

The dark hair framing the pixie face was identical to the one that had been revealed earlier. The woman turned and looked at Dana, and her face was apologetic.

"Hey Dana," she said with a weak smile. Dana looked from one Asha to the other.

"This is June," Bryce said, indicating the original Asha.

"My twin sister," the second Asha – the actual Asha said.

"June, your girlfriend, your identical twin," Dana said. "And a murderer." There was a pregnant pause for a moment and then a voice from behind her spoke.

"I think you should meet with the Four-Fold Crown," it said with a distinct Russian accent. Dana didn't bother to turn to see who spoke. She just headed towards the entrance to the pyramid, feeling disappointed, stupid and just plain tired.

At the top of the pyramid above her, the chimpanzee seemed to laugh.

SEVENTH REPORT: REMAIN SILENT

The weird aroma of burnt flowers permeated the entire pyramid, weaving its way through the corridors and getting stronger the closer Dana got to the center. At least she assumed it was the center. The inside initially looked not dissimilar to the outside, with the grey-purple bricks that had been used to build the thing clearly the same on the inside, however as they started to go deeper, the rooms became less archaic and more like what she would have expected Asha to live in.

Bryce had been correct, it was most definitely a cult of women, and many regarded Bryce with a degree of concern, ranging from contempt to fear. Dana remembered a time when she had visited a friend after she had fled from an abusive father; the girl and her mother moving into a women's shelter to stay safe. Colonel Spectra had dropped her off and signed her in, but when Indigo had entered the reception, the few women who had been there gave a similar vibe. This was more than a cult; it was a refuge.

Except, Dana wondered, how did Asha fit into this, and how did her sister, June, become an assassin. How had she never even heard of June? When Dana had first discovered Asha, she had gone through a lot of the girl's social media, but there was never a hint of a twin sister. In fairness, there was never a hint of any family, but surely she would have made some mention of having a twin. Unless that twin didn't want to be in the limelight.

Which an assassin probably wouldn't want to be, Dana reflected.

"You knew," she suddenly said, looking at Bryce, and felt a flash of anger which surprised her because she thought she was too tired to feel anything. "You knew it was June when you saw her."

"He knew before," Asha said softly. "June told him she'd be there."

"You knew André was going to be murdered and you did nothing?" Dana said to Bryce, and this time she couldn't keep the anger from her voice.

"My girlfriend is a top tier assassin," Bryce said. "I couldn't stop her." Dana stopped to look at him, her mind working overtime as she wondered how Bryce and June had possibly got together. It was borderline insane.

"Keep moving," the Russian girl said, shoving her gun into Dana's back, and Dana turned to her in annoyance. She had taken off her hood as well, and she looked about 15, with a round face, brown hair that curled slightly at the fringe, and full red lips. She probably wasn't 15, Dana thought, but she wondered what the hell was going on. Fighting the urge to make a break for it, Dana turned and continued the journey they were being pushed down.

They passed a number of different living areas, all of which had the comforts of home, and even the kitchen they walked through was clearly not cheap. Money had been poured into this, though if June was getting a lot of money for killing

202

people that would explain where…

Dana suddenly stopped as her brain made a connection that was probably obvious, but had only just occurred.

"She's not the only killer," Dana muttered. "You're all assassins." She stopped again and turned to Asha. "Oh god."

"I'm not, honestly," Asha said, touching Dana's arm as if to reassure her. "We're not all killers. Some of us train to be. That's what June wanted. I wanted to make money from being an influencer. There are hackers here…it's a whole operation."

"I don't," Dana started, but Asha just shook her head.

"It's not for me to explain," she said. "The Four-Fold Crown will."

Dana found herself being marched down corridors, Bryce following as though he were not with her, which was curious. Though with that being said, Dana also noticed that the guards that were escorting them were focusing their weapons on Bryce more than her. It was if she had been given something of a free pass. Because she was a woman?

The place was curiously bigger on the inside. Not literally, of course, it wasn't a TARDIS, but on the outside the pyramid had seemed a little small than the inside would suggest. Dana realized that they were certainly moving downwards, but the corridors seemed longer than she would have thought, which meant that the outside was quite deceptive.

There were more chimpanzees hanging around on the inside of the pyramid as well, although Asha told her there were actually bonobo, or pygmy chimpanzees. They were about the size of a three-year-old child, though were probably a little heavier, and while they had the heavy brow of a chimpanzee, their eyes were thoughtful, regarding the humans around them cautiously but unfearfully.

The corridors themselves changed, and when Dana and Bryce had first started down them, they were bricked on either side by the same grey-purple bricks, though on the inside there were different carvings which seemed to be artistic, and the wording engraved was written in everything from English to Japanese and Russian. After a short walk, they entered a door and things changed dramatically.

Now they were no longer in dusty corridors, but rather clean, wooden corridors that were well lit with electric lights. Women walked back and forward dressed in casual attire, from jeans and shirts, to bikinis (which Dana briefly envied given the heat, though she realized that there was also air conditioning in this part of the pyramid). Most didn't spare a second glance to Dana and her guards, though the presence of Bryce caused some concern, and Dana noticed that a few of the girls in bikinis hurried to ensure Bryce hadn't seen them.

If this was a refuge, then the girls were clearly scared of the outside world. Perhaps justifiably so.

They passed by rooms which were clearly communal, including a lounge room of sorts where the women sat around watching tv or just playing on tech devices, and then past a swimming pool, before coming to two large double doors, with a strange cube-like logo on it, that seemed somehow to twist in on itself.

"The Four-Fold Crown," Dana murmured, when she saw it. Two of the guards pushed the doors open, and Asha stepped through, beckoning Dana and Bryce to follow here. June brought up the rear, but the reminder of the entourage remained outside.

Inside, Dana could smell the scent of the burnt flowers even more, and was now wondering exactly what it was, and what was the point of it. The light was low, and as Dana looked around, she realized she was in a room that seemed like it was some sort of giant diamond shape, with the middle of the room clearly reaching towards the natural roof of the pyramid, while the bottom was an inverse pyramid.

At the center, where the two negative pyramids met, each side had an enclave, three of which were dark, while the fourth held a figure. She had long dark hair, full lips shaped like Cupid's bow, and her eyes were almond shaped, with impressive lashes. She seemed to be dressed in expensive designer clothes, but Dana couldn't tell what the labels were, and wondered if perhaps they were designed specifically for her. She was sitting on a stone throne, made from the same brick as the outside walls (and indeed, Dana noticed, the inside wall of this…she hesitated to use the word, but temple seemed strangely appropriate), and to her right was what appeared to be a bowl of some description. The woman lifted a facemask, like the ones you see on ventilators, to her face and breathed deeply. Her fingernails were astonishingly long.

"Who are you?" came a voice, and Dana swung around from where she was looking to look at the enclave directly opposite the one she had been examining. There was another woman with a round face and long brown hair. She wasn't particularly tall, but her outfit was high cut giving the impression of long legs. Like the other queen, this one seemed to be of Asian origins, but unlike her partner she wasn't seated and almost seemed to be the voice of the room.

"I'm Ian Bryce," Bryce said. "I'm June's husband." Dana's eyes widened in surprise at this new revelation, but before she could say anything, another voice rang out.

"June has no husband!" Dana turned to her left to see another woman bathed in light in her enclave. This woman was taller than the second woman, with short blonde hair and bangs, but was dressed in the same astonishing style, with the same glitz and glamour of the other two, though this one's outfit seemed almost militaristic, with a collar that wrapped up around her neck, and the colours more beige and green. Like the others she seemed of Asian origin, but she spoke English without an accent and while the second woman was commanding, this one was fiery.

"No not yet," Bryce started, but June cut him off.

"This is the man I spoke of, Fi," she said. "I met him on a mission. I sought permission from Gongi to pursue the relationship. He wishes to marry me and speaks out of turn, but he does so only from love."

"Gongi gave no permission to marry anyone," came the fourth voice, and Dana now had a better understanding of what the Four-Fold Crown actually was. An organization, a refuge, a temple – all parts of the same thing, as well as the Four-Fold Crown who were the priestesses of this temple, the crowned queens. "She, like me, simply didn't object." This voice belonged to another blonde woman, with long hair, her outfit as amazing as the other three, but black. Her face was the softest of the four, oval-shaped. Dana suddenly realized it was impossible to place the ages of the four women. They could have been in their twenties or their forties. Poised above them in their enclaves, they looked like four great birds of paradise, brightly coloured and dangerously alluring.

"I am sorry, Eau," June said, lowering her head. "I don't ask to leave the Four-Fold Crown, but I do ask to spend time with my love. But I will do as you wish." She didn't raise her eyes as she said this.

"We will consult," the second woman said.

"Thank you, Whenua," June said bowing even lower. The lights bathing the four enclaves disappeared and the four queens were plunged into darkness. Dana looked to Bryce and June, the latter of whom refused to raise her head, while Bryce was looking distinctly nervous. No one said a word, though Asha gave Dana a sympathetic smile. It felt like they were standing before a judge in a trial, and Dana supposed that for Bryce that was exactly what was going on.

Suddenly the lights were activated again and the four queens were visible. To Dana it looked like they hadn't moved an inch.

"We are not without sympathy for your love," the woman June called Eau said.

"But we will not tolerate him within the pyramid," the woman named Fi added.

"He will be banished from the pyramid but remain under the protection of the Four-Fold Crown," the Whenua announced.

"I can't go out there by myself," Bryce protested.

"You'll have the bonobo for company," Eau said, a small smile on her face, and Dana suddenly got the feeling she'd get along well with the woman. For the first time she also thought she could detect a slight trace of an Australian accent in her voice. Whoever these women were they were definitely from a variety of locations around the world.

"But I'll die!" Bryce cried out.

"Then maybe you need to work harder to stay alive," Fi said. "I'm happy to withdraw the protection of the guard if you wish to prove your love without them."

"Because you'll need to prove your love if we are to give our approval of your relationship," Whenua said, and there was a note of finality in her voice that made it clear she wasn't going to listen to any more discussion about the matter. June had clearly worked this out as well, as she had taken her boyfriend's hand and was trying to communicate to him either through the power of thought, or just by squeezing the hand. Bryce did obediently remain silent, which was probably for the best. However, it was clear that the Four-Fold Crown had turned their attention to Dana.

"I'm Lara," Dana started to say, but Whenua held up her hand.
"You are Dana Spectra," she said. "We know who you are. Asha has spoken of you in glowing terms."

"You are welcome to stay in the pyramid," and Dana was forced to turn to see the first queen – the one perhaps named Gongi – speak for the first time.

"Thank you," Dana said, a little astonished.

"Enjoy our hospitality and decide whether you wish to return to civilization," Eau said. "Because if you would prefer to remain with us, we would welcome you into our fold." Dana's face must have betrayed her surprise at this.
"We welcome all those with specialist skills and amazing talents,"

Whenua said. "You definitely satisfy those. Enjoy your time and then return to us and we will answer any questions you have."

Again, the note of finality, though this time it was reinforced with the darkening of the enclaves. The double doors they had entered through opened, as did another set, and through each of those four women entered, wearing the dark activewear that seemed to be the guards' de facto uniform. Two of them grabbed Bryce by the arms, and as he protested, he was led away, June following, trying to keep up but not interfere. Asha watched her sister leave, her eyes betraying her concern.

"Will they be OK?" Dana wondered.

"I'm sure they will," Asha muttered, but she didn't seem entirely convinced. Nonetheless, she took a deep breath and turned back to Dana. "Come to my room. We have a lot to talk about."

"Don't we just."

EIGHTH REPORT: RELINQUISHED CONTROL

Asha took Dana from the temple, and Dana was a little surprised to find that she headed directly to an elevator built into the pyramid. There was a strange mix of ancient and modern about the pyramid, and as the elevator slid smoothly and noiselessly to the fourth floor, Dana decided she could easily have assumed that they were no longer in the middle of the Democratic Republic of the Congo, but were instead back inside one of the massive office blocks in the middle of Paris.

She also noticed that there were quite a few floors on the elevator panel, and notably several seemed to be below the ground level. Given that the ground floor was clearly a living space, and presumably the fourth floor was the accommodation, the top floors maybe were reserved for the Four-Fold Crown. So, what was on the bottom floors? Storage?

Dana reminded herself that she had conveniently forgotten precisely why she had come to the Congo in the first place. There was a very real purpose, to discover precisely why June had assassinated Thomas McAteer. The journey here had consumed her to the point she had totally forgotten that fairly important point.

"Are all the living areas on the fourth floor?" Dana asked, not quite sure where the conversation might take her.

"Oh, third and fourth," Asha replied. "You move up the

pyramid the more you contribute."

"So, the higher you are, the more important you are?" Dana asked, and Asha picked up on the thoughts that were betrayed by Dana's tone of voice.

"It's not like that," she said, shaking her head, as though Dana were pre-school.

"But the four..."

"The queens are at the top, yes, and yes, the more you contribute the higher you go, but that doesn't make you more important. It's a goal, I guess."

"Except for the queens. Because they are the most important," Dana added, and Asha shrugged, unable or unwilling to justify the point. "So, the living area are the bottom two floors?"

"No, the computers and storage are on the bottom. Living is on the ground and above. Oh," Asha suddenly paused. "You didn't know that there were levels below."

"Oh, well," Dana lied, playing into her bimbo personality, "I thought we were going down. I just thought that the bottom floor was sunken."

"No, no," Asha smiled, "not at all. Do you want something to eat, or have a shower or something? No offence, but you look like shit." Dana opened her mouth to be outraged, but then stopped. They had arrived at a door, and Asha pushed it open, revealing the room beyond, which was clearly hers. In fact, as Dana looked around at it, she suddenly realized she recognized the room from a number of Asha's videos. The bed, the wall, the posters of One Direction, the bedside lamp which was a strange Christmas tree shape, and also green. And the mirror.

Oh, the jungle video! That makes so much more sense

now...

"I don't get why, Asha," Dana said. "Like, why join a cult?" Asha looked at her, rolling her eyes at the word, but at the same time she wasn't defensive of what she had done.

"It was a joint decision," she said. "Me and June. We both..." She paused, searching for the right words. "We were looking for something. A purpose, maybe? I don't know. Mum was...well, she was great and all that. She tried hard to be the best mum she could be, but it was never going to happen. She just..." Again, Asha gave up, the words not there for her to explain whatever it was she was trying to. But she didn't have to, Dana reflected. The meaning was clear. "June was angry a lot, I wanted to be someone better. I'd started vlogging and stuff, and then someone contacted me. They'd heard my videos, and had an opportunity. They would support me, help me. Had the money to do so. And then I could help mum. I asked if I could bring June, and suddenly it was there. She did her thing, I did mine."

"Her's being to kill people for money," Dana said pointedly. This point Asha seemed unwilling to confront.

Like admitting your sister is a junkie?

Dana bit her lip intending to withdraw, but Asha had something to say all the same.

"The Crown aren't perfect," she said. "But they are better than every other option I've seen. And they have built something here that people like me and June need. I'm sorry if that disappoints you, but...it's what it is."

There was a long pause as the two waited to see what the other would do. At one point, Dana caught a look at herself in the mirror. She did look an absolute mess. Her hair was dank, her arms scratched from the trees, she was sweaty and she felt hot despite the air conditioning.

"I do look like shit," Dana giggled, hoping to break the ice. "Shower and then food would be a dream come true." Something akin to relief passed Asha's face, and she came forward and took Dana's hand.

Dana wasn't sure how much Asha contributed to the Four-Fold's little cult, but she suspected it was a lot, because the bathroom was something else entirely. When Dana opened the door to go to the en suite, she briefly paused, wondering if she slipped into a parallel world. The bathroom was made of rock, the shower behind a stone archway with double glass doors giving access. The sink was a ceramic bowl atop a plinth, and two discrete metal bars held the towels. Dana had no idea where any of Asha's toiletries might be kept, but she saw soap in the shower and decided she didn't really need much more than that. She had her own shampoo and conditioner, of course. Never travel without it.

Stripping off the t-shirt, and then the activewear, she looked at them as they hit the ground and felt a twinge of sadness seeing that they had become stained throughout her journey. As soon as she was out of the Congo, Dana decided to treat herself to a shopping spree.

She stepped into the shower, and noticed a button, which she depressed and was surprised when water gushed down like a waterfall over her. The whole thing had the vibe of a health clinic, which was a very odd vibe for a place that was apparently running an assassin-for-hire organization from, well, presumably the basement.

That was her next objective, she reflected. She needed to get into the computer systems and get the information on who hired June to kill McAteer, and in the process put her little sister at risk. As the water cascaded down over her tired body, Dana wondered what Dr Prass would say about her current obsession. Even at this moment in time, she was struggling to justify why she had become so determined to find McAteer's killer. It's not like she felt a burning desire for justice, or guilt over his death.

Oh.

Dana stood still as the water crashed over her, and her brain finally pointed out what she had refused to see until this point. So, what to do about it? Bringing McAteer's killer to justice wouldn't resolve anything if her actions continued to put Bella's life in danger.

Had she really reached a point in her life where, having decided maybe being part of the espionage world was something that she wanted to do, she'd now found a genuine reason not to?

Her thoughts were interrupted by a pair of hands reaching around her body, up her belly and over her boobs. Surprised, Dana turned around and saw Asha standing before her, equally as naked. She was very attractive, Dana decided. Not that she hadn't seen the girl in a bikini before, but now, fully naked, Dana appreciated the musculature on her body. She had a surprisingly well-defined Adonis' belt, which seemed counterpointed by the small, pert breasts.

"And what do you think you're doing?" Dana asked, the smirk coming to her face without even trying.

"I just thought we should save water and shower together," Asha said, her eyes playful. This, Dana thought, was when maturity should kick in and a special kind of focus required, so she could turn to Asha and say, "No! I have important things to do, and your sister is an assassin." But when Asha stepped forward, and stood on tiptoe to reach up and press her lips against Dana's, the model's brain switched off and she grabbed the smaller woman's ass and pulled her close.

It was surprisingly sweet sex given that Dana had a feeling it was fueled by the adrenaline of the last twenty-four hours, for both of them. They had kissed and groped in the shower, exploring each other's bodies with their hands and enjoying the feel of the curves and swell of each other's breasts. As Asha concentrated on Dana's nipples, it was though the smaller girl had never tried such a thing with another woman. On the other hand, when Asha had finished, Dana dropped to her knees, kissing underboob, then belly, then below the belly and finally using her tongue to bring her friend to the first orgasm of the night.

They had dried each other down, unable to keep their hands off each other, and as soon as they were in the very spacious bed, Asha pushed Dana down, determined to repay the favor. Her mouth worked its way around Dana's body, paying attention to any area that elicited a moan from the older woman and for a while, Dana lay back enjoying the pleasure that Asha was giving her. Soon Asha changed her position, grinding into her friend, and the thrill of the rapture ripped through each of them, causing Asha's leg to shake slightly, and Dana to grip the bedsheets.

When they had both orgasmed, Dana pushed Asha onto the bed, face down, and pushed her legs apart with her knee. She enjoyed the grunt that Asha gave, unable to react, forced to obey. As Dana leaned forward to kiss the girl on her neck, she reached down and grabbed Asha's ass again, delighted at the feel of the tight bum. Each time Dana exerted pressure with her fingers she heard Asha gasp in pleasure. When Asha's body shuddered again, Dana smiled to herself, and relinquished control, allowing Asha to take the top position.

Asha repositioned herself so that she was above Dana's face and soon they seemed to be in competition, with each girl holding back, despite the extreme pleasure that they were forcing upon the other. When they were unable to hold back, at almost exactly the same time they bucked and felt the energy go through their bodies.

Dana wasn't sure how long it lasted, but she didn't care. For a moment she lay in the bed, suddenly aware of how dark it was, the younger girl wrapped around her, breathing into her neck. Dana smiled slightly and turned to kiss Asha.

"Why are you here?" Asha asked softly, and Dana felt a small stab. Fucking was over, it was time for truth.

"Your sister tried to kill my sister," Dana said, deciding to simplify it.

"You're here to kill June?" Asha said, shocked.

"No," Dana replied quickly. "No, of course not. I would never. I just want to know why. Who organized it, why would it even happen."

The lay in silence for a few moments, each perhaps wondering what the other as thinking and trying to work out how to move forward with their conversation. Dana traced her finger over the heart that was tattooed on Asha's hip, impressed at the weird

216

geometry of it. It wasn't the only one, either. There was a tattoo on the woman's upper arm, with the same swirling features, and one under her left boob, though this was just text: "art is passion, passion is everything."

"I might take a walk," Dana said, and she gently moved Asha, though the smaller woman sat up and looked at her.

"Walk to where?"

"I'm not going to do anything silly," Dana said. "Honestly your sister is more likely to kill me than I'm going to kill her."

"That's what I'm afraid of," Asha mumbled, and Dana couldn't help but smile.

"Maybe there's an alternative," Dana said with a smile, and lent forward, giving Asha a kiss.

"Really?"

"You stay here," Dana said, and stood up, looking around briefly to see where her clothes were.

"I'm coming with you," Asha said.

"It's not a good idea. You're part of this place. It's best you don't do anything I can comfortably take the blame for." Dana paused, a little frustrated. "Where are my clothes?"

"Oh, I can get them for you," Asha said with a smile.

"Thanks," Dana grinned.

"If you let me come with you." The grin was quickly replaced by an eyeroll, but Asha sat smugly and finally Dana flung up her hands.

"Fine. Let's just go."

Dana moved down the corridor, reaching into her bag and feeling for the specialized gun case inside. Not for the first time this trip, she decided to get a backpack as soon as she returned to Australia. Or actually just any old airport. The size of her current bag was useful, but it was definitely not convenient.

Her hands seized around the case and she opened it, pressing her finger against the recognition lock and feeling the case snap open. With the gun in hand, she eased the case shut again, but kept her hand in her bag. For the entire time she kept her eyes on the corridor ahead, though when she finished, she briefly wondered what had happened to Asha. Looking back, there was no sign of the girl, and Dana wondered if she had given up.

Or had she a change of heart and was going to alert the Crown? Dana paused for a moment, considering her options, and then decided she had little choice. She set off in the direction of the elevator.

Once at the elevator door, Dana reached forward and summoned it, repositioning her bag at the same time. As the door opened, Dana stepped in, but was surprised to see Asha quickly join her.

"Where have you been?" Dana asked, surprised.

"Oh, sorry. I needed the toilet," Asha said, not particularly apologetically.

"You could have said," Dana retorted, annoyed.

"Sorry," Asha shrugged. "Where are we going?"

"Basement, I guess," Dana mused, pressing the lowest button. The elevator went down smoothly, though not spectacularly quickly, and Dana found each second dragging out more than it should, as she held her breath, desperately hoping no one would stop the lift. She was grateful that there was no lift music piped though, but that made her concentrate on a number of other things, including her own face staring back at her from the mirrored walls. Also, she could smell the burning flower smell again.

"What's that smell?" she said, and Asha looked at her curiously.

"What do you mean?"

"Can't you smell something like burning flowers? Like a weird incense?"

"Oh," Asha said, understanding. "Sorry, I don't even notice it anymore. Yeah, there's a flower that they burn out here. It's got healing powers, apparently. There's a heap of it, so we burn it and let it waft around the pyramid. We don't all need physical healing, obviously, but there's plenty of mental healing we could use." She gave a lopsided grin, and stuck out her tongue, and Dana couldn't help but laugh.

When the elevator pinged, and came to a jolting halt, both women gave a jump and looked at each other, before laughing again. The doors slid open and the pair stepped out, the atmosphere beyond immediately shushing them.

It was dark and definitely sleepy. If a room could be an animal, Dana felt they had just walked into a cat. It was quiet and asleep, but there was a tension about it that made you think if you touched something incorrectly it would bite you.

"Where are we?" Dana wondered.

"I think the computer room is in there. It's where all communications are monitored and information is held, apparently. I don't know. I just use my phone. But I suppose the Wi-Fi is down there." Asha grinned weakly.

Dana moved to the door opposite the elevator and

opened it, curious to see that beyond were stacks of crates. She wondered what they might be, but pulled the door shut. She had to focus. Going to the door that Asha had indicated, Dana pushed it open and stepped through.

The new room was lit more brightly, and there were more computers scattered around. Dana went over to the nearest one and tapped it, the screen coming to life, seeking a login. For a moment Dana bit her bottom lip and then turned to see what Asha was doing. She was clearly bored, and Dana felt slightly guilty at dragging her all this way.

"Bored?" Dana asked cheekily. Asha pretended to yawn, and gave an exaggerated stretch, reaching to the skies and exposing more belly and the hints of the star tattoo on her hip and the text under her boob.

"I'll survive," she replied with a grin.

Dana finally released her grip on the golden Glock, and then reached around the bag to get her phone out. She pressed her little finger to the small dot in the corner and watched the phone interface change to the hidden operating system behind her own and scanned through the apps, hoping to find something useful. To her surprise there was a "copy system" button, and Dana pressed it.

"What are you doing?" Asha asked.

"I'm not sure," Dana admitted. With the button pressed, the screen suddenly brought up a number of different options. There was a "visual display" button, and when she pressed it, a red dot appeared, with lines connecting to a number of blue dots. It was a curious 3D model, and Dana realized that she was the red dot, and the blue dots were the systems available to her. She pressed the blue dot closest to her, and her phone leapt into life, as did the computer in front of her. While the login didn't budge, she could see the little green light on the computer start to flicker and the machine hummed into life, occasionally growling as it worked. Her own phone displayed a list of files.

"Go out and check no one is coming," Dana whispered to Asha urgently, who looked puzzled, but then did as she was told. Dana waited for a little bit, watching her phone download the information, and then placed it down on the table.

"There's no one out there. Honestly, it's nighttime and people do sleep here," Asha announced as she walked back in the room, but her voiced trailed away when she felt the gun barrel at the back of her head. She glanced around and realized that it was definitely Dana standing behind her; there was no other sign of her in the room.

"You know I fucked your sister, right?" Dana said pleasantly, not lowering the gun.

"You fucked June?" Asha asked, puzzled.

"Oh, please," Dana said, and yanked down Asha's shorts, leaving the girl standing in nothing but her G-string. "Cut the act. I do pay attention when I go down on somebody, and that star was not what I saw." There was silence.

"I had heard you were a slut," June said, finally giving up the pretense.

"Were you watching me?" Dana asked. "Did the Crown ask you to?"

"Get fucked."

"Fair enough," Dana said, and pushed her gun forward into June's head. The girl moved forward, and Dana circled her, collecting her phone off the table. It was green, indicating the download had completed. She tapped the screen, returning it to its main mode, and slid the phone into her bag, which she bent to pick up.

Immediately June moved forward, but Dana fired her Glock, and the bullet whistled past the top of June's ear.

"I am a *very* good shot," Dana said, and June looked at her stoically, though she was a lot paler than when she was a few seconds earlier. With the bag now over shoulder, Dana pointed indicated the exit. "Move. We're leaving."

"Leaving where?"

"The pyramid." Dana stepped forward, indicating with the gun, but wary about getting too close. June refused to move, but Dana cocked the weapon and June narrowed her eyes, but decided it was safer to lead the way out.

NINTH REPORT: VICTOR FOXTROT

As the elevator ascended, Dana kept her gun pointed at the back of June's head. She wasn't entirely sure why, because she was fairly certain she wasn't going to use it, and she strongly suspected June thought the same thing. But then, perhaps it was that degree of uncertainty in both of them that kept the gun where it was, and June obeying.

"Why?" Dana said.

"Why what?"

"You almost killed my sister! Why did you do it?"

"Your sister was never in danger," scoffed June. "I'm as good a shot as you are. Maybe better. There was no chance I wasn't going to hit my target."

"So why kill McAteer?" Dana asked.

"Because I was told to. I do what I'm told all the time. It's the way we work for the Four-Fold Crown." She said it as though it answered all Dana's questions. Dana couldn't wait to be away from the June and the whole horrible organization.

"Is Asha all right?"

"I wouldn't hurt my sister any more than you'd hurt yours."

As the doors to the pyramid opened, Dana pushed June forward. She wasn't entirely sure she had memorized the path back to the main entrance, but as they continued along their path, Dana saw more and more clues that convinced her she had got it right. When they approached the double doors, she gave June a slight shove with the gun.

"Open the doors."

"As if I can," June objected. "I'm not important enough."

"Well, you'd better find a way otherwise you're not much use to me anymore, are you?" Dana pointed out. June looked at her and Dana held her gaze, hoping she didn't show a flicker of doubt. She couldn't afford for the other woman to think that she wouldn't hesitate to pull the trigger. The seconds seemed to drag out to hours, but finally June scowled and turned to the door, putting her hand against it, and Dana heard several clicks as locks released. June pushed the doors open and Dana shoved the smaller girl.

As they stepped out into the field, Dana looked up to see Bryce standing before them. She felt a slight sigh of relief, but when June attempted to run, Dana grabbed at her, remembering that the pair were in a relationship and he was unlikely to be particularly sympathetic to her cause.

Suddenly the area lit up, causing the bonobos to whoop as they were disturbed. Dana heard the sound of the grass being pushed aside at the same time an electric whine came from above her. She looked up to see that further up the pyramid, part of the wall had slid aside and there was a landing now visible to her. Standing on the landing were the Four-Fold Crown, looking for all the world like superstars about to perform for an adoring audience. The two blondes were on either side of the two brunettes, and Dana struggled to remember their names.

"You disappointed us, Dana," the softer faced blonde – Eau? – said, though Dana felt the sadness that was being shown in her face was more sarcastic than genuine. "We hoped that you would join us."

The rustling in the grass had stopped and when Dana turned back to Bryce, she saw that he was now joined by a number of women, all in the black activewear. The Four-Fold Crown's guards.

"You're not the only one who disappointed us," one of the brunettes said. Dana distinctly remembered she was Whenua, and as she spoke, she turned behind her, and when she turned back, she had Asha in her grip. With a vicious shove, Whenua pushed Asha forward, and the girl tumbled down the pyramid, falling from the platform. She was grateful that the pyramid had obviously been built more recently than any of its mirrors, as the slide down was bumpy, but not harmful, and though she hit the ground roughly, Asha was bruised and battered, but not badly wounded.

"You abused our hospitality and our goodwill," Whenua continued. "And you were helped by one of our own. I don't know whether you corrupted her or whether she joined you freely, but Asha is no longer welcome here."

"I didn't..." Asha started, but she was interrupted.

"No more!" the quietest of the four said, her voice ringing out. Gongi looked down at them. "You are banished from here, Asha. Do not return."

"Please, forgive..." June said, but like her twin sister she was also interrupted.

"You are also banished," Gongi announced, and June

audibly gasped.

"You wish to be with your man, then go with him. But you have chosen him over us," Eau said.

"And me?" Dana asked, and for the first time, the fiery blonde spoke up.

"You will die," Fi said. "Kill her!"

Shots rang out, and Dana squeezed her eyes shut and fell to the ground, but as she did, she realized hadn't been hit. She rolled over in the grass and raised herself up a little, somewhat surprised to find that the guards were firing their weapons, but not at her; rather they were shooting at something in the forest beyond.

Dana watched as several of the guards dropped, bullets flying out of them as they passed through limbs that weren't protected by their Kevlar.

"Close the pyramid," Whenua was shouting, while at the same time Dana could hear Fi bellow "Fall back!"

Bryce had dropped to the ground, trying to get to June, who was crawling towards him, and Dana saw that Asha was huddled against the pyramid, clearly terrified for her life. The doors to the pyramids behind them had opened, and more of the guards were spilling out. Dana kept her head down in the grass, letting the guards race forward, hoping desperately that they would ignore her.

"Dana!" called out a voice, and Dana peeked up to see Max Travere calling out for her. He was dressed in camouflage gear, and was carrying a very big gun that he held against him as he called out.

"You have to help me," Bryce ran up to him, but to both

Dana and Max's surprise, blood started spilling down Bryce's, and Dana twisted around to see where the shot had come from. Standing at the entrance, getting her guards back into the pyramid, was Fi. Her short blonde hair was now sticky with sweat and she had an AF 2011-A1 double barrel pistol in her hand, which she had used to deal very quickly and efficiently with Ian Bryce. Dana watched as Eau came up behind her, whispering something in her ear. Fi looked annoyed, but reluctantly turned. Before she did, she caught sight of Asha, and the look on her face changed.

"No!" screamed Dana, working out exactly what was going to happen, but as she wriggled around to get a clear shot, Fi had already brought the AF2011-A1 up, and Dana blindly fired her gun, not even sure whether she was aiming or not. She saw the AF2011 go off, but at the same time it flew out of Fi's hand, and Fi screamed in pain. Eau grabbed at her fellow queen, pulling her inside, and somewhere in the panic, Dana heard Asha scream as well.

"Dana!" Max called out again, and Dana pulled herself up out of the grass, trying to get across to Asha to see if her friend was OK.

"Dana," Asha called out, weakly, and Dana reached down to her friend, seeing that blood was spreading out over the girl's t-shirt around her abdomen.

"Come on," Dana said, reaching down. She sensed, rather than saw, something looming over her, and as she turned, she saw one of the guards looking at her, a face full of horror and anger. Her gun was coming into position, and time slowed down as Dana bitterly regretted not being able to tell her sister that she loved her. She wanted to see her dad and step-mum, and even Kimba to make things right. She didn't want to die, not like this.

Her body reacted, trying to get out of the way, hoping that there might still be a chance for survival, but to her surprise, a hole appeared in the guard's forehead, and the woman slumped to the ground.

"Dr Lara Muller, I presume?" came a very American, very sarcastic voice. Dana stood up, a look of shock on her face. "I'm not sure I like you as a redhead."

Standing before her was Justice Kennedy.

"Pleased to see me?" Justice asked with a grin.

Dana opened her mouth to say something, and then punched the other woman as hard as she could in the face.

Max had scooped up Asha and was carrying her into the jungle, Dana and Justice following. There was no time for fighting about past issues – that was something that could be dealt with later. Max had assured Dana that there was a helicopter waiting and they needed to get to it as quickly as possible. As it turned out, Justice had also brought with her an Incident Response Unit, and it was those that had started firing at the Four-Fold Crown's army. The team only consisted of the five troops, and soon all of them were on board the light grey helicopter which almost immediately started its engines and moved into the sky.

"I had to use a lot of pull to get this," Max shouted over the roar of the chopper, handing Dana a set of headphones, which she slid over her head. Max and Justice did a similar thing, and Dana found hearing what Max had to say much easier. "It's one of our Airbus copters," Max said, a smile on his face. He was clean shaven and Dana wondered if the man ensured he was perfect before he so much as encountered any person. She couldn't imagine what she was looking like at the moment.

"How did you know?"

"When I left you in Brazzaville it was to ensure I had a bit of backup in case I needed to get you out of her in a hurry. I also had a little bug on our late friend Mr Bryce. Did you notice?"

"Him mentioning the cult of women?"

"Yeah, that was odd, so I thought I'd keep a track on him. It wasn't great reception but what I got back was enough to know things weren't quite the way they should be. I was about to move out and collect you when Interpol contacted me."

Dana turned her head to look at Justice, who was not impressed, rubbing her jaw where she had been hit, and though Dana felt more than a modicum of satisfaction she did wonder what the hell the other woman was doing. She looked over to Asha and noticed that one of the team that Max and Justice had brought with them was attending to Asha's wound, trying to make her comfortable. Asha was clearly in a lot of pain, and when the soldier caught Dana's eye, he gave a less than encouraging look. Dana bit her bottom lip, afraid that they were too late for her.

"I was on my way to Guiana," Justice's voice came over the headset. "We've had problems. When I heard you were in trouble, I thought I'd help out. You might have just said thank you for saving your life." Dana looked at the American.

"Seriously, you think I'm going to be nice to you, after what you did?"

"Fuck's sake, Dana," Justice growled, but she kept her mouth shut and said no more, glowering ahead of her.

"Did you manage to sort out anything at all?" Max asked Dana, and Dana looked at him, wondering if she should share the information she had.

"I'm not sure," she eventually settled on. "I think I need to contact a friend. I have a feeling that maybe I can find out some information." Dana paused and then turned to Justice. "Why were you going to Guiana?" Justice looked at her for a moment, and then Dana saw metaphorical shutters close.

"It's not important," Justice said, and sat back in her chair. Dana wondered what she was moody about, and guessed that it was probably her own fault.

"Where are we going?"

"We need to get out of the Congo, quick smart," Max said, and he was looking a lot more cheerful than when they were on the ground. "I have flight plans for *le Côte d'Ivoire*, but it won't be much good to us if we're shot down before we can get there."

As if to mock him there was a sudden click and a new voice was heard.

"You might want to hear this," the voice said in somewhat stilted English, but before they had any time to dwell a new voice came over the headsets.

"You need to supply us with information now, or we will shoot you out of the sky," the voice was saying. Max cast a quick glance at Justice before making a hand signal to the pilot, who nodded at him.

"This is a Red Cross mission. We're using French helicopters and dropping off much needed medication," Max said, giving a grimace to the others in the cabin. Everyone looked at each other, and Dana glanced at the pilot who seemed to be

230

looking at his displays. He leaned back to Max and tapped the agent on the soldier, holding up five fingers. Max clearly understood, but said nothing further.

"We have no record of your flight," the voice came back. "You need to set down."

"Check your records again," Max replied swiftly. "Romeo Charlie 4-1-5 Victor Foxtrot." There was an extended pause and Dana could feel the tension in the air. It was clear that they were waiting on something, and there was the possibility that they were going to get shot down, but the pilot and Max knew something she didn't, and that seemed to be what everyone was on edge about.

"Set down, Victor Foxtrot," came the voice again. "We definitely have no record of your flight, and you are in violation of international air space."

"Please repeat," Max said, and leant forward to the pilot, who held up two fingers.

"Set down immediately," came the response. "We will target you if you don't obey. You have been warned."

"We are not in Congolese air space," Max said. "You have no jurisdiction over us. If you fire upon us, I have been instructed to inform you that you will making an aggressive move against the French government, and they will respond in kind."

"I thought you were a Red Cross mission," came the somewhat startled response after a few moments.

"You need to listen better," Max said with a savage grin. The pilot tapped him on the shoulder and gave a nod, which made Max grin even more. "Don't test me on this," Max added. Everyone waited expectantly, but nothing happened and then suddenly they heard the voice of the pilot.

"They've gone, we're fine."

Max and Justice looked at each, and the look of relief was palpable.

CÔTE D'IVOIRE

FIRST REPORT: SISTER'S CONCERN

It was raining when the helicopter finally set down in Yamoussoukro, though one of the soldiers – a nice guy with amazing hair named Louis – told Dana that was pretty much standard in the Côte d'Ivoire for the time of year. For four months it was hot; for the rest of the year, it was hot and rainy. Yamoussoukro was one of two capitals of the country, and was, Dana decided as the car drove them from the airport to their hotel, surprisingly small.

It was not a terrible place either, though Justice warned her that violent crime was pretty standard in the city. The rain may have greyed the clouds, but the land was verdant and the city was dominated by the tan Basilica of Our Lady of Peace of Yamoussoukro, a giant church with a massive central white dome, surrounded by four slightly smaller domes. As they got closer to the city, more and more skyscrapers began to appear and the traffic built up.

The city did, however, still feel as though it were something out of time, as though perhaps it hadn't quite let go of the 1980s, and really didn't want to. A car took them via the Houphouet-Boigny Ave towards their destination which was, Max informed her, the Hôtel President. Asha had been whisked away with the soldier that had tended to her aboard the helicopter remaining with her. She was going to a hospital to be treated for her wound, and though Dana thought that was a positive move, she couldn't help but feel the others seemed to be making the best of the situation.

Of course, where Justice was concerned, Dana was dubious about everything.

She was trying to put that out of her mind, however, because as soon as she got the chance to go to her room, she was going to have a shower, get changed and then contact someone. With the information on her phone about the Four-Fold Crown, she needed someone who had a skill with computers and she thought she knew exactly who that person might be.

They crossed the Lac de Yamoussoukro and Dana sat back in the car, looking out of Justice's window, who sat beside her, to see the lake – though once they passed through the Rivera Garden and into the actual city itself that view disappeared, replaced by streets, shops and skyscrapers. Sighing, she looked out of her own window and was a little surprised to see a building with a familiar logo – Silhouette Moreau had a building in Yamoussoukro. He had buildings everywhere, Dana reflected, but given how it all started it was interesting to come full circle to see his logo once again.

Not too long after that, Dana looked at her naked body in the mirror of a room that was definitely yearning to go back forty years, and gave an exaggerated groan. She had become a piece of modern art, painted in bruises. She turned to look at her butt and was a little dismayed to see she was right; a big black mark was on the left cheek. No bikini shoots in a hurry.

She had run herself a bath and having convinced herself

she still looked decent, she slid into the water and let out another groan, though this time it was of pleasure, as the water wrapped itself around her, trying to massage every part of her body.

God, it felt good.

She instructed her phone to call Bella, and to her surprise the phone was answered immediately.

"Holy shit, are you OK?" came her sister's excited voice, and Dana scowled.

"Stop swearing. What happened to your standards?"

"Oh f...please," Bella groaned. "Are you OK?"

"Yes, I'm fine," Dana grinned, a little pleased at her sister's concern. "What time is it there?"

"Ten in the evening. Where are you? What time is it?"

"Midday in Yamoussoukro. That's the Côte d'Ivoire for the uneducated."

"Like you knew where Yamoussoukro was before today," scoffed her sister. "Mum and Dad say hello. They want to know you're OK."

"Tell them I'm fine," Dana said. "I mean, I am, but I feel like I've been beaten very badly. Haven't though. Just shot at. A lot."

"You found the shooter!"

"I did," Dana said. "And you'll be pleased to know we were both right."

"What?"

"Asha has a twin sister named June. That's who the shooter was." As Bella whooped for joy, Dana shook her head.

"I fucking told you!"

"Bella!" snapped Dana.

"Sorry, but still. I was right."

"I have to go. Have some things to do. Just wanted to tell you…" Dana paused. "I just wanted to tell you that I love you. Tell Dad and Mum that too."

"You are OK, right?" Bella asked, and the concern in her voice was obvious.

"Yeah, I am. Definitely."

"OK," came the cautious response. "Love you too." The phone call ended, and Dana waited a few more minutes before dragging herself out of her bed and pulling a towel around her. The hotel may have had issues, but the towels were definitely not one of them.

She went into her bedroom and lay down, closing her eyes for a moment, but her body was not accepting of this deal, and instead, Dana crashed into a deep sleep.

Hôtel President is, on the face of it, two separate entities, which could be defined as the seventies section and the eighties section, based on when they were built. The tower, built in the 1980s to complement the longer building beside the pool, was notable for a distinctive restaurant at the top that gave a 360-degree view of Yamoussoukro. Over time, of course, the buildings had lost some of their appeal, but refurbishment seemed to be an ongoing process in the hotel, and despite an abundance of tiles, Dana had to admit that her room wasn't all that bad really.

Slightly off-white walls and ceiling matched the bedsheets, while the tan pillowcases matched the curtains on the windows. Dana pulled the curtains together, though did pause to see that the pool down below looked inviting. She decided that if time permitted, she might even go for a swim, though as the clouds in the sky reminded her that rain was only a second or so away, she wondered if it would be worthwhile.

Sure enough, the heavens opened and the rain began to fall again, so Dana closed the windows and then the curtains. There was a unique desk made of three curved units, two more of which were set to the side below the television. The little corridor to the front door had shuttered cupboard doors to the left and the entrance to the bathroom on the right. Five stars it may have been, but Dana wasn't certain by whose standards that was applied.

Rather incongruously there was a red phone on the wall, and she lifted the head set to listen to the dial tone. On the table was a room service menu, and Dana took the phone again, pressing the buttons to get room service. She ordered herself a cheeseburger, complete with fries, hoping that it would be fairly straightforward, and also took the opportunity to get a vanilla milkshake.

With that done, she took out her mobile phone and dug around in her bag for the charger to connect it. Then she scrolled down her contact list looking for a specific name.

Ashley Frost.

She pressed the facetime button and waited patiently.

Her phone came to life with a face far too close to the camera for anyone's liking, as the person in question struggled to put her glasses on and squinted at the phone, her dirty blonde hair a tangled mess on her head.

"Wha?" Ashley Frost managed to get out, blearily. "Wait? Dana? Dana Spectra?" The incredulity in the woman's voice had her struggle to sit up in bed, while at the same time protect her dignity. "Oh my god, like…wow! I can't believe…you called me!" The two had met relatively recently in Mongolia of all places, and Dana had been given Ash's details in case she ever needed a computer expert. Ash had been star struck from the moment she had set eyes on the model, and that clearly hadn't disappeared in a hurry.

"You told me to call you if I needed a good hacker," Dana smirked, and Ash nodded furiously, finding a baseball cap to slam on her head.

"Yep! I'm your girl, definitely," Ash agreed.

"Where are you?" Dana asked, puzzled.

"Oh where, I'm…" Ash paused as though trying to remember. "Baku!" she announced triumphantly.

"Mission?"

"Uhm, well, maybe," Ash shrugged. The purpose of their last meeting had been an attempt by an organization called the Doves to kill Dana – an organization that Ash belonged to, though thankfully they came to the conclusion that executing Dana was a mistake. "Do you need me?"

"Oh, if you're busy," Dana mimicked Ash's shrug.

"No, I can help. Honestly."

"I need to find some information and I have a chunk of data that I think it's in. It's big," Dana said, apologizing in case it was a big job.

"Can you send it?"

"Via phone? Is that OK?"

"Mine can take it. As long as yours can, we should be fine," Ash said, and Dana nodded.

"I may have to hang up to do this. And it may come from a different number. But it'll be me," Dana said.

"And I'm looking for?" Ash asked.

"Anything about the assassination of a man named Thomas McAteer," Dana replied, and Ash nodded again.

"Urgent?"

"Please."

"Talk soon," Ash said. Dana disconnected the call and then began tapping on her phone, changing over to the sleeper OS beneath her phone and finding the data hidden away on it, before sending it to Ash's phone. She wondered if she should wait on the secret phone, but then decided it wasn't worth it. She flicked it back to her own phone, and looked around for the remote to the television set. She wasn't tired enough to go to sleep, so she decided to watch tv until the call came.

The phone rang less than forty-five minutes later, when Dana was about to embark on her third episode of an American sitcom that was definitely not as funny as people raved about on the internet. Maybe she was being harsh, but old people definitely didn't have the same sense of humor as normal people. When she realized her father's opinion might be on the positive side, she chided herself.

"Yes," Dana said, raising an eyebrow. Ash was still in the hat, though she seemed much more awake that she had been previously.

"OK, so whoever owns this data was employed to assassinate Thomas McAteer," Ash started and Dana clicked her tongue in irritation.

"I know that," she muttered.

"The money was paid from an account that I haven't checked yet, but I didn't need that to find out who employed them," Ash said.

"It's not important, I know where the money came from. Who employed them?"

"There were a few emails back and forth, all encrypted, all pseudonymous, blah, blah," Ash said, flicking through something on a tablet. "However, I did a little reverse search on them. The final one confirming McAteer's exact location came on the day of his assassination, from Canada."

"*From* Canada?" Dana asked, wondering if she had heard correctly.

"Yeah, that's a surprise?"

"Yeah, though," Dana paused for a moment. "I dunno. I just didn't think it would come from Canada."

"Well, he was in Canada, so it makes sense."

"He?"

"The guy who sent the email. The guy who wanted McAteer dead," Ash said.

"Being?"

"They all came from the same computer. It pings right every time."

"Who?" Dana asked, struggling to contain her impatience.

"Silhouette Moreau."

SECOND REPORT: TOTALLY WORTHLESS

Dana stood on the white pathway leading towards the Basilica of Our Lady of Peace, and had to admit that it was one of the single most impressive things she had ever seen in her life. The sheer size of the temple was absolutely astonishing.

She was approaching the courtyard at the front of the basilica, much wider than the church itself, and bracketed on either side by two semi-circular rows of columns, the beginning and end of each row topped by a white dome with a cross on the top. The church with its own colossal dome stood in front.

It was nine o'clock in the morning and people were starting to mill around, keen to see the church. Some were obviously tourists, but Dana suspected that many of the faces were locals who wanted to go in and have some time with God. There were columns everywhere, including what looked like six sets of double columns at the front of the church.

"Did you catch the name of the street that we drove in on from the airport?" Max Travere asked, materializing at Dana's side and making her jump slightly.

"No," she said. "Is it important?"

"Houphouët-Boigny Avenue, named after Félix Houphouët-Boigny, the first President of *Côte d'Ivoire*. President for 33 years until he died of cancer in 1993. Won seven elections.

Loved by the French. Although things started to go wrong. They always do." Max seemed wistful as he said this, and Dana wondered what that might have been about. "He was the one that wanted Yamoussoukro to be the new capital of *Côte d'Ivoire* and wanted to have a massive church based on St Peter's Basilica in the Vatican. It's not as tall, but it's certainly wider. Biggest church in all of Africa, allegedly." He turned to her with a smile. "Shall we go in?"

Dana nodded, and the pair walked up through the courtyard, making their way to the Basilica.

"You seemed sad when you said things always go wrong," Dana said cautiously.

"Oh," Max smiled, though it didn't reach his eyes. "It's been a rough year, if I'm honest."

"Being a spy?" Dana asked cheekily, and he grinned at her.

"Actually, I try to make my job as relaxing as possible," he rejoined. "But there were things. Parents, girlfriends. You don't want to know."

"Girlfriends plural? I definitely have to know now," Dana said, and was a little shocked when she realized there was a tiny sting of jealousy.

Where did that come from?

"Girlfriend, singular," Max reassured her. "Which is hard enough in my line of work. But I suppose I sort of talked myself into the idea that I could make it work." He stopped and looked at her, though he seemed to be looking into the past. "I couldn't. Obviously. I thought I was very James Bond, but it turns out I definitely wanted a proper relationship."

"But you chose the job in the end," Dana said.

"My mum died last year," Max replied, as though it were an explanation. "I think I just came to the conclusion that maybe an entire chapter of my life was ending. So when she broke up with me, I let it happen, because…it was the end."

"I'm not sure that's valiant or not," Dana said, not trying to be mean.

"Definitely not, I assure you," Max said. He stopped again to turn to her. "So obviously there's history between you and Justice," he started.

"Oh, yeah," Dana said, and she rolled her eyes. "I do not trust her as far as I can throw her."

"I should ask for her to be replaced?"

"Oh, no, her loyalties are in the right place," Dana said. "But she has her own goal, and that's what she'll follow. Anything you want on the side is not something she'll pursue. In fact, sometimes she'll just get rid of it completely because it suits her."

"Ah," Max said, pulling a face.

"Oh, it's fine," Dana touched his arm, hopefully reassuringly. "I promise I won't punch her again."

"That was an impressive punch."

"My Dad is Army." It was enough explanation for Max, who continued to walk beside her as they approached the church.

If she had been impressed by the expansive exterior of the basilica, the interior took her breath away. For the first time in her life, she understood the inherent respect that came with entering religious temples. All those inside seemed to understand it as well, as everyone moved as though they were afraid that the blanket of somberness that lay over the church was ridiculously fragile and like some sort of thin glass, would crack if anyone were to make too loud a noise.

The temple was relatively dark, with the light that shone through the many windows muted into various colours by the stained-glass windows that were different shades of blue, purple and pink. Rows upon rows of wooden pews were arranged in eight sets that spread out from the center to the edges of the building. The centre itself was another mini temple, with a roof that reached up to a point, above a vivid blue domed chandelier. The columns supporting the roof were intricately patterned, with gold snaking around them towards the tops.

Columns were a strong feature inside as well as outside, with a range of columns from small smooth ones to much larger fluted columns at the end of each of the eight sections of pews. People were scattered around, some lost in their own contemplation, some simply taking in the beauty of the basilica.

If there was a God, Dana mused, and that God were to touch the souls of his followers, this was definitely the place she expected it would happen.

"It seats 7,000 people," Max whispered. "But I've heard there have been over 10,000 in here at some points. You can see Jesus meeting with Félix Houphouët-Boigny on one of the windows, apparently."

"Oh, so he wasn't really self-aggrandizing?" Dana asked with a smirk.

"I should know that word?" Max said, slightly puzzled.

"Sorry, like…full of self-importance," Dana explained.

"Ahh," Max nodded. "My English is good, but not perfect. He was a dictator. I think that should explain it."

"Oh."

"His fortune was left to the country, so maybe he tried to redeem himself. Though his family are in court trying to get a proper share. Death brings out the worst in people." Max paused, then realized what he had said. "Sorry, that wasn't me being mournful about my mother's death. Just an observation."

They sat in silence for a few moments, breathing in the room of believers as their faith seemed to create a bond between them and the others in the room of the same mind. Perhaps that was the point of religion, Dana reflected.

"Were you really sent to help me?" Dana asked, curious.

"Justice's boss...Broadsword? He seems to genuinely worry about you. He agreed to lend me Justice if I did him a favour and helped him out. I think he likes to collect favours, so I was asked, rather than a request being put through to the DGSE."

"Sorry to be a pain," Dana said, but was reassured by the adorable smile of her new friend's face.

"It's fine. Sometimes you work on an assignment for a long time, but your brain reaches a still point and doesn't know where to go from there. My brain had hit that point, so I was glad to relax a bit. Did you end up finding out anything your shooting?"

"I know who ordered the hit, but I don't know what to do with that information." Dana sat back in the chair and huffed slightly, earning a look of annoyance from the people around her to which she hastily nodded an apology.

"You are so strange," Max whispered with a small smile.

"You don't know how to talk to women," chided Dana. "You should be telling me how beautiful I am. That's the deal." She gave him a grin, and he shook his head.

"You know how beautiful you are," Max said. "You don't need me to tell you. But I don't get why you're doing this."

"This?"

"This, all…this." He shrugged and indicated the room they were in. "What makes you want to get involved in this sort of thing. I'm guessing it's not the first time if Broadsword is involved. But you're not actually Interpol."

"No," Dana agreed. "I think it would help sometimes."

"That's shifting the focus," Max replied, pulling a face.

"Oh, well, I wasn't sure what you were asking me." Max shook his head again.

"Come on Dana," he said, and as Dana turned to look at him properly, she was struck by how good looking he was. He was almost stereotypically hot, with his casual hair, firm jaw and deep blue eyes. "What makes you run around almost getting killed, trying to find out who assassinated someone you were nowhere near?"

"I," Dana started and then wondered if there was any point in lying to the man in front of her. What would it achieve?

But do you know the truth?

"I think it's a number of things," Dana said, hoping it sounded conclusive, but suspecting it was simply opening up another can of worms. Max was indeed looking expectantly, and Dana wanted to go with him away from the basilica, but she couldn't entirely justify having come all this way for nothing.

And yet, she wasn't entirely convinced of Max's motives. It wasn't exactly like she hadn't been asking this of herself at each step of the way, but after a while her words seemed to ring hollow.

"I'm sort of defending my sister," she finally said. "Plus, I was there, and I didn't do anything."

"Didn't you chase the killer?" Max said, a trace of amusement in his voice.

"Yes, but," she started, but he shook his head, and she wondered if she had got too loud. She lowered her voice and lent forward. "Don't you think I should have done something extra?" she asked.

"Not really," he replied.

"Well, I do," Dana said, and turned to sit back in the pew, regretting the fact she probably looked like a petulant child. They sat in silence, and Dana looked around, wondering if the second row of stained-glass windows represented a second floor. Was there a balcony of some sort up there?

"Do you want to go and get something to drink?" Max suddenly asked. "I'm not sure if there's much more to see here."

"Oh," Dana said, feeling a little disappointed. "I thought that we were going to do something like meet someone undercover or something."

"No," Max replied, looking a little crestfallen. "I just thought you might like to see the church." Dana looked at him for a moment, raising an eyebrow.

"Fine," she said. "But I need some pictures to post on my IG or it will be a totally worthless visit."

"Oh, to be a model," Max said, shaking his head.

"It's all about advertising, baby," Dana grinned.

THIRD REPORT: DEFINITELY SPECTRA

"Our operation was compromised!" Fi's face shouted angrily from the large monitor hanging on the wall of the office. She was standing, pointing as she let loose her fury, somewhat impotently on the camera she was addressing. The other members of the Four-Fold Crown sat behind her, impassive but clearly visible. What they were thinking was anyone's guess, but none of them contradicted their sister.

"You were the one that chose the assassin. We paid you, and made sure that the money came siphoned from a source as far away from us as possible. And then you chose an assassin who was sleeping with someone from the company that we used. How did *that* happen?" The scarred face of Heroux leaned into the camera to give the same emphasis that Fi had, his cold blue eyes not giving an inch to the women.

"Don't turn this on us," Whenua suddenly spoke up, her brown eyes matching Heroux's. "We had no idea what company you were using, so how would we possibly know who to avoid sending?"

"It's why we pay you," snarled Heroux. "And it wasn't a small amount. We would expect you to get it right. And we didn't ask you to deal with Hémery. You took that upon yourselves."

"Our assassin was tracked down by someone who was

an associate of Hémery's," Whenua shot back. "What did you expect us to do? Sit back and let her follow a trail that led directly back to us?"

"It's exactly what you did!"

"Ladies, Heroux, please," came a smooth voice, and Heroux sat back, allowing the camera positioned on the monitor to take in more of the room, including the dark features of Silhouette Moreau sitting comfortably behind a desk. "This blame game serves none of us. Mistakes were made, and certainly we hadn't anticipated Dana Spectra's connection to André's niece. That's definitely on us, for which we apologise. How about another payment equal to the last to accommodate the difficulty we've put you through?"

"That is more than generous, Mr Moreau," Gongi said, and Fi immediately returned to her chair as the older queen spoke. Everyone saw the barely contained anger of Heroux, but wisely all chose to say nothing, though the Crown perhaps noted the quick look that Moreau gave Heroux.

"The fact is a single Australian girl is unlikely to be a big problem to any of us," Moreau continued. "We are very powerful organisations that cannot be beaten down by a girl, no matter how tenacious she may be. And, admittedly, she is very tenacious."

"She's here on the Ivory Coast now," Heroux said, and the Four-Fold Crown wondered if the signal was responsible for the momentary look of concern that flashed across Moreau's face. "She arrived by French military chopper. The only crewmember we were able to identify was the pilot, who's definitely French. The others, it's hard to tell but one was definitely Spectra."

"You appear to have a problem on your hand, Mr

Moreau," Eau said, her found face suspiciously calm as she spoke.

"I don't see it as a problem," Moreau replied. "May I ask a small favour?" The queens glanced at each other.

"What is it?" Whenua asked.

"Your assassin's lover. Do you have him? Is he still alive?" They looked at each other again, but this time the nod from Gongi was much clearer.

"We do." Whenua said.

"He has a slight head injury," Fi said as though she were discussing the fact she had been given scones with dates, when she had specifically asked for plain. "But he's alive and capable of communication."

"For now," Eau added, and this time the smile on her face was much more obvious.

"Would we be able to have him? I'd quite like to ask him some questions, if you had no objections."

"Of course," Gongi replied. "We'll send him to you."

"Thank you so much," Moreau said, his smile lighting up his face. "I do hope we'll be able to do business again at some point." He reached forward to hit the disconnect button, waiting for the queens' acknowledgement to do so.

"Fucking bitches," Heroux shouted, unable to restrain himself any longer. "They fuck up the operation and then expect us to have to pay the price?"

"It's unimportant," Moreau said. "But when he arrives, I would like to know who gave out the information about us. I want to know how much McAteer told people before we tie up another loose end that might be tighter than we thought it was." He strolled over to one of the walls of his office and used his phone to make the windows go clear. The view he had of Yamoussoukro was spectacular. At the top of his building he could see across the city, including the awe-inspiring Basilica.

"Spectra?" Heroux asked. Moreau remained silent as he studied the city, pretending he wasn't really paying attention to what was going on. Heroux waited as patiently as he could, urging his boss to turn back and give him an answer, but Moreau continued to take in the view. He could repeat himself, but he had long experience knowing full well that it wasn't the sort of thing the billionaire tolerated.

"Do you think a model from Australia is going to be a problem?" Moreau wondered.

"She chased after the Crown's assassin, and then tracked her to the Crown in the Congo," Heroux argued.

"She's an influencer. Have you seen her socials?"

"Not really, if I'm honest. I saw some photos, but…" Heroux shrugged.

"She's an influencer (and he made it rhyme with shit), more interested in showing off her new bikini and what's between her legs than she is actually paying attention to the world."

"She made her way to the Congo!" protested Heroux.

"She's like one of those people who climb buildings and then take selfies from the very top," Moreau said.

And yet…

"Perhaps we should invite her to the launch tomorrow," Moreau said. "After all, having one of our brand ambassadors there would be good, given as how Asha has disappeared."

"Maybe Spectra knows what happened to Asha?" Heroux

mused.

"Precisely. Let's track her down and invite her to the bash. It's short notice, but her arrival here suggests we might get lucky. And she can use it to get more likes." Moreau went back to the window to look out over the city again. Perhaps it would be better to be safer than sorry. "Take care of it, and let me know the moment Bryce arrives here."

"Of course," Heroux nodded, and turned to exit.

Yes, Moreau reflected, given the timing perhaps it would be better to have all bases covered.

As Dana stepped up onto the sidewalk of vue Basilique she turned around to look back at the view that was afforded her – the central white dome of the Basilica of Our Lady of Peace stood above the trees across the lake, giving her an indication of how far they had just driven. Even from this distance the Basilica looked noble and serene, as above her, the clouds gathered and rain began to fall once again. The Ivory Coast was nothing if not predictable regards the weather, Dana reflected.

"Coming?" Max asked, his hand pointing forward to the restaurant ahead of them. He had offered to take her out for a meal after she had taken some selfies and sent them to her sister. "I know the best place in Yamoussoukro," he assured her, but as she got into the car that was waiting for them, he elaborated and added "Lower your expectations though. You're not in Paris, so things are done a little differently here." Dana narrowed her eyes at this, and wondered what she was letting herself in for.

La Brise, however, was an interesting place, on the vue Basilique, the street that runs around the Lac de Yamoussoukro across the water from Rte De Daloa, the other great highway running through the city. Truthfully, Dana was finding it difficult to wrap her head around Yamoussoukro, which seemed to be split into several different sections that weren't all necessarily related, which seemed very strange for a city that was purportedly the capital of its country.

The restaurant itself was a long building with a red tiled roof and orange awnings (though Dana wondered if perhaps there was a time they had been red as well). There were a couple of chairs out the front, but once they passed through the carved wooden poles that formed the entrance, they saw a number of tables with white tablecloths and red cloths over the top of those. African figures were dotted around the room on their plinths, managing to look arty, despite their strangely inhuman appearance. Some of them were accompanied by animals, such as elephants or zebras.

As they moved further inside, she saw that there was a blue staircase that led upstairs, where the tablecloths weren't quite as nice as the ones on display under the wooden roof. Wooden masks leered at them from around the room and everywhere there were fans moving slowly to sluggishly guide the humid air around. It was sticky, Dana reflected, and she wished that she had changed into shorts and a t-shirt, but travelling the distance back to the hotel was out of the question.

"Shall we sit?" Max asked, and pointed to a table that was free. Dana was acutely aware that she was attracting attention, being the only red-haired, white woman in the restaurant. A number of people glanced at her curiously, while a couple of children were fascinated by her clearly foreign appearance.

"We can sit inside if you would like," Max offered. "There's some tables inside, might be a bit nicer, though I don't think there's any air conditioning here."

"You seem to know this place pretty well," Dana said, slightly surprised.

"Well," Max grinned. "My grandmother was from the Ivory Coast, so I have a connection. It's not a bad place, all things told, and I have been here a few times for work." He waved over a waiter who appeared quickly and Max spoke to him in French. "Do you mind me ordering for us? I'll make sure it's good." Dana smiled and nodded, slightly impressed by the confident display of arrogance.

"So, to be clear," Dana said as the waiter left, "You're definitely not Interpol?"

"Directorate-General for External Security," he said, and Dana looked puzzled.

"French secret service," he grinned. "But don't tell anyone. Action Division, even."

"Seriously?" Dana asked.

"Seriously," he replied. "But also seriously, don't tell anyone. Justice vouched for you, so I am trusting you."

"I might plaster it all over Instagram," Dana smirked.

"Ah!" Max said. "Yes, that," and he pointed at her.

"What?" Dana asked.

"That smirk, yes? That's your thing, your trademark? When I was doing some research, you do it a lot."

"Oh," Dana said, and felt herself go a little red. "Well, it's…"

"*Trés sexy*," Max grinned, and Dana sat back in her chair.

"Oh shush," she said. She turned when she thought something was caught in her hair, and she saw a young child had been reaching up to touch her hair. "Oh," she said again, uncertain how to respond, though it was made easier for her when a stern voice called to the child.

"How does it feel being the only white face in the room?" Max asked, not unkindly.

"It's a little weird," Dana admitted. "But I'm not freaked out or anything."

"The kids here wouldn't see someone of your complexion around her very often," Max continued. "It's all a bit new to them."

"When I was younger, we went to Japan, and I remember a lot of people wanting to take their photo with me," Dana said.

"I like the idea of welcoming strangers with fascination and a desire to get a photo with them, rather than despising them for being different," Max said.

"Fair," Dana admitted. "Why are you here, though? I mean, seriously?" Max looked at her, clearly weighing up options in his head about how he wanted to proceed with the conversation.

"What are you planning on doing from here?" he asked, apparently changing the subject.

"So that's an off-limits topic? And that's how you tell me?" Dana said, raising an eyebrow.

"No, no," Max shook his head. "It will inform me as to

what I tell you." Dana regarded him and wondered exactly what she wanted to say to the man. He was hard to read, she decided, but there was something definitely likable about him. And it wasn't just his gorgeous accent.

Or his gorgeous ass.

"I think," Dana started to say, but was interrupted by her phone ringing. She tilted her head slightly at this and took out her phone, surprised to see it was Christa Adams. She was about to silence the call, but then changed her mind. "Excuse me," she said, and slid her finger across the screen.

"Dana? Are you in the Côte d'Ivoire?"

"How could you possibly know that?" Dana asked, her voice squeaking in astonishment.

"So you are," Adams said, ignoring the question. "Yamoussoukro, I believe?"

"I don't even…"

"Silhouette Moreau has been in touch with me. He's doing a Shadow launch in Yamoussoukro tomorrow night. He was wondering if you'd be interested in being the special guest. All the usual buzz, benefits and the like. Apparently the other one – what's her name? – is unavailable."

"Asha?"

"That's her. I don't really know, nor care, but I'm happy to take the money. I'll say yes, unless you have some life-threatening emergency."

"No, no I don't."

"Good. I'll text the details. Do you have any *Digné*, on you?"

"Yes…"

"Excellent. Make sure to wear it. I shouldn't have to tell you. Oh," there was finally a pause from the other end. "Do you have something to wear?"

"No, of course not."

"What are you doing there anyway?" Adams suddenly asked.

"I'll try and find something to look good."

"Chic, not good. And something that people will want to talk about. The more brands the better."

"OK."

"Excellent. Details coming. Well done." The phone rang out and Dana put in on the table in front of her, an appropriate shadow crossing her features. Max gave her a curious look and Dana shrugged slightly.

"I just got a job," she said. "A request to attend a function."

"What? Here?" Max asked, his astonishment echoing hers.

"Yeah." Dana paused for a moment, and then looked around. "Are we getting food anytime soon?" Max laughed.

"Welcome to Yamoussoukro," he said. "Nothing is done in a hurry here." Dana looked around and realized that, indeed, all the staff were relaxed, standing around, some joking with each other, while others looked for something to do. Every so often someone would appear with food and a table would get to eat, though Dana realized that people were expected to enjoy the ambience before they enjoyed food.

"So," Max continued, "the question becomes...who knows you are here in Yamoussoukro?"

"The answer," Dana replied, "would appear to be

Silhouette Moreau."

"You seem concerned by that," Max said, and Dana looked at him, wondering how to deal with him. There was no denying the man was hot and she very much enjoyed his company, but it wouldn't be the first time in the last few years that she had fallen into that trap. But at the same time, how did she approach the situation she was in?

"When I was at the Four-Fold Crown's pyramid, I obtained their data," Dana said.

"What data?"

"All of it, I think," and Max looked genuinely surprised.

"So, you were successful then, in your excursion."

"More than you think. I was trying to track down the person who hired the Crown to assassinate McAteer," Dana said. Max pursed his lips as he sat back in his chair, looking at her.

"I'm guessing that there's no such thing as coincidence," and Dana shook her head. "Well, we really do have a problem then," Max said. Dana looked at him and Max seemed extremely reluctant to say what was about to come next. "The thing is, I haven't been fully upfront."

"I suppose as I wasn't that's fair enough," Dana admitted gracefully.

"The," he paused and then chose his word carefully, "*thing* Justice is helping me look into seems to be related to a man named Heroux. He's…" Again, Max seemed to be choosing his words with particular care. "Shall we say he's got an interesting past. He's currently in *Côte d'Ivoire*. We tracked him here, and I suspect I don't need to give you more than one guess as to who he is working for."

"There's no such thing as coincidence," Dana repeated.

"Not in my world," Max affirmed. "And at the center of all these coincidences…" Dana sat back in her chair and bit her bottom lip. The spider in the middle of his web.

"Silhouette."

FOURTH REPORT: BECOME CULTURED

There was a knock at the door and it almost seemed hesitant. Dana wondered who it could possibly be, and then wondered if she wanted it to be Max. Would he be hesitant in knocking? He didn't seem like the sort, more the kind that would give a deliberate bang, announcing his presence.

Dressed in a green bikini that she had been dragging around on the off chance she might get the chance to go swimming at some point (and that was always a possibility – a girl should never go anywhere without a bikini), Dana had decided that she might make the effort to have a swim in the pool of the Hôtel President. She had come to terms with the fact that her trip to Africa was not going to be full of the sort of places she had stayed at before, but that didn't mean that she wasn't going to enjoy herself.

Risking the possibility that it was indeed Max at the door, Dana walked up the small corridor to the front door and opened it.

"Well, I can't say I'm disappointed by the view," came the immediate response, and Dana scowled when she saw Justice Kennedy standing in her door.

"Wow," Dana drawled, vaguely mocking Kennedy's accent. "What a surprise." She turned and walked back to the room, though she didn't close the door, which Justice took as an invitation.

"You know, I didn't come here to make your life miserable," Justice said, hoping it might be a somewhat peace brokering start. Annoying, Justice found herself slightly mesmerized by Dana's gorgeous ass. It would not be unfair to say the two had a complicated relationship, which had started with a great night of sex in Singapore, and ended with a murder in Monaco. Those sorts of things can create a fundamental difference in your approach to life. "This isn't quite the Larmes d'Athena, is it?"

Dana turned to look at Justice, her eyes veiled.

"Are we doing the nostalgia thing?" she asked, and there was venom in her voice.

"Fucking hell, Dana," Justice said, giving the impression of a boiler that was no longer doing its job properly. "I know we're never going to see eye to eye about Guin," Justice started, but Dana was already for the fight.

"Not about Guin," Dana said. "About the fact you murdered her." She said nothing more, just held the challenge and Justice took a deep breath but then let it all out.

"I don't know what to tell you," Justice finally said. "We're never going to agree on this, and that's fine. I get it. We're not friends, you can never forgive me. And frankly, I don't want your forgiveness anyway. But you and I have a mutual problem to work on, and we can either do it individually, maybe getting in each other's way and messing it up, or we can work together like adults. And the difference between us is that I'm not going to let you get in my way." Justice's blue eyes flashed at Dana, and the redhead frowned a little.

"We can work together," Dana said. "I'm happy to be professional." Justice noted that Dana made the word sound like an insult.

"Melissa Andersson, the agent you met in Singapore a couple of years back," Justice said, and Dana sat down on her bed, crossing her legs. Justice looked around and found the single chair in the room, which she pulled out and sat down on. "There's a weird place in the waters off the coast of Cayenne in French Guiana. A gendarme called Benoît Royer was investigating it. Sort of like an oil rig that is using up a lot of power that it probably shouldn't be. Royer called in the DGSE, and they sent Max, who called us, and we sent Melissa. The two went over to the rig and, uh, technically broke in, but neither came back."

"So, you think they were murdered on the rig?"

"We haven't had a single trace of their bodies turn up anywhere," Justice said. "And we've been looking. We aren't going to allow someone to just kill an Interpol officer and get away with it. However, the thing is, we know who runs the rig." Justice pulled out her phone, and after a small amount of tapping, turned it to Dana, who saw a picture of a middle-aged man with scars on his face. He looked, she thought, like someone who had been quite literally thrown to the dogs. "Heroux," Justice said. "Just the one name, not a lot of information about him. However, we do know one thing that might interest you." Dana gave the American a look, but was curious despite herself. "He's currently in Yamoussoukro and he's on the guest list of Silhouette Moreau's Shadow launch tomorrow night."

"Silhouette pays to have Thomas McAteer murdered, a

man who was working for him. Heroux murders two law enforcement officers who break into a private rig that is using power for a reason no one knows."

"Two different problems, tied together by an energy drink that a relatively famous Australian model is promoting."

"There's no such thing as coincidences," Dana mused. "Relatively famous?"

"When you make a movie, then I'll consider you properly famous," Justice said, giving a wry smile.

"So, you want me to find out what sort of a connection there is between Silhouette and Heroux?" Dana asked.

"If you could. I mean, if you could find out what's on that rig at the same time, we'd be eternally grateful, but I don't expect you to pull off miracles."

"But why?" Dana asked. "I don't quite get that."

"Heroux is an underground figure," Justice said. "Well, former underground figure. But the rig is allegedly for legitimate archeological research. Which might be true. I've no doubt there are all sorts of things off the coast of French Guiana. But Heroux has to have got the money to build that rig somehow. Sure, he might have got it illegally; we suspected he was gun running, so maybe that's true. But maybe he has a billionaire financier."

Oh, that makes sense, Dana reflected. "But how does that tie in with McAteer's death," Dana mused, this time out loud.

"You tell us," Justice shrugged.

"I'll see what I see, and let you know. Anything that comes up, I'll pass it back."

"Thanks," Justice said. "I really do appreciate it. I'll let you have your swim. You'll no doubt want to be showing off that hot bod to all the doting admirers down by the pool. In hindsight, maybe I was wrong about the hair, as well. Red does sort of suit you." Dana raised an eyebrow at the comment, wondering whether she was being complimentary or catty. Maybe even both. Justice got up and headed for the door.

"For the record," Dana announced, stopping Justice in her tracks, "it's been a hot minute since we last met. Don't think you'll get the chance to get in my way." Justice turned and was surprised to see Dana's hand resting on the golden Glock that had appeared on the bed.

Justice opened her mouth to say "My baby girl's all grown up," but the look on Dana's face stopped her.

Not that she desperately wanted to get out of Africa, but Dana desperately wanted to get out of Africa. The people were lovely, the food was lovely, the countries were...well, mostly lovely, though there were some quite terrifying occupants in some of them, but she wasn't going to hold that against an entire continent.

But as she strolled into the Shadow event wearing a Gaurav Gupta sculpted corseted black dress (it had a sheer black which cut into her right waist, and a very long slit up the left side), complete with silver Tony Bianco Anja heels, and some matching silver Digné jewelry around her neck and wrist, she realized that she had reached the bottom of her seemingly bottomless bag that she had packed a few weeks earlier.

She was coming to the conclusion that active wear and a very expensive black dress were an absolute necessity whenever packing was involved. These days it seemed she never knew when she might need to go to an expensive dinner, or just generally look a million dollars.

As she walked the red carpet towards Silhouette's headquarters, where the launch was taking place (Dana suspected that there was nowhere in Yamoussoukro that quite suited Silhouette's needs for the launch, which did beg the question why was he doing in Yamoussoukro rather than Abidjan, which, while no longer the actual capital, was still a bigger and arguably more impressive city), there was quite a lot of paparazzi to take photos.

There was also a great deal of military presence. A large number of black-clad men stood around, their faces stony and their black berets rammed onto their heads. They were carrying machine guns, and Dana was surprised to find that she didn't really recognize what they were. Her father had once told her that machine guns were really only for military use and should never be in the hands of civilians, but she had got a recognition of them over time. These seemed newer and more impressive than most of the ones she'd encountered.

If the Australian Travel Advice website had seen this lot, they would downgrade the Ivory Coast's status from…oh. Dana suddenly realized the obvious; they weren't military. They were private security, probably Silhouette's own.

Or maybe, Heroux's? Justice had suspected him of gun smuggling, but maybe he was more into manpower.

They certainly were putting the paparazzi at ease, and she heard a number of shouts of "Dana, this way!" and "Dana, can we seem from behind?". She paused, turning left and right for the cameras, angling her head to ensure that she wasn't going to be photographed awkwardly, and making sure that her Saint Laurent uptown pouch (in grain de poudre leather!) was held comfortably in both hands.

"Who did your hair and makeup?" a photographer called out, and Dana inwardly winced, realizing that this question was probably inevitable.

"I'm trying something different," she said. "It's done by me, but it's a more natural and relaxed vibe. Do you think it's working?"

"It's very different," the photographer replied.

"You don't think it looks good?" Dana asked, and she put just enough punch into her words for the photographer to quickly back down.

"No, you look beautiful!" he said. Dana gave him one of her smirks, and the flashes went off again. She would have to get Bella to find out what the response was to her new style, she reflected.

As she entered the building, she couldn't help but feel guilty at the opulence she was entering. Silhouette Moreau had clearly not spared a cent on the function, or indeed his Ivory Coast headquarters. The reception area was a large open space with the front an expected wall of glass, while the back was a fascinating mosaic in different shades of blue. For this event, the glass front was now covered with dark drapes that bore the Shadow logo on it, and beautiful men and women wandered around, their bodies painted black in the same style that she and Asha had done for the publicity photoshoot, offering a variety of different Shadow-based drinks, as well as themed food. The stylized "S" logo had been rendered in 3D and hung from the ceiling, light embedded in it to create the lighting around the room.

Dana took a drink from one of the waitresses, double

taking slightly as she realized the woman's breasts were bare. She was tempted to make a comment, but decided that it she would be better off closing her mouth. The woman caught Dana looking and gave a shy smile, so Dana smiled back.

"I hope you like," the waitress said.

"Absolutely," Dana replied, and realized she had instantly gone into flirt mode. The waitress gave another small smile, and walked away. In the G-string she was wearing, her buttocks were also clearly on display and Dana bit her bottom lip.

Behave Dana!

"Dana Spectra!"

Dana turned to see Silhouette Moreau walk up to her, wearing nothing but black – a black Dolce & Gabbana double-breasted silica-fit jacket (which was absolutely gorgeous), with a black Dior Homme oblique long-sleeved shirt, buttoned to the neck, but with no tie. His arms were outstretched, and she turned to embrace him. She was surprised at how firm his embrace was, as though they were old friends.

Behind him was his head of security, the tattooed woman, also dressed in an elegant Viscose stripe three-piece suit; jacket, waistcoat and trousers. Interestingly there was no shirt, which gave her a sexy, deadly appeal, and displayed the tattoo on her chest very clearly – a set of bat wings.

Chillo, was that her name?

Chillo scared Dana, but she couldn't quite think why. Perhaps, though, that was the point of a head of security.

"Dana, I cannot thank you enough for this. Honestly, we had Asha lined up for this event, and then she informed us that something had come up, and she couldn't make it, but I found out you were here, and…well, here you are. You are an absolute gem. The effort you're making for us is above and beyond, and I promise you that we will do everything we can. But, how are you, and how is your sister? I hope you've both recovered from your ordeal in Canada?" Not for the first time, Dana realized that Silhouette preferred to make a speech rather than engage in small talk, and every time he talked, it felt a little like she needed to take a breather.

"Oh, we're fine. Honestly, we're all recovering slowly, but life goes on. And I'm more than happy to help out. My Dad has always told me that if you have a little loyalty, you'll find out who your real friends are."

"Well, I hope that we can definitely describe ourselves as real friends, *oui*?" He was about to continue when a man walked up to him, dressed much simpler in a black tuxedo that seemed more off the shelf, but it was the scars on his face that drew Dana's attention.

"My security consultant, Mr Heroux," Silhouette said, confirming Dana's identification. "Would you excuse me for a moment, please?" The two walked away, heads close as they discussed whatever it was, they were discussing, and Dana watched them with a little curiousity. As she turned back to take in the room, she was surprised to find the waitress from earlier approaching her.

"A refill?"

"What exactly am I drinking?" Dana asked, with a smile.

"Oh, I think that's vodka and strawberry Shadow," the waitress said.

"Are you not cold?" Dana said, her smile not dropping.

"Honestly?" the waitress said, and Dana nodded conspiratorially. "My nips have been hard all night. It's genuinely embarrassing. I don't know how you did it!"

"Well, mine were strategically covered in the photos, but I had much the same problem," laughed Dana. "Your accent doesn't sound French or, uhm…" Dana paused, wondering how Ivory Coast was turned into an adjective.

"Ivorian? I know, doesn't make sense. I'm not though. Australian student." Dana tilted her head in surprise. "Of course, I knew who you were way before the Shadow thing. I'm from Brisbane as well, so I've followed you."

"Why here?"

"Followed a boyfriend for a bit, came here, broke up, now I'm trying to get money to get out. Thankfully this place started up, because otherwise I'd be stuck."

"What did you do in Brisbane?"

"Stripper," the woman laughed. "Girl's gotta do."

"Oh, so you're used to this," Dana grinned, pointing at her bare breasts. The woman looked across the room, and grimaced.

"Gotta get back to work. Let me know if you need anything."

"Find me later," Dana said. The waitress frowned, and then nodded. Dana wasn't quite sure why she said what she said, but there was a part of her that wanted to help the girl out. Whether she could or not was another matter entirely, but she could at least try.

The real question was what to do next. She would do some mingling to ensure that she was fulfilling her contract and promoting Shadow to those that were milling around. She rarely recognized the elite that Silhouette was trying to impress, but she suspected that today she'd have even less chance of knowing who everyone was. Would the rich and famous really make their way to Yamoussoukro to investigate a new energy drink?

But, with that being said, there seemed to be a lot of very rich Arab men wandering around, clinking glasses and giving each other rich belly laughs. So far Shadow had been rolled out in places like America, the United Kingdom, Australia, Russia, Japan, France…Different countries in different continents or regions to ensure what seemed to be some sort of maximum distribution. Yamoussoukro was obviously the African hub, though it made her wonder why he didn't bother with somewhere in Egypt.

The truth was she wasn't any kind of business woman so she probably didn't understand what the plan was. Still, he'd made some interesting choices. A tall man dressed in an elegant royal blue suit stepped forward and politely asked if he might introduce her to someone, and Dana put on her game face and allowed herself to be guided.

Silhouette Moreau had his first real encounter with racism, not at school or in the workplace, or just walking down the street – though all of those would definitely come as he got older – and not at the hands of a white person – though, again, there would be plenty of white people who would be more than eager to make fun of the colour of his skin in later life – but with his own aunt. At the age of five he had been swept away from his mother's family and taken in by his father, a French man of some note (notoriety? No, that wasn't fair) who had decided it was time for the young Silhouette to become cultured, and more than just a common

Ivorian.

At that time, he went by a different name, one that these days he struggled to remember, precisely. Sometimes he wondered if he had repressed the name, but then there were times he would close his eyes and drift off to sleep, and the face of his mother would appear to him and she'd whisper his name – his original name – but when he woke up, the dream would dissipate, along with the details. He could find it; it was hardly going to be difficult for a man of his means, but he simply couldn't be bothered.

But the younger Silhouette had walked into his father's living room, where his extended family had gathered to welcome the newest member.

"Oh," crowed an aunt, who actually looked like a bird, dressed in something that seemed far too feathered, and far too coloured, "He's blue-black, isn't he?" The rest of the family either giggled, or nodded in agreement, except for his father who looked irritated, but curiously, the irritation seemed directed towards the young Silhouette, rather than anyone else. He hadn't really understood what they had meant, and later one of his cousins – a young girl by the name of Marie – explained it to him.

"You're *so* black," she said, and pointed to his skin. "Look," and Marie put her coffee-coloured arm beside his to highlight the distinction. "You're like a silhouette!" Marie didn't seem to hate him for it, but some of his other relations seemed to be embarrassed by him, and family affairs weren't common, but Silhouette was never sure whether they had been common before or not. Ultimately it didn't matter; he wasn't really welcomed into the Moreau family. Truth be told, it rather suited them if he just

273

metaphorically did what they expected him to do literally – fade into the shadows.

His father later asked him if he would like to choose a different name, now that he was in Paris, and even by that point, the young Silhouette had begun to understand that "would you like" really meant "do it", and so he had selected the name Silhouette, and his father looked angry as though he thought his son was mocking him. But then he smiled, and laughed, and agreed it was a suitable name for the boy. Looking back, Silhouette realized that his father was just as racist as his aunt had been; arguably even more so. After that, time with Moreau Snr was earned, and rare, and by the time he was 12, Moreau decided he didn't really want to earn the time.

The only family member he really spent time with was the only one who wanted to – Marie, but when he turned fifteen that all changed. Sometimes the memory of why surfaced, and Silhouette, sitting in the dark looking back at his life and unable to stop what would rise, unbidden, to the surface, would physically flinch at what had happened. Marie would never look him in the eyes again. If they ever met again, Moreau suspected he would have Heroux kill the woman. It was a time of his life he never wanted to think about again. A time when he realized that he needed far more control over himself than he actually had. A time when he realized that human beings were far too close to the animals that they hunted.

But it was a turning point in his life. His father died a blessed few weeks later, and he inherited enough money and his father's business. Almost immediately he made the decision to move back to Yamoussoukro to his mother, where he would run his late father's business, and expand into the Ivory Coast. It was a surprisingly wise decision for a boy who was only just about to turn sixteen, and one that was ridiculed by everyone. But his father's company – a software firm – was about to go places, and the Ivory Coast needed it as much as anyone else did. By the 1990's, Moreau Systèmes had become a force in the industry, before becoming Silhouette Systems. By the 2000s, it was the leading computer technology firm in Africa.

And then, Silhouette found something else for the business to look into. He smiled to himself at that. Research and branching out into new fields was something that Moreau had always thought was a good idea. He certainly wasn't against it now.

He breathed in deeply, and then turned to the closed door that was in front of him. Placing his thumb on the small black panel, the door slid open and he stepped through. In front of him, he saw Heroux standing with a number of his men, all dressed in cheap black suits, to make sure that no one thought they weren't security for a single moment.

You had to admire that sort of dedication to banality, Moreau reflected.

"Mr Moreau," Heroux said, as he turned to see his boss. "Allow me to introduce Ian Merryweather Bryce."

He stepped aside and indicated a chair, to which was tied a man who didn't look as though he was in the best of health. Ian Bryce was not only unshaven, sweaty and generally unkempt, but he clearly had a bullet wound which probably needed more treatment than the rough bandage that had been put around it was going to provide.

"Mr Bryce, you have been something of an annoyance to me," Morea said, and he looked around for a chair, before Heroux provided one. "I rather thought I had most things worked out in the removal of Mr McAteer, but then you go and spoil it all…" Moreau paused for a moment. "Well, yes, indeed, by saying something stupid like I love you." He smiled at this and looked to Heroux who nodded a small smile back.

Moreau felt disappointed. That had been rather a good one.

"The thing is, Mr Bryce, we paid a lot of money to ensure that the money for the Four-Fold Crown came from Hémery's company, and then you started digging into things that you should have kept to yourself and the next thing we know, your girlfriend becomes the centre point of a plan you helped to unravel. I also feel that technically, you weren't so much loyal to the Crown as you were to your girlfriend." Moreau sat back and regarded the accountant with a degree of annoyance.

"I didn't know," came the weak response back, and Moreau sighed a little. He detested stupidity more than he could say. It was one of the few lessons that Moreau Sr had taught his son, and it stuck with him for the rest of his life – "Always surround yourself with people who are on the same intellectual level as you, because you can't converse with the stupid people, and you shouldn't have to lower yourself to their level." He had said it with such haughty disdain, that the younger Silhouette hadn't, not for one moment, considered that it wasn't ingrained into his father's behaviour. It was the reason that both he and his father had nothing to do with his mother. She was a simple person, one who had no desire to push herself beyond running a simple market stall in Yamoussoukro, selling necklaces and bangles. Of course, both

Moreau's had kept her in money; she wanted for nothing, which probably explained why she was more than happy to do very little. But even if she had, she wouldn't have got far.

He realised the thought of his mother had brought a sneer to his face, and when he looked, he knew that one or two of the men wondered why. They wouldn't ask. They wouldn't dare.

"Betrayal is a complicated thing, Mr Bryce," Moreau intoned, as though he were reading from a hymn book. "We all set limits on what we think is betrayal. You think you can't betray us because we weren't working together. In fairness, I would say that betrayal is not as black and white as that."

"Hémery knew that the money…" Bryce began, but ran out of breath, and began coughing, blood starting to bubble around the man's lips. He was definitely going to die, and probably quite soon, but it would be annoying if he died before they had a chance to kill him. Bryce had turned out to be a very damaged cog in an otherwise perfect machine, and Moreau wanted nothing more than to boil that cog down to its constituent components.

"Who else knew?" Moreau snapped. "Who did you tell? You gave people information that you actively helped one of them find the Four-Fold Crown, bringing them closer and closer to me."

"Hémery ordered me to look into the books…" spluttered Bryce, and Moreau gave a snort of derision.

"Who else did you tell?" Moreau repeated, and Bryce shook his head. Clearly, however, things weren't moving quick enough for Heroux who whipped the back of his hand across Bryce's face with such savagery that he left a welt.

"Who else did you tell?" bellowed Heroux.

"No one…" Heroux hit him again.

"You're lying!"

"No," Bryce protested weakly, but it came with bubbles, and Moreau knew they had very little time left.

"Listen to me, Bryce," hissed Moreau, getting out of his chair and whispering into the man's ear. "Let me make this absolutely clear to you. You will tell me the truth right now, or I will kill you and your lover."

"No!" Bryce said, and this time some fight returned to his eyes as he struggled to right himself in the chair.

"Tell me!" Moreau said with as much force behind his voice as he could muster.

"You won't…" Bryce said, but Heroux gripped him around the neck, and the man weakly reached up to fight back, flailing and failing.

"Speak!"

"No one," Bryce tried to gasp out.

So well planned out, Moreau reflected. Details checked off, back up plans put into place, trapdoors to ensure that pathways simply led to the wrong exits, but there was always the human element, and that meant there was always room for error. You could never trust anyone completely. No plan could account for the unexpected human emotion.

Why couldn't humans be reliable?

Moreau felt rage grow inside of him, something that he rarely let happen. It was a mixture of frustration and anger, a fury at his impotence in controlling those around him. Moreau tried to breathe deeply; tried to nullify the red haze that seemed to be creeping into his vision, but his usual tactics weren't working. He tried to turn the rage into noise, letting out a bestial howl, but still he saw red. Almost without thinking he grabbed Bryce, and pushed his thumbs into the idiot's eyes, pushing and pushing until he felt them give way, turning into jelly and mush that wrapped itself around his digits like some sort of silly putty.

Somewhere in there, he was fairly certain he heard Bryce scream, but he wasn't entirely sure and the moment had passed.

When he properly looked, he realised that Bryce had as well.

Good. He didn't deserve to have an easy way out.

"Take him to the plant and get rid of him," Moreau said, not even looking at Heroux as he did. Someone passed him wet wipes, which he used to clean his thumbs. Thankfully there was no other mess. He still had to return to the party upstairs.

"Immediately," Heroux said. "Also," he started, but Moreau held up his hand.

"Not now, Heroux, there are guests still here," Moreau said. "I have to get back to them. We still have an energy drink to sell, don't we?"

FIFTH REPORT: NO TANGIBILITY

Dana Spectra spent the next hour introducing herself – or being introduced – to people all around the room, shaking hands, having photos taken (and desperately hoping she wasn't having a photo taken with someone who would turn out to have a very shady past that would come out and she'd be talked about as his friend for the rest of time) and imbibing a lot of Shadow-based cocktails. The music continued to pump as the DJ added a cool African sound over the top of what sounded like standard Western pop rerecorded by local artists. In truth, it went off like a typical launch.

As time ticked on, Dana suddenly realized that there was no sign of Heroux anywhere in the room. She continued to mingle, making small talk and having her photo taken with those that wanted it, but she made sure to keep a look out for where Heroux might have gone. Having done a circle of the room though, he was nowhere to be found.

She chided herself slightly, reflecting that the room was far too large to reasonably assume that he wasn't there, and yet it wasn't like he didn't stand out. She bit her bottom lip, wondering whether to just leave it and not stress, or to act on his disappearance.

"Drink?" came a voice, and Dana turned to see her topless waitress from earlier, a welcoming smile on her face.

"Uh, no," Dana murmured, her mind working overtime. "I was wondering," she said, and her conscience fought with her brain as her mouth worked, "is there anywhere we can go?" She left the sentence hang, and the waitress looked at her, slightly agog. Wrong play, she thought to herself. "Sorry, sorry, it's fine, don't…" Dana said, but the waitress shook her head.

"We could go upstairs," she said, and she looked inviting. "I do have access to the elevators to get drinks, but we could go upstairs, rather than down." Dana cursed herself slightly, as she felt her hormones kick in and mix with the adrenalin. It was wrong to use the girl, definitely wrong. But maybe she could find out where Heroux was and what he was doing.

"You didn't tell me your name," Dana said, coyly, a little disgusted at her own behaviour.

"Liseth," the waitress replied. "Why don't you step this way, ma'am, and I'll show you where you can go." Dana grinned and followed Liseth, as she walked her past the security guard near one of the glass doors that led to the interior upper floors of the building.

"It's so weird," Dana giggled, as Liseth stood in front of her, totally nude, yet covered from foot to neck in black paint. She reached out and traced her finger underneath Liseth's belly, before moving down to between her legs. "Like, I totally want to go down on you, but I'm terrified my tongue will get black and it'll be really obvious." She laughed, and Liseth laughed with her, before the waitress changed positions with Dana, pushing her back against the desk in the office they'd turned up in.

"Then I guess I'll have to do the work, and you'll sit back

and enjoy it," Liseth said playfully. "Typical model snobs. Afraid to get a little body paint on their face for a hot bitch." Dana was slightly surprised at how good Liseth was. The Agent Provocateur black lace G-string was on the floor in a matter of seconds, and Liseth was already underneath the dress, working her magic.

As soon as they had got in the elevator they had started making out, and on a whim, Dana had pressed the top floor button, Liseth far too busy trying to get her tongue down Dana's throat to care about what was going on. As they stumbled out of the lift, Dana was surprised to see that there were on a floor with an open plan, meeting spaces and a single desk scattered around them. If this wasn't either Heroux or Silhouette's office, then it was definitely not what she had been expecting. But given where she was surely there'd have to be something useful around?

The main office area was marked out by a large, Toledo desk on a what appeared to be a silk rug with fascinating African designs. Dana wasn't sure how much the rug cost, but she was willing to be it was five figures – he may have been about conservation, but Silhouette was determined to prove you couldn't do that stylishly. Behind the desk were a number of bookshelves and two closed cabinets. As Dana now sat back on the desk, her legs apart and a hot brunette between them, she closed her eyes, no longer really interested in the space around her. Rather she was more interested in exactly what Liseth would be able to do.

She still felt a little guilty about the situation, but in truth she really hadn't planned on seducing a waitress to get into Silhouette's office. She wasn't even sure why she thought it might be a good idea in the first place. Really it was Heroux that she needed to investigate, and yet even as Justice had spoken about the security chief, Max's idea that Silhouette was the spider at the center of a global web still hit home.

For more reasons than she cared to mention, when she opened her eyes and saw the digital display on the elevator changing, her brain – which had clearly abandoned her earlier to let her sex drive take the con – immediately told her what to do.

She pulled back and closed her legs, getting Liseth up off her knees.

"Someone's coming," she hissed and Liseth's face went pale. Dana grabbed the girl and went behind the desk, grabbing a few of the cupboard doors and opening them. To her delight, her second choice was a cupboard for clothes, with a set of draws and a hanger on the inside. Dana shoved the girl into the cupboard and started to close the door.

"Do not say a word," Dana said, and closed the door on the frightened girl. Hoping against hope that there was a chance Silhouette had mirrored his office furniture, Dana raced to the opposite side of the room and grabbed what she thought might be a matching door and pulled it open. She was wrong; it wasn't exactly the same piece of furniture, but it was a drinks cabinet, and though there wasn't a ton of room, there was enough for her to climb into the cabinet, and sit on the top of it, pushing glasses as far back as they might go, and pressing her head into a wooden piece of shelving that jutted out. She then pulled the cupboard doors closed and released her breath, waiting for what would happen.

The elevator pinged and Dana's heart sank. She had been hoping against hope that it wasn't Silhouette, but she heard the doors slide open and she heard someone step out of them.

Very cautiously, she pressed against the doors so they both started to open a little, but didn't push too far; just enough to create a crack between the two doors that she could see through.

She saw Heroux standing in the room, looking around, before he crossed the floor to one of what appeared to be the meeting spaces. He had crossed out of view, and Dana would only be able to see him if she rearranged herself, but with the glasses of the drink cabinet at her back, she was acutely aware that if she moved, she was going to give her position away very clearly.

There was nowhere to move from where she was without making a noise, and Dana cursed slightly, letting the doors move back into position. She had no way of getting out without drawing attention to herself.

Was that her G-string on the floor?

Dana pushed the door ever-so-slightly and sure enough she saw her satin lingerie on the floor. She needed to get that back. Not just because it gave away her position, but also because it was comfortably over $100, and she wasn't throwing away that money because she'd not bothered to clean up after herself.

There was no sign of Heroux, but Dana kept her ears pricked for the slightest sound. When she heard the elevator door ping, she waited, listening and waiting for the doors to slide shut, hoping that Liseth would have the common sense not to come out of her cupboard. There was a pneumatic hiss and another ping, and Dana waited again, listening to see if there were any more footsteps in the room, but there was nothing.

Deciding to take the risk, Dana pushed the cupboard door open, and stepped out onto the floor. She was grateful for the soft carpet below, and she walked over to her G-string, and bent down to pick it up. As she moved her head up, she felt something touch her head; a small round thing, and she knew exactly what was being pushed into the back of her head.

"Well, don't I feel like a dick," Dana said conversationally.

"Indeed?" Heroux replied, and Dana wondered what his accent was. She had heard him speak French fluently, but she had no idea if he spoke with or without an accent, but there was something about his English that didn't seem quite as though it was from a French speaker.

"Can I get up?"

"I don't see why not." Dana stood up, keeping her panties in her hand, and turned around to see Heroux pointing a gun at her.

"Springfield Hellcat?" Dana said, identifying the weapon instantly.

"You know your guns," Heroux replied, and there was admiration in his voice.

"My Dad knows his way around a pistol," Dana said. "I get that from him. Guns and fashion labels."

"Everyone has to have a hobby."

"May I ask why you're pointing it at me?" Heroux smiled at her.

"Oh, come on," he said, as though they were two old friends trying to kid each other about how great their cars were. "I thought we were going to treat each other with a bit of respect."

"Fair," Dana nodded. "I suppose I probably shouldn't be in this office."

"Are you alone?" Dana's face kicked into neutral, very quickly.

"Who would I come up with?" she asked, staying as bland as possible.

"How did you get up here, if I may?"

"Pick pocketed a pass card from one of the waiters. Don't fire him," Dana added. She reached into her clutch, and Heroux reacted sharply, but Dana withdrew Liseth's pass card and handed it over. "Honestly it's not his fault." Heroux took the card and regarded it for a moment, before sliding it into his pocket.

"Why, though?"

"You wouldn't believe me if I told you," Dana said, wondering what sort of a lie she could possibly come up with.

"Try me," Heroux said, raising an eyebrow.

"I," Dana started, hoping her brain would catch up to her mouth, "have a thing for…well, it's hard to describe. Maybe places of power?"

"This office is a place of power?"

"Well, Silhouette is pretty powerful, this office is his…I came to…" Dana left the sentence hang in the air, hoping that Heroux's imagination would fill in the details she couldn't be bothered too. He looked at her, a smile coming to his face slightly, then he chuckled. Dana gave a small laugh, and his laugh got a little bigger.

"I like you, Spectra," Heroux said. "You're inventive, I'll give you that. But here's the thing, I was at the Miss Green Earth pageant. I was at the Casino de Monte Carlo when you made a scene, as I recollect. Honestly, I thought not much of it, but I also knew that Cisneros had then died, and there was always something about the incident at the Casino that bothered me. You just seem a little too unreal, I think. I've read a lot about you, and the idea that you came up here to get off in Mr Moreau's chair isn't that unbelievable to me. But I also know that you've been on a big hunt for the person who killed McAteer, and someone like you, with your interest in sex and booze wouldn't waste that much effort going to Congo-Kinshasa of all places. So, there's something about you that just doesn't sit right."

"That pageant is going to haunt me," Dana joked, but it was a little soulless. Heroux had the look of a cat who had finally cornered a mouse, and even though the mouse was almost definitely going to exhaust all possibilities of escape, the fact was that the cat would almost inevitably be able to catch it. And then break it. No, less a cat and more a dog.

A wolf.

His face was lean, his eyes narrow, and he had a lupine smile on his face that made him look evil. It was a dramatic word, hyperbolic and overstated, but Dana couldn't think of any other word to describe the man in front of her. He had definitely killed people. There was nothing in his face that suggested any form of understanding or sympathy for the person he pointed a gun at.

What could drive a person to see life as something so meaningless?

"I might take that," Heroux said, and indicated the sheer panties Dana was holding. She sighed, deeply, and then handed them across.

"I had you pegged for a pervert," she said. "I'm guessing it has to do with scars, right? You want your revenge against the society that turned its back on you when you became disfigured.

No woman would sleep with you, so you forced them to, and the power gave you a thrill. When did you realise you couldn't come without looking at the terror in her eyes?"

The amateur psychologist trick worked, which was surprising, because Dana hadn't really thought she could pull it off, but the anger on his face was real, as she had touched a very sensitive nerve. For a moment she thought he would simply hit her, but instead he lunched forward, his hands going between Dana's leg, and she wondered what he planned.

Rather than grab her, however, he had gone for her dress, his hand grabbing the side of the slit, and he went to rip it back, but before he could he was interrupted.

"Heroux, please, please. That dress is comfortably $1500 US, I would have said," came a smooth voice, and Heroux released the slit, standing up to acknowledge the entrance of Silhouette Moreau. Dana hadn't even heard the elevator that time.

The ever-present Chillo a step behind; though this time she was carrying – a Walther PPK Black. Dana had to admire the gun; single and double action trigger, .380 calibre, 6 rounds capacity with 1 in the barrel, and weighing 584 grams. When Dana had been introduced to guns, she had shot a Walther very early on, and she had always been impressed with it.
Heroux, meanwhile, had not enjoyed being put back on a leash.

"She has her own scar that she can't live with," Heroux spat, and Dana winced, appreciating how personally Heroux had taken her attack.

"She has indeed," Silhouette said. "Hello Dana. I think I have the right to ask you what you're doing in my office."

"Apparently she came here to masturbate," Heroux said,

laughing hollowly.

"Interesting," Silhouette said, clearly disinterested. "Dana, I don't know what is going on. I honestly don't. But I do know you met with the Four-Fold Crown, and as much as I would like to think they kept their mouths shut, I'm not sure I can totally trust them too. Particularly as Asha has disappeared. Which makes me think that maybe you know something that you shouldn't."

"I don't get why," Dana said abruptly. "McAteer, why? Why target him?" Moreau gave a slight smile.

"Dana, Dana, Dana. I'm sure I don't know what you're talking about." He grinned, and his white teeth shone brightly. With the dim lighting, Moreau melted into the shadows perfectly, with only his eyes and teeth picking him out. He was like a wraith, moving around the room with no tangibility.

"What do we do with her?" Heroux asked.

"Yes, what do we do with her," Moreau mused. "The thing is Dana, and this hurts me because I really do like you, I need to get rid of this building. I've a feeling that my operation in Africa has been compromised. You going to the Congo, then coming here...it's just too risky to assume you're really that lucky. Mr Heroux is right. You were clearly an albatross to dear old Librada Cisneros. I don't think I want you becoming one to me."

"So that means, what? You're going to kill me?" Dana asked, fear gripping her, though she was determined not to show it.

"No, no, not at all. In fact, you being here is rather convenient." Moreau turned to summon the elevator. "There's a fire starting on the floors below, maybe arson by an intruder? And then you came up here. Because you were going to break into my office, I suppose, but the thing is, you had badly miscalculated and while you were up here, the building below burned. You are a silly thing." He walked up to Heroux and removed the panties, turning to Dana and handing them over. "I think I do believe the bit about you masturbating on my chair. Maybe you should to that. It might take your mind off being burnt alive."

"Thanks," Dana said wryly, taking the underwear. "You're sick."

"Sick in a good way?"

"No." Moreau smiled at her.

"I'll accept that," he conceded. Behind him the elevator pinged, and he turned and entered it, followed by Heroux. "Good luck Dana. I'm sorry it had to end like this, but on the plus side, we will dedicate all future Shadow activities to you. In fact, we'll start a charity in your name. It will be wonderful. You're an inspiration to us all." Chillo gave her a final look, and to Dana's surprise there was a slight grin on her face. Then she followed her boss. Silhouette reached forward and pressed a button, and the elevator doors slid shut.

SIXTH REPORT: GOING OUT

Dana pulled the door to the cupboard open to find Liseth cowering in the corner, her hands over her eyes.

"Come on," she said, and then quickly went to Moreau's desk and took out her phone, swiping and tapping so she got the download app again, and synched her phone to his computer, starting the download.

"What are you doing?" Liseth asked, panicked, but Dana just shook her head.

"See if you can call the elevator," Dana said, without looking up. The data transfer on her phone was surprisingly slow, and she began to wonder if Moreau's systems might have something in them that was stopping the download. Seventeen percent. This was going to take forever.

"Won't they be at the bottom waiting for us, if we take the elevator?" Liseth said, still not quite keeping a grip.

"I don't think so," Dana said. "I'm more worried about the fire." Liseth looked at her, eyes wide and this time she was clearly about to lose control.

"What fire?" she bellowed.

"Did you not hear that in the cupboard?" Dana wondered, but Liseth's look was enough to answer the question.

"I think I'm just terrified out of my mind right now, and I

can't work out why you're not!"

"I'll be terrified later," Dana said, giving a tight smile to the other woman. Twenty-two percent. Fire alarms started going off around them.

Bloody hell!

"The elevator isn't coming, I don't think," Liseth said.

"How many floors up are we?"

"Nineteen."

Farrrrkk...

"OK," Dana muttered grimly. "Guess we aren't jumping out of a window then." She looked up to see Liseth at the doors of the elevator, seemingly trying to pry them apart. "What are you doing?"

"Can't we open the doors and climb down the shaft?"

"Not like that, I don't think," Dana said. "We'd need like a crowbar or..." She trailed off as she looked around the office, hoping to find something that they might be able to wedge between the doors and then force them open. Table, chair, paper, pen...Oh... Dana grabbed a tablet off the table, realizing that it was clearly not powered up. She came over to Liseth, and the pair tried to slide the tablet between the doors, and to Dana's surprise they were successful. Together, their hands on each door, they dragged the doors open, and Dana stuck a leg up and angled herself so she could push the door open, but not destroy her heels.

Liseth scrambled underneath the leg, and looked down, but Dana didn't need her to confirm anything. She could hear the sounds of a fire in the shaft, and even from this high up, the heat was being funneled up and out. As was the smoke. Dana waited until Liseth had pulled her head back, and then withdrew and fell on the floor as the doors slid shut behind them.

"What the fuck do we do?" Liseth asked, now clearly panicked beyond belief.

What the fuck indeed, mused Dana. Though not for long, because she could feel herself becoming just as panicked as her new friend. There was no time to be sitting around. She jumped up and quickly dashed to the table, only to be tremendously disappointed to see that the download was up to thirty-one percent. She wasn't going to get the data and get out alive, she thought. She then dashed across to one side of the room, cursing the fact that the room seemed to take up the entire floor, and that it was way too far to get across it in a hurry.

The windows didn't open – of course they didn't – but there did seem to be a door that led onto a balcony of some sort. She tried the handle, relieved to find that it actually opened, and then stepped out and looked over the balcony edge, before almost losing her balance.

The nineteenth floor was much higher up than she thought it would be. In the back of her mind, she had an idea that maybe they could make their way down the building one floor at a time, if somehow, they could find rope and swing down floor by floor.

If every floor had a balcony.

If they could get down nineteen floors before the building was consumed in fire.

Because by the time they made it lower and lower the floors would definitely be a fireball.

Dana cupped her face in her hands, which was

something she had taught herself never to do when you were wearing makeup. It just wasn't worth the risk. Now, though, when things genuinely seemed a little bit helpless, smudging makeup was the least of her concerns.

She went back into the open floor office, her mind wondering if there was any point checking the other side of the building to see if it was any different, and even though she thought it was pointless, she still decided to race across the room (brief pause – thirty-five percent…was it going slower now?) to pull the door to the other side. She looked over the edge, and realized that it was the same situation.

As she walked inside, she realised Liseth speaking to her.

"What's the situation like?"

"Not good," Dana replied, a little distractedly.

"The doors to the elevator are getting hot," Liseth added, not very helpfully, and Dana sort of took note of what she had heard.

"Does Silhouette live in Yamoussoukro?" Dana asked, and Liseth looked at her blankly.

"I don't know."

"Surely not. At least not all the time. Like, even if he does, he's always everywhere else, right? So, he comes here. And he's definitely a private helicopter man, right?" Dana looked at Liseth, not sure what answer she was expecting.

"You think there's a helicopter on the roof?" Liseth asked, hope suddenly filling her eyes.

"Well, there's definitely gotta be a helipad up there, right? So there has to be a way to the roof."

"So, we find our way to the roof?" Liseth's voice was suddenly filled with excitement, and both women went to the balcony door, Dana pointing Liseth to one end, while she took the other. They raced to the respective corners of the building, and to Dana's delight she saw a stairway leading up. She was about to check it, but then turned and remembered her phone. It was all or nothing now.

"Stairwell around the corner. Go," Dana urged Liseth, as she passed the woman on her way back inside Moreau's office. She grabbed her phone from the desk, disappointed to see that it had only reached forty-eight percent, but sighed and stuck it in her clutch, which she also grabbed. With a quick look back at the room, she headed out again, following Liseth up the stairwell to the roof.

Silhouette Moreau had allowed himself to be escorted from his building by security, and indeed everyone else was being led out. Photographers were still busy snapping, but fire was wrapping itself around the base of the building, creating a strange sort of flower-like effect, where the fire was the petals of a concrete and glass stamen. It was an oddly beautiful site, and Moreau hoped that someone was capturing it. He wanted to put an image of it in the new building that would ultimately take its place. Silhouette Systems always had its heart in Yamoussoukro and even if that physical heart was burned, the spiritual heart would wait until it had a new body to fill.

Oh, he rather liked that. Yes, that would be in the speech he would give to the board members tomorrow.

"We got Bryce's remains into the car and we're taking

him to the facility," Heroux murmured, standing beside his boss so that he could speak at a volume that no one else would hear.

"Good, good," muttered Silhouette. "I want to blame it on him."

"We can't really do that without the corpse, can we?"

"Of course we can. If he got incinerated in the building, that's on him, isn't it? Anyway, it's not like the police will question us too closely about this. There's a reason we have the arrangement we have." Heroux nodded at this. It was certainly true they had an understanding with the police in case something like this should rear its head.

"What about the girl?" Heroux asked.

"Hmmm," Silhouette murmured. "I think I'll keep my promise. We shall be devastated by her death, and we'll definitely start a charity in her name. All the rest."

"Do we inform the family?"

"Oh, no. That's the police's job. No, it's time we made our exit, I think. I have places to be, and you have a job to do." Heroux nodded and turned to go back to the car. Moreau took one last look at his building and sighed. He had quite liked the building to be honest. But its destruction solved a lot of problems in one fell swoop, and any other irritants could be swept away and blamed on the fire.

It really was cleansing.

Now twenty stories above the city, Dana braced herself as the wind blew at her, and glanced across to Liseth feeling sorry for the girl. She was, after all, wearing nothing more than a black thong and black paint, and from the look of her nipples she was clearly very cold. They needed to be out of the area as quickly as possible.

And for once, things seemed to be working out OK, because on the helipad in front of them was a helicopter.

Dana's father had taught her about guns, and she had taken an exceptional interest in fashion, but vehicles were low down on her list of things to memorise, and even if she had them higher, the truth was that helicopters were unlikely to be high up on the list anyway. As a result, when she looked at the helicopter all she saw was a black helicopter, with the distinctive Silhouette Systems logo on it.

It had a cabin, obviously, like all helicopters, and there was a single rotor on the top with a smaller one on the tail towards the back. It looked...well, not small (and relatively small), but also not big. It wasn't one of those massive ones where you could get an army into. This was smaller than the chopper that they had flown to Yamoussoukro in, but still not tiny.

Dana ran up to the door to the cockpit and pulled, somewhat astonished to find it opened for her.

"Hey!" she called back to Liseth. "Quick!" and she climbed in to the cockpit. A part of her – one of those ridiculously cocky parts that could confidently predict you would be able to name at least thirty American states before you got to seven and realized that it was pretty unlikely – thought that flying the plane would be simple. She had definitely seen the pilot of the other chopper fly it, and he didn't seem to be doing much more than pushing his joystick back and forth.

There was obviously more to it than that, though as she looked across the panel in front of her, filled with lights and switches, she hoped that it wasn't *that* much more. Rather delightfully there was a key on the panel and Dana turned it, hoping that something might happen. Liseth had now got in on the other side, and was looking expectantly at her, so Dana gave the panel some more scrutiny and decided to take a gamble. She lifted the little red plastic covering beside the key and flicked the switch underneath it, whereupon the blades above them started to slowly revolve, and Dana looked to her side and gave her partner a confident smirk.

Across the panels lights were flicking on, and dials were springing into life, along with the small monitor, none of which made any sense to Dana at all, but as she glanced out the window, she could now see that smoke was billowing up around the building and the fire was clearly growing at an exponential rate. The noise of the rotor began to drown out the noises around them, and Dana wondered if she heard a crack…or was she just imagining it? If the roof was about to cave in, she needed to get them up quickly.

Beside her there was what appeared to be the handbrake in a car, and thought it was down, Dana wondered if perhaps it served a similar function, but acted in reverse. Swallowing, she grabbed the lever and pulled. To both ladies' astonishment, the chopper began to rise, and Liseth quickly grabbed the seatbelts to wrap around herself.

The chopper continued to rise, and Dana released the handbrake (though that was almost definitely not what it was) and pushed the joystick forward, to which the machine responded in kind, moving forward. Feeling more positive, she stretched her feet forward, but when her right foot pushed on a pedal, the helicopter swung sharply to the right, and Dana heard Liseth squeal in fear.

"Don't push the pedals," Dana said, but she couldn't be heard. Oh! Headphones... She shook her head trying to sort out what she was thinking, and pushed the left pedal gently, relieved that the helicopter responded and bought her back around to where she was.

Looking out ahead of her, Dana could see Lake Yamoussoukro, and she wondered if she could get to the other side of the lake and somehow land the helicopter.

There was a sudden rush of smoke and wind, and Dana twisted around to look back, watching as the building began to crumble in on itself. Below, through the smoke and fire, bathed in merrigold, amber, squash and bronze, the streets below were gathering vehicles and spectators. Dana suspected that Silhouette Moreau and his lapdog were definitely away from the drama at this point. There was no way they were going to hang around on the off chance that they might be killed, or at the very least spoken to.

Dana pushed the joystick forward, and the helicopter moved in response, but she noticed that some of the lights that had been green were now amber, or worse, red, and a dial was dipping.

Of course there was no petrol in the machine. It was probably a piece of rubbish anyway, which is why Moreau didn't care that it was still on the roof when the building came down. If something seems too easy, it probably is. Dana sighed heavily and wondered if it was worth putting on a headset to communicate with anyone.

Would the police have helicopters in Yamoussoukro?

Probably.

She didn't initially notice the helicopter start to dip, and when it did, she pulled the joystick up, but rather than pull up, the machine started to reverse a little, and Dana realized that the joystick was working on one particular plane while the pedals and "handbrake" worked the other two. She grabbed the "handbrake" and pulled it up, pushing the joystick forward, but it did little to address the steadily downward motion the helicopter was taking, and Dana risked a brief glimpse up to confirm what she already knew deep down – the rotor blades were definitely getting slower.

Lights began to blink, and Dana pushed forward, hoping against hope that it might move them forwards faster. By now she thought they only had really one option – if they crashed (and that was more a when than an if) into Lake Yamoussoukro they might be able to walk away relatively unscathed.

"Hey," Dana turned to Liseth and shouted, trying to remain relatively calm. "I think we're going to land in the lake."

Actually, it was quite impressive how calm she sounded. *Maybe I should ask Christa to get me an acting job.*

"On what? I thought you needed to land on solid ground?"

"Well," Dana paused, trying not to inspire fear and panic, "I think we're running out of fuel."

"Right," Liseth said, and Dana looked at her in surprise. "What?"

"I thought you'd be more bothered by that," Dana admitted.

"Oh, I'm sitting virtually naked in a helicopter that's about to crash into a lake full of crocodiles. I am fucking freaking out." Dana looked at her, a sinking feeling in her stomach.

"What do you mean, a lake full of crocodiles?"

"All the lakes in Yamoussoukro are connected. The crocodiles can get from one to the other when they are smaller, and so they are all full of crocodiles." Liseth returned Dana's look, and Dana could feel herself wanting to cry.

"So, we crash, and then if we survive that, we have to get out of that lake before the crocodiles get us?"

"I guess so," Liseth said.

"This," Dana started and could feel her voice tremble.

Cut it out, Spectra. Get a hold of yourself!

"This is not a great day," she finished. To her surprise, Liseth reached across and took her hand, squeezing it.

"We got this," Liseth said, smiling at her.

"Do we?"

"Well, if we don't, we're going to get eaten, so...we got this." Dana looked at her, a little surprised at how the woman was so calm.

"OK, well...let's do this," Dana said. She looked forward, taking in the path ahead of them, though it didn't look particularly good. Ideally, she wanted to crash the helicopter as close to the edge of a lake as possible, but if it was too shallow, they might end up getting badly hurt. Too deep, and it would take too long to escape the crocodiles.

Oh, if only I'd minded my own business.

Behind them, the Silhouette Systems building had been brought completely to its knees, and emergency services were out in full force trying to contain the blaze. Buildings on either side had presumably been evacuated, but the Silhouette building had been designed well, and when it collapsed it had done virtually no damage to the smaller buildings around it.

The helicopter continued to dip, and Dana pointed it towards what she hoped would be the best place to set down. It was far enough from the shore that it wouldn't do any damage, but not too far that they would have to risk the crocodiles. If they were lucky, the blades might cause enough disturbance to force the animals back.

"Brace for impact!" Dana shouted, and then couldn't help but smile. She'd always wanted to say that. She was fairly certain that the helicopter had lost all motive power, as though the lights were all on, she couldn't really hear the blades rotating. With a rough bump, the helicopter hit the water, throwing its passengers back in their chairs, but in truth, it wasn't that bad. Liseth was already unbuckling her straps and Dana abandoned her controls, pulling at her own safety harness.

Stagnant water started seeping into the cockpit, pooling around their feet, and Dana wondered what exactly it was that she was smelling – the water, or perhaps fuel. She was fairly certain she could tell the difference, but at that moment she didn't entirely trust her senses. A part of her was absolutely convinced that she could see a crocodile just outside the cockpit, but when she looked properly, she couldn't see anything. Panic was definitely playing havoc with her senses.

Free from their straps, Dana pulled her pumps off (devastated that they were clearly now ruined), and pushed at the door to the cockpit, though it remained firmly shut.

"What's going on?" Liseth asked, but Dana simply grunted in response. Opening the door was the top priority and she suspected that the crash had pushed the frame of the vehicle out of shape, locking the door firmly in place.

"Can you open your door?" Dana asked, and Liseth turned to twist the handle, which popped off in her hands. Dana issued forth a sound which was distinctly unladylike, and then with a howl of anger, kicked out at her door, which gave a resounding thud, but refused to give way. Twisting around, she kicked out at the opposite door, and this flung open, though her temper almost saw her kick her new friend in the face. Once the door was open, Dana grabbed her clutch – feeling the reassuring rectangle of her mobile – and moved forward, coming face to face with a crocodile.

Since encountering Interpol for the first time, Dana had thought she had become much braver, and was able to take a lot more things in her stride, and in fairness she stood by that belief, despite the fact that, in many ways, it was undermined by her screaming ridiculously loudly at the sight of the horrid, Cretaceous face. It opened its mouth and Dana immediately concluded that she had reached the end of the line. Nice life, well done – you enjoyed it a lot, had lots of sex, alcohol and partying, but everyone has to tie it up sometime. Bonus points for going out in style; after all, who could say that they were eaten by a crocodile in a helicopter in the Ivory Coast? It was nothing, of not unique.

She was, however, loath to throw it all away without a fight. Always go down screaming, her biological sister had once said, and armed with only a shoe and a clutch, Dana swung the heel with her left hand, and pierced the crocodile's eye. The reaction was immediate, though surprisingly without fanfare. It didn't howl or even grunt, rather it snapped its jaw shut, blowing a putrid stench in the women's direction, from which they both recoiled, and pulled back into the water. The effort to seek out this prey had become, it decided, a little too difficult, and so it went to rethink its strategy, sinking into the gloomy depths it had come from.

"Come on," Dana said, grabbing Liseth's arm and pulling her forward, as she stepped out of the chopper and into the water in front of them. They were quite close to the shore, and so the journey to safety would be quick. Quite why she thought there wouldn't be any other crocodiles showed a surprising naiveite on Dana's part, and she felt foolish as she planted a foot directly onto another crocodile, which twisted with surprising force, knocking her back into the helicopter.

However, before the crocodile could claim a victim, the side of its face exploded, and like its friend from earlier it sank into the depths, though whether it was as alive as its fellow was a matter up for debate.

"Come on!" came a thick French accent, and Dana grabbed Liseth's hand again and this time they pelted forward onto the shore, up to Max Travere, whom Dana hugged instantly, before turning and pulling Liseth into the hug. It felt very reassuring to feel the two live bodies beside her after everything.

"You coming out of the water with a topless woman, having killed a crocodile with a high heel shoe is very on brand for you," Justice Kennedy said with a wry grin, and Dana looked at her with all the disdain she could muster.

"Why don't…" she started, but Justice held up her hand, which had a clearly smoking gun in it.

"Before you tell me to fuck off, I just saved your life," Justice said. "Again." For a moment it looked as though Dana

304

might have another fight, but Justice was surprised at what came next.

"Thanks," the Australian said. "Thank you. I appreciate it. A lot."

"Don't tell me you're going to hug me," Justice replied in mock shock.

"Let's not go too far."

"Too late," winked Justice, but Dana just shook her head.

"We should probably go," Max said, and Dana turned to see a crowd was gathering on the sidewalk. "We can get away with a lot in Yamoussoukro, but there's still a limit." Justice quickly hid her gun, and Max walked them to a nearby car. No authorities seemed to be coming, though they were probably dealing with the collapse of Silhouette Systems. Discretion being the better part of valor won out, and the foursome disappeared into the night in a very old, yellow Toyota Corolla.

SEVENTH REPORT: RATHER PERFECT

"It's pretty corrupted," Ashley Frost said, and Dana buried her head in her pillow and tried not to scream.

"I didn't exactly have a lot of time on my hands," she pouted, when she pulled herself back to the conversation.

"Oh, the building thing, and the fire..." Ashley started, but drifted off as she continued to analyse the data she had been given.

"Is there anything there?"

"You know I'm still sifting through the Four-Fold Crown's data, right? There's *lots* there. I mean *lots!* I could spend hours on that stuff."

"Ashley, focus," Dana growled. "This is important now. Then you can go back to the Crown's stuff."

"I am focused," Ashley grumbled. "There's not a lot of information here, except I can tell you that there's a research station for Silhouette Systems not too far from where you are. There's a lake or something nearby, I dunno..." She trailed off again, sifting through data, and Dana tried her best not to interrupt the hacker. "There's something odd about the data though, I have to admit. Maybe it's just missing or...it's..."

"Odd?" Dana wondered.

"Well, yeah, exactly," Ash agreed, and Dana buried her

face in the pillow again.

"Please tell me what is odd," she finally said.

"Oh, right, all the plans and promotionals are squarely aimed at the under 70s."

"That's not exactly unusual," Dana said, wondering if she was missing the point.

"No, I mean, the current promotionals are geared towards a complete audience, worldwide conquest, etc, etc. Shadow in everyone's fridge by the end of the year."

"Oh, Shadow," Dana said, surprised at this. "Well, that makes it more normal that it's not targeting the over 70s."

"Except I just said it is," Ashley said, and her glasses looked up, giving a strange reflection that made it look like she simply had two glowing orbs in her face. "But next year's strategies don't mention the over 70s at all."

"Maybe they are going to test the market for that age group, but aren't doing any long-term planning?"

"Or maybe the information is missing," Ash carried on. "I dunno. It's just odd. I'm not sure why it's annoying me. But there is a research project going on there."

"At the research station?" Dana asked, and bit her tongue, wishing it hadn't come out quite so bitchy. Fortunately, Ashley didn't seem to notice.

"Yeah, which is very close to the Shadow bottling plant." Both women looked at each other through their phones, their minds coming to the same conclusion.

"What would you guys do?"

"Oh, we'd go in and investigate for sure," Ashley grinned.

"Take a look inside a research station that's probably highly guarded and definitely has something worth protecting from the rest of the world."

"Even if there isn't something suspicious going on, and let's face it, that's highly unlikely," Ashely said, managing to drawl out "highly" for more seconds than was necessary, "you could very legitimately be accused of industrial espionage."

"Well, that makes things a lot easier," Dana mumbled.

"Is there another towel?" a voice came from the bathroom, and Ashley's eyes widened in surprise.

"Did I interrupt something?" she asked, seeming both mortified and horrified at the same time.

"It's just a," Dana paused wondering what to say. "IT's just a friend I met when trying to escape a fiery inferno in a crashing helicopter before almost being eaten by a crocodile."

"Oh, thank god," Ash grinned. "I mean, rumours of your feminine wiles are a little legendary, but I don't know if I want to see them up close."

"Oh, you definitely want to see them up close, babe," Dana said, giving Ash her "total smirk" look. "I'll talk later," she added, and switched off the phone, suppressing her laughter at the look on Ash's face, which was a priceless mask of absolute shock.

"This is not a bad hotel, is it?" Liseth said, coming out of the bathroom, wrapped in a towel. Dana realized it was the first time she had seen her without the black paint all over her body, and as a result, the bruises were now on display.

"You've taken a beating," Dana grinned, and Liseth echoed her, before twisting to display a particularly nasty bruise on her thigh.

"Crash," she said. "And the shin one is where I banged it backing away from the crocodile. Honestly, I think I'm about ready to go back to Australia."

"I might know some people who can help you out with that, if you'd like," Dana said, and Liseth smiled gratefully. "Order some room service, and I'll go and talk to people who know people." Dana grabbed her phone and then got up and headed for the door, hearing Liseth flop back down on the bed gratefully.

"Enjoying a little bit of downtime, we're we?" Justice smarmed and Dana just shook her head at the older woman.

"Downtime?" Max asked curiously.

"Dana has a reputation to uphold," Justice said. "Well, more a body count."

"At least mine are satisfied when they leave," Dana snapped back.

"Weren't you?" Justice asked, and Dana wondered if she physically portrayed her mental flinch.

"I'd prefer to have a sexual body count than a corpse body count," Dana said, and Justice remained stony, the smile on her face no longer reaching her eyes. Dana wasn't sure why she had said it, reflecting that Justice had indeed saved her life recently, but every time she looked at the American, she thought about Guin and how that relationship had been snatched away from her by Justice. Even now, when she closed her eyes, sometimes the pale redhead would appear before her and Dana would feel the stab, tears pricking at her eyes at the unfairness of never being able to see Guin again. Justice would remain a constant reminder of Guin's death, and Dana wasn't sure if she would ever be able to let it go.

"OK, so clearly a lot of unresolved issues," Max said, and Dana thought she detected a slight note of jealousy in the man's voice. "You said you were going to have some data scanned. Did you get anything?"

"Maybe," Dana replied. "There's a research project going on at a Silhouette Systems laboratory not far from here."

"How far is not far?" Justice asked, and Dana looked a little guilty.

"I'm still working on that. But the laboratory is very close to where they actually produce Shadow."

"What does that prove?" Max asked, and Dana paused. It had all seemed quite logical when she had been talking to Ash, but now that she was being faced with questions that seemed to undermined the entirety of what she was saying she felt...well, undermined.

"You can't deny he tried to kill me," Dana pointed out, trying to get back onto safer ground.

"Well, we can, because only you saw that," Justice replied.

"OK, well, in that case, bye, I'll see you later, sorry to be wasting your time," Dana snapped, and Justice had the grace to look shamefaced.

"I believe you," Justice said. "I'm just being a bitch." She paused for a moment and then, to Dana's surprise said "Sorry." Dana tried not to look surprised but failed. Justice gave a little shrug and Max clearly felt it was time to intercede again.

"We accept he tried to kill you, but that doesn't

automatically mean that a secret research project he's working on is illegal. Lots of companies do that."

"I assume you want to break in and find out what's going on?" Justice added, and Dana felt flustered, unable to defend her desire, but equally unable to deny that was exactly what she wanted to do. She felt her phone buzz, and was about to ignore it, but frustration made her grab it out and look at what had been sent to her. It was from Ash, and she was about to put it away when she noticed that it was an image.

Odd.

Dana swiped her phone open and looked at the image that had been sent to her.

"The Project is called The Solution," Dana said, and the two agents opposite her looked slightly surprised. As Dana scrolled down the image she saw something which utterly convinced her she was on the right track. "Take a guess who was the lead researcher on it." Dana looked at the other two who exchanged a look, before shrugging and turning back to Dana.

"Go on," Max offered. Dana turned her phone around, the image on it now expanded, clearly making out exactly who was the head researcher.

Dr Thomas McAteer.

Dana approached her bedroom, followed by Max, who was in full flow.

"Once Justice has clearance we can head straight on in," he was saying, suddenly quite enthusiastic about the idea of breaking into a Silhouette Systems office.

"Do you think Justice will actually get permission?" Dana

asked. "I thought that maybe we were pushing our luck by suggesting it. You were the one that pointed out it was a loose thread we were following." Max shrugged, clearly not going to be put off his new plan.

"Well, it might be a loose thread, but there's no denying what he did to you, and if we can get the proof that we need, we'll be able to act more formally." As he spoke, his hand connected with Dana's back and she felt a slight frisson from his touch. He was very good looking, she decided. His dark wavy hair complemented the brown skin, and his eyes were a gentle amber colour. His lips, though…they were a really nice shape, not too wide, not too thin. Her mind wandered, wondering what it might be like to kiss him. There was definitely something engaging about the man.

At her hotel door, she slid the key into the lock and twisted it, but the hair on the back of her neck stood up. There was something not quite right. The television set was on, quite soft, and she could smell food that had been ordered, but there was something off that her senses were alerting her to. How long ago would Liseth had ordered the food?

Dana stepped into the room, placing her hand on Max's chest as she moved. He, on the other hand, reached around and pulled out his gun from the back of his trousers, leaning around to see over her. He didn't try to push forward, and Dana appreciated the consideration.

Liseth was on the bed, and she heard Max breath in, clearly embarrassed. The woman was on the bed completely naked. She was rather perfect, Dana reflected, and noted that her full breasts sat upright, clearly the result of plastic surgery. The rest of her body was nicely toned, giving great shape around the stomach and thighs. Her legs were actually apart, and it was that more than anything else that made Dana realise something was wrong – if Liseth had been hoping that something more would happen between Dana and her that night, she might indeed remain naked on the bed, but she wouldn't leave her legs open.

Dana looked at the woman's chest and noted there was no movement. She set her jaw, hardening her heart, and focused on making sure the room was empty. The windows were open, the curtains blowing out. Max pushed open the door to the bathroom, and so Dana moved across to confirm her initial verdict. She placed her fingers under Liseth's nose, but there was nothing. Gently she ran her fingers over the body, and realized that she was still warm, the skin still slightly goose-fleshed, the nipples still hard. Had Liseth been raped? There were bruises on the woman's body, but they may very well have been from earlier. She hoped that the legs being apart was more a message than proof of anything else.

Max had joined her, and moved Liseth's head from side to side, looking at Dana when he touched Liseth, clearly coming to the same conclusion that the Australian had. Dana ran her hands over Liseth's arm, sliding her hand into the dead girl's and squeezing it.

Poor Liseth. She gently kissed the girl's forehead, a tear forming in her eye. They had barely known each other, but…once again the unfairness of life reared its head and Dana wanted to rage against it.

As she pulled her hand from Liseth's, she noticed a mark on the deceased girl's wrist. She turned the hand to look at it more clearly, and Max leaned forward, running his finger over it. Dana did the same, feeling the little bumps around the two pin pricks.

"Poisoned?"

"Maybe paralyzed first," Max murmured, and his hand gently moved across the lower part of Liseth's body, his meaning clear.

"Two pricks," Dana said. "I hope she fought back." Max pursed his lips, and shook his head.

"Fuck permission. We go to Silhouette now."

EIGHTH REPORT: SAN PÉDRO

Locating Silhouette Systems' research and development building was not an easy task, until Justice had pointed out that it was allegedly right next door to the Shadow production plant which would be extremely easy to track down, and she was – of course – absolutely correct. As Justice pointed out the location on Google Maps, Dana and Max had rather shamefacedly nodded in agreement with the adroit logic.

They were on a plane in a surprisingly short time, though Dana did pause to find out how Asha was doing. She had called her friend, and was reassured to discover the influencer was fine, though Asha said they needed to talk.

They certainly did, Dana reflected. Asha had a lot of explaining to do, but ultimately it would be for another time.

San Pédro Airport was more impressive than Dana had expected it to be, given they were going to a city which had a population of about 160,000 people.

"It's a commune," Max said to her on the flight. "It's made up of about, oh, I want to say thirty villages. None of them are particularly big; in fact, I think one might be quite tiny. Maybe only about 150 people? But they are all clustered together and called San Pédro. Gbamin is from there." Dana looked at him blankly when he delivered this fact. "Gbamin? Jean-Phillipe

Gbamin? The footballer?" Dana's blank look became withering. "You don't like football?" The astonishment in his voice was palpable and Dana heard Justice laughing. "You like football, right?" Max said to Justice who gave a slight smile and shrugged. "An Australian and an American and neither like football. How is that even possible?" Dana was both surprised and amused that he remained quiet for the rest of the trip, as though the fact was too much for him to get past.

Once back on land, they checked through the airport which was quite lax in its security protocols, and were soon on their way into the city in a rackety old taxi cab that was both yellow and extremely quaint. They were grateful that the driver spoke French, though he assured Max, who then passed the message on, that they might not get as lucky with other places in San Pédro. It was a small little city and foreigners didn't play a big part. Once again, Dana noticed the ever-present rough dirt roads painting the city in a distinct shade of tawny, something that felt like it might be the national colour of the *Côte d'Ivoire.*

Max had given her a little more information about the city on arrival, all of which boiled down to the fact that it was heavily reliant on fishing, and also was the second biggest port in the country – which was arguably not saying much. It did, however, explain why the Shadow factory was located where it was.

San Pédro wrapped itself around the Lagune Digboué, with San Pédro airport sitting neatly between the two parts of the city. The smaller part – the part that was directly on the coast – had the Port Autonome de San Pédro on the west side of the city, as far away from Lagune Digboué as it was possible to get. On the coastal side of San Pédro the city sort of stopped before it got to the lagoon, but then seemed to suddenly remembered it existed, and a small little village bridged the coast and the lagoon on its western side. The eastern side was their destination, however.

Squatting in front of the lagoon on the eastern side, and contrasting strongly with the emerald and amber of the countryside around it, the grim grey block of concrete looked like God himself had dropped something particularly unpleasant and wasn't keen to pick it back up again. Standing on the edge of the lagoon, Dana lifted her binoculars to take the sight in again.

She and Justice had worn a long dress over their long shirts and trousers, and an equally long scarf wrapped around their heads to hide their features. Dana's backpack was hidden under dress as well. As they had got out of the taxi and Max paid, they noticed the looks of suspicion from the locals, who regarded them with a very healthy disdain.

"Don't take it personally," Max shrugged. "The Ivory Coast doesn't have a healthy relationship with white people. We abolished slavery in the early 1900s, but that doesn't mean much when you have companies who still effectively enslave the population to harvest the cocoa. People in San Pédro have it a little better because they have their fishing industry, but if you're struggling, there's always the option to go and work for the big American chocolate companies and get paid just enough to survive." He was angry, but Dana wasn't sure who at exactly. She had to admit it was a little hard to connect, but not for the first time since her quest to discover who had killed Thomas McAteer, Dana realized that her life in Australia which was better than most generally, was a long way removed from what was going on in

Africa.

The decision to leave the village and head to the lagoon was something both women were keen on; even Justice seemed a little outside her comfort zone when confronting the stark reality of life in *Côte d'Ivoire*.

As such the three of them stood (well, Dana stood, the other two sat) on the lagoon's beach and examined the Shadow production plant. It hadn't taken any of them too long to see the smaller building to the left of Shadow. A brief glance gave Dana the impression it had been made out of some white plastic, as though it were designed by a 1970s science-fiction television designer.

"That looks familiar," Max murmured, and Dana wondered if he was going to elaborate. It seemed to be built into the lagoon, but it was clearly accessible by the same rough road that had been created to get to the factory, so it wasn't for boat access. The trucks travelled along the small coastal path, and made their own roads to get there. "I think," Max suddenly said, "that it's in the lagoon in case it needs to flood the complex."

"In case something that they are researching gets out of control?" Justice asked querulously. "What do you think they are doing in there?"

"It looks a little like the rig that Heroux has in French Guiana," Max replied. "The same sort of design, the same sort of material. I wonder if perhaps whatever they are doing there – here – in both places, might be dangerous enough that if it got out of control, they would simply flood the building."

"Maybe," Justice conceded, "although maybe it might just be that if they need to destroy it, flooding is the quickest way

318

of going about it."

"Why would they need to destroy it?" Dana asked.

"You tell us," Justice replied, looking at her, and Dana felt a twinge of irritation. She was beginning to wonder if Justice would have preferred her and Liseth to stay longer and download more information rather than escaping and surviving.

Sort of surviving. The softness of Liseth's skin came back to her senses far too quickly and it definitely hurt. She remembered grabbing Asha's bum and squeezing it and a wave of guilt rolled over her. If Asha died as well, that would be a second person she had spectacularly failed to save.

"You OK?" Max asked, taking her hand as he stood up.

"Fine," Dana nodded. "What's the plan?"

"Well, I suppose we could try and go in from the front," Max reflected.

"Just walk in?" Dana said, shocked.

"Maybe," he said, and Dana realized he was serious. "I mean, if that laboratory is designed to be flooded, then we might be able to find a way to get in from the lake."

"No," Dana shook her head. "We're not going in via the lake."

"We don't know that there are crocodiles in the water," Justice said, a cruel amusement playing on her face.

"Great, you can go in and let us in through the front then," Dana retorted, and this time Justice actually laughed.

"So obviously we're not going to go and knock on the front door," Justice said. "How do we get in?"

"We could knock on the front door," Max shrugged. "They must have buyers."

"There's no way they'd believe we came here on a whim," Dana said. "And for all we know there are posters of me all around that building."

"Slightly egotistical," Justice sighed.

"She has a point," Max agreed. "She is one of the brand ambassadors, and they probably do get guests from time to time, so there's a fairly good chance there's a poster in there with her on it. But we could always say we had an appointment but there was a miscommunication."

"Or," Justice said, and pointed to the coast, "we could hijack a van and then drive straight in."

Tariku Kayode was very tired. It had been a long day and he simply wanted to go home and eat. He might spend a few moments talking to his wife, he would not go in and check on their children. He just wanted to eat and sleep, because he had to be up early the following morning to go back to work. At present his life seemed to be a constant, never-ending cycle of work, food and sleep. Tariku's father had been a fisherman when San Pédro was a simple village with barely a hundred people, but he had been there when the port had been built in 1968, and as the city had opened up to include the little villages around it. Rather ironically, Tariku had seen what it had done to his father. The old man had spent his life waking up early to go fishing, and then desperately spend the rest of the day preparing and trying to sell the fish. Despite all the changes that had been made, in San Pédro, however, there was very little option except to follow in his father's footsteps.

And then, along came Silhouette Moreau's factory,

promising new jobs for everyone, and opportunities to do more than just what tradition dictated they should do. Suddenly the doors were open for new jobs, some of which didn't need a lot of skill. You could be taught how to bottle, and you could be taught how to repair the machines when they broke down. Tariku wasn't inclined to do either of those, because he could drive a truck. It was something he had learned from his uncle, and the Shadow factor needed drivers to transfer the crates of shadow from the factory to the port. It was a dream come true, and when Tariku had told his wife the good news, the pair had celebrated all night long.

That was a long time ago. Or at least it seemed that way. Now, as he drove along with the music blaring at him from his radio in the hopes that it might keep him awake, and the heat doing battle with the air conditioning – a battle which the heat seemed to be very close to winning – Tariku vaguely wished that he could have lived his father's lifestyle. Fishing may have been a hit or miss job, but at least the hours were better and Tariku would have been able to spend some actual time with his family.

Sighing heavily, he wiped the sweat from his forehead and checked to see the time. 7.30 pm. Only an hour and half more and he could finally end the day.

Then, rather surprisingly, he saw a white woman standing on the road in front of him, wearing shorts and a t-shirt, and looking lost. He blinked a couple of times, not entirely convinced he had seen what his eyes had told him, but sure enough, the white woman didn't disappear.

For what seemed like an awful long time in his head, Tariku argued with himself about what he should do, but then he decided that he couldn't really drive on by. White *étrangères* being

321

out on the lagoon at this time of night could probably result in death, and he didn't really feel that much ill will to someone that he wanted them dead.

"*Pardon!*" he called out of the window as he slowed the car down. "*As-tu besoin d'aide?*" She answered him, her face looking vaguely hopeful, but he couldn't understand her English, though at one point she said city, which was definitely something he knew. "City!" he nodded at her, and then thumbed backwards. It would be rough road back, but she would get there. If she was still there when he was on his way back, he could give her a lift, but not on his way to the factory. He couldn't afford to be late and get reprimanded, or fired, depending on who was working.

Or, if Heroux was there, maybe even worse.

The woman was shaking her head, waving her arms and saying something, but again all he could pick up on was the word city and as he'd told her where that was, the conversation wasn't going anyway.

Unless she hadn't understood the thumb gesture. Shaking his head, he stuck his arm out the window and pointed back along the makeshift road.

"City! City!" he repeated, and pointed. He swore to himself briefly when he saw a mosquito land on his arm, and slapped at it. He couldn't leave the woman on the road dressed as she was, really. The mosquitoes would eat her alive. He paused to think of some way to communicate to her that she could get a lift with him, but as he turned to look into the cabin for inspiration he was surprised to see someone sitting beside him. A handsome guy, dressed in a long-sleeved shirt and jeans.

"*Bon jour,*" the Frenchman said (and he was definitely

French, Tariku thought – no matter what the colour of his skin, there was no way this guy was Ivorian, or even African). "*On peut monter avec vous*?" He had a smile on his face, but he was holding a gun at Tariku, and it was clear that the whole thing had been a set up. When he looked back out, he saw that the woman was pulling jeans and a long-sleeved shirt on as well, so she had just been trying to get his attention. When the cabin door opened and a third, redhead person got into the cabin, Tariku suspected that his life was forfeit.

"*Où voulez-vous aller*?" he asked, hoping that they wouldn't kill him.

"*L'usine*," the Frenchman said, pointing towards the Shadow factory. "*Secrètement*," he added. The third woman had climbed into the cabin, which was now getting increasingly crowded, and there were definitely mosquitoes getting in as well. Tariku nodded, and the man spoke, this time in English, presumably to the women, who nodded, and then they got out of the cabin. Tariku guessed they were going to get in the back of the truck.

"*Tu garderas notre secret*," the Frenchman said, and it was definitely a threat rather than a question. "*Je veux que tu vives*." His politeness and concern made him more terrifying than if he'd simply threatened to kill him. But the Frenchman got out of the cabin and closed the door, joining his friends in the back. Tariku remained still, wondering what he should be doing exactly, but then there was a bang on the back of the cabin, and he guessed that he was supposed to drive. Taking a slightly exaggerated gulp, he set the car in motion.

"How do you know he won't give us away?" Dana asked.

"I was really nice to him," Max grinned. "I said I hoped he would live. And I do." Dana frowned, and lent back against the wall of the van. It was a fairly standard box truck, but it was definitely old – comfortably older than Dana herself. There was precious little inside the actual van, so presumably the driver was on his way to the factory to stock up and then take it…to the port? She wasn't sure, but assumed that everything would be shipped out.

The driver had clearly been terrified, so he probably wouldn't give them away, but Dana was worried that he would be more scared of Silhouette and Heroux rather than them. Heroux was the sort of person who could easily convince someone that their anger would have much worse consequences than someone simply pointing a gun at your head. That was the problem with threats; if there was someone higher up the food chain threatening your victim, your threat paled into insignificance.

Dana gritted her teeth as the truck bumped over another rough patch, and she looked at the other two who were grimacing as much as she was. This guy may have been a driver but the standards were pretty low if that were the case.

Justice pulled herself to the back doors and released the inside catch pushing one door open a little so she could peer out at their progress. Dana caught a quick glimpse of a fence line before Justice pulled the door shut and locked it.

"We're through," she said.

"He'll drive into the factory," Max mused, and Dana looked at him. "We might need to get out before they find us."

"We'd better hurry," Justice urged. She unlocked the

door again, swinging it open, and turned back to them before falling out of the van, much to Dana's horror. Max raced up to the door and then beckoned her to follow, before falling backwards as well. Reluctantly, Dana followed him and looked out. She could see the side of the factory and realized that they were getting far too close. It had seemed insane, but as they had both done it, Dana put her hands to her chest and fell backwards. She hit the ground with a thud, and let herself roll to absorb some of the momentum. A hand was thrust towards her and she grabbed it, feeling herself get hauled up. To her surprise she was face to face with Justice.

"Haven't been this close in a while," the American grinned and Dana rolled her eyes. She did not shove the other woman away, however, and Dana wondered if she beginning to forgive the Interpol agent.

No. Not yet.

Perhaps unsurprisingly, it started to rain, and the three pulled back to the wall of the factory in the hope of gaining some protection. The truck continued on its way and a large roller door opened up to allow it access. Even as it was going through, Dana could see that the driver was trying to communicate to whoever was on the inside, presumably letting them know that there were three people in the back of the van.

"Should keep them occupied for a bit," Justice said with a wry smile. Dana turned to her, only to find that Max had disappeared.

"Where's…" she started, but Max appeared around the corner.

"Entrance over here," he said, though he was barely

audible above the sound of the rain, which hammered down on the steel roof of the factory which such force that the noise was the most dominant sound around. Dana could only guess at how loud it would be on the inside, and wondered how the workers could stand to tolerate it.

The two women made their way to the side of the building Max was on, and found a standard metal door that had been locked in place by a singular padlock, which Max had obviously picked. He pushed it open and they crept inside, immediately moving to the right where there were copious shadows.

Early on in her career, a friend of Dana's had asked her if she would model for him, and she had accepted. His location of choice was an abandoned factory that he had found in one of the Brisbane suburbs. Dana remembered creeping inside, her blood a little chilled by the cracked windows with bits of glass missing (though it turned out most of it was on the floor inside). There were gantries with dodgy scaffolding, and rails that didn't necessarily seem like they would support the weight of anyone who leaned on them. Light had pushed its way through the dirty glass, casting moody shadows and sickly yellow light all around them. Dressed in a short white dress, Dana had looked like some sort of angel that was walking through hell. It was probably the first photoshoot she had actively fallen in love with, and she rather wished she could shoot with him again.

The Shadow production facility wasn't that far removed from what she had shot in, though it was full of machinery that was definitely not first rate. Metallic gears grinded as cogs turned, but didn't immediately fall into line with the next one along. Sometimes there was a thud, that reminded Dana of a bike changing gear, but on a much larger scale. She could see jars being filled with a variety of coloured liquids – different flavours of Shadow getting different murky colours – which were then capped and a label applied. The conveyor belt moved the bottles along, jumping every so often as it came across an uneven connection, though surprisingly the bottles remained upright. A man was standing near each of these connections, presumably to make sure any bottles that didn't quite make it were put back into the upright position.

The truck driver was at the far end of the factory, and Dana couldn't make out what was going on there, though it did seem to have the attention of two burly men in black uniforms.

"Only two security?" Dana whispered, and Justice and Max scanned the room.

"Looks like it," Max mused.

"For a rich guy, he does things on the cheap. I would imagine it wouldn't be hard to find security guards in a place like San Pédro," Justice muttered.

"We're on the wrong side of the building," Max said, and he pointed towards the opposite end of the building where there was a door which was clearly a new addition. Even with the lights around it not working, the door was still clearly a bright white.

"The rain should make it easier for us to get across," Justice said, though Dana thought she might be hoping against hope a little. To their right there was what was presumably the office, and one of the few areas in the building where the lighting was actually pretty brilliant.

"So, if we go that way," Dana whispered, "we have to go

around the office, which will put us into the light for a minute or so. If we go the other way, we ultimately have to get to the truck exit where security is currently waiting for us."

"Or we swap halfway through," Justice said.

"I don't think we're going to get away with crossing the room without getting noticed," Max replied. "I don't reckon those workers will raise the alarm," he added.

"Security is really close," Justice pointed out. "They might be worried about getting a beat down from them if someone is on the premises and they don't mention it."

"Look," Dana said, and pointed to the roller door. The truck driver had obviously made his point and security now headed out of the building. "They've gone looking for us."

"We weren't in the back of the truck, so they think we're outside," Max grinned. "That worked better than I hoped it would."

Without a word, the three knew immediately what they needed to do, and quickly skirted the walls of the factory to their left, going back past their entrance point, and making their way to the truck entrance with as much haste as they could. Dana briefly smiled at the irony of using the shadows to remain hidden from the workers. Shadow had become their weapon against Silhouette, though probably not the shadow he was thinking of.

Justice had led the way, and when she got to the roller door, she held up her hand and peered around to see if they were able to make it past. When she whipped her head back again, Dana instinctively clung to the wall, but when she looked up it was straight into the eyes of one of the factory workers. She gave a weak smile, and put her finger to her lips, but the man's response didn't inspire a lot of confidence. When he looked more panicked,

Dana looked to Max, and was surprised that he had produced his handgun. On her left, Justice had done the same, and Dana sighed slightly to herself, and reached behind her, under the long-sleeved shirt she was wearing.

She had decided to wear her little backpack, a Pacsafe Petite Econyl backpack that proudly boasted it was an anti-theft backpack, thanks to things like a slash-guard strap, a TurnNLock hook and interlocking zip pullers. She reached back, a little awkwardly, but was able to grab her golden Glock, which she removed, her sense of security increasing slightly with the new weight in her hands.

Sure enough a security guard had entered – a big, beefy man whose vest barely fit across his broad chest and whose shirt most definitely didn't fit across the rounded belly. He had a bushy beard, which his stubby fingers rubbed as he seemed to be hoping it might bring him some form of mental massage.

It was all largely irrelevant, as when he took a few more steps, Justice stepped forward and clubbed him savagely on the back of the neck with her gun, and the man fell to the floor. Max swiftly joined the Interpol agent, and the two worked to move the big man out of the way.

Dana watched them go, and then turned to see that the worker she had made eye contact with had not only ratcheted his fear up another notch, but had also gained friends. This time there was no reassuring gesture Dana thought she could make, but when she turned to her left, she was shocked to see the second security guard standing in front of her.

"Hi?" she asked, but he had already grabbed at her arm, and Dana swung with her right hand to punch him, but quite aside from the fact she was as good at punching with her right hand as she was writing with it, he had another hand free to swat her away. Deciding to turn the tables on him slightly, she grabbed the free hand with her own, and he looked a little surprised as she used the security of the grips to angle herself in such a way she could kick out with her right foot, straight into the man's face.

It wasn't enough to knock him out, but it was enough for him to release his grip, and she fell slightly, but lashed out again, this time connecting with the man's testicles. As he doubled over, Dana pulled herself up and lashed out with her Glock, cuffing the man under the side of his left ear, and this time he dropped to the ground.

To her surprise, she could hear a round of applause, and she looked up to see the workers all clapping, making enough noise that even the sound of the rain wasn't able to drown it out. Dana smirked a little, and when she looked to see where her friends were, she saw that they two were standing there giving applause. Dana bowed slightly to them.

"Maybe we should have done this from the beginning," Max shrugged. Justice was looking around, and she pointed out a number of different security cameras that were watching them. "Let's hope keeping an eye on the feed was these guys' responsibility," Max said. "Come on."

When they approached the white door at the far corner of the factory, Dana shook her head slightly, annoyed that the fact it was finger-print locked should have been obvious to her from the very outset. Of course it was. They weren't going to just leave it open on the off chance that anyone could stroll in.

Unlike the factory. Dana frowned at that thought.

Whatever was behind the white door and in the research and development building was clearly far more important than a simple bottling plant.

"If this falls apart, they can simply...claim it on insurance?" she thought aloud.

"Whatever's behind that door, they don't want people digging too deeply," Max said, picking up on her thinking. "This place they would be happy to admit what was happening. But behind that door are industrial secrets that they don't want to have to talk about."

"But even those can be insured," Justice pointed out.

"But there's a greater chance of it getting out if something happens," Max pointed out. "Better to beef up security so nothing does and you don't have to get into pesky discussions with the insurers and the law."

"So how do we get past the door?" Justice asked, and Max pursed his lips. There was a fingerprint scanner on the door, but there was also a keypad, on the off chance that the system failed to recognize the print. It could happen, Dana reflected, remembering when her phone suddenly stopped recognizing her face and wouldn't open for her, requiring her to enter her code and setting up the facial scan again.

"Six-digit code," Max said, looking at the six red lights that were above the fingerprint scanner. "The odds of us breaking that aren't particularly good." Seemingly on a whim, he entered in six digits, but the door remained firmly locked, and Max shrugged, almost to himself.

"I can't believe we didn't plan for this," Dana sighed.

"Well, in fairness, it was a very late in the day plan," Max said. "Under normal circumstances we would have spent weeks planning this, and made sure that we got the door code. We needed to act fast, and here we are."

"We can't force the door," Justice said, but it wasn't clear whether it was a question or a statement. Max assumed the former, and shrugged, but as he pushed at it, testing for where the door was secured, he shook his head.

Suddenly, to their surprise, one of the workers came over, a look on his face that still wasn't secure, but he nodded apologetically, and Dana, Max and Justice all stepped back, noticing that he was afraid to go near them. He swiftly moved to the door and pressed in six digits, and at the end, all lights went green and there was a distinctly satisfying clunk as the door unlocked. Their new ally turned to them, nodding and bowing, and started to move back, without a single word. Dana reached out to thank him, but Justice put her hand on Dana's arm and shook her head.

Over the past year, Dana had begun to realise that there was a lot that took place in the world that she simply wouldn't be able to understand. Or, more accurately, would never have enough information to provide the understanding. Their new friend's motivations would probably remain a mystery, but Dana suspected that it wouldn't be too hard to guess what was going on. After all, to think that none of the workers had ever paid attention when the code was being keyed in was arrogance on behalf of whoever was behind the door. Equally, if you're going to treat your labour badly, then they would be less likely to show you the respect and loyalty you might be hoping they would. Not for the first time, Dana vowed to make sure she treated all people with the respect they deserved. You just never knew when they might be in a position to make or break you.

As Max pushed the door open, they three looked into the brightly lit corridor beyond.

"Here we go," Max muttered.

NINTH REPORT: IMPRESSIVE FIGURE

Dana ran her fingers over the smooth finish of the white, plasticky wall, and was surprised that it felt a little more velvety than she thought it would. It was probably a special type of plastic, she reflected, but the corridor looked like something out of a science-fiction movie her dad had shown her when she was younger. Interestingly, there didn't seem to be any security cameras, and she wondered if that was a misplaced confidence on Silhouette's part, or perhaps she simply didn't see them. If it was the latter, she guessed that she'd find out soon enough and look particularly stupid. Also, she got the rather strange feeling they were going *down*. She tried to think back to what they had seen from the outside. How much of the laboratory was underwater, exactly?

"I think," Max said, "that our aim is to find out exactly what is going on in this research laboratory, and then we get out, as quickly as possible."

"Do we have any place to start, realistically?" Justice asked.

"Just one," Dana said, and the other two looked at her in surprise. "Well, we know that Thomas McAteer was a nano-tech specialist, so I'm guessing that if he was working on something that Silhouette had him killed for, it was probably some sort of nano-tech, right?"

"Makes sense," Justice agreed. "Let's hope that there are signs then." She marched to the end of the corridor, followed by the other two, and to her surprise the door in front of her slid open. She paused and looked back at her colleagues.

"It might be automatic," Dana said, but she could see from the look on the Interpol agent's face that her tone of voice was clearly far from reassuring. Cautiously the three stepped into the corridor beyond.

It clearly went in both directions, and as the three looked at each other, Max and Justice came to the same conclusion, and without even speaking, Justice headed off to the left, while Max went to the right. He gave Dana a little look, and she nodded, following him.

The corridor, however, wasn't as a featureless as their entry point, and Dana realized that this was an observation corridor of sorts, with large windows set into the wall regularly, allowing a view into a laboratory. Max paused at the first one, peering around to see what was in it in such a fashion that those inside wouldn't see him. When Dana looked back, she saw that Justice had made a similar decision, and was on all fours, crawling under the window she was at. Max had also ducked down and was now crab-walking his way across the corridor, refusing to get on his hands and knees. Dana peered into the laboratory and decided that it was strangely exactly like she had seen in countless movies. There were scientists in lab coats, walking around with chemicals, heading to machines that could shake and spin the test tubes that were being slid into them. She wasn't sure if she was disappointed or not but ultimately she decided that science was simply just something she probably wasn't going to understand particularly well.

One thing, however, did stand out to her, and she realized that there was someone in the room that wasn't in a lab coat. Instead, he was dressed in jeans and a white t-shirt, with a check, flannel shirt over the top. He was sitting back in a chair, checking off different things on a clipboard he had, and occasionally a scientist would come over to him and ask him a question. Dana scanned the room again in the hope of finding some sort of clue as to what they were researching, but she realized that most everything seemed to be written in French, for a start, and there were certainly no big signs indicating what exciting new project Check-Flannel man was working on today.

There was also a door on the wall with the windows on that they were currently moving along. So, the corridor was a ring, she thought. Sure enough, there was a door on the opposite wall leading into…

Her thoughts were interrupted by Max who hissed at her like she was a stray cat, and Dana gave him a look, before crouching down and crawling across to him.

"Did you work out what they were doing in there?" Dana said.

"What?" he replied, puzzled by this comment.

"We're looking for a nano-tech project, aren't we? Was that it?"

"I don't think so," Max replied and Dana looked at him through hooded eyes.

"How would you know?"

"Well, I would have thought that the computers might be displaying nano-tech designs and the like. It all looked chemical to me." It was a fair point.

"I suppose you think you're pretty clever," Dana said.

"A little," he grinned back at her. "But you're right. I'll make sure to read what I can in future. I'm gonna look like a right fool if the nano-tech is also chemically based." Dana matched his grin, and the pair stood up, able to walk a little more before they had to duck down again.

They passed by two separate laboratories, and Dana guessed that Justice would probably be doing the same, which meant that there were probably five to seven different laboratories in total, which seemed like a lot of different projects to be undertaking for a company that was principally working on saving the environment.

"This one is definitely some sort of easily recyclable container," Max whispered as they cleared the second laboratory. "I read stuff about different plastics, but you could see the design of a container on a computer." Dana looked in and saw that there was some sort of can on the table, and as she watched, a machine descended a small slim tube into the can before removing it. Were they injecting something into the can to break it down? Dana waited for as long as she could, but then Max pulled her below the window, mouthing to her about someone else in the room.

There was, however, a new surprise on their journey, and this was in the form of a corridor leading off from the one they were on. The pair paused as they looked at the new corridor, and Dana noticed that, rather grimly, this one wasn't quite as white as the one they were in. This one, actually, seemed to be of a darker, almost jet-black plastic.

"Do you think that's a design choice?" Dana asked, as they looked down what seemed to be a corridor of darkness.

"You've noticed the feel of the plastic, right?" Max asked.

"Yeah, like sort of...velvety, I guess. Like those board games that have that smooth, soft feel to their boxes."

"I think it's a new plastic design. Part of the whole recycling thing."

"Have they discovered something like that? I don't recall them talking about it."

"I think it's a secret," Max said. "I reckon that maybe they've built his here because it's a whole lot easier to skip over building approval in a country like the Ivory Coast. You throw enough money the government's way and they'll just let you do what you will. So, they use their new plastic, build it here where no one will question them and there aren't the same regulations..."

"Maybe save a fortune in the process," Dana guessed, and Max nodded.

"So, when they build this place, they just use the plastic that they have. Some of it was molded in white, some in black. They just took what they had and built it. Screw aesthetics."

"Well, haven't you just been putting the jigsaw puzzle together." This prompted a smile from the Frenchman.

"I'm not totally useless at my job," he said, with mock indignation.

"Just enough to stay working with Interpol," Dana replied and this time Max stifled a laugh.

"I'm hoping I won't be replaced by a sexy supermodel," he shot back, and Dana raised an eyebrow.

"I can't help it if people think I'm amazing," she said, but the sound of a door closing stopped them both, and they pressed themselves back up against the wall they were on, in the vain hope that they might not be discovered. Fortunately, the footsteps they heard moved away from them. Dana shook her head, and saw that Max had obviously reached the same conclusion she had – this wasn't the time for flirting.

"We should split up," Dana said. "You see what's going on down there, and what else is in the labs, I'll go down into the darkness." She made it sound silly, but the look on Max's face was clearly concerned.

"I don't know if that's a great idea. We don't know what's down there."

"Yeah, but I can't speak French, so I won't have any idea what's going on in the labs. You actually might. And we are here to find out what sort of secret technology is being developed." Max's face didn't change, but she could see that he understood what she was talking about.

"*Merde*," he said.

"I can't speak French, but I know what that's supposed to be," Dana scowled.

"Be careful, Dana," Max said. "Silhouette has already tried to kill you once. This isn't a game."

"I know," Dana replied, and this time the sharpness in her voice wasn't playful. "I'm doing this for a reason, Max." He nodded at her one more time, and then turned to follow whoever had walked up the corridor. Dana felt annoyed, and wanted to go to him to make sure that things were OK between them, but instead turned to walk down the dark corridor. Time to be an adult.

The corridor was not dissimilar to the one that she had walked down earlier, though obviously in black rather than white. The one big difference, however, was that there were no windows, so while it was peppered with one or two doors on either side, there was no way of looking into the rooms and seeing what was going on in there. Equally, there were no markings on the doors either, which meant that if someone was looking for a specific room, they would have to know exactly what that room was. There were no signs to give you an indication on where you were going.

At the first door, Dana tentatively pushed against it, but it didn't open and she could see a glossy black panel set against the door – another fingerprint lock. The few other doors she tried responded in the same way – or more accurately didn't respond – and Dana began to suspect that she had wasted her time walking down the moody corridor.

At the very end there was a single door, and despite the spectacular lack of success so far, Dana walked up to it and gently pressed it to see if it would open. To her surprise, it slid open. Beyond was an office, and Dana cautiously stepped into it.

In some ways the office seemed set up in a manner that wasn't too far removed from the one at the Silhouette Systems building that so recently burned to the ground. However, that office was part of an open floor which contained more than one room. This was definitely a singular office – the desk and chair were directly in front of her, while to the left were shelves and what was obviously a mini bar of sorts. To the right, a number of comfortable chairs gathered around a small table, obviously for meetings. But it was the same Toledo desk on a silk rug that would have cost a fortune.

340

"Drink?" came a smooth voice from behind her, and Dana jumped slightly as she stepped forward and looked back to see Silhouette Moreau standing behind her. "So good to see you Dana," he continued, heading for the minibar.

"You literally tried to kill me," Dana pointed out.

"Please," he said dismissively. "I left a helicopter on the roof for you to escape. I could have used that myself and then you'd have to be burnt to death. But instead, I knew you'd get out of there." He didn't look at her at any point while saying that, and Dana decided he was just talking rubbish to make himself feel better about her escape. "Seriously, though," he repeated, "drink?"

"Uhm, can I have a Sex on the Beach, please," she said, deciding to go all in.

"Vodka girl?"

"Actually, I just like juice-based cocktails, if I'm honest," Dana said. "Peach, cranberry, orange...sweet as."

"I learnt bartending once," Silhouette continued, as though they were the best of friends. "Wasn't a requirement, but I thought it would make me look cool if I could mix drinks for people. I was going to say friends, but I don't really have a lot of them." He held up his hand, as he continued, "No, that wasn't a plea for sympathy. When you're as rich as I am, whining about having no friends is a little disingenuous. But also, when you get to be as rich as I am, you suddenly have supposed friends popping up all over the place, and those ones are definitely not who you would want to invite to your birthday party." He took a clear rod and swirled it around the drink he was making, before turning back to Dana and giving her what she asked for. "We would have these big parties and I would make drinks, and then it ended up in the press as they would say things like…ooo, uhmm…*Silhouette Moreau cuts an impressive figure as, dressed all in black, he stands behind the bar making his guests the drinks of their choice. It's just another of the skills the billionaire possesses, and he makes it look as easy as he makes designing the technology that will lead us into the future.*"

"There's no way anyone wrote that," Dana said, taking the drink. She sipped at it and had to admit that it was actually made very well.

"Oh, it was something like that. It got a bit clunky towards the end there, but you get the idea. A better journalist would have come up with something more impressive." He gestured to his side where there were two comfortable armchairs, and Dana moved to sit down in one. It was very nice, she decided, as she felt herself slide into it, the chair adapting to her shape.

"I didn't even notice these when I walked in," Dana said, taking another sip of her drink.

"It's a big office. I like to be comfortable wherever I am. A nice meeting area, a proper desk for a conversation with the boss, and a little area where two friends can have a chat about life and the risks that it brings." He sat down in his chair, and raised his glass to her, before taking a sip. He seemed to be drinking an Espresso Martini, Dana decided.

The room fought against the black of the plastic walls, Dana noticed, as a lot of the furniture seemed to be white, while a number of the other dressings contained the strong colours of African art. It gave the room the feel of a sixties movie, where the sets were coloured with strong, primary colours.

"You weren't around in the sixties, were you?" Dana

342

asked, and Silhouette looked offended.

"As if I'm that old, Dana," he smiled. "You're talking about the design of the room? Or just the plastic of the walls? A lot of plastic in the sixties, I know. It was a whole thing then. And the colours are bold, I agree. But no, it's not a desire to go back to the past. There was nothing particularly great about the past, no matter what old people tell you."

"Dad does like to tell me how we have it good these days," Dana agreed.

"Oh, we do, we do. But then they go into the old complaints about how we no longer have old fashioned values, and ideals have changed, as though that never happened before, and the world doesn't shift with every generation. I say, though, we have it much better now, because we're more interested in trying to keep the world alive, rather than trying to destroy it with every new bit of technology we develop." He sat forward, suddenly quite keen on this new topic. "You know this entire building is recyclable? This plastic is designed in such a way that you can easily remold it into something completely new. It won't break into microplastics, because it's designed to melt in such a way that it stays together, unless forcibly separated. Breaking off tiny pieces of it would be impossible because of the bonds that it has, so you have to break it off into chunks. And then you can remold those chunks into new...well, into new anything, really."

There was a genuine passion in his eyes when he spoke, and Dana decided that the man did genuinely care for the environment and the planet that they lived on. But at the same time the passion was almost a fiery intensity, like a preacher trying to convince his flock that he had spoken to God, and he knew the way forward. It was a certainty that he was right, a manic conviction that betrayed a madness behind the logical rationale that was being spouted.

"So why try to kill me? Or not kill me?" Dana asked. "I mean, if you're so great, and all this is so good, why try to kill me?" Silhouette sat back in his chair and mused for a moment, before taking another sip of his martini.

"You know that there's a guy, I don't remember his name, that is concerned about decline in population on the planet? (Dana stifled a chuckle at this, suspecting that Silhouette definitely knew the name, but didn't want to admit he did) He's worried about the number of births, or something. The birth rate has declined. There aren't enough people being born, in his opinion. Though if I'm honest, and admittedly as a black man I might be biased, I think what he really means is that there aren't enough white people being born. The thing is, though, there are over 8 billion people on this planet. In 1800 there was 1 billion people. Can you imagine that? For a moment, just imagine every group of people you know, but divided by 8. The population of your country would have been just 3.5 million people. That's not even the population of Sydney today.

But it doesn't stop there. In 1950 the world population was 2.5 billion people. In seventy years, we've increased the world population by 5.5 billion people. We've more than tripled the world population in seventy years, and this idiot is concerned about the decline in birth rates? People are still having babies; the birth rate is still positive, which means the population is growing, albeit at a smaller rate, and that's not necessarily a bad thing, Dana, not at all." He took another sip from his martini, and then put it on the small table beside him, before leaning forward and putting his fingers together.

"You asked me about Thomas McAteer, and why he was killed. OK, let's not play games anymore, Dana. I have a vision for the future, and it is all to do with this planet remaining a viable biosphere for our race. And if that is going to happen, there needs to be some changes made, because this planet is incredible at rejuvenating itself, if given the chance. There were rivers in Fiji, filled to the brim with plastic, that choked the life out of those rivers. But those rivers were cleaned up, and the rubbish removed, and in just under twenty years, the systems had recovered and were able to support life once again. Twenty years! Imagine that, Dana. Our planet can regenerate if it were given the chance. And that's what we need to do. Silhouette Systems is going to be a world leader in that area, because that's what we do. We aim to regenerate the planet."

"Thomas McAteer disagreed with you," Dana said.

"He did," Silhouette agreed. "So, I had to remove him."

"Why couldn't he just resign?"

"Sometimes you have to acknowledge that someone you trusted has let you down. The person that you trusted has a lot of information that you really can't afford to get out, so unfortunately you have to do the only thing you can to stop him from talking. And in this case, it was a bullet. I'm sorry Dana, I really am, I never meant to put your sister in harm's way. And I promise you that we hired an assassin that was perfect for the job. We were assured that there would be no error, and there wasn't. I made absolutely sure that it was only McAteer that was going to get the bullet. There was never a time when your sister was in danger."

"How old are you?" Dana suddenly snapped. "That's the kind of immature thinking my friends would use, and even I'm not that dumb that I can't see the possibility of something like that going wrong. You can never know for certain that this assassin is going to be absolutely perfect, because you can't predict all the eventualities. All you care about is that this guy needs to die, and so you'll pay for someone who'll do the job, but you still can't predict what's going to happen."

"This isn't chaos theory, Dana," Silhouette objected. "A butterfly flapping its wings halfway around the world won't change the accuracy of a professional assassin."

"What if a bee stung her in the face?" Dana said, and Silhouette laughed out loud. "Well? There were flowers and plants on that rooftop. There were insects. Something that might have bitten her or stung her. How do you know that wouldn't happen? How do you know that a bee wouldn't sting her at just the right moment and then the shot goes wide and my sister gets killed? You don't, do you? Because at the end of the day you don't care. My sister is a risk you're willing to take in order to make sure you get to do what you want."

"That's not true, Dana," protested Silhouette. "I am very experienced in these things, trust me. I see the eventualities. That's how I'm so good at my job, because I can expect the unexpected."

"Like me?" Dana asked, and he looked at her. Once, some time ago, Dana had seen a snake approach her cat. She had been much younger, and the cat was not particularly big, but was fluffy and an off-white colour that gave him the look of a cat that was perpetually dirty. The snake, on the other hand, was more generic to a child's eye. It was a brown snake – an Eastern brown, to be precise – and it managed to sneak up on Tissa, thanks in part to the fact its tan flecked brown skin camouflaged it in the undergrowth. Tissa (named because Dana's sister Kimba had been unable to say Tigger, thanks to her missing front teeth), had turned and seen the snake far too late. Tissa hissed, and then did something that seemed like a last-ditch decision; it lashed out at snake. Before the snake had opened its jaws, the cat batted it across its face. It was, as events transpired, the best decision to make. The snake paused and regarded the cat, and decided that the attack might not be worth it, given the pain it had just been inflicted. It turned and fled, speedily, not noticing that Tissa had done exactly the same thing.

But the look that the Eastern brown had given Tissa was the same look that Silhouette Moreau regarded Dana with now. Unlike the snake, however, Dana suspected there was little chance Moreau was going to run.

In which case, in for a penny...

"You didn't anticipate me finding the Four-Fold Crown. You didn't think I would try to find out who attacked my sister. You didn't factor me into anything," Dana pointed out.

A darkness settled over Silhouette as he sat back in his chair. There was no congenial smile anymore, but a determination that would ride over any obstacle. No, not ride – go through. He was an unstoppable force, and anything in his way needed to move aside or be destroyed.

"Do you know what a Pyrrhic victory is?" Silhouette asked, softly.

"Sort of," Dana shrugged. "Winning, but losing?"

"Winning at great cost, to be precise. Trying to prove that I don't anticipate what's going to happen will probably result in your death. That's a Pyrrhic victory." He remained still in his chair, and said nothing, and then suddenly he was forward again, and Dana took a gasp, shocked at the speed he moved, the speed of the Eastern brown snake surfacing once again. "Perhaps I didn't anticipate you. Perhaps I did think that your sister's life was worth the sacrifice. Perhaps I would make even greater sacrifices. Perhaps a treacherous waitress is worth the sacrifice." At this, Dana fought the surge of anger in her belly.

Silhouette stood up, putting his martini glass on the side bench where his makeshift bar was, and went to his desk. Dana guessed what was going to happen, but reflected that there was no real way to stop it now.

Sure enough, he appeared to lean on his desk, and within two minutes, Heroux appeared at the door. It was the longest two minutes of Dana's life, as the logical part of her brain wrestled with the part that had hope and optimism.

He's not doing anything. If we were fast enough, we could take him!

He's literally waiting for us to do that. We have to wait. If we're alive we actually have a better chance of staying that way.

"Mr Moreau?" Heroux said, sliding a glance at Dana before he spoke.

"Look after Ms Spectra," Moreau said. "She wants to see our research. Afford her every courtesy. You can even show her the grimier areas of the laboratories. It won't matter if she gets her hands dirty. She's not leaving."

TENTH REPORT: LITTLE OPTIMISM

Justice wasn't particularly disappointed to be going alone down the corridor, principally because she knew she worked much better when there wasn't someone looking over her shoulder, trying to point out whether there were rules or regulations she needed to follow. Dana would question her nonstop about the morality of what she was doing, while Max (and admittedly she didn't know him all that well), seemed to be more of a by the book kinda guy than she was.

However, by the time she got to the first window that she was able to look through, she realized that she had one big disadvantage, and perhaps, yes, it was due to a degree of arrogance on her part, but why the *fuck* did these people not use English? She stood there for a moment, looking through the large glass observation port, seeing the computers inside, and tried to guess what the experiment might be. On the table was a black can with a neon yellow logo on it that looked like two S's forming a weird L shape. The computer monitors all had a lot of diagrams showing what Justice guessed were molecules, which would disassemble and reassemble, resulting in small red code coming up, and a much larger, flashing sentence.

Échec de la simulation.

Well, she could work out what three of those words were. The most important one, however, was the one she couldn't.

But if the text was in red, she guessed that it probably wasn't good.

They were running simulations...to break down compounds? To break down pollution, maybe? This was an eco-preservation research station, after all. But was it worth killing for?

Justice decided it probably wasn't, and so she crouched down and scuttled along the corridor to avoid being seen by any of the scientists inside the laboratory.

The corridor was largely featureless, but Justice had to admit she had the nagging feeling that she was being watched, and truth be told, she would be surprised if there weren't any cameras recording things at all here. Silhouette may be inclined to keep his work hidden, but it seemed unlikely that he would abandon all security completely. Especially if something had happened to Melissa at the other facility.

She peered into the next window, and looked at a new laboratory, but surprisingly it was one that seemed to be shut down. There was no one inside and the stations were all asleep, even though she could tell from the little green lights flashing around the room that power was still flooding through them. Shrugging a little, she strolled down the corridor, not needing to keep herself a secret as she passed by.

Each laboratory, she noticed, had two observation windows and a door between them. She did a little maths to herself and reflected that if not the actual next laboratory, then after it she would come across Dana and Max, on the condition they kept to the corridor and didn't go wandering off. Max had been right, had they more time, they would have prepared better and Justice wished that she had some sort of drone that they could have flown over the top of the building to work out the shape and how far it extended. There were no other corridors coming off that ring that she was walking through, and yet from the outside across the lagoon, she was sure that the building seemed to be wider than what was on the inside. Which would suggest that there was more on the other side of the building.

She paused at the next observation window, looking in and seeing what seemed to be a broadly similar setup to before, though this one seemed to have more chemicals on shelves, and there was a curious design on one of the monitors. It seemed to be like a gun, of some sort, and Justice wondered if they were developing weapons.

A movement caught her eye, and she quickly moved away from the window and looked down the corridor, only to see the handsome face of Max, as he gave her a little wave. She shook her head, miming having the shit scared out of her, and Max gave a small smile. He held up his hand, and then crouched down, coming across to her, where upon he stood up again.

"What's going on in there?" Justice whispered, though she realized that the walls might be soundproofed and there would be no need to do so.

"I think they're working on a delivery system of some kind," Max replied. "That device looks like you slide a capsule into it and then inject it into something."

"Or someone," Justice muttered.

"I don't know. I can think of a number of uses for eco-preservation," Max said. "But I thought that jet injectors were no longer used for humans. Perhaps you're right, perhaps they're developing a system for humans that is safer than the old one."

"Did you find anything interesting?"

"*Non*, it was all fairly boring. Proper research, most of which went over my head. What about you?"

"This is my third. The first one I think was just chemical breakdowns or something. The second lab was empty."

"Empty?" Max said, slightly surprised.

"The project probably ended," Justice replied.

"We could have a look then," Max suggested. "After all, if it's empty, there's no one there. We can actually go in without causing an issue."

"The computers were all still active," Justice nodded.

"Let's just hope it isn't their lunchbreak," Max replied. Justice was about to respond, somewhat sarcastically, when she checked herself. It was a good point – there was no reason to think that each team would go on a break at the same time.

"Tea break," she settled for, and Max grinned. In the brightly lit interior of the research station, he'd almost forgotten it was night time outside. His body, fueled by adrenaline, wasn't remotely feeling fatigued.

The pair walked back to the door of the previous laboratory, Max getting the opportunity to look into the room beyond, shrouded by inertia. Justice examined the door for the first time, and realized there didn't seem to be any sort of handle, but there was a black panel which clearly required a fingerprint. She looked back at Max who sighed. Each of them remained silent as they went through the options that were laid out before them, but at a certain point, they looked at each, recognizing that they had come to the same conclusion.

Breaking in would be impossible, and putting the station

on high alert to get security to come and open the room seemed like an unwise decision as well.

"Each team probably only has access to their lab," Max guessed.

"But the team leader might be able to access the others," Justice said, finishing his thought.

"We can't just walk in, because then one of us would have to keep the scientists under guard."

"So, we wait for someone to leave their lab," Justice said, and Max nodded in agreement.

"By the toilets, because that's presumably where they'll go," Max said.

"Did you find toilets?" Justice asked, a little astonished.

"Come on." He led her back to where he had come from, and what seemed to be like the center of the ring, based on where they had parted company, there were a set of doors – four in total, but all clearly stalls for toilets. The pair took their place against the door of the laboratory they were standing near, and both removed their weapons.

"Where's Dana, by the way?" Justice suddenly asked, realizing that they were one down on their team.

"We found a corridor; she went off to look."

"Of course she did," Justice said, more bitter than she meant it.

"You two really have a past, don't you?" Max said, and she could hear the judgement in his voice.

"Her naivete shits me," Justice said. "She needs to grow up." Max laughed.

"Oh come on, she's barely past twenty, right? You don't

think that affords her a little optimism?"

"Not in this game, it doesn't."

"Maybe you're just annoyed because she's more positive about the future than you are," Max opined.

"Now you sound like the naïve one," Justice retorted. Max opened his mouth to say something, but Justice held up her hand. It was soft, but they could definitely hear the sound of footsteps coming down the corridor. Max crouched down and retreated a little way, hiding himself from the scientists behind him, and hopefully from the person approaching. Justice followed, though she dashed across to the other side of the corridor, keeping a close eye on the window to make sure no one was looking through.

They heard the figure make its way into a toilet, and Justice crept forward, pausing to listen at the doors to make sure she got the right cubicle. Max joined her on the other side, and the pair waited patiently, both successfully shutting out the sound of whatever was going on in the cubicle.

When the door opened, someone stepped forward and Justice, who was on the right side, quickly put her hand on the person's mouth and shoved the gun into the side of their head. As Justice bundled them back into the toilet, Max followed, pulling the cubicle door shut behind them.

She was a short, dumpy looking woman with a slightly podgy face and eyes that definitely couldn't get any wider. With the two guns pointing at her, tears were already flooding the woman's eyes. Interestingly, Justice noted that she was white, which would suggest she wasn't Ivorian. Which meant...

"Do you understand me?" Justice hissed, releasing her

354

hand a little to allow the woman to speak.

"Yes, yes," came the response, and Justice realized she was American. Maybe mid-western.

"Who has access to the laboratories?" Max asked.

"What? Uh, everyone," the woman replied.

"Everyone as in you can open any laboratory door here?" Max asked.

"I can, because I take results from room to room, but each group have their own lab they can access." Max glanced at Justice, who gave a small look of relief. They might have been wrong about the idea that team leaders could access all labs, but fortunately it appeared they had found someone better.

"We're going to leave her, and go to the empty lab, and you're going to let us in," Justice said.

"You're not going to kill me, are you? I'm just a scientist. Not even that really, I'm just a messenger. I don't know anything about the projects really."

"We won't kill you, *madame*, if you do exactly what we ask you to do," Max said, spelling it out. He wrinkled his nose as he smelled the rather rancid aroma of urine. "Did you piss yourself?"

"I'm sorry," the woman said, breaking down in tears, no longer able to hold it together. "I just don't want to die. I didn't mean to do anything wrong. I just needed this job, and it paid well, so I just thought I'd come over, but I didn't think it was bad, and I knew that they said if Africa things could be really bad and you might be killed because all the blacks are fighting each other..."

"I was sympathetic for a moment," Max growled. "If you're going to be racist, I might just kill you all the same."

"But it's true," she whimpered.

"The *blacks* are not all fighting each other," Max snarled. "Militia groups are fighting each other. You think that the civilians want to be involved in that?" His gun was now under her chin and she was clearly shaking. "Let's go," he said. "Before I do something you might regret." Justice remained quiet, though there was the hint of a smile on her face. There was no world in which she would describe herself as woke, but she had to admit she had little time for racism.

Max and Justice slipped out of the toilet, the research scientist between them, and they swiftly made their way back to the empty laboratory, hoping that no one would notice them as they walked past. In truth, there was a sense of nervousness from both of them as they walked past each window, despite being on the opposite side of the corridor. At any moment, Justice was convinced a scientist would look out the window and see them.

Happily, nothing happened, and both agents let out a deep breath as they finally found themselves in front of the empty laboratory. The research scientist approached the door and put her thumb on the black panel, which lit up with "Lauren Roberts – Welcome", and the door slid open smoothly and silently. Max gave Lauren a rough shove, and she stepped into the room before them.

"This all works, right," Justice asked.

"Yeah, it's all active. Is there something specific that you wanted?" Lauren asked, and Max narrowed his eyes, examining her.

"Why should you help us?"

"I don't want to die," Lauren replied, clearly trying to be

helpful, and Justice chuckled a little. She sat down at one of the computers and pressed the space bar, bringing the screen to life, but as she saw nothing but French on the screen, she groaned, and turned back to Max.

"Do you want to take over?" Max nodded, and Justice replaced him keeping Lauren at gunpoint while he tapped on the computer. Surprisingly, nothing was password locked and the screens opened up for him without any stumbling blocks. "What's with this?" he asked, turning to Lauren.

"What do you mean? The French? Mr Moreau insists on it," she said.

"There's no password protection," Max pointed out.

"Oh, yes, well, everyone on a project should be able to access all information, and Mr Moreau and Mr Heroux might want to access it as well, which means that we don't password lock anything. They can just enter and do their thing," Lauren said, but Max had lost interest during her explanation.

"I wish we could get a copy of the data," Justice mused. She looked around, trying to see if there was a USB of some description.

"Is the data for all projects here, or is this just one project?" Max asked.

"Just the one. It's wrapped up. The first couple of phases have already gone through, and it's pretty much ready to go to proper manufacture," Lauren said.

"What is?" Max asked, and Lauren looked at him dumbfounded. "What's going to manufacture?"

"I have no idea," Lauren replied, fear filling her voice a little. "I haven't worked on this project at all. I just take USBs from different rooms to other rooms. I'm just a messenger, honestly. I'm not really a scientist, just a menial."

"USB," Justice said to her, holding out her hand, and again Lauren looked blank. Justice fought the urge to slap the woman, and repeated her word with a little more force, before adding: "If you're carry them around, you must have one at least on you."

"Oh, uh, right," Lauren nodded, and started patting down her pockets.

"You're taking quite a while to get something out of a pocket," Max said, and his gun was back in his hand, pointing at her.

"Oh no, no, I'm...here!" Lauren pulled her hand out of her right coat pocket, brandishing a USB with a grin, and she handed it over.

"You're very untrustworthy, you know that?" Justice asked and Lauren blanched a little. "Don't worry. Not in my interests to kill you." Then she paused and turned back to the scientist. "Just yet."

"Should we make a copy?" Max looked turned away from the computer monitor and looked back at the Justice.

"It's just one project," he mused. "How much information would we really get." Justice huffed a little.

"What is this project, then?"

"Nanobots," Lauren said, and the two looked at her. "I don't know the specifics if I'm honest, but it's creating nanobots that have, uhm, a program or instruction," she faltered. "I'm not totally certain," she admitted. Justice rolled her eyes, and put the USB in her pocket, agreeing with Max about the futility of making a copy. She looked around the room and her eyes alighted on something that she had noticed earlier, but had almost forgotten about.

"What's behind that door?" she asked, pointing to the door on the opposite side to the entrance they had used.

"Oh, that's the incinerator," Lauren said.

"Incinerator?" Max said.

"Incinerator somewhat undersells it," came a voice from behind them, and the two agents turned to see Heroux in the doorway. "Lauren, have you been telling tales?"

"I'm sorry, Mr Heroux, they came in and they pointed a gun at me, and I was on the toilet so I almost..." Her babbling was cut off as Heroux gave her a look.

"Let her go," Heroux snapped, as he strolled towards Justice, his hand outstretched. Justice looked behind him to see a thug held Dana at gunpoint, along with two other security guards and a burly, bald man in a white coat with a grey goatee. Justice hesitated, but realized the futility of the situation and placed her gun in Heroux's hand.

"Hey Dana, having fun?" she asked, casually.

"Yeah," Dana said. "It's been amazeballs."

"Justice Kennedy and Maximilien Travere, I presume?" Heroux said as he walked up to Max to collect his gun.

"You're very well informed," Max said, handing his gun over without a second's hesitation.

"I know some people, who know other people. There were conversations had, etc, etc. People talk."

"Do people?" Justice said, and there was an edge to her voice, as though she were expecting an answer but knew full well she wasn't going to like it.

"Oh yeah, most definitely," Heroux said. "I asked around and pretty soon I found out who might have been associated with an Interpol agent and a gendarme attempting to break into one of our other research stations." He paused and then turned to the burly man.

"This is Dr Paul Wilcox. He's a pretty bright guy. The forefront of eco-preservation, and more importantly the development of plasma pyrolysis, which Mr Moreau is pretty keen on because it can destroy plastic completely."

"Plasma pyrolysis?" Max asked, and Dr Wilcox looked at Heroux who nodded, and stepped back to allow the scientist to speak.

"We can generate extreme heat with a plasma arc, and once applied to the plastic waste, it will convert it to various carbon oxides and water, but it breaks down the entire thing, destroying all the plastic and not leaving any microplastics at all." He spoke with a British accent, sounding, in Dana's opinion, tremendously intelligent. The British always made science sound impressive, she reflected.

"It can work on other things as well, because it's extremely good, but there's a difference if the waste is organic," Heroux paused, somewhat over dramatically, as if trying to remember something that he clearly forgot, or never knew. "What was it, Paul?"

"Oh, we use a non-transferred arc if the waste is organic. We do have two different types of torches, and if the electrodes are inside the torch, it's non-transferred, but if it's outside it's transferred, because then the arc forms over a larger distance. It's quite complicated," he finished almost apologetically, and Heroux shrugged as though he were accepting the defeat of knowledge that was far beyond him.

"Should we step inside and show our guests your device? The one in Guiana is much better than the one here, but this works just as well, doesn't it, Paul?"

"Oh yes, absolutely," Wilcox said, and he crossed the room, pressing his thumb to the door, which swung open.

"You killed Melissa Andersson in one of these?" Justice said, her voice cold and dispassionate.

"Her and Benoît Royer, I believe his name was," Heroux said, and his voice held amusement.

"You animal," Max said, and Dana noticed how similar to Justice he seemed to be at this point. Both were agents doing their job, emotion no longer involved, and yet there was a sense that both of them were holding a tight rein on their anger.

"Do you know what the penalty is for trespassing in French Guiana?" Heroux asked.

"Jail time or a fine," Max replied, his voice like steel.

"Oh, I thought we were allowed to do as we wished to trespassers," said Heroux, looking around as though he were expecting someone to answer. "I'm pretty certain that we can do it right here, though." He smiled – a twisted affair given the scarring on his face, that only served to make the man more of a nightmare figure. "Why don't you step into the room?" he asked, and with his guards, made it clear that there was little choice. Dana, Justice and Max all moved towards the door, with Dana stepping through, taking the plunge.

The circular room they were in had a large well at the

center, and Dana looked down into it, seeing that there was nothing particularly exciting about the metal cylinder. She looked up and it was there she saw what was presumably the plasma torch. There were clearly two different devices hanging above them, and as she watched, the one that was currently the closest moved back and the other one came forward, lowering into position. It looked like a long metal cylinder that came to a large blunt end.

"We basically just toss the waste down the tube and then switch on the machine. There's a timer, so we can activate it, step outside and let it do its thing. I know what you're thinking," Heroux gave his twisted grin as he continued, "You're thinking if the controls are on the inside, you can change them. Can't, because you have to fingerprint activate it to bring up the controls in the first place, and your fingerprints aren't in the system." He turned to Wilcox who was working the controls. "Let's give them ten minutes, Paul. I think that's fair."

Wilcox had the decency to look nervous, but nodded at the instruction and turned back to the controls, and after he finished, there was a hum around the room, and Dana could feel the hairs on her arm start to rise slightly. With a degree of indecent haste, Wilcox gave the room one more look over and then quickly stepped out.

"The plasma arc will activate, and blast down the tunnel. You're probably thinking you'll escape alive, because you won't be in the tunnel, but," Heroux shook his head, taking in the entire room. "The thing is the heat buildup is incredible. We worried about the controls actually getting damaged, but then we found a way to make sure that they would stay safe. You guys...well, the heat in here is going to get to pretty extreme heats. It's like an enormous acetylene torch is just hanging above you, and here's the thing: the tunnel will start to rise up so that it can make sure everything falls to the bottom, and that will include you. And once that happens…well, at least it's quick." Heroux smiled one more time, and then stepped out of the room. "Goodbye," he said politely. "Give my regards to Melissa and Royer, won't you?"

With a final chuckle, he slammed the door shut.

ELEVENTH REPORT: TWISTED SMILE

Dana could feel the floor below them start to move almost as soon Heroux closed the door, and even though they knew it was futile, Max immediately crossed to the control panel, but it remained steadfastly blank, a little orange countdown playing out in front of them.

9.37...9.36...9.35...

Dana, however, had something else on her mind and to the surprise of her companions, she went to the edge of the tunnel, and taking something of a leap of faith, she lowered herself into the well area. Thankfully it wasn't too deep and though she couldn't touch the floor as she hung from the edges, when she let go, she didn't fall too far.

"What are you doing?" Max called down to her, looking nervously at the mouth of the plasma arc that was starting to glow a little.

"Do you remember what we were saying when we looked at this place from the outside?" Dana called back. She placed her hands on the walls of the well and began to feel her way around the well.

"Not particularly," Max called back, and by now Justice had joined him, looking down into the well.

"Dana, we don't have time," she said. "You must have

felt the floor moving."

"It's going to angle up and force us to fall into the well, so I figured I might as well get that process started early," Dana called back. Her hands were still on the walls of the well, clearly looking for something.

With a thud, Justice landed beside her, and Dana broke away from what she was doing to look at the American.

"What are you doing, for the love of God," Justice said, her face a mask of annoyance.

"We thought there was some sort of door that opened into the lake," Dana said, and Justice immediately caught on.

"If this experiment got out of control they could flood this and the plasma arc would, if not stop functioning, then do no damage at all until it burnt itself out," Justice said, and Dana grinned at her.

"Find the hatch," Dana continued, "and we either get out, or they open the doors to see what is going on."

"You're one crazy bitch," Justice said, but like Dana she began to press her hands against the wall to see if they could find the hatch.

"What are you doing?" bellowed Max down to them, but neither woman replied.

"Justice," Dana said, and indicated a small indentation in the wall. Justice came over to her and wrapped her fingers into the hollow, her face a mask of concentration. Then she turned to Dana.

"There's a button. It's probably the release for the hatch. Dana, if this opens, we may get a lot more than we bargained for. I don't think we'll get out. The force of the water…" She left the sentence hang, but Dana just shook her head.

"What have we got to lose?" Justice risked a glimpse up and saw that the arc was starting to spark, and the hum from the machine was now clearly audible.

"Brace yourselves!" Justice screamed, and Dana pushed herself up against the wall beside Justice, seeing that above Max had opened his eyes, suddenly realizing exactly what the intention of the women was. He disappeared from view, and Justice depressed the button.

The result was not only immediate, but so much more than the women thought it would be. A klaxon began to sound, ringing around the room, and beside Max the main doors flung open. The lights went down, to be replaced by dull red lighting. Most importantly of all, though, the wall panel beside Justice blew inwards, and water did what all liquids did – it moved into the empty space to fill it. The force was impressive, and it was moments before both women were up to their waists in water.

"We'll have to ride it up," Justice hollered to Dana, and Dana nodded, preparing herself to tread water to get to the top of the well and rejoin Max.

It took a surprisingly short time for the water to fill the well, and the women scrambled over the edge, picking themselves up.

"We have to get out of here," Max said. "This room is below the water so that it floods completely. We have to get back to the factory." Dana nodded at him, unable to get the breath to respond properly, and they headed for the now open door. When they stepped through, however, they received a rude shock, as someone slammed a gun into the back of Max's head, knocking him to the ground. Dana noted in her periphery, that Justice was under attack from another guard, but standing before her was Heroux.

"Moreau was right about you," he snarled. "You're way more resourceful than we gave you credit for. Certainly, more resourceful than that waitress bitch I put out of her misery. But now, I think, you've used up all that resourcefulness." He raised his gun, and with little option available to her, Dana thew herself at the man's legs, the gun going off and the bullet flying over her head ineffectively. Heroux hit the ground roughly and tried to keep hold of the gun, but his hand smashed against a lab table on the way down, and he instinctively dropped the gun.

However, he was much stronger than Dana, and when he was able to punch her in the face, his fist connected solidly, making Dana wonder briefly if she'd been hit by a sledgehammer. His second punch connected with her stomach, knocking the wind out of her, and she collapsed to the floor, struggling to draw breath.

Dimly, she noticed that Max had engaged in a fight with the guard that had attacked him, and Justice was on her feet fighting hers. They were probably the easier fights, she consoled herself with more mirth inside than she could possibly manifest on her face. She needed an advantage, but she could barely draw breath, let alone try to work out what she could use to fight back.

Her brain, however, suddenly realized that this wasn't the lab that they had entered through. This was one of the active labs. They had five or so doors to escape from, and they had chosen the one that Heroux and his thugs were waiting in? Had he got lucky or were they just unlucky. It was largely irrelevant.

367

All of this went through her head in less than half a second, which meant that she was still musing on her bad luck when Heroux swung at her again, presumably having decided that beating her to death was going to be far more entertaining than shooting her. She flung herself away as he came down upon her, and though she smashed her face into the leg of the lab table beside her, a number of things tumbled down, both onto her and onto Heroux.

She grabbed the nearest thing she could and slammed it against Heroux, but was disappointed to find that it was nothing more than a test tube which she struggled to keep hold of, and which simply slid out of her hand. Heroux lashed out again, and Dana ducked, a little delighted when he connected with the table, causing him to growl in pain.

Pulling herself away from Heroux, Dana was finally able to bring herself to her feet, and as she stood in front of Heroux, she decided to go down the horror movie route of grabbing what was on the table in front her and throwing it. Heroux knocked the test tubes and keyboards aside, though when she placed both hands on the table, she was a little surprised to find that under one of her hands was a pair of scissors. The other had landed on a mouse, which she threw at Heroux, and he knocked aside, but by now he was almost upon her and she stabbed into him with the scissors.

Heroux looked down at his stomach, blood pooling out of him, and then, to Dana's astonishment, he looked at her and smiled. He reached up and in a display of manliness that Tarzan would have been proud of, ripped off his shirt exposing his chest. The scars on his face went down much further, and Dana was a little horrified to see the spider-web of scarring across the man's body.

"You know why they call me Heroux?" he asked, mockingly. "I was with a group in Iran a long time ago. We were working on a gun deal. I had just got into the business." He was stepping forward with each sentence, and Dana made she stepped back, willing herself not to get sucked into this story. "One night we were camping, because there was nowhere for us to stay. So, we were in our tents. I didn't even know they had wolves in Iran, but they do. And they came at night, as only wolves do. You know that they say there's no honour among thieves? It's true, Ms Spectra. They threw me to the wolves. I fought back, and lived, but I was marked for life. This," he said, and pulled out the scissors, not even wincing in pain. "This is *nothing!*"

She had got sucked into the story. As he mimicked her attack, and thrust the scissors into her stomach, she realized she had done exactly what she had told herself she wasn't going to. Now she would have a scar on her stomach.

Christa Adams was going to be pissed.

If she lived.

Actually, if she died, Adams would be pissed as well.

"*Nothing!*" Heroux roared on her face, and he wrapped his hands arounds her throat. She could hear that Max and Justice were still fighting, so there was going to be no last-minute gunfire to save her life this time. And there were no real weapons to hand to fight back either. She was going to get strangled to death with a pair of scissors in her stomach.

Oh.

Dana let out a scream of pain, and Heroux's twisted

smile grew, a look of satisfaction across his face that he was finally going to end the girl's life.

And with the last of her strength, Dana drove the scissors straight up through Heroux's jaw and into his brain. He released her, staggering for a moment, a look of utter incomprehension on his face, before he fell to his knees and then to the floor.

Dana bent over, her hand to her stomach, feeling the blood oozing through it. All around her the room seemed to be going a little hazy, but, irony of ironies, she saw Heroux's gun on the floor. Wincing at the discomfort, she bent down and picked it up and then took a deep breath before standing back up again.

The pain was excruciating. Dana blinked a couple of times, and then, gritting her teeth, she raised the gun and fired two shots, one at Justice's attacker and one at Max's attacker. She was a good shot, she thought. She probably just saved their lives. Maybe.

And then everything went black.

UNITED STATES OF AMERICA

FIRST REPORT: MEDICAL ATTENTION

Dana Spectra opened her eyes, and was a little surprised to find that she was in a hospital room that was rather lush. She didn't remember falling asleep in such a room, or travelling to one. Very, very odd.

The door opened, and a young woman in a nurse's outfit came in, giving her a little smile.

"Wow, the celebrity's awake," she said, with a distinctly American accent. "I'll have to spread the word. How are you feeling?"

Dana opened her mouth to respond, but was surprised at how dry her mouth felt. She blinked a couple of times, and the nurse – who Dana noted was named Hannah, thanks to the handy name badge – handed her a glass of water, which she sipped at gratefully. There was an IV in her arm, she realized and a monitor on her finger.

"Not bad," she finally said. "What happened?"

"What happened, when?" Hannah replied, as she looked at the screen that the monitor on her finger was connected to.

"Why am I here?"

"Apparently you got stabbed in the stomach in the Ivory Coast," Hannah said. "I won't lie, that sounds like the most incredible story that I've ever heard, but the people you were with wanted you to have the best medical attention they could get, and you were flown here, post haste. I mean, I won't lie, I don't know who would do that for me."

"I would," Dana said weakly, and then felt a little ashamed of herself for her bad habits. Though speaking of bad habits, she could go a Blue Lagoon. And a meal, a proper meal. Something that was full of carbs and was decidedly bad for the health.

In fact, just some McDonalds would do fine.

"Are you flirting with me?" Hannah asked, a little grin on her face. "I'd sort of thought the rumours of you being a bit easy were exaggerated." Dana felt weak, but held out her hand, and to her surprise the nurse took it. Dana squeezed it, and then put her head back on the pillow, her eyes starting to close. The drink in her other hand was rescued by Hannah, who put it on the table.

"How about you have a nap, and then we can talk about a date after?" Hannah whispered, but Dana was already back in the land of morphia.

"The nurse said that you were making the moves on her," Justice said, and Dana raised an eyebrow.

"That doesn't sound like me," she said, but found it hard not to grin.

"How are you feeling?"

"Good, fine. The scar is going to be a pain," she moaned.

"Can't you get plastic surgery to fix it?" Justice asked.

"I already have the one on my thigh. What's another?" Dana said, though in truth she wasn't happy about it. She was already embarrassed by the scar on her leg; a second one didn't fill her with joy. But, in some ways, she had got into modelling to overcome that particular self-doubt, so a new scar would be a smaller hill.

Besides, it wasn't like there weren't other models with markings. She would definitely still be employable.

Hopefully.

"Your phone has been going off, so you probably need to spend some time addressing that," Justice said, handing it over, and Dana opened it to see that there were a few people she expected to see on the list. Her parents, her sister, her manager, Karim Narogin and, rather interestingly, Ash Frost.

"Where's Max?"

"Oh," Justice's smile broadened. "A little sweet on him, are you?"

"I'd like to know if he made it out alive," Dana said.

"He did, no thanks to you."

"What the hell's that supposed to mean?"

"Well, you did a spectacularly good job of shooting my attacker in the head. Max's you were a little off, and the bullet went between them, scaring the living daylights out of both of them. Fortunately, Max recovered quicker." Dana felt herself go red.

"I was blacking out at the time," Dana murmured, feeling ridiculously embarrassed.

"I'm grateful that you saved my life," Justice said sweetly, and Dana narrowed her eyes.

"I'm also grateful," came a voice that sounded not unlike honey pouring onto toast.

"I'm so sorry," Dana said, turning to Max.

"What for?"

"I didn't mean to almost shoot you!"

"You didn't," Max said, puzzled, and Dana turned to see Justice wetting herself with laughter. "You killed my attacker. Just in the nick of time, I might add."

"Well," Dana said sourly, and Justice snorted.

"I missed a joke, didn't I?" Max said.

"Not really," Dana replied. "Jokes are funny."

"I'm glad you're well, because there's something we have to talk about." He took out a small device which he switched on, and then switched off again. "We should be fine here. Justice and I tried to put together what we saw in the labs, and honestly most of it was nothing. But the empty room, was definitely a project being overseen by Thomas McAteer. It's definitely nanotech, and it's some sort of heart monitor. I couldn't get heaps of information, but it seemed to be some sort of heart monitor, or maybe a pacemaker."

"There was a logo as well," Justice said. "Did you see it?"

"What sort of a logo?" Dana asked. Justice pulled out her phone and showed Dana the picture that she had taken earlier.

"That's the Shadow logo," Dana said. "The drink."

"What's a pacemaker got to do with an energy drink?" Justice wondered.

"There's more," Max said. "Silhouette Moreau left Côte d'Ivoire and went straight to French Guiana. I think we know what the oil rig is doing, and why it uses so much power."

"It's another plasma arc," Dana said.

"I can't see the connection between eco-preservation, plasma arcs, energy drinks and heart monitors," Justice mused, sitting back in her chair and putting her foot on Dana's bed. "Well, I mean, I can see the connection between eco-preservation and plasma arcs. The other two…I just don't see it."

"I'm not that old," Dana said, and the other two looked at her.

"That old for what?" Justice asked.

"It's something," Dana started to say, then stopped. "I don't know. Maybe. I…" She frowned as her brain tried to make a connection, but didn't quite get there.

"I think we need to go to French Guiana. And by we, I mean Justice and I, obviously. Not you, Dana," Max said, and the look on his face suggested that he wasn't going to listen to any further conversation, which Dana had to admit that, in hindsight she thought it was a bit weird. Surely, he couldn't have been that unaware of her personality at this point?

"Seriously?"

"You're wounded."

"I'm going to be discharged this afternoon," Dana said, with a confidence born from lying about her height when she was younger to agents.

"They aren't serious?" Max said in astonishment.

"Well, I'm sewn up, there's not much more they can do, is there?" Dana looked at him, with the same attitude cats give when they remain on the middle of a street as a car drives up to them. Max had a similar chicken-instinct as the drivers, and he was the first to turn away.

"Fine," he said, but before he could continue, Dana had interrupted him.

"I started this, Max, I think I'm entitled to see it through!" she said.

"You heard me say fine, right?"

"I'm just saying, it's not unreasonable to want to put an end to this, and I saved both your lives, *and* I killed an international gun runner." She folded her arms and sat back on the bed, slightly regretting her actions as a stab of pain went through her gut.

"I said fine."

"Just saying."

"You are a pain in the ass," Max said, though there was the hint of a smile on his face.

"Right?" Justice said, throwing her hands up in the air. "This is what I was saying!"

"We'll get things ready. You recover. We head off tonight." Max moved forward and took her hand, squeezing it, and she responded the same way, smiling at him.

He was genuinely hot, she reflected. How much older than her would he be? 10 years? Probably more. Over thirty, but probably not past forty. Though, maybe he just looked good for his age.

"Yo, let's go," Justice harrumphed, and Max released her hand and walked out after the American.

Dana watched him go, taking a moment to have some optimism in her life for a short while, but it was rudely interrupted by her phone ringing.

"Hello?"

"Where the fuck have you been?" Bella's voice exploded in her ear.

FRENCH GUIANA

SECOND REPORT: CONVERSATION REPLAYED

Maximilien Travere stared out from the window of his third-floor room in the yellow (and slightly dingy) Hôtel Des Amandiers and mused that it looked like it would be yet another stormy night for the mission. To the right he could see Anse Nadau, and to the left, Anse de l'Hôpital – Nadau Cove and Hospital Cove. They looked not entirely dissimilar, with the beautiful green grass and dull grey sand separated by serious black rocks that weren't moving for any man or beast. Some of the rocks reached a hand out to the sea, their jagged black fingers getting absorbed by the dull grey water that seemed to reflect the sky above it, despite the desperate attempts by the sun to bring some colour to a sea that wasn't in the mood.

The hotel was 3 stars, which Dana had mentioned the moment they had arrived, and the two spies had looked at her as if she were mad. She apologized, quickly saying that she wasn't that sort of girl, though Justice had given her a look that said "No, you definitely are that sort of girl." It was interesting, Max reflected, because he wasn't entirely sure what kind of girl Dana really was.

His life was fairly straightforward, and though he sort of wished for a normal relationship, he had resigned himself to the idea that perhaps it was never going to happen. But he clung to it, a little like a lifesaver, because when he looked at Justice he saw someone that he didn't think he ever wanted to be. There was an emptiness to Justice; a hole that had been created, maybe by the job or maybe by something else in her life, but either way it was a hole that she had decided could only be filled by the job or by... well, by a vice, whatever that vice would be. And he recognized the fact that such a hole was starting to appear in himself.

Not too long ago, he had seen a counselor, as mandated by the job, and when they had spoken, he had asked Max how long his career might continue.

"Do you think there's an issue?" Max had replied, curious as to where the question had come from.

"Not at all," the counselor said, a smile on his face (practiced, reassuring). "But a lot of jobs have a life expectancy. Mine does. What about yours? How long do you think you will continue to live this life?"

"Why does yours?" The counselor didn't break at all, and his response was just as quick as all the others.

"I think that if you spend your entire life dealing with the issues of other people, you can't always just be a sponge and absorb it, because all sponges sort of fall apart after a while. Surely that would happen to me as well? I'm not Superman. I don't have the ability to just laugh off the pain and drama of other people, and if I could, I doubt I would be very good at my job. So, at some point, I will need to sit down and say, how much more of this heartache can I take? How much longer can I watch people struggle with life, trying my best to help them cope, while perhaps not coping myself? But if I can be realistic enough to accept that, I wonder can you? How much longer do you think you can live this life?"

Max had looked blankly at him, because he didn't have an answer, and the counselor had smiled that same beatific smile and reassured him that he wasn't going to have a mental breakdown tomorrow, but perhaps he should give some thought to the question.

Meeting Dana and Justice had made him think about these things a little more. Dana was fun, and alive, and had a heart and a soul, and though she probably drunk a little too much if she wanted to take this job seriously (or perhaps she didn't...), and she definitely flirted a lot, she wasn't as shallow as Justice liked to paint her. There might be a time when the two of them had some adult fun, but it certainly wouldn't last – she was a butterfly and would move on as soon as she got bored, and he was far too old to pursue any serious sort of relationship with her. But she was certainly more captivating than Justice Kennedy. Kennedy was gorgeous, without doubt, drank and fucked more than she should as well, but there was that hole. She had seen too much, and it had taken something from her.

Max wasn't sure if he was older than Justice, but she had a lot of street years, and even if she were younger, she seemed to be the Ghost of Christmas Future, reminding him about the decision he needed to direct his life in.

"You worked out where we're going from here?" came a voice with a distinctive American twang, and Max turned to see that Justice had walked in.

"Yeah, *Phare de l'Enfant Perdu* is up there," and he pointed up the coast, though it was just a direction. "There's a little commune up there called Macouria, and that's where we got to the lighthouse last time. We don't have to do it this time, but that's where we'll get a boat and then we head out to sea and hopefully to the Silhouette Systems second research station, which is definitely not some sort of archeological rig."

"How long will it take us to get there?" came the Australian voice, and Max turned back to the room, a little surprised to see Dana there. For a moment his voice caught in his throat, as with the sunshine making her hair blonde, the white singlet and the denim shorts, Max briefly thought that Melissa Andersson was standing in the room with him.

"An hour or so," he said, once he got his bearings back. Dana joined him on the little balcony outside the room, and the three stood there, looking up the coast.

"It's going to rain, isn't it?" Justice said, feeling as down as the weather.

"It tends to around here. That sort of climate."

"I think I like it better than the Congo," Dana said, a little unnecessarily.

"There're few places I don't like better than the Congo," Justice replied.

"Are we going to hire a car?"

"Yeah, I should go and do that," Max said. "And probably check in with the office. They might want to know I've arrived safely."

"I should do that as well, before we set off," Justice agreed. "See if the analysts have any useful information that might save us some time."

To Dana's surprise, the two got up and walked out, leaving her in the room alone – a room that wasn't even hers.

There was not much else for her to do, and so she

decided to leave the hotel and go for a walk on the Place opposite the hotel. The calls to her family in America had reassured them somewhat – particularly her sister who had rather lost her mind with fear – and calling Karam back also revealed that ASIO were a little concerned about what she was doing.

"Obviously I can't tell you what to do," Karam had said, though there was a note in his voice that made it clear he was going to tell her what to do, "but ASIO and ASIS would prefer it if you didn't bring Australia into disrepute."

"Is this some cool bit where you say if I'm captured, knowledge of me will be disavowed..." Dana said, but she was interrupted.

"You're not going to be disavowed, because you're not working for the Australian government, are you?" Karam said petulantly.

"You sound annoyed."

"Oh, ha ha," Karam replied. "Seriously Dana, we know who you're with. ASIS have been monitoring you and have seen you leave and enter several different countries with an Interpol agent and a DGSE agent. Interpol are being surprisingly unforthcoming in regards to what Justice Kennedy is doing, and the French are pretending they don't know what we're talking about. It's making some people very nervous. And I'm one of those people."

"Is it the Australian Defense Minister? Because I can't remember his name."

"Dana, please, for the love of fucking god, be careful," Karam said. "Better yet, take a back seat and let the other two deal with whatever it is that they want to deal with."

"I can't," Dana replied, and it was a sentence that wasn't an invitation for any discussion. "Honestly, I can't. I was going to let it go, but I can't now."

"Why?"

"If I were to tell you that this was something big and something scary, would it change your mind?"

"How big and how scary?" Karam replied in a shot, and Dana paused. "Dana do you even know what is going on?"

"Have you ever had an instinct play out in your gut that you're sure about, but you're not sure why, but you're just sure about."

"You're not sure why?"

"Exactly," Dana felt triumphant, though a part of her wondered if he was mocking her.

"You think this is big and scary, but you're not sure?"

"Yes," Dana said. "Thank you for believing in me."

"Didn't say that," Karam replied pointedly. "Do you know where Trinidad and Tobago is?"

"What? No, why?"

"Because that's the nearest Australian Consulate. It's not close." There was a pause, before Karam said "Just letting you know."

"Thanks for the info," Dana replied, her voice dripping with sarcasm. "I'll try to make sure I don't need any help."

"Good luck," Karam said.

"You're genuinely pissed with me," Dana responded, slightly surprised.

"Yes, I am. This is foolish. You're about to do something for...I don't even know what reason, and you can't even tell me if it's worthwhile. So, yeah, I'm pissed." And he rang off without saying anymore. Dana was tempted to call him back to berate him for being rude, but decided instead it was hardly worth it. She didn't bother ringing Ashley. That was likely to be more anger.

The conversation replayed itself in Dana's mind as she strolled across the Place des Amandiers, enjoying the afternoon sun and the quiet burble of the sea in front of her. Cayenne seemed quite quiet all things told, and even though there was the standard noise a city made as it settled itself in for the night, in Cayenne – on the beachfront at least – that noise was muted and respectful.

She took some selfies and sent them to Bella for posting on her socials, and then on a whim, lifted up her singlet and snapped a shot of her belly with the new scar. It was a lot nicer than the one on her thigh. At the moment it was reddish and raised, but the doctors had informed her that would go down and fade, and so ultimately, she would be left with little more than a white line across her belly. That was quite different to the long scar on her inner thigh, which, while white, was not smooth, but bumpy and depressed. She paused to run her fingers along her thigh and scowled at herself, not only for the scar but her response to it.

Grow up.

She realized she had walked some distance, and across the road from her was a small convenience store, in a slightly dilapidated building that had a metal bar security door across the front, held open until the store closed. What caught her eye, though, was the large black poster with the Shadow logo on it, plastered across one of the windows, taking up far more room than it needed to. It was one of the posters with her and Asha in nothing but the black paint, seductively holding the cans in such a way that their modesty was protected. Shadow was everywhere, Dana mused.

She watched as an elderly couple exited the little convenience store, two young children running around their feet, and the older pair playfully ruffled the hair of their, probable, grandchildren, before handing them the Shadow drink to have a sip from. Only a little bit; they were far too young to be drinking that sort of drink. The grandparents then gave each other a little cheer as they then drank it down.

Everyone was drinking it, Dana thought. Sometimes it didn't take that much to capture the mood of the audience. Though the taste was amazing. Not for the first time, Dana's mind wandered back to that Justice had talked about the other day... what on Earth was the connection between Shadow and a plasma arc?

"Our planet can regenerate if it was given a chance..." Dana mused.

"I beg your pardon?" Dana twisted around and was slightly surprised to see an older lady standing beside her. She was in a dress that was definitely older than Dana was, but it was clearly comfortable, and it wrapped around the lady as easily as a Dana's favourite black dress.

"Oh, I'm sorry," Dana said, smiling at the lady. "I was just thinking aloud."

"You thinking right, child," the lady said, her face creasing with the smile that lit it up. "This ole planet could easily get better. We just gotta give it a chance. We gotta help it. You kids, you got the idea, right?" She reached out and tapped Dana on the arm, hefting the big bag on her other arm to make sure it didn't slide off. Dana put her own hand on the lady's, smiling at the contrast between the two hands. The lady took Dana's hand and squeezed it. "You keep thinking those thoughts and make this place better for everyone, you hear?" She squeezed Dana's hand one more time and continued on her path, heading towards the convenience store.

"Make this place better..." Dana played the thought over in her head. Then, her mind set, she headed towards the store herself.

THIRD REPORT: IMPLACABLE FORM

When Max pulled up in front of the Hôtel Des Amandiers, he was driving what appeared to be a burnt orange Hummer H3, which sounded impressively loud. As he eased it into the parking bay, it gave off a surprising bang, belching out black smoke. Justice breathed it in with a smile, but Dana could see she wasn't keen on inhaling the diesel fumes for a long journey.

Max had personally been quite impressed with his skills as he talked to the rental car agency, and they promised him the newest SUV they had, though as he walked out, waiting for them to bring the car around to the front of the shop, he realized that most of the cars that were parked and awaiting hire were clearly twenty years old or more. Sure enough, the Hummer H3 looked to him like it was a 2005 model ("No, no," the service staff member had said, holding up his hands and shaking his head as if to ward off evil, "this is 2010." It was definitely not a 2010 model), though in all fairness, the staff member probably hadn't lied when he said it was the newest car they had.

He had paid in cash, and no further questions were asked, which was pretty much exactly the way that Max wanted it. That said, he was aware that the women wouldn't be overly keen on the car, and he braced himself for a lecture from Miss Green Earth, whose face made it patently clear what she thought of his car hire.

"I hope the wind is against us," Dana said sweetly, and she thought she was displaying enormous self-control, though the spies both noted her impressive ability to be passive aggressive with just a smile.

"Are we ready?" Max asked. The question was a simple one, but it was meant clear in two ways, and both women nodded, understanding. For Dana it was the golden G48 Glock. One of the problems that she encountered was getting ammunition for the weapon, and so in Australia had shown her father the weapon (which he was reluctantly impressed by) and thanks to him, she had managed to obtain some ammunition. While she was in America, though, she was forced to ask Justice if it was possible to get what she needed. Justice had given her a broad smile and Dana knew that she was making another mark in the ledger. Justice Kennedy was not a something-for-nothing kinda girl.

She had also taken the opportunity in Los Angeles (her short stay in hospital had been a pleasant surprise), to get some new clothes for her journey, and as such she was now dressed in G-Star 3D black jeans (boyfriend fit), a Uniqlo brushed jersey oversized blouson (also black), and an AIRism sleeveless black top. She'd packed her gun and additional ammo into her backpack, all of which Justice regarded with a raised eyebrow and asked if she was going to ninja school for training. Dana had been tempted to comment on the American's combat trousers and singlet, asking if she was auditioning for an army movie, but then decided to say nothing, just in case Justice had actually been in the army.

Might explain a lot.

Kennedy herself had her custom Nighthawk Agent 2 on her, her personal weapon of choice, but while that was tucked into a holster that sat under her left arm, stuffed into the back of her combat trousers was a Sig Sauer P320, a brown semi-automatic pistol with a 10-round magazine. The black singlet she was wearing was covered by a white lightweight Lululemon running jacket, and happily the underarm holster didn't create an obvious bulge. Over her arm was a bag that held additional ammo, but more importantly it had a Draco Pistol in it; a crude gas-operated semi-automatic pistol, which was starting to grow in popularity among gangs in the US. It was not a weapon that the authorities approved of, but Kennedy wasn't going to be taking it back to any country she might call home.

Max was already prepared, but unlike the women, he had been satisfied with denim jeans and a dark blue polo shirt. There was a jacket – a Harrington navy one that Dana guessed was Next. It was the only concession to extravagance she had ever seen the man undertake, which was odd for what she thought spies would be like.

"Suits you," Dana said with a smirk, and pulled at his jacket edge, playfully. He smiled at her.

"Well, I try," he said.

"You succeed," Dana said, and then climbed into the Hummer.

Their journey out of Cayenne took longer than they expected, as the traffic fought against them thanks to the fact they were leaving around 3 pm in the afternoon. The rough roads were suddenly filled with cars heading in different directions, very few people feeling the need to justify their actions, or indeed alert fellow drivers as to what their intentions might be. As such, as they approached Pont du Larivot, the bridge that crossed over the Cayenne River, it was getting close to 4 pm. The city had long since given way to overwhelming greenery, though as they approached the bridge, Max told them that some offices were to their right, almost on the coast and hidden from view by the forest around them.

The bridge was smaller than Dana expected – not a rough road, of course, but not much larger than two standard lanes. As they started across the *Pont*, the moody grey clouds that had threatened them all day finally followed through, and great big splotches of rain began to appear on the windows.

"I don't think it's going to be as rough as it was the last time I went over," Max said, "but it certainly doesn't look like we're going to have a pleasant run." By the time they reached the other end of the bridge, this turned out to be true, as the rain was now coming down in full force. The dull yellow lights picked out what was ahead of them, but there was no other lighting providing them with any help to see where they were going.

Dana had the impression they hadn't really left Cayenne, as there were still roads and clusters of houses dotted on either side of them while they drove along, but when they passed through an area that was, most definitely, a town of some description, Dana briefly wondered if they had possibly made it to their destination.

"Soula," Max supplied. "Anybody need to eat?"

"After the mission I'm going to stuff my face," Justice said. "Before then, though, I'm fine."

"Yeah," Dana agreed. "I'm OK." They had driven past a McDonalds back in Cayenne proper, and with hindsight, Dana wished they had gotten something there. She had a mild craving for rubbish food, but she was reluctant to indulge until she knew exactly what she was getting into.

French Guiana was an interesting country, she decided. Not as poor as the countries she had been in over the last few weeks, and if anything defined a country's wealth it was definitely the state of their roads. Bitumen roads were a luxury in the Congo and the Côte d'Ivoire, but they were the norm in French Guiana. That being said, the cars owned by the locals didn't suggest a huge prosperity.

Her reverie was broken as the lights faded again, the Hummer once again on the road to their destination, skipping past the little roads that snaked off from the N1 motorway they were on. At one point, Dana was surprised to see them pass a bus stop, at the corner of a larger road that headed inland.

Another smaller town – Malmaison – interrupted their featureless journey, and this time Max did stop to grab some water from a white roofed convenience store that had a large yellow sign with the word Proxi in big, friendly blue letters.

"We're almost there," Max informed them. They got back into the Hummer and set off for the final part of their journey. At almost six o'clock exactly, the car drove into Macouria.

Max had outlined what was going to happen, and said that he had phoned ahead to get them a boat that would be ready for them when they arrived. Rather shockingly, instead of heading into Macouria, he swung to the right, heading off the road and into the growth to their side. For the first time, Dana understood why he had got the Hummer, as it comfortably navigated its way through the bushes and scrub with ease. Before too long they had broken out of the forest and were on the beachfront. Max pulled the car up, and the three of them looked out their windows, the rain falling around them.

"That," Max said, and he pointed out to sea, "is the Atlantic Ocean. Wild, huh?" He pointed slightly to their left and giving Dana a look said, "Trinidad and Tobago. Nearest Australian consulate." He swung his hand about 100 degrees to his right and said "Africa." He looked at Dana with a compassionate smile. "You've had quite the journey." Dana couldn't disagree, and for a brief moment she wanted to lay down and properly rest. Sadly, that would have to wait.

Max moved the car forward a little, using the high beams to pick out what was along the beachfront ahead of them, and he gave a small sigh of relief when the light picked out an older man with an impressive belly, standing beside a rope that kept a firm grip on the little boat that was floating off on the sea beside him.

"*Bon jour!*" he called out to them, his voice as deep as Dana suspected it would have been. The trio climbed out of the car and headed towards their contact, who was much bigger than Dana thought he would have been. He comfortably stood above all of them, probably around 6'5". "Travere?" he asked.

"*Oui*," Max nodded and walked up to the man, who engaged in an animated conversation, pointing out to the boat, and making a number of hand gestures which were presumably explaining what was going on. At one point he rubbed his thumb and middle finger together, and Dana didn't really need much explanation about that. Max nodded at him, before taking out a wad of cash from his pocket, and counting out several notes. He then counted out a few more and handed them over, but this time there were some serious instructions that went with the money. The big man nodded his understanding and then turned to wave at the girls.

"*Je me casse!*" the man said, and set off up the beach towards the forest.

"The boat's over there," Max explained, pointing out to sea, and when Dana followed his finger, she saw a dinghy.

"You cannot be serious," Justice said, voicing exactly what was going through Dana's head. "I mean, I have to ask, why the fuck could that not be on the beach?"

"Can someone bring it to the beach?" Dana wondered.

"It's not that deep," Max said, a trifle defensively. "We can just go out to it."

"Is it not just collecting water right now?" Justice asked, and she looked up at the sky dramatically, as if to remind herself it was pouring rain.

"I'm assuming we aren't going to just stay here and hope it comes to us," Max grumbled.

"Lucky you bought your amazing new shoes," Justice said, and Dana rolled her eyes at the older woman. Resigned to the fact she had just spent a lot of money on clothes that were clearly going to get damaged very quickly, Dana followed Max into the water, and Justice brought up the rear, grumbling at every step she took.

Max had been right about one thing – when they got to the dinghy, they were only up to their knees in water, and after hauling their bags into the boat, the trio climbed in, Dana nimbly bouncing in, but she and Max both helped Justice get into the boat.

Max leant across to start up the engine, and was secretly delighted when it instantly responded. The rain started to get heavier, and Max pointed out to sea in a certain direction, though it was all meaningless to Dana who wasn't seeing much thanks to the sheets of water, though if she squinted into the night, she did think she could possibly see a light glowing in the distance.

Max steered the boat forward into the darkness, and they proceeded forward, presumably to their destination.

"How do we get in?" Dana asked.

"Melissa and Royer went under water to do it, but I've been studying it for a bit. Even sent a drone over there. There's an entrance on the side that's away from us, so we can go around and get in."

"What sort of an entrance?" Justice asked.

"There's a ladder, it goes up to a door, and then we open it and *voila*!"

"The other lab had a finger printed doorway and a code," Dana protested.

"My drone had a good camera," Max grinned. "I've had the code for a while."

"Oh, the code you tried at the other lab, that didn't work," Dana said.

"It was worth a try," grinned Max.

Silence descended on the trio as the boat disappeared into the darkness of the night, guided only by Max's apparent excellent sense of direction. Max and Justice were getting into the right mindset for their mission, prioritizing their goals and making certain decisions based on what was required and what they might need to do. Dana was in a world of her own; the knowledge that Max knew the code to the rig made her realise that so much of the mission they were now on had been taking place without her knowledge. She was still working on coming to terms with the fact she wasn't going to know everything about what was happening in her new life, so it seemed a little strange to discover that something she had been pursuing so doggedly had been worked on from at least one other direction. Two, given that it didn't seem likely Justice and Max had worked together for a long time before she had encountered them in…gosh, in the *Congo?* Had it really been that long ago?

Actually, how long ago had it been? Time had started to blur together and she hadn't really sat down to get a good idea of how long she had been away. She would need to get back into work with a vengeance when she returned to Australia, not just to make Christa Adams happy, but also to remind her fans that she was still alive.

Oh, and the money.

Should she get a house away from her family?

Slightly annoyed with herself, she shook her head, as if to force out a number of pointless details, and brought her head back in the game. She reached behind her to see how quickly she could get to her Glock and reflected it might be a little difficult to do. She should probably take it out and place it somewhere else. Looking across, she saw that Justice had pulled out of her bag, what seemed to be like a mini machine gun; she was clearly ready for whatever was going to come at them. Max was piloting the boat, so he hadn't done anything yet.

As she looked up, she saw that the rig was coming into view, the dull lights on it shining through the rain as it continued to fall upon them. She had been a little worried that the boat would start to fill with water, but happily that wasn't the case, and the dinghy was doing very well under the circumstances. Thanks to the rain, however, everything looked ghostly and ethereal, despite the consistent noise of water slapping against water all around them.

Dana narrowed her eyes suddenly, bringing a hand up to shield them from the rain. Had she just seen something in the sea?

"Is there something out there?" Dana said to Justice, who frowned at her.

"The rig?"

"No, something else?"

"In the water? There's nothing too terrible I don't think. Like some big fucking fish maybe but nothing else."

Dana rolled her eyes slightly, feeling she was wasting her time with the conversation, and turned back to the ocean. Had there been a shadow?

"Almost there!" Max shouted, and Dana reached for her backpack to get her Glock ready.

The darkness was opaque and Dana felt fear grip at her heart. Her instincts screamed that there was definitely something out there.

"Guys," she shouted, but it was far too late. Suddenly

flood lights illuminated around them, from two boats to one side and one behind, as well as from the rig itself.

"Dana!" came a cheerful voice, and she looked to the boat to the right to see the immaculate form of Silhouette Moreau standing there. Beside him, the implacable form of Chillo, her long dark hair matted to her head thanks to the rain, the carving knife in her right hand glinting thanks to the lights reflecting off it. "Would you like to come in out of the rain? Your friends as well, of course. Come on, come on. Chillo, would you help them aboard?" Chillo grinned, the piercings in her face highlighting the cute dimples that formed.

It was the third of Silhouette's offices that Dana had been in recently, and he was right – they were all much the same. The design, the layout, the furniture. Consistent and, relatively dull, really. Dana sighed slightly, and glanced across to the drinks cabinet, thinking that she could really go a drink.

"Dana, Dana, Dana, Dana," Moreau said, as he rested himself against his desk and regarded her. She stood between Justice and Max, and was acutely aware of how close Chillo was behind her. So close she could feel the woman's breath on her neck. It was bizarrely erotic, and Dana chided herself – place and time, for fuck's sake, woman.

"When I was informed by my employees that Mr Heroux had been murdered, I knew immediately who did it. It was obvious, of course. I underestimated you," and Silhouette actually chuckled at that comment. "I'm prepared to admit when I'm wrong. I'm a big enough person to do that. I thought Heroux would successfully take care of you…the three of you…and I'd be able to push ahead with my brilliant plan." Two of Silhouette's thugs came forward, carrying three bags, two of which Dana identified as hers and Justice's backpacks. The third she assumed belonged to Max, and this seemed to be confirmed as the bags were emptied out onto the floor, with Justice's machine gun, her own Glock and two more guns that were presumably going to come from Max. "Chillo?" Silhouette said, and Dana suddenly felt the smaller woman's hands running over her body, between her legs, up her bum and then her sides. She did the same for Justice, but paused as she found the Sig Sauer in the waistband and the Nightwing holstered under her arms.

"Who's got the better boobs?" Justice said to Chillo as the killer's hands ran over Justice's breasts. "It's Dana, isn't it? But just say me to boost my ego." Chillo stared coldly into Justice's eyes and then conducted a similar search of Max, resulting in two more weapons being produced – a Smith & Wesson M&P, and a M9A3 Beretta. Weird, Dana reflected. She hadn't picked him as a Beretta man. Perhaps he was simply going with what he had available. Chillo tossed the guns onto the pile at Silhouette's feet. The business man had picked up the golden Glock and was looking at it with interest.

"Whose is this?" he asked. "No, wait, let me guess. Flamboyant, modified, I'm guessing it's yours," he said, pointing the gun at Justice. "It seems like your sort of thing. Flashy and American."

"Actually, it's hers," Justice said, smugly, indicating with her thumb. "Though to be fair, she was given it. She didn't choose it."

"Oh, that makes sense. Your father's military, isn't he?"

"Don't talk about my father," Dana said emotionlessly, and Silhouette raised his eyebrows, but was stopped from saying anything by Max.

"How did you know?"

"Excuse me?" Silhouette turned to him, confused.

"How did you know we were coming? We didn't tell anyone."

"You had to arrange a boat," Silhouette said with a smirk, and Max rolled his eyes, though Dana suspected that underneath the cool façade he was cursing himself. "Yes, the *travailleur* who rented you the boat works for me. He let us know as soon as you met him that three *étrangers* had just rented a boat and was heading out to sea. He talked about a beautiful white woman and I was fairly certain I knew who was coming."

"*Fils de pute*," Max growled and Silhouette's grin grew.

"I don't disagree," the businessman said, the smile never leaving his face. Then, with a slight frown, he bent down to the pile of rubbish at his feet and picked up two cans that were in there. They bore the distinctive Shadow logo, and he looked at them puzzled. "You brought these?" he said, looking at Dana.

"Well, I am the brand ambassador," she said.

"Oh, so true, so true. And we will be very sorry when you die. You know that Silhouette Systems is really going to donate to a charity on your behalf when people discover you've died. So sad, so sad, but it is what it is. You understand." He walked up to Dana and gave a little smile. "You know it's not personal."

"I know you talk a lot of shit," Dana said.

"Do I?" Silhouette seemed to think this over for a bit, and then took the two cans of drink to his bar, where he placed them upon it. "You know, you're a clever girl, but you're not as intelligent as you think, right? Otherwise, you'd know what is going on."

"Well, I wish you'd fucking tell us," muttered Justice. "This is definitely the lowest point of my day. Getting captured I can deal with, but you pretending you're some sort of clever, cryptic mastermind is just killing me." Chillo grabbed Justice by her jacket collar and pulled her back, the knife going straight to the back of Justice's neck.

"Chillo," chided Silhouette. "I'll happily tell you."

"No, let me," Dana said, and Silhouette turned to her, his face mirroring the confusion that both Max and Justice had.

"I beg your pardon?"

"I think I've finally put it together. The plasma arcs, the Shadow, the eco-preservation, the nano-technology. I think I know what you're planning to do. There's only one detail I don't know, but I reckon you can supply that."

"Oh?" Silhouette looked at her curiously.

"How old is too old?" Dana asked, and Silhouette seemed genuinely thrown by the question.

"What?" Max asked, but Dana held up her hand.

"He knows what I mean. How old, Silhouette?"

"I don't think I'd like to live past 70," he said, but his voice lacked the previous authority.

"Then that's the last piece of the puzzle."

"Being?"

Dana glanced to her right and left, seeing her friends looking at her with the same mixture of puzzlement and concern as Silhouette Moreau. It was a precise moment as she captured the attention of everyone in the room.

"You're going to kill everyone on the planet over the age of seventy." The two spies turned to Silhouette, their faces now trapped between shock and disbelief. Silhouette looked at them and then turned his attention directly to Dana.

"Oh, very good."

FOURTH REPORT: FRENEMIES MAYBE

Silhouette Moreau held his hand out, inviting Dana to continue her explanation, as he wandered back behind his desk and sat down in the chair there, sitting back to enjoy the show.

"It's all about giving the planet a chance to regenerate itself," Dana said. "The planet can do it, it just needs the chance, but if the population continues to grow, it never will, right?" Moreau nodded graciously, but didn't interrupt her. "So there needs to be some way of curbing the population, and what better to simply chose an age and kill everyone over it. I mean, obviously we don't get that decision to make, but our betters will. And by betters, I mean Silhouette Moreau." Moreau held his hands up in a "what can I say" gesture, but again said no more.

"But how?" Justice asked, no longer sure who she should be directing the question to.

"You asked about the nanobot pacemaker, and what it's purpose is," Dana said, emboldened to take a step forward, a little theatrically. "Designed by Thomas McAteer, it sends an electric pulse that forces the heart to beat, right?" Moreau nodded. "Except it can do the reverse. It doesn't just start a heart, it can easily stop it. The nanobots have a base programming, and can perform more than one function, I assume. It can assess the age of its target, and then issues the pulse if the target is over seventy.

The Shadow factory was putting nanobots into the drink, though I don't know how," she paused, looking at Silhouette.

"Dr Paul Wilcox," Moreau said, and pointed to the back of the room where a familiar bald, burly man with a goatee was standing. "He's our expert in this particular field. Well, not just ours, the world's now that Dr McAteer is dead."

"Most nanotech has a single function programmed into it because it's so small, which is to connect to a Wi-Fi source to gain further instructions. From there it can build more, create simply machines, etc, etc. We haven't sent out the worldwide signal just yet, because we need to ensure maximum coverage, but we have tested it..." Wilcox seemed to be about to speak more, but Silhouette held up his hand.

"We don't need to bore them with more details. I'm more interested in Dana telling us what we're missing." He sat back in his chair again, the smile not quite on his face anymore.

"So, people die, a massive amount of the population dead, and the planet gets the chance to rebuild because the population has diminished a lot."

"A lot?" Max said incredulously. "We're talking millions."

"Only when we activate," Silhouette protested. "I conservatively estimate 600 million; just seven-point-five percent of the population."

"600 million people will die at once?" Justice said, and Dana had never seen her quite so horrified before.

"But the planet wouldn't be able to cope with that many deaths at once," Max said, the scope of what was happening building in his mind even as he spoke. "Even if that were split evenly, one half of the world will be in summer, and that means

300 million corpses lying in streets, rotting in the sun, because morgues can't take them. Millions of people, trapped in their homes with their deceased partners decaying in front of them because there's nowhere for them to go. Panicked people calling upon emergency services which aren't going to come, because they can't handle the load." A hint of a smile was now on Silhouette's face as he seemed to enjoy the scenario Max was painting.

"Electricity costs going through the roof because the air conditioning will be on full blast in the hopes of keeping the temperatures down," Silhouette said, warming to the theme. "Maybe some buildings will work together and turn an apartment into some sort of faux morgue. Some countries would have to send out the national guard to commandeer refrigerated trucks, which would mean food delivery stopping, diary, frozen meat..." Silhouette said no more, leaving those in the room to come to the same realization. "Flower delivery would stop. No flowers for funerals."

"And then the next day everyone who turns 70 dies?" Max asked, trying to wrap his head around what was being proposed. "Every day another couple of million to add to the list?"

"The electrical grids would collapse," Max said, as he thought more and more about the consequences. "Garbage wouldn't be collected because there's just too much for services to deal with. The bodies would simply expunge the shit and piss everywhere; people wouldn't be able to clean it up. Crematoriums would be overrun, there'd be mass graves just to cover up the bodies, but cities still wouldn't be able to cope with the demand."

"Unless," Dana said, "there was somewhere you could

quickly and efficiently get rid of the corpses. A machine that would be able to reduce piles of bodies to nothing quickly and quietly. You'd only need to see the value of something like that, and then governments would be throwing their money at anyone who had one, because screw getting scientists to develop that technology. If it exists, pay the man what he needs. Because it does exist, doesn't it?" Dana turned back to Silhouette Moreau who started to giggle slightly.

"The plasma arcs," Justice breathed, the horror in her voice not remotely hidden.

"Now to be fair, this part is entirely Dr Wilcox's area of expertise," and the burly bald man took a little bow at Moreau's words. "He may be learning on the spot about the nano-tech, but the plasma pyrolysis is all him."

"We think the governments may take a few days to take advantage of our resources," Wilcox said, "but once the flies and rats start taking over the streets, they will be pretty eager."

"You're fine with this?" Max said to him, almost unable to comprehend what he was hearing.

"Our planet has been treated very badly. It's not going to be around for much longer, so if we have to cull the population and cause a bit of chaos and havoc in order to allow the younger generations to live on our planet, then I think it's a good cause."

"The voice of reason, Mr Travere," Silhouette said, standing up. The look on his face seemed disinterested with what was going on now. "Dr Wilcox, would you be so good as to show these two what happened to their friends a few weeks back. Chillo will help you with that." The burly men grabbed Justice and Max, both of whom immediately squirmed, though when they met

410

Dana's eyes, there was something there that suggested that neither had any real idea of what they would do if they managed to squirm out of the grasp of the thugs.

"Consider what you're doing a test run, my friends," Silhouette said, and Justice fought harder, managing to briefly escape and landing a solid punch on the face of her captor, but Chillo's knife was at her throat and the American forced herself to step down. "It's the end of the line, Ms Kennedy," Silhouette said. "You've done very well. You've found out what I intended to do. But that's it, I'm afraid. Thanks for playing."

Chillo and Wilcox lead the thugs out of the room, their two captors now walking, temporarily submissive, as they were led to their executions. Aside from a single guard, Dana and Silhouette were now the only two people left in the room, and a silence fell upon them, like someone throwing a dust cloth down. Dana could almost feel the weight of it upon her.

"Will it be worth it?" Dana asked, finally breaking the silence.

"There will be a lot of chaos," Silhouette said. "Riots and the like. Looting, governments trying to work out what to do with themselves. America will lose their president."

"What if they blame someone specifically? What if they decide it's a terrorist attack?" Silhouette shook his head at her solution.

"World War 3 will only break out if America decides to go after China or Russia, and the deaths will sweep across the land at the same time, so that they will know it's not either of them responsible. They might suspect aliens. I'm sure someone will suggest it. But someone will offer their services and discover that the Earth might have had a pulse in its magnetic field which caused everyone over at certain age to have a heart attack."

"People won't be that stupid," Dana protested.

"Oh please," Silhouette laughed. "You're not serious? People will be desperate for an answer, and they'll take whatever they can get. The change in field might be permanent so the next day when everyone who is newly seventy dies, they'll realise what's happening. There'll be other deaths so it'll be confusing at first to work out what's going on, and laws might need to be suspended. It will be a very rough time for the planet, and no mistake, but when we come out of it, the world will be a better place and one that is ready to be more serious about preserving the planet. And everyone will know that they now have a time limit and they'll make the most of that."

"You don't think that it will encourage people to work harder to find out about this so-called magnetic field change, whereupon they'll discover what you've done?" Dana challenged him, glaring down at him, but to her surprise he just shrugged.

"Look, it's not that bad. If someone gets too close, we'll deal with them and stop the deaths. Getting rid of all the old people will be an excellent start, and if we can't continue because people get too close to the truth, well…we just dial it back. Shadow will still be out there, and it will still be ready for action. But we can stop the nanotechnology as quickly as we start it." Dana shook her head, and turned to the one guard standing by the door. He seemed disinterested in what was being said, as though he had perhaps heard it all before. "You think we haven't tested this, don't you? You think that we've been very cavalier. I assure you that Dr McAteer was very thorough about it." He looked around on his desk and then found what he was looking for – what seemed to be like a slightly smaller phone, or perhaps a folding phone.

Silhouette took the device and touched it, and Dana saw his face go blue as the screen lit up. There were clearly two red dots on the screen, and Silhouette frowned for a moment, turning the device the other way around, though the dots didn't move. Satisfied he pressed the one furthest away from him, and the dot went white. Then Silhouette pressed a finger on the white dot and it went black.

A sudden gasp made Dana turn to see that the guard behind them suddenly grasped at his chest, wincing in pain.

"Sir, I'm," he started to say, but he was struggling to draw breath. Dana watched in horror as Silhouette watched his security guard flail in front of him, his face going slightly blue. In just a matter of minutes it was clear the guard was dead.

"What do you think? We can send a broad signal, or this device allows me to target a specific bot. Well, I say specific, I've got big thumbs so it's hard to pick a single one out of the clump. It was probably a few hundred." He grinned, as he held up the device, and Dana realized that the single red dot remaining wasn't a single red dot at all, but rather a collection of much smaller dots gathered together.

No prizes for guessing who that might be, she reflected drily.

"May I get a drink after that?" Dana asked, and Silhouette's grin didn't disappear, as he put the device on the desk and then grabbed the cans of Shadow that Dana had brought.

"Shadow?" he asked, proffering them. Dana took them,

but raised an eyebrow.

"I don't think so," she said. "I might try a wine. I'm assuming you have something good."

"It'll be your last drink, so I think that's fair," Silhouette said. "Should I?"

"I know my wines," Dana said witheringly, as she headed to the bar on the left-hand side of the room.

"I'll have one as well, thanks," Silhouette said. Dana placed the cans on the table and grabbed two wine glasses, then took a look at the wines that were sitting on the cabinet in front of her. She reached forward and grabbed the Casanova di Neri Brunello di Montalcino Giovanni Neri 2019. She was about to pop it open, when Silhouette interrupted her.

"Dana, not that one! You shouldn't drink that until 2026. It's a keeper. If I were you I'd go the El Enemigo Cabernet. There's a 2019, and it tastes incredible now. That's what I'll have." Dana moved to the other wine and she pulled the cork out, enjoying the slight hiss. She poured a glass suspecting she'd poured more than the 150 ml, but doubted he would care. She was about to pour her own glass when she saw the Shadow.

It was when she had seen the old couple drinking the Shadow that she remembered the injection system that she had seen in the warehouse, the Shadow logo that Justice had snapped a picture of, all of which finally allowed her to make the connection that the nanobots were in Shadow, which prompted her to buy two. A vague plan had started to form, but it was nebulous and the details weren't remotely exact. She'd needed more information before her brain could properly lock the idea into place. Silhouette revealing that he could very specifically target the nanobots was the key to firming up the plan. Finding out that he had none in his system meant she finally knew what she could do with the Shadow she had.

She could change that.

"I'm more of an Italian wine person, myself," Dana said.

"Oh, well, there's a Siro Pacenti Brunello di Montalcino there, but I'd give it another three years before drinking. Up to you though." He shrugged and turned to go back to his chair. "I should do something about that body," he muttered to himself.

Dana grabbed the Siro, and then, angling herself to hide her actions, she opened the muselet, and then tugged at the cork, working it so that it was almost out. Then she placed her right hand on the cork, and the left on a can of Shadow, and timing it, she popped the cork and opened the can, at the same time as faking a sneeze.

She paused, wondering if she had been too over the top.

"Bless you," came Silhouette's voice. Dana exhaled softly.

"Thank you," she said tartly. Then as she poured herself a glass, she added Shadow into Silhouette's glass. "Is that enough?" she asked, turning to Silhouette and holding up his glass.

"Are you hoping I'll get drunk?" Silhouette asked with a smile. She brought his glass over to him.

"I've seen you drink. I'm fairly certain it would take more than that," Dana said.

"You're right," he agreed, and drank from his glass. He screwed up his face and looked at her. "Is that really the El

Enemigo?"

"No," Dana lied, trying to adopt an attitude she'd seen Bella use. "I just thought I'd give you the Siro as well." The look on Silhouette's face reminded her of the look on her mother's when Bella tried it on.

"I was right about giving it a few more years," Silhouette said, and put the glass on the table. He got up and headed over to the bar, and Dana saw him stiffen when he got there. He turned back to look at her, and in his hand, he had the open Shadow can. There was no need for words, though Silhouette opened his mouth to say something anyway, and Dana instinctively reacted by throwing her glass at him, and he recoiled, attempting to avoid it, though as a consequence the wine sprayed him, and his white shirt turned a rich crimson, giving the impression he had been shot. To her delight, her glass hit the counter behind him and smashed, sending glass towards him, again ensuring she wasn't the center of his attention.

With the small advantage she had, Dana turned to the desk and grabbed the device, pressing at it, and was gratified to see there was now a third colony of lights on the device, in the same red as the second; a stark contrast to the black one which seemed to be getting paler.

Silhouette looked at her, clearly weighing up his options, and Dana stared back at him, her heart in her throat.

"I will not let you," Silhouette said, raising his voice in anger for the first time Dana had ever heard him. He leapt across the room at her, and Dana pushed her finger on the moving red button, but was horrified when it refused to change. She stabbed again, hoping to anticipate the movement, and to her delight it

416

turned white, but Silhouette was now upon her and he threw a punch at her face, which connected and caused her to see sparkles of light.

The device had been flung out of her hands, and she was knocked to the floor, but Silhouette was scrabbling for the device, and Dana scrambled across the floor, trying to ignore the pain. With some effort she managed to launch herself at his legs, knocking him to the floor.

Shoved to the side, Dana was able to get hold of the device, and Silhouette roared furiously. She pressed the white button and watched it go black, but to her shock, it didn't seem to affect Silhouette at all. Instead, he continued his new charge, and within seconds his hands were around her throat, tightening and causing the lights to sparkle back in her eyes again.

She clawed at his face, kicking out with her legs at the same time, but nothing seemed to have an impact on the man, whose face now filled her vision, twisted and garish.

What a sight to be your last, she thought, a little depressed.

Wait, was his grip weakening?

Sure enough, sweat was starting to build up on Silhouette's face, and he relaxed his grip, struggling for breath. He released her as he fell back, rubbing his left arm and trying to catch his breath.

Oh, the nanobots needed some time to get to the heart, she realized.

"I thought," Silhouette gasped, "that we were friends." He looked at her, before struggling to draw another breath and then fell against the table.

"Frenemies, maybe," Dana said. She should do something, she reflected. She could save his life. Torn by indecision, she looked at the device and pressed the black colony of dots, but nothing happened.

"No," Silhouette said, shaking his head. He reached out his hand, and Dana, strangely, took it. "Best brand ambassador we have," he said with a smile, and then his hand went limp.

Dana found herself feeling guilty as she looked at him. She didn't know CPR so couldn't help in that regard, but she could maybe call an ambulance. Except they were on a rig at sea and so that wasn't likely. Also, what was the emergency number in French Guiana?

Max probably knew CPR, Dana reflected, and then paused.

Max and Justice! She jumped up and headed for the door, then turned back and grabbed her gun from the pile on the floor, and the control device for the nanobots.

Sorry Silhouette.

But maybe it's for the best.

FIFTH REPORT: AMAZING RECIEVE

Max and Justice were getting a very strong sense of déjà vu as they watched the plasma arc above them hum into life, energy starting to collect around the base. They knew they had a little time, and Justice had already begun searching for the catch to flood the well, but as she began searching, a bullet ricocheted off the wall, and she spun around to see a guard had fired at her.

"Don't make us kill you," Wilcox said, and Justice looked at him incredulously.

"What the fuck are you talking about? That's exactly what you're going to do."

"Yes, but with the arc," he said, waving his hand at it. "I mean, it's a sort of band-aid approach; just a blast and you won't even know about it. But if we have to shoot you, you'll be in a lot of pain towards the end, and I don't want that." He was English, Justice reflected, noticing the accent for the first time. There was a veritable range of nationalities on Silhouette's payroll. She was slightly impressed by his diversity drive.

Wilcox turned to the guard.

"Probably best to keep an eye on them. I'll give you proper warning when the arc is about to fire," he said, though the guard was looking a little nervous. In fairness, it wasn't the first time. Early tests had caused a couple of deaths, which meant that

Wilcox was about to lose his funding, but more importantly his credibility. When Silhouette Moreau had contacted him about what he was doing, he had been enthusiastic and tried to convince Moreau that what he was doing was worthwhile and a boon to the Earth. Moreau had told him he had to say no more after just five minutes, and the next thing he knew he had a new boss; one that was happy to clean up a few loose ends if they ever occurred.

"Another guard?" he would say, shaking his head, and the first time Wilcox was worried he was genuinely concerned. "Well, if he's been vaporized by the plasma arc, I suppose that's going to save a lot of paperwork." And Silhouette had laughed, looking expectantly at Wilcox, who also laughed a little uncertainly. Not least because he wasn't sure exactly when he had to stop laughing, which was awkward. After that, Silhouette would make the same joke, until Wilcox didn't even bother to laugh politely.

Truth to tell, Dr Paul Wilcox was slightly nervous. Up until now everything had been going quite smoothly, and though there were some people who raised concerns, those concerns went away, or the people went away, and then everything was easy again. No stress, which suited Wilcox fine, because he was beginning to suspect he had high blood pressure, and he could remember Tom McAteer at the board meeting, complaining about how he was worried that there was something going on with the programming of the nanotech which he couldn't understand and he needed reassurances that everything was fine. Then he had pointed at Paul and asked questions about the pyrolysis, and *then* he asked about some personnel issues that cropped up in Wilcox's department, and Paul Wilcox could feel the burn in his eyes as his blood pressure rose.

Then Tom was shot dead, and though Paul was upset about it, because they were friends at the end of the day, there was a part of him that was relieved. Except things started to get weird. Heroux was suddenly on site a lot more, and he was asking questions and doubling guards. There were rumours that someone was after them. When the blonde woman and the seedy little French gendarme turned up, Paul had complied with Heroux and thrown them to the reactor, but he didn't feel good about it. Obviously, it was murder, and he wasn't really comfortable with that, at the end of the day. But more than that, if these two people had started to ask questions – and one was a gendarme – then might that not suggest that others would ask the same questions?

Suddenly there were *whispers*. When Moreau turned up on the rig, he would be in huddled conversations with Heroux, or they would disappear into his office, and then occasionally Chillo would appear to escort Paul to give answers in regards to what was going on with the plasma arc project. Also, could you take over the nanotechnology project? It just needs supervising, nothing more. Wilcox couldn't exactly say no, and then the headaches seemed to be coming far more often. Not to mention that both Chillo and Heroux scared him. A lot.

Except now he was beginning to find Silhouette just as scary.

However, Wilcox did agree with what Moreau was suggesting. The planet was their planet, and no matter what people thought about somehow colonizing other worlds, the fundamental truth was that there were insurmountable pragmatic problems to overcome. It made far more sense to actually clean up the planet humans had than to simply dump it and move onto another planet in the hope they didn't screw that one up. And perhaps culling the population was not an unwise choice. People might learn to appreciate the seventy years they had more, rather than wasting it on performing activities that were both illegal and hurtful to other people.

No, broadly speaking (and no plan was perfect, let's face it) Silhouette Moreau's vision was a worthwhile one. And if he could deal with killing a *lot* of people over seventy, Paul Wilcox could deal with killing a couple of government spies.

Hence, having rationalized it rather nicely in his head, the headache that was building up began to fade, which made life much better. That was until he felt a metallic barrel pushed into the back of his head, at which point the headache came back again with a vengeance.

"Turn the plasma arc off," came a voice with an Australian twang, and Wilcox wondered what he should do. He still needed time for the arc to fully charge, but once it did the conversation would be moot. He was about to start a conversation that would distract the woman, when she seemed to read his mind. "You can turn it off now, or I can kill you one of two different ways. And I've already killed your boss so I'm pretty certain I won't be too bothered about killing you as well."

This, of course, changed the narrative completely, and so Wilcox deactivated the arc, much to the puzzlement of the guard who was watching.

"Now, I'm going to need you to deactivate the programming of the nanobots so nobody accidentally switches them on and kills 7.5 percent of the population," the voice said, and Wilcox felt brave enough to turn around. It was the Australian model (of course it was) and she had a golden gun trained on him as well as a small device that he recognized all too well. McAteer's last contribution to the project was the plans for the personalized nanobot activation pad (the PNAP, which was not a name that had caught on).

"We can just make sure that the deactivation signal is disabled so it can never be sent," said Wilcox, extremely disappointed in his lack of loyalty or indeed commitment to the project he had only minutes earlier been gushing about. Spineless, Wilcox, he chided himself.

Though both Moreau and Heroux are dead, so... spineless but alive seemed to be a better option than committed but dead. After all, both had the same outcome, but one was considerably less appealing than the other.

"You're going to do both," Dana said. "I want this project dead and buried, sunk so no one ever can reestablish it again." She suddenly swung around to where the guard appeared to be sneaking up on her. "Please don't make me use this and kill anyone. Because I will. My friends are definitely going to live, but I have no desire to end your life." The guard looked at her for a moment, and then dropped his gun.

"No, that's fair," he said. "I was getting sick of living here anyway, to be honest. Thinking about moving back home."

"Oh, where's home?" Wilcox asked.

"New Zealand," the guard said.

"You are a long way from home," Dana admitted.

"Tell me about it," the guard said. "Honestly, it's been niggling at me for the last few months that I'm really not enjoying the job, and wouldn't mind going home again. It was a break up, and you think, oh, fuck it, I'll just change countries and it'll be like a massive move that will be good for me, but it doesn't take long to miss your friends and family. A girl isn't worth."

"I would say it depends on the girl," Dana said, cheekily, and the guard looked at her.

"Are you…?" he started, but Dana cocked her head.

"Come on, mate," she said, and he put his hands above his head, just slightly disappointed.

"I'm a fan, you know," he muttered, and Dana resisted the urge to hug him.

"I'll sign something for you," was what she started to say, until Justice Kennedy screamed: "Dana, move now!"

There was a brief moment, and it was genuinely very brief, where Dana thought she wanted to argue with Justice for the sake of…well, for a teenage temper tantrum, really. But Justice sounded very insistent, so Dana threw herself to the ground, and rolled. A lot of things were happening at once, and she registered the fact that Max and Justice had pulled themselves out of the arc well. She was also aware that Wilcox and the guard were also panicking. It was, however, the presence of Chillo that she was focusing on, the tattooed woman was wearing a singlet, and for the first time, Dana appreciated just how muscular the woman's arms were, and how tattooed she was.

She stood over Dana, a sneer on her face, and Dana stole a glimpse of the PNAP and mentally rolled her eyes. Of course, this bitch hadn't drunk any Shadow. That would have made things so much easier.

Chillo launched herself at Dana, and the taller girl lifted her legs to hit Chillo in the stomach, but despite the impact, Chillo was waving her blades (she had a blade for each hand?) and Dana recoiled, slightly afraid that she'd get sliced up by the thug. Desperately, Dana looked around and saw her golden Glock some way from her, but unfortunately it looked like it was the only weapon that she had available to her.

Quickly she rolled away, trying to avoid Chillo's attacks from what was clearly now a much stronger position of power. The guard had run at Chillo from behind, and tried to grab her by the arms, but the woman was smaller and much slipperier, managing to slide down, swing around and drive a blade into the guard's stomach. Dana felt a stab of pain in sympathy, and hoped she get the man some help before he died.

Nonetheless, the guard's actions gave her a little time to pull herself to her feet so she was ready when Chillo came for her again. Dana ducked and swerved around the woman, but she was clearly a street fighter and had a lot of practice with her craft. When Dana pulled back, she saw the knife slice across her jacket.

"You bitch," Dana said, a little shocked. "Do you know how much that jacket cost?" Slightly angrier that she probably should have been, Dana kicked out at her opponent, and caught Chillo in the shin, which barely made the woman flinch, but there was a flash of pain in Chillo's eyes and Dana's common sense returned as she backed away from the killer.

"Hey!" Dana heard Max shout, and she turned to see he had thrown her the Glock. Had he lost his mind, she wondered. Instinctively she reached out and to her absolute delight the grip slid into her palm. Without even thinking she spun around, subconsciously aimed the gun and pulled the trigger. The bullet went straight through Chillo's heart, and the woman looked genuinely shocked before slumping to the ground.

"Holy fuck, did you see that?" Dana called out, and looked around at her audience. Wilcox was on the floor, terrified, the guard was clutching at his stomach, and Max and Justice were both looking at her, a little shocked.

"Time and place?" Justice asked.

"Right," Dana agreed, and raced over to the guard, sliding her gun into the back of her pants. "Are you OK?"

"It was a fucking amazing receive," he said weakly, smiling at little.

"Don't you fucking die now," Dana said. "You've actually made me guilty enough to possibly go out with you sometime."

"Right, right," he said, the smile growing. "I'd like…"

"Hey," Dana said, gripping the man's hand. "Hey!"

"Dana," Max said, and she felt his hand on her shoulder, the smallest of squeezes.

"I didn't want him to die," Dana said, numbly.

"I know," Max said. "He knew."

"He saved my life," Dana muttered. "I didn't even tell him. I didn't say thank you." Max squeezed her shoulder again, and when she turned to him, he had his hand out. She took it and stood up, a weight on her that felt heavier than anything physical that could be offered.

"Dr Wilcox here is going to take me to the control room so we can end this nanoshit," Justice said. "Then, I suggest, we get the fuck out of here."

"We need to evacuate this complex," Max said.

"We can activate the emergency alarms," Wilcox supplied, and Justice grinned.

"You get more and more useful every day, professor," Justice grinned. They headed for the room and exit, and Dana paused to look back, looking at the body of Chillo splayed out on the floor, still in what appeared to be a state of shock, while the guard was on the floor, lying in a pool of his own blood.

She hadn't even found out his name.

UNITED KINGDOM

FINAL REPORT: JUST FINE

"To be honest I was worried you weren't going to make it," Christa Adams said, and Dana sighed a little, feeling the exhaustion of the last month weighing down on her. This, she thought, would be what a blanket felt like when it had been left out in the rain, and it was waiting for the sun to come out and dry it, so that extra, depressing weight was lifted from it.

"Are you listening?" Christa snapped, her face a mask of annoyance. She pursed her lips, and Dana felt chastened, which was an amazing habit the woman had. She was dressed in a pant suit (Carla Zampatti, Dana guessed. It tended to be Christa Adams choice of brand.)

"Yes of course," Dana said. "That's why I'm here. I always listen." It was a very smooth lie, but the moment she had gotten back to proper cell service, her phone had gone off, demanding to know where she was and would she be ready for London Fashion week. Horrified, Dana quickly booked flights for London, with Max and Justice assuring her that they would be able to clean things up from here.

She felt tired and worn out, and Christa had burst into her room as she was getting changed to head out.

"What the hell is that?" had been the first thing out of her mouth as she saw the new scar that Dana had acquired. "Is that our new look? Pin cushion?"

"It's not that bad," Dana had protested to which Christa had arched an eyebrow and replied tartly:

"It's not that good." Dana rolled her eyes, which had launched Christa into her onslaught about arriving in London.

"We can't afford to throw away anything at this point. The brand is starting to snowball. People are taking an interest and they want you involved. Do you know how many invites we've been getting?"

"Not really," Dana admitted.

"It's a lot. I have you booked up for the next few months at functions, and not just walking. There are some that you've simply been invited as a guest to. Also, there's been a nibble."

"You know I struggle when you talk like you're from the 1990s," Dana moaned, returning to getting her new clothes on.

"A nibble. There has been interest from a couple of studios in you. I've had a few casting directors call me and ask if you can act."

"Are you fucking kidding me?" Dana said, and she genuinely couldn't describe the excitement that surged within her. "What sort of films?"

"I'm not sure. I ignored the first two, as they were more interested in whether you'd do full nudity or just toplessness." The disdain in Adams voice couldn't kill Dana's enthusiasm though.

"Is it a horror film? I might go topless for horror," Dana said, swept up with the idea of appearing on the big screen.

"No," Adams said simply. "That is not going to happen. We'll wait for something worthwhile. In the meantime, you have a job to do, and you'll be doing it."

432

"Right," Dana nodded. She knew which events she would be walking in, and what she had been invited to, and there was a ton of preparation that went into some of that, all of which would begin in the afternoon.

"I'll be in touch."

"I mean, obviously you'll be busy as, running around events over the next week," Dana chuckled.

"As it happens, I will. I do have other clients who are actually on time, doing the jobs I arrange for them and not getting cut up every five minutes," Adams said. She turned to walk out, and then suddenly stopped and turned back. "Dana, you have the chance to be one of the biggest models on the planet. And quite frankly I can get you there. And it very much suits me to get you there. But for some reason, it doesn't seem to suit you."

"It does," protested Dana.

"You had a hunger for this job just a few years ago. Now you seem distracted," Adams said. "I told you when you started the life could get to you."

"It's not that, honestly. I'm focused. I promise." There was, Dana reflected, no way that she was going to be able to convince Christa Adams that the drive was still there, and as Adams gave her one last look and turned to leave, Dana got the feeling she might come close to throwing away her dreams. Truth to tell she couldn't afford to lose Adams; she was genuinely one of the best managers in the business. Signing up to her agency had been a big win.

No more distractions, Dana reflected. This week needed to be all about this part of her life and everything else would be just something she could come back to.

Her phone gave a little tingle, and Dana looked at it curiously.

Hey! Just woke up. Been sleeping for days. Not sure where u r but if ur in London wanna come visit? Guys hospital.

At the top was the one word: Asha.

It was enough to make Dana pause and recheck her phone. She hadn't realized that Asha had been sent to London for help. In fact, the truth was, after the Congo she'd sort of lost track of her friend. They'd left the Ivory Coast without a lot of time to think, and it had all been a case of hoping that things had gone well with Asha. But they'd transferred her to London.

She rapped her fingers on the table that the phone had been settled on and chewed on her bottom lip. She couldn't afford not to do her job tonight, but at the same time, this was a friend who had almost died.

Dana almost jumped out of her skin when the phone in her hand rang, and after pulling herself together she slid her finger across the screen.

"Hello?"

"Is this Dana Spectra?"

"Yes, it is," Dana replied.

"Ms Spectra, this is Grace Wells from the British Fashion Council. Just ringing to let you know that tonight's schedule has been cancelled due to illness. We do apologise and will definitely be rescheduling, but at the moment things are a bit up in the air. We will be in touch as soon as we have a new schedule, which we're hoping to be tonight, tomorrow morning at the very latest."

"Oh, that's fine, thanks for letting me know," Dana said.

"You're very kind. Apologies again for the late notice and the inconvenience."

"No, that's honestly OK."

"Good day, Ms Spectra."

"Bye," said Dana, though the phone had already rung out.

Cancelling an entire schedule, suggested something quite bad. Dana wondered what it might be, but then decided it was probably nothing to do with her, really. She just went where she was told, put on what she was told to wear, walked where she was directed and tried to make the outfit look amazing. So…free afternoon? Fate had spoken, surely?

Her nostrils were assailed by the overwhelming scent of disinfectant as she stepped into the lobby of Guy's Hospital. And the aroma was the least of it, because the hospital had turned out to be a lot busier that she expected, with a multitude of people milling around, in various states of decay, as they waited patiently or spoke with the people at the counter. Dana, dressed in a comfortable A-line black minidress with white collars and cuffs, as well as a Boss belted wool trench coat, felt a little out of place. Well, perhaps over-dressed was a better description; most of the patients were wearing jeans and jackets that had seen better days. The weather wasn't really cold enough to necessitate a jacket, despite the day having the first bite of winter in the air, and Dana wasn't in the mood to give in.

In truth she had been a bit concerned about her trip to the hospital, worried that she had made some bad decisions on her journey. It seemed simple enough to go to London Bridge

Station and then, she assumed, walk to the hospital, but having stepped into the streets as the rain decided to make its regular appearance, she set off down Tooley St, in the hope she was going in the right direction.

When she decided to turn, it was down into an old brick tunnel with dull yellow lights desperate to reassure travelers that they were entirely safe and there was no need to panic. Dana felt a little guilty as she pulled her coat tighter while young men with shaved heads, tattoos and cigarettes walked past her. It was an irrational fear, she knew, but she also knew that it was unwise to take chances. She had left her gun in her hotel room back in Russell Square, where she was staying, and briefly wished that she hadn't.

But, with that being said, regardless of her fears, very few people gave her a look beyond an initial glance which barely raised a flicker of interest.

She had got out into St Thomas St and found herself under the watchful gaze of The Shard, the tall monument of concrete and glass that towered over the buildings around it, and gave stark contrast to what was across the road. If the Shard represented the modern world, directly across from it were the dull brown bricks of...

Oh. Dana realized that she was looking at the dull brown bricks of Guy's Hospital. The white letters sat against the building alongside a blue sign with arrows showing the direction of the main entrance. She set off down Great Maze Pond, walking past the oddly shaped metal panelling that twisted and curved around what appeared to be the service area of a building – presumably the tall concrete building to the side. For a brief moment, Dana lost her sense of direction, but when she walked a few more steps, she saw the entrance to Guy's Hospital on her left; a small inlet where the twisted metal panels continued until they bumped up against the smooth white of the NHS' hospital.

"Can I help you?" asked the spectacularly British lady behind the desk with a look on her face that suggested she had been behind the counter for far too long that day, and she was dealing with *a lot* of stupid people.

"I'm here to visit someone. I was wondering if you could tell me which room she might be in," Dana said. The lady behind the counter didn't even bother looking up.

"Name," she simply said.

"Asha," Dana said.

"Surname?"

"Harvins." There was a pause as the admin lady looked at whatever was on her computer and then looked up at Dana.

"What's your name?" she asked, and there was a note in her voice that suggested that if Dana said the wrong thing, security would descend upon her like a lion on a gazelle.

"Dana Spectra," Dana said, a little softly.

"You need to leave here, turn left, head down the street, turn right, and keep walking til you come to Nuffield House. That's where your friend is. I assume I don't have to explain anything else to you?" Truthfully, Dana very much wanted to say yes to that question, as she had no idea at all why the lady was speaking to her as though they were both walking through a minefield. However, it seemed that she *should* know what was going on, and so Dana gave a small smile and shook her head.

She had wanted to complain about having to trek to

some new building, but Dana decided that today was not the day for whinging, and so she headed back out the doors to the main entrance of the hospital, and followed the directions given to her, pulling her lapels up in the hope they might afford her a little more protection from the rain, which had decided it wasn't going to give up on its never-ending war against the United Kingdom.

Turn left, head down the street and turn right. That didn't seem too difficult. Dana scanned the buildings as she walked along, and was pleasantly surprised to find a blue sign that had "Guy's Nuffield House" on it. Unlike the towering hospital that she had just left, this particular part of the complex was a simple single story that definitely looked as though it had been around in the 1980s, if not earlier. There were two wooden doors, and Dana walked up and pushed them open, though before she did, she took in the big sign to the right of the doors that had the various floors of the building on it. Frowning, Dana assumed that the building to the right that was about four stories high was presumably the actual hospital ward itself.

Certainly, having gone through the wooden doors, Dana was in a very pokey little lobby that was separated from the staff by frosted glass, and had that weird musty smell that reminded her of her grandmother's home.

Mothballs, that would be it.

Dana walked up to the counter and tapped on the glass, and after only a few seconds it was pulled apart by a bored looking man.

"You alright?" he asked, pleasantly, and Dana wondered if the reason he had grown his mustache was to do that thing some men did of trying to look older.

"Yeah, I'm here to see," she started to say but was interrupted.

"Fourth floor," he said, and pointed to the other side of the room. "Through that door, take the elevator, bed 4."

"You know who I'm here to see," she asked, puzzled.

"Sure do," he said, with a lazy smile. "You Australian?"

"Yeah."

"Where you from?"

"Brisbane," Dana said. "In Queensland."

"Oh, right. My cousin lives in Brisbane. Veronica Walsh." Dana looked at him, wondering if he genuinely thought she would know who he was talking about. "Oh, you probably don't now everyone in Brisbane," he said sheepishly.

"Not really," Dana confirmed. "I actually live in the Northern suburbs anyway."

"Right," the guy said. "Fourth floor." He pulled the frosted glass back, saving them both from any further awkward exchanges, and Dana headed to the elevator. The carpet was fairly threadbare, and the seats were definitely decades older than she was. It was like she had stepped into an old movie, but in truth she wasn't totally surprised. Most of her time in London was spent in the areas that were keeping up with the times, but she knew there were parts that were just content to be left behind. The NHS was no exception to that, and while new wings shot up, with the most up-to-date medical equipment and care, some of the older wards were left behind.

She pressed the button on the elevator and stepped in, selecting the fourth-floor button. The elevator wasn't particularly big, and the mirrors didn't really help that, despite what initial appearances might suggest. It was also a fairly slow elevator, and Dana felt a small niggle in her belly as she wondered what might happen if she got stuck at some point. After what seemed like a short eternity, the elevator judded to a halt and Dana waited patiently while the doors separated and she was able to step out.

The floor itself wasn't any busier, and the windows at either end of the corridor didn't let in enough light to make the corridor seem welcoming. Instead, fluorescent lights seemed the create a starkness that was strangely not hospital-like at all.

Each door was numbered and Dana walked along until she found the one that had a black four on it. Tentatively she knocked at the door, and from inside she heard a voice calling out.

"Come in?"

Dana tentatively entered the room, which had the same smell of disinfectant that the rest of the hospital had, and the same dull yellow lighting, which didn't do much to improve the state of the largely pale-green room. However, there was the reassuring beeping of a machine of some description that presumably was linked to the clip-on Asha's finger.

Because Asha herself was on the bed, smiling weakly and looking for all the world like she had been stabbed in the Congo, shipped to the Ivory Coast and then finally onto London. Or, as Dana more succinctly put it: "You look like shit." She grinned at her friend, and put her bag on the floor near the bed, to lean forward and gently hug her.

"Ohh," groaned Asha, "I do feel like shit."

"What did the doctors say?"

"I'll be fine," Asha nodded, reassuringly. "I went into surgery to make sure that everything that happened in the Ivory

Coast was fine, and for the most part it was, so they think I'll make a full recovery."

"And then back to the Four-Fold Crown," Dana asked, and tried to keep her voice neutral. Asha reached out and grabbed her friend's hand.

"In my defense," she said weakly, "they do good things for women. It's a good retreat, honestly. But the cult side of things makes it a lot worse, I grant you." Dana shook her head, and then looked around for a chair, which she found nearby, and dragged it closer to the bed. There was an IV tube, Dana noted, alongside the vitals monitor, and Asha did have a tube running under her nose, supplying, presumably, oxygen. "Did you sort everything out?"

"You haven't spoken to Max or Justice?" Dana asked, curiously.

"I don't know who they are," Asha replied. "I met a guy called, uh, well, it seems silly, but I think he said he was Broadsword. I must have been high. But I thought that was his name. He organized my transfer from Yamoussoukro to London. Then he came to visit me a few days later to make sure I was OK, but he said he couldn't tell me anything about you, because he wasn't sure exactly what you were doing."

"Oh," Dana waved her hand slightly. "Nothing exciting. I went to French Guiana. It was unique."

"Unique," Asha chuckled, and then coughed slightly, wincing in pain. "Can't laugh very much."

"Was there a place to get food or something?" Dana asked, suddenly realizing how hungry she was.

"You've only just walked in the door!" Asha protested.

"Also, aren't you here on work or something?"

"How do you know that?" Dana asked, surprised.

"I'm assuming you have your sister back on the case," Asha grinned. "I'm following on IG."

"Oh," Dana mused. "I should probably thank her for keeping me in the public eye. While I'm doing stupid things."

"You and me both," Asha sighed. "I need a Bella. There's a vending machine on the second or third floor, I think."

"I'll be back," Dana said, and leaned forward to kiss her friend on the forehead, before heading out the door. Friend. Her mind briefly flashed back to what they had done in the Congo, and she scowled at her lack of control. Though, nothing was going to take away the awkwardness of a night of passion more than a brutal stabbing.

She headed to the elevator and went down a floor, delighted to find that there was indeed a vending machine there, and quickly grabbed herself a drink and a packet of chips. For a moment she deliberated, wondering if she should risk it. Broadly speaking she didn't usually have a break out if she ate a packet of chips, and she could do some exercise at the hotel tonight to make sure she could work it off. Screw it, she thought. Besides, she'd already purchased them.

Back on the fourth floor, she wandered down to room 4, but paused. Something wasn't quite right. Everything seemed in place, but then she realized it had been a sound, and when she heard it again, she raced to Asha's room.

It was a muffled thump, as though something had fallen or been knocked over, and when it happened a second time, she knew there was a problem. Dana dashed inside and was horrified to see Asha standing beside the bed, injecting something into the IV.

"What are you doing?" Dana started, and when Asha looked up, she realized it wasn't Asha at all. Of course it wasn't. June gave a veritable hiss, and then obviously realized she had to choose between finishing off what she was doing, or attacking Dana. The hesitation was enough, and Dana flung her can of drink at June, hitting the assassin solidly in the side of the head, leaving an angry red welt.

It had the desire effect, and June let go of the IV, before moving around the bed.

"I don't mind saying, I'm sort of glad you're here," she said.

"I don't mind saying, I'm fucking sick of the sight of you," Dana responded. June growled, and leapt at Dana, who dodged out of the road, but found herself backed up against Asha's bed. Asha wasn't looking good, her face now pale, but June was causing enough problems to make Dana leave her friend's welfare for the moment to protect her own. If she wasn't capable of defending them, June would kill them both.

June's lunge was met by Dana grabbing both of the girl's arms and trying to force her back. Despite being considerably taller than the assassin, June was impressively strong, and Dana winced as June fought back, but Dana was able to twist around, and by dropping she could slip away from June who hadn't anticipated the action.

Annoyingly, for a hospital, there weren't any obvious weapons that Dana could make use of, but now at the end of Asha's bed, she found a towel, and grabbed it, twisting it into a flexible club, which she lashed out at June with. The assassin recoiled a little, but as Dana grabbed the other end, she used it to push back June's next attack.

It was around this point that Dana realized June absolutely had something in her hands, but she couldn't quite work out what it was exactly. It was metal and sharp, and her brain kept saying "You can't afford to get a mark – you're walking in the next few days!"

Taking the risk, she lashed out with the towel, and clipped the side of the other woman's face, causing her to fall back in pain. Dana looked around and came to the conclusion that the only real weapon she had was the can she had brought in. She dived to the corner of the room where she saw it lying, and couldn't help but swear as June was on her in an instant.

Viciously, Dana swung around and clubbed her again in the side of the face with the can, but was horrified when she realized she had made an error of judgement. The can must have split when it hit June the first time, and this time as she slammed it into the other girl's face, the split was now a savage blade that sliced through June's skin, and June screamed as it cut her eye open.

Dana jumped up and raced across the room, seeing something that might just give her the advantage that she needed. On the wall was a blue button, and though she wasn't sure exactly what it was going to do, she slammed her hand on it. Disappointingly, absolutely nothing happened.

June was on her again, and Dana gave her own squeak when she felt something penetrate her arm. She turned, and was finally able to see what June had been trying to attack her with –

444

the syringe that she had pushed into the IV earlier. A surge of adrenaline allowed her to shove June with a significant amount of force, and the smaller woman was sent reeling across the floor as Dana pulled the syringe out of her arm and tossed it towards the door.

June went to scramble for it, but Dana was on her, her knee in the back of the other woman's back, as she pulled June's hair. However, June's training kicked in, and she took up the slack, bending back so that the hair wasn't taut, and twisted, allowing her to give Dana a savage punch to the gut. Rather than continuing her pursuit of the syringe. June, instead, walked straight over to Dana, and quickly and efficiently kicked her in the knee, before delivering another blow to Dana's stomach. Her next punch was for the head, but clearly the fact she was now missing an eye threw her aim off slightly, and as Dana twisted to avoid the punch, June's fist went straight into the floor.

June turned to Dana, her face twisted into a snarl, and Dana couldn't help but draw back. The face had become the most horrific version of her friend's that she had ever seen, with one eye nothing more than a collection of cells and goop, dribbling down a face that had become scratched and ripped, blood congealing over the wounds, but also dripping down her face, and seemingly coming from her nose and mouth. She looked for all the world like a strange zombie version of Asha, and Dana lost the ability to think clearly.

As June stood up, a gunshot rang out, and a wound opened in her shoulder, blood dribbling down the front of it, staining the white t-shirt that she was wearing. June turned, and Dana looked in surprise to see Max standing there, his gun smoking slightly from the shot he had just fired. June took one more step forward, and the gun rang out again, this time, the bullet burying itself in June's stomach. A second step, but June's knees gave out and she crumpled to the floor, her hands following and with what seemed almost like a wistful sigh, she fell flat.

Max was pushed aside by a number of people in white, and two of them went straight to Asha's bed, while another one went to June.

"We need to get this woman to a surgery," the man kneeling said, his Indian accent betraying his heritage, and one of the people at the bed looked up and grabbed her phone and dialled.

"She injected something into the IV," Dana said, as she pulled herself back up to the chair that she had been sitting on earlier.

"Are you OK?" the nurse asked.

"Yeah," Dana said, though admittedly she was feeling quite weak. Christa was going to be furious if she had wounds. Might have to call Jeremy and see if he can get a flight to London to help sort her out.

"There are problems with the vitals here, doctor," the nurse by the bed said. By this point, Dana guessed that the man kneeling was the doctor, and sure enough, he replied.

"Tell surgery to get ready, and we're bringing two across immediately. It's urgent," he added, and the female nurse on the phone, started speaking again.

"Are you sure you're alright?" Max asked Dana, and she was surprised to see him kneeling beside her.

"Hey," she smiled, weakly. "How you doing?"

"Dana?"

"She stuck a needle in my arm," Dana murmured, and realized that her mouth felt quite fluffy.

Was fluffy the right word?

God she was tired.

"I think Dana might have been injured," Max was saying, and the next thing Dana knew the Indian doctor was talking to her.

"Can you hear me, Dana?" he said, and she acknowledged him.

Did she? He seemed concerned.

"I think there was some sort of poison in the needle," the male nurse was saying, and Dana grimaced slightly.

So tired.

"Dana, can you hear me?"

Dana smiled and grabbed Max's hands. Maybe. Definitely someone's hands.

"Just fine."

THE END

Also by Ryan Alcock

Dana Spectra

Death On Ice
Poisoned Chalice
The Killing Label

Dana Spectra Universe

Justice
Man Hunt
The Doves - Target: Dana Spectra

Monster Trappers

The FIrst Three Traps
The House at Skylar Falls - Special Edition
The Curse of the Black Spectre

Non-Fiction

I'll Explain Later
The Unofficial and Unauthorised Guide to the Doctor Who
Universe
It's All Connected: The Infinity Saga
It's All Connected Vol Three: Phase Four
The Unofficial and Unauthorised Guides to the Marvel Cinematic
Universe
X-Celsior
The Unofficial and Unauthorised Guides to the Marvel Cinematic
Multiverse